S0-BNJ-937

THE MESSENGER

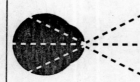

This Large Print Book carries the
Seal of Approval of N.A.V.H.

THE MESSENGER

SIRI MITCHELL

THORNDIKE PRESS

A part of Gale, Cengage Learning

GALE
CENGAGE Learning

Detroit • New York • San Francisco • New Haven, Conn • Waterville, Maine • London

GALE
CENGAGE Learning®

The internet addresses, email addresses, and phone numbers in this book are accurate at the time of publication. They are provided as a resource. The publisher does not endorse them or vouch for their content or permanence.
Thorndike Press® Large Print Christian Historical Fiction.
The text of this Large Print edition is unabridged.
Other aspects of the book may vary from the original edition.
Set in 16 pt. Plantin.

LIBRARY OF CONGRESS CATALOGING-IN-PUBLICATION DATA

Mitchell, Siri L., 1969–
   The messenger / by Siri Mitchell.
     pages ; cm. — (Thorndike Press large print Christian
  historical fiction)
   ISBN 978-1-4104-4979-5 (hardcover) — ISBN 1-4104-4979-3 (hardcover)
  1. Quakers—Fiction. 2. Philadelphia (Pa.)—History—Revolution,
1775-1783—Fiction. 3. Large type books. I. Title.
PS3613.I866M47 2012b
813'.6—dc23
                                                 2012014528

Published in 2012 by arrangement with Bethany House Publishers, a division of Baker Publishing Group.

Printed in Mexico
1 2 3 4 5 6 7 16 15 14 13 12

To the girl with an enduring fascination
for George Washington's spies

# # # #

JANUARY 1778
PHILADELPHIA
UNDER THE BRITISH
OCCUPATION

# # # #

1
HANNAH

It was the last thing I had expected to see.

I'd left Meeting just after it had ended, this first day of the week. My mind was too agitated, my heart too full of turmoil to stay. Once more, it had been a silent Meeting. God had not given a word to any of us to speak. If He had any opinion on the great conflict that had overtaken the colonies, He was not of a mind to share it.

My soul longed for peace.

More peace than a city filled with red-coated soldiers could afford. And so, passing Amy Newland and skirting Betsy Evans, I pushed out into the morning's chill alone.

I'd taken up the habit of keeping my eyes fixed upon the ground as I walked. In that manner I could not see the emptied, looted houses that now blighted our fair city. If I kept the hood of my green woolen cloak pulled forward over my head, I could pretend not to hear the British soldiers cursing as they strolled through the streets. And if I walked fast enough, I would soon be safe at home, where nothing at all seemed to have changed. I would be able to enjoy a few sweet moments of solitude before everyone returned for dinner.

Rounding the corner from cobbled Second Street onto unpaved Chestnut Street, I was nearly home. But halfway down the block I became aware of a great goings-on. Lifting my head and pushing back my hood, I realized that it was happening in front of my house.

When I'd left for Meeting that morning with my family, we'd filed out of a large brick house, well built, boasting imported windows that were bordered by trim black shutters. We had walked through a yard girded by a recently raised fence. The undisturbed grounds had been pristine, the fence posts covered with hoods of snow and the shrubberies pillowed with drifts. But now all was in disorder.

Red-coated soldiers and an army of street urchins were swarming over the place.

I ran down the street, cloak pulling at my neck, just as fast as the slush-slick street would allow. As I came to a sliding halt in front of my house, I had to throw out my arms for balance. "Stop! Stop this at once!"

10

I called out before I even thought to wonder whether I ought to speak. It did not do to protest anything too loudly, not in these difficult times. The patriots had once accused my father of being a Loyalist and had even gone so far as to arrest him that September past. But we Friends had been treated no better by the British. They accused us all of being rebels.

The safest course had been not to draw attention to ourselves. And despite my outburst, it seemed in that I was still successful, for the soldiers and the boys in the yard paid me no mind. They did not even pause in their labors. With protesting creaks and groans, boards were levered away from the fence. The snow that had once laid undisturbed had been churned into mud. One of the soldiers was at work chopping up our boxwoods and throwing them up onto a cart. They lay in a pile, their leafy branches waving at me as if in supplication. I heard a shout in the direction of the house and saw a young boy climb up the portico in order to help some men pull down the shutters.

Regardless of the fear that had squeezed the breath from me, a most un-Friendlike rage began to build within my soul. "Thee can't just take things that don't belong to thee!"

A soldier at work tearing up the fence spit into the sludge beside me and then reached down to scratch at his groin. "Why should you care? Aren't yours, neither. They belong to one of those rebels."

"They are too mine. This house belongs to me." And these thieves seemed bent on dismantling it one timber at a time!

"You?"

"Aye. Me."

"So you're the rebel." He looked at me with no little malice.

My stomach roiled at his assessment as memories of other mobs and past destruction brought the taste of bile to my tongue. Where were Father and Mother? "I am not a rebel." How dare he accuse me of being one of those who had nearly sent my father away from us in exile! "I am a Friend." A Friend that tried to keep to her own business and ignore the turmoil of the rebellion.

"A friend." A gleam sparked his eyes as he looked at me with sudden interest. "No friend of mine. If you were, I'd have remembered. Though I wouldn't mind making your acquaintanceship right now." He put a finger up to his hat and tipped it toward me.

Another soldier, one who had succeeded in freeing the gate from its hinge, threw it in the man's direction. It was caught hold of with a grunt. "She doesn't mean *friend,* you oaf. She means to say that she's *a* Friend. One o' them Quaker sorts."

All along the fence, the soldiers stopped their work at those words and straightened to look at me.

The soldier I was speaking with threw the gate onto the cart. It landed atop the box-woods. "Don't really see as how there's much difference between you people and those rebels. And besides, we've used up all our firewood. They're paying us five shillings extra to go find some. Consider it your contribution to our cause. And much obliged." He winked at me and then went back to work.

Was there no one who could stop this injustice?

In earlier times I might have gone across the street to the Mortons, but they were no longer there, having fled to their country house. The neighbors next to them would be no help; they'd long despised my father's peaceable ways.

I turned from the fence, determined to search for aid. Down at the end of the street I saw a man cross the road. I began to call out to him, but seeing his coat askew at his shoulders and his untidily drawn-back hair, I realized it was only Jeremiah Jones. A man with no loyalties, he'd served the raucous patriot crowd at his tavern just as ardently as he now served the British. The men that arrested my father had been known to frequent his establishment. He would be of no help to anyone protesting an injustice; especially not to a Friend.

When an officer on horseback came posting down the street, I ran toward him, hoping that his commission had conferred upon him common sense in addition to rank. "Please! Thee must help me!"

The man reined his horse and removed his hat.

"Thee must tell these people to stop. They've mistaken our house for that of a rebel's, and they're taking things that are not theirs."

His gaze passed from me toward the house and lingered there for a moment. Then it came back to rest upon me. "Yes. Yes, of course you're right. They must be stopped."

Praise God! Someone who understood. Someone who would put an end to this madness.

"You there." He addressed the soldier to whom I had spoken. "Whose regiment are

14

you from?"

The soldier answered, eyes sullen. "The Queen's Rangers. Sir."

"You're rather far from your precincts, aren't you?"

The man didn't answer, but some of his fellow soldiers had already begun slinking away. The boy atop the portico leapt down, leaving the sole shutter still attached to the house dangling. He darted around the corner.

The soldier flung one last picket onto the cart and then moved to grasp the handles. The officer called out to him. "I rather think I'd like those to stay." The words sounded ambivalent, though the tone did not.

The man let go the cart and, with a muttered curse, took himself off down the street.

I turned, hand at my heart, toward my savior. "I owe thee much by way of gratitude."

The officer dismounted his horse, tied it to the one post that remained standing, and surveyed the destruction the soldiers had wrought. "A thorough bunch. If I can say nothing else about the Queen's Rangers, they usually take the best of everything for themselves. This will do quite nicely."

Quite nicely for a barn, perhaps. "My family will be returning presently. May I ask

15

thee to dine with us?"

He raised a brow. "Now? I'm expected at the officers' mess for dinner."

"Then may I invite thee to tea tomorrow? I'm certain my father will wish to give thee his thanks."

"I suppose I could. I could join you for a cup of tea before I bring my men over."

Men? "How many would that be?"

"Several." He walked through the mud and up onto the front stoop, then turned and surveyed the wreck of our yard. He looked past it toward the street. "Aye. This will do quite nicely."

Several men in addition to this officer? I'd meant to thank just this one. Food was so scarce these days . . . but Mother always seemed to somehow come by a loaf of bread or a jar of cream when none was supposed to be available. "I'll tell my mother to expect . . . three, then? For tea?"

"For tea?" He barked a laugh. "Well, why not. For tea and room and board."

"Room and board?"

"I've been ordered to secure myself quarters for the winter, dear girl. In a city of twenty-five thousand, one would think it would not be so difficult as it has been. But your place looks as fine as any I've seen."

"But thee cannot just . . . *our* place?"

He frowned. "Let's call it my place then, shall we? Since that's what it is now. In any case, I thank you for the invitation. I'll return for tea tomorrow."

The officer returned precisely at four o'clock the next afternoon. He was followed by an adjutant and two servants leading two horses, one cow, three goats, and two chickens. Father met him at the door. I took refuge, with Mother and the children, on the front stair.

Father barred his entry with an arm across the door. "I must protest. I've already told the Superintendent General of the city that we're not to quarter troops."

"Colonel Beckwith at your service." The man lifted his hat from his head and bowed. "I've only myself and two servants." The colonel noted the direction of Father's gaze. "And some assorted livestock as well."

"We've no room for them."

"But you've a stable."

"For our own horse."

"Horse? A singular animal? Then I'm certain there will be room for mine." The colonel nodded toward the servants. They moved off toward the stable.

"The superintendent will not countenance the breaking of his rule."

"The superintendent serves at the pleasure of His Majesty, and His Majesty's pleasure is that his troops be quartered comfortably for the winter." He put the tip of his crop to Father's chest and pushed past him into the hall.

We, all of us, moved farther up the stair.

We could hear the colonel walking the length of the front parlor, boot heels striking against the floorboards. He crossed the front hall, sending a glance up at us. As his gaze came to rest upon me, he paused and bowed. After stepping into the other parlor, he returned to address my father. "These rooms will do quite nicely."

"I cannot allow thee to stay here."

"And I simply cannot allow myself to stay anywhere else. I shall take these front two rooms for my use. And one of your bedrooms as well."

"I shall protest!"

"I suppose you will do as you must. In the meantime, I'll tell my men to start bringing in my things."

In the time it took the colonel's five trunks and sundry crates to be brought in, Father had gone the two blocks down to Superintendent Joseph Galloway's and returned. After a hurried conference with Mother, he gathered us all into the kitchen. "There's

18

nothing to be done. We shall just have to try and get along with them."

We'd been trying to get along with them for three months now, ever since the British had occupied the city. More than that even, we'd been trying to get along ever since the rebellion had started. But Loyalist or patriot, they all looked upon us the same. We were not one of them.

As Friends, we were suspect. Getting along did not seem to be working very well.

2
JEREMIAH

". . . so Colonel Beckwith put a pistol to the rebel's head and the fellow dropped clean away. Right to the floor. Didn't even stop to soil himself on the way down. And he said, the colonel did, 'The only thing rebels are good for is dying.' " A ripple of laughter passed through the public room of my tavern. It was followed by the stamping of feet. Both sounds of a normal Monday's business.

Clamorous crowds were not unknown to my tavern, even though the loyalties of my customers had changed with the occupation. But any tavern owner knew that a man who drank three mugs of rum paid more for his pleasures than a man who only drank one. As I collected an empty tankard, a hand reached out and grabbed my sleeve. Had I not seen it, had I not stopped, that pull might have stripped the coat from my shoulder. "Don't you think so, Jones?"

I turned toward the voice. The same one that had told the story. "Unhand me, you loathsome brute." I hoped the smile at my lips would temper the venom in my words. "I think the only thing you're good at is getting your mates to pay for your drinks."

Another wave of laughter. Another call for drink.

I summoned the cook's daughter from her corner and went back to my daybook, protected by the wooden cage that framed the bar. I had no illusions about the refinement of my guests. The cage had sheltered me a time or two during brawls and it kept my customers from pilfering my spirits. I watched the girl's progress, noting when she served the tailor. He was sitting alone at a table in the corner, sunk into the Windsor chair as if he did not want to be noticed. I wished I did not have to.

A round of applejack for the noisome soldiers and a mug of rum for the tailor in the corner.

Rum.

I filled six mugs with applejack. Pushed them across the counter toward the serving girl. Then I took up a bottle of rum, pulling the cork from it with my teeth, and poured a drink with my good hand. My only hand. The hand that hadn't been shot off fifteen years earlier during Pontiac's War.

It didn't bode well that the tailor had ordered rum. Not when he usually drank Madeira. But a man couldn't refuse to read the signs just because he didn't like the message they bore. I walked across the room and set it down in front of the man. Turned to leave.

"I can't do this anymore."

I paused. Cast a glance down at him. "This is not the time or place."

He nodded, jerkily, eyes darting about the room. Though nearly half the city had fled as the British approached, they'd brought double the number of soldiers with them. Nearly twenty thousand, some said. The room was rife with redcoats. He tossed back the liquor and threw some coin onto the table, then dabbed at his forehead with a handkerchief as he rose to go. "Meet me at the shop. After supper."

He pulled me into the shop just as soon as I put my hand to the door. Locking it behind us, he retreated behind his counter, frowning. He unfolded a length of material, put a hand up to his queue and fiddled with the bow that secured it, then refolded the material once more. Finally he placed his hands atop it and sighed. "The thing of it is, I can't do this anymore."

I had been hoping that I hadn't understood him correctly earlier. "You can't — ? But . . . if you're not going to do it, then who is?" That was the question, wasn't it? Who was going to do what he had been doing?

The tailor shook his head and unfolded the material once more. Then he put his shears to the fabric. "I don't care. They'll figure something out. They always do."

"You're just going to abandon your position?"

"Too dangerous."

Too dangerous for a man who stayed hidden inside his tailor's shop for most of every day?

He let the shears rip into the fabric, pulling the material through the blades.

"At least tell me who your contact is."

"You are."

"I mean the other one. The one you pass my information to."

The tailor's apprentice walked into the workshop, arms filled with colorful lengths of fabric. He dumped them onto a table and brushed off his hands on his apron.

The tailor sent a look of consternation my direction before addressing the boy. "I need you to run down to the wharf and see if our ship has come in. I'm anxious to receive those trims I ordered."

The boy nodded and ducked out of the shop, leaving the door to bang shut behind him.

"It's a country girl. Comes into the city to sell eggs. That's one of the problems."

"Eggs?"

"When is the last time you saw eggs at the market?"

When was the last time there'd been milk or butter? The cost of food for my tavern had increased steeply since the occupation. If I hadn't developed contacts among the occupiers themselves, I doubted I would have been able to obtain flour of any quality. Or cheese or meat either. Effectively, Philadelphia no longer had a market. It had mercenaries who crept in through the lines before dawn and sold their wares for a fortune.

"I don't have the nerve anymore to skulk about the market waiting for her. You know what they do to you if they catch you?"

I'd heard.

"What she sells me are quail's eggs. That's where the general hides his messages. Do you know how much a quail egg cost before this infernal mess? And I haven't been given any money for my expenses in months." He folded the material he had just cut and swept the scraps into a basket. "Though I *am* partial to a good quail's egg."

If truth be told, he was partial to a good many things that cost an extravagant amount of money. Being the best-dressed man in town couldn't come cheaply, even if one had the ability to make the clothes oneself. But he was going to let good intelligence go undelivered for want of egg money?

Had I had another hand I might have used it to strangle him. As it was, all I could do was clench the hand I had and shove it straight to the bottom of my coat pocket. Useless and ineffectual. That's what I'd become. "*I'll* give you the money." The one thing the redcoats knew how to do was drink. And they were willing to pay handsomely for the vice. I figured they owed me. It hadn't bothered me a bit to change the name of my tavern from Patriot's Arms to King's Arms to lure them to my business.

"Even if I had the money . . . it's not that. It's what they want. What *he* wants. General Washington."

I raised a brow.

He shook his head.

"If you're going to abandon all this, the least you can do is tell me what the general wants. I might be able to do it." In any case, from time to time I heard useful information. It would be a shame not to have the means to pass it along.

"There's no one could do this." He shut up the blades of his shears, placed them into the basket, and clapped the lid down on top. Poking at the bottom of the basket, he pulled a scrap of parchment from a hole. Handed it to me. "He wants to get this message into the jail."

A message into the jail? That's what the general wanted? No wonder the tailor had decided to quit the cause. He was right. There was no one who could do that.

I returned to the tavern in low spirits. Though I hadn't actually ever spied for General Washington, I had been able to provide helpful information now and then, helping the cause in my own way. But now, all that was finished. My support for the war effort had just been reduced to squeezing shillings from the soldiers who frequented my tavern. It might add to my fortune, but it wasn't nearly so satisfying. I drew the door open and walked into the smoke-shrouded public room.

"Jeremiah Jones!"

I blinked. As I tried to block that too-familiar voice from my ears, the years fell away. I was transported back to Devil's Hole. I'd been a colonial in Gage's Light Infantry then. We'd been dispatched to rescue an ambushed wagon train that had been bound for the fort near the falls. But the Indians had surprised us, attacking from the high ground, under cover of the brush. Everything had happened so quickly.

"Jeremiah Jones!" John Lindley had yelled across the road at me. Lieutenants both, we were sworn to protect the men we led. But he was pointing his musket behind him, appearing as if . . . as if he wanted to retreat?

The way of battle wasn't backward, it was forward!

I don't know who got off the first shot, but suddenly the air was filled with the pop of musket fire. The drift of smoke began to obscure my vision. Beside me, I heard the terrible thud of bullet penetrating flesh. One of my men crumpled onto my feet.

"Jeremiah — retreat!"

The haze had enveloped my platoon. We were fighting in a world where there was no sight. There was only sound. The whine of bullets, the groans of the wounded. And there were smells. The peculiarly pungent smell of terror. And the musty scent of fear.

I kicked at the dead weight of the fallen

soldier and freed my feet. Turned, cupped a hand to my mouth, and shouted a cry. But no one answered. No one rallied to my call. It was as if the entire world had fallen away. And without the advantage of sight, I no longer knew which way was back and which was forward.

In that swirl of smoke and nightmare, a bullet found my elbow. The pain was so fierce that I lost hold of my musket. So piercing I fell to the ground.

When the shooting stopped and the smoke had dissipated, I found myself face-to-face with a dead man, staring into a pair of eternally startled blue eyes. Trying to scramble to my feet, I put out my arm. Biting back a scream, I fell to my knees as a web of darkness threatened to envelop me. When my vision cleared, I beheld a scene of carnage. The whole of my platoon had fallen around me. Good men all.

Stumbling, I made my way through the forest back to the fort. At least that's where I hoped I was headed. But nothing in that forlorn and desolate place looked right. Despite the warmth of the day, my arm was cold. I put out my other to cradle it and encountered a tattered, sodden mess of a coat sleeve.

Somehow I managed to lurch to a tree

stump before I collapsed.

Eventually they found me, two privates looking for survivors. They rolled me onto a blanket and then dragged me through the wood. Endless tree branches waved above my head.

Daggers of pain.

Teeth gritted against the agony.

Fingernails digging hollows into the flesh of my palm.

Less trees, more sunlight, followed by blue sky, clouds . . . and finally the smells of the fort. First woodsmoke and then the latrines. Even worse, the surgery. The sounds of the army echoed around me. The grunts of men at work. The clatter of tin and pewter ware. And the rasp of the surgeon's saw. They dragged me toward that sound, toward those terrible smells. Paused in front of an open tent.

"Bring the lieutenant in."

I felt the warmth of relief wash over me. If the surgeon could get the bullet out and bind me up, then I could collapse in my tent. Sweat out the pain for a while in privacy.

The blanket began to move once more.

"No! Not that one."

They stopped.

"That one's come up from the colonial

militia. Take this other one: he's one of the British regulars."

My head banged against the ground as the privates dropped the corners of the blanket, pitching me onto my wounded arm before I passed out. When I came to, I was lying in front of the hospital tent, with bloody rags piled beside me. As I lay there, an opossum slunk out from the forest's edge, tugged a severed hand from the pile, and returned to the brush with it, fingers waving from its mouth.

I used my good arm to push myself to sitting.

Behind me, someone cursed. Boots scuffed against the ground. I heard them venture around me. A face peered down. "We got another here, boys!" Strong hands beneath my armpits lifted me to standing. The world turned gray for a moment as I gained my feet. Those same hands supported me while I lurched toward the tent.

"Another for the surgery!" The soldier who had helped me pushed me down onto a stool.

The surgeon came over, wiping his hands on his blood-smeared apron. He peered at my arm, poked at my elbow.

I swore as the world faded to white.

He pulled a knife from his belt and slit

the sleeve of my coat, releasing a sudden and alarmingly putrid stench. "Take him to the table."

I knocked away the soldier's hands and walked over to the table myself. As I sat there trying to recover my wits, they poured me a mug of rum. I couldn't seem to get my hand to take it up. And even when I used my other hand to bring it to my mouth, most of it dribbled down my chin onto my chest. As they pushed me down and tied me to the board, I saw the surgeon take up a crescent-shaped saw.

The next time I woke, I was in my tent. I could tell by the stains on the ceiling and by the way straw prickled at the back of my neck. I tried to swallow, but my mouth was too dry. I tried to lick my lips, but my tongue felt ten sizes too big.

John Lindley's face loomed above me.

I blinked.

He smiled. "Want some water?"

I nodded.

He lifted a canteen to my lips. Most of it ran down the back of my neck. But with subsequent drinks my tongue seemed to shrink, and increasing amounts of water made it down my throat.

John lifted an arm that had been wrapped in gauze. "They patched me up as well." He leaned closer. "I have to admit, I probably kept the surgeon longer than I should have . . . it hurts like the devil to have an arrow plow a furrow in your arm. Hurts more than one might think."

Arm.

There was something about an arm. Something it seemed like I ought to remember.

"But look at it now!" He flexed his arm through the gauze. "And nothing to show for it but a scar."

A memory tickled at the edges of my mind. "Were you the first one into surgery?"

"What's that?"

"Were you the first one?"

He attempted to shrug. Winced. "I was there before you, in any case. One of those beetle-headed privates dumped you over by the refuse pile. They didn't realize you were even alive for a day or two. You'd passed out like a drunkard. That's why they couldn't save your arm. It was too far gone."

Couldn't . . . ? I turned my head and lifted my wounded arm, but . . . it was no longer there. I blinked. I could feel it. I could have sworn I could feel my fingers flex. And I knew I wasn't imagining the pain shooting from my elbow, but there was nothing there.

It took three days and two bottles of

whiskey for me to understand what had happened. Eighty-one men had been caught up in the ambushes by the Indians. Indians who had been shooting *arrows*. Only eight men had survived. But even then I didn't accept it. I couldn't. I couldn't believe I had been shot by my own army. And I wouldn't accept that a man who had been grazed by an arrow had been rushed into surgery before a man with a bullet-shattered arm. For the sole reason that he was a British regular and the other man a colonial.

Never before had I so desperately wanted to murder someone.

"Jeremiah Jones! It is you, isn't it?"

When I turned at the greeting, I half expected to find myself back at the fort. But I was still at the King's Arms and my arm was still gone, though my forehead had gone slick with sudden sweat.

I nodded to return his greeting. "John Lindley."

"Jonesy!" He smiled as if he was delighted to have found me. "If I'd known you were in the city, I might have looked you up before now." He extended his own hand and moved to clasp my arm, but his grip only closed on an empty sleeve. To his credit, a flush colored his cheeks. "Well. How about this! Can't hardly believe it took a rebellion to bring us back together."

How about this. How about a man's sworn enemy walking into his tavern and greeting him like a long-lost friend.

John clapped a hand on the shoulder of the man he was with. "This is that colonial I was telling you about the other day. The one that survived Devil's Hole with me."

"Ah! The one that might have been worth a commission." He glanced pointedly at my useless arm. "Some bad luck there, eh?"

Some prejudice disguised as bad luck. "Can I get you something to drink?"

"You buying?" John lifted a brow as if he couldn't believe his luck.

"I'm selling. I own this tavern." Only its size and its spirited crowd distinguished it from the other hundreds of King's Arms that kept the colonies supplied with spirits. It was drawing Tories and soldiers like flies. And that was my goal. To make them pay for everything they'd taken from me.

"Then you fell out of the army and onto a golden egg. I'm glad for you!" He slapped me on the back as if we could pick right up where we'd left off.

As if he wasn't my enemy.

3
HANNAH

It was as awkward a tea as I had ever been
party to. The mahogany furniture in the
front parlor had been bought from the city's
finest craftsmen, but the simple lines of the
tea table and glass-paned secretary, even
the dark blue upholstered French chairs,
seemed to quail at the colonel's bright
finery. His gleaming boots, glimmering
gilded gorget, and scarlet-colored coat did
not belong here in our quiet, dignified,
simple world. The colonel, Father, Mother,
and I sat, speaking not a word to each other.
Indeed, my knees were shaking beneath my
skirts, and I had long before abandoned my
cup to its saucer due to the trembling of my
fingers. It was unthinkable that a Friend like
my father who had denounced both sides in
this rebellion, who had firmly chosen not to
support either cause, would be forced to
quarter a soldier. It was an outrage!

An outrage we had no choice but to endure.

We Sunderlands knew the price exacted for our peculiar convictions. In a time of war, there was very little tolerance for peace. My grandfather had paid for his Quaker beliefs with his very life, protesting the treatment of the colony's Indians to those who now called themselves patriots. He'd been clubbed to death while British soldiers stood by and watched. And just this past September my own father had been dragged from the house by rebel soldiers while crowds looked on. Friends would be forever watched and never safe. It did not matter who helmed the government or who controlled the land. I feared the rebels just as much as the Loyalists.

As we sat there in discomfited silence, I heard the front door open and saw a flash of blue in the front hall as someone offered a cloak up to the maid. My friend, Betsy Evans, appeared in the doorway. She started forward, but as her gaze came to rest upon the colonel, she stopped.

Mother rose and drew her into the room with a hand to her elbow. "Thee must take tea with us."

She had already slipped from Mother's grip and was backing toward the hall. "No.

I cannot stay. I had only come to pass a message."

"A message!" Father came to his feet, urging Betsy to come in and sit. "Do tell. Has there been word from our Friends exiled to Virginia?" The plight of those Friends seemed to weigh heavy on his heart. I suspected it had to do with his originally being numbered among them back in September. Since our paper manufactory had closed for want of materials, he spent his days advocating on their behalf to anyone who would listen.

Betsy shook her head. "Perhaps . . ." She closed her mouth with a frown and then opened it to speak again. "I'm to see John James and Isaac Jackson this afternoon. Perhaps they will have had some word from Virginia." Be that as it may, I knew my friend. I knew there was more to her visit than she was saying. But she declined both a cup of tea and a chair. "I'll stop by later. After I've been to see the others."

Mother caught her by the hand. "If thee have something to say, please, say it."

She eyed the colonel once more. Then she enclosed Mother's hand with her other. "It's Robert. He was taken in a skirmish and —"

"He wasn't — ?"

"No! Thee are not to fear. He's alive.

37

That's what I've come to say. He's been put into jail. The new one on Walnut Street."

"Jail?" Mother was swaying now. Betsy moved to take one of her arms while I took the other; we helped her back to her chair.

"And who is Robert?" The colonel was looking with a keen eye at me and at Betsy.

"My son." Father's voice made it clear that he rather wished it weren't so.

"Your *son?* There are more of you?"

Father's frown and a dismissive wave of his hand told all that need be known of Robert Sunderland, father's firstborn son and my twin. Robert had been born and raised a Friend, and then he'd turned his back on his faith and joined in the rebellion.

"So. This Robert is both your son and a rebel. My. That *is* interesting. I thought you people were supposed to be above that sort of thing."

The tops of Father's cheeks had gone red. "Each man must make his own choice."

"Could his choice be your choice too? Do you wish to see His Majesty's rule abolished?"

"We wish nothing more or less than a peaceable end to this conflict."

"Don't we all!" The colonel laughed and raised his teacup in Father's direction. "Well said: a peaceable end. That's exactly what we'll have, even if I have to shoot every rebel in the colonies myself."

When Betsy slipped from the room, I followed her. I stood beside her, silent, while the maid placed the cloak about her shoulders and opened the door. As Betsy stepped out onto the front stoop, I went with her.

"Oh, Hannah!" Betsy buried her head in my shoulder and wept. Robert's own Betsy — the girl he had meant to marry until this conflict had taken him from his faith and from his home. "He's lost to us. General Howe isn't allowing visitors to the jail. And even if he were . . ."

Even if he were, no Friend would go. It was forbidden. To aid a soldier in any way was to support his cause and that we could not do. Our sole purpose was peace and the capacity of man to maintain it. Yet what if Robert had been wounded? Surely an exception could be made in that case, couldn't it? To be so set on peace in a time of strife was a terrible trial to the soul.

"They say the prisoners are starving . . ." Sobs overcame her words.

"Surely they're not starving. General Howe could not refuse them food." Could he?

"I don't know what to hope for. Not now."

Hope. A good Friend would hope that through this tribulation Robert would come to his senses, renounce his actions, and return to the faith. But a sister, or a true friend, would hope — pray, even — that Providence would allow him some sort of comfort or some kind of mercy. That he might receive no penalty, no punishment for his sins. But what sort of sister or friend could pray for mercy when the soul was in danger of eternal damnation? "It will turn out. All will be well." I took Betsy's face between my hands and kissed her on both cheeks.

She held up a trembling hand to mine. "All will be well?"

"Aye. Thee will see."

"I just . . . I don't know what to think." She seized my hand and squeezed it before giving me a tremulous smile as she turned to leave.

"What can he be thinking?" Father had roared the words across the table last autumn after reading the letter Robert had left behind when he'd joined the rebels. Once he had flung it from his hand, Mother hastily pulled it from the table. It had disappeared into her lap. "Of all the foolish

—" He pushed to his feet and stalked from the room, leaving his chair upturned in his wake.

I knew what Robert had been thinking. I knew exactly why it was that he had gone.

It had to do with Fanny Pruitt.

We had fled the city for the summer house the spring past because Father had thought it safer. And it had been for us. But not for Fanny, the hired kitchen girl. One morning when he'd gone out to saddle his horse, Robert had found her, bloodied and beaten, hiding in the stables. He'd coaxed her into the house and enlisted me to tend to her.

She would not speak — and never did speak so far as I knew — about what had befallen her. But as her belly had swelled with child toward summer's end, it became quite clear what had happened. And the fits she went into whenever she saw a British soldier pass by on the road told us who had done it. We couldn't keep her in service, of course, though Robert had protested strenuously against Father's dismissal of her. When we had moved back to the city in August, someone else had been found to replace her.

It was Fanny Pruitt who had made Robert take up the rebels' cause as his own.

I knew what he was thinking; I'd always

41

known what he was thinking. At nineteen years, his decision wasn't a rebellion of youth and it wasn't a fascination with arms or some misguided search for adventure. It wasn't any of the things that the Friends in Meeting had later decided upon in explanation.

I knew the reason was Fanny, because he had told me so.

"I heard it, Hannah. That night I heard her. There was a terrible mewling outside as if some poor kitten had gotten lost and couldn't find its way back to its mother. I knew something was wrong, but I didn't do anything about it. I'm a Friend; I'm not supposed to. I pulled my pillow over my head and willed myself back to sleep." He spoke the words with a regret sharpened by guilt.

I laid a hand on his arm. "It's not thy fault, Robert. It wasn't thee that —"

"Did it?" He looked at me with eyes just as gray as my own. "No. But what am I to do now? How am I to look at her? How can I walk by Fanny Pruitt every day of my life knowing what I allowed to happen?" He beseeched me as if I might have some answer. "It isn't right what those soldiers are doing."

Of course, I argued with him. "The rebels

do the same. The very same things, Robert. They steal and rape and plunder under protection of the name of General Washington. Thee know that they do."

"Aye. But to my way of thinking the British ought to hold themselves to higher standards. They're here to keep the peace, Hannah. They're here to enforce the king's law. If the king doesn't care that his soldiers molest innocent country girls, if he allows such crimes to go unanswered, then he's no king for me."

"The king doesn't even know Fanny Pruitt!"

"But there are ten thousand in these colonies just like her. And if he cannot protect the meek and the poor, then why should I obey him?"

"Thee cannot just choose whom to serve, Robert! 'Tis treason. And worse, 'tis rebellion!"

"And what of the king? He's a tyrant. What of that?"

I could feel his fury, his outrage, his anger. I had always felt what Robert did. And so I understood that to him, the conflict had become personal. But then he always took everything so personally, as if it were he himself the king had somehow misused. It wasn't two days later that he slipped out of the house at night. He hadn't a musket to take with him, but he'd packed what he had: his plain, unadorned coat and his uncocked, wide-brimmed hat. He hadn't been thinking of kings or war or anything else. He'd been thinking of Fanny Pruitt.

As I stood there watching Betsy go, I took in a shaky breath of winter air and then gave it back with a swirl of frost. I walked back into the parlor and found the colonel had finally put those long legs of his to use and left us. In his absence, Father had gathered the family together. I sat in a chair, took up little Jonah, and put him on my lap.

Father was speaking. "Perhaps this time in jail will remind Robert of his testimony."

Mother's hand was fingering her pocket. I was certain she had Robert's letter hidden there inside. "We must pray that it is so."

I would pray, but I could also act. "I can take the hired girl and try to visit in the morning. They ought to allow me to leave some broth or some whey." If I were there first thing, perhaps I might also be allowed to see him.

"Broth or whey . . . ?"

"Something of sustenance in case he was wounded in the capture."

Father shook his head as he frowned.

"He's in that sorry place because of the choices he made. We cannot forget the Yearly Meeting's admonishment: We must have nothing to do with this ungodly conflict. 'Tis rebellion that placed those soldiers where they are. It's up to those who enticed them into this conflict to find a way to succor them."

"But —"

"We can pray for his soul. But he gave himself over to those rebels; now those rebels have the charge of keeping him."

I woke at the night watchman's call of two o'clock, trembling. Though I slept under cover of several blankets, my back pressed up against my sister Sally's, my limbs had gone stiff with the cold and my bones ached from it. Though I pulled the sheets up over my head, and though I pulled my knees up to my chest for warmth, I shivered for the rest of the night as if I were sleeping outside in the snow.

That morning my fingers were numb with cold. As I went down the back stair to breakfast, I nearly stumbled. My feet had gone numb too.

Mother gave a cry when she saw me. "Thee are near to blue!" She laid a kiss upon my cheek, gasped, and then grabbed at my hand. "Such cold thee have!" She turned toward the hired girl. "Sadie, draw a chair up to the fire!"

Mother wrapped scarves around my neck and piled cloaks upon my shoulders, but nothing helped. And as I sat there, a burning restlessness grew inside of me. Finally I shed the cloaks, keeping only my own. Pulling it tight at the throat, I fled the warmth of the kitchen for the door.

"But where are thee — ?"

"Out." I had to get out.

I nearly ran right into the colonel's Hessian as I pushed through the door, but I didn't stop. I didn't want to give him any of my time because I needed . . . something. And I needed it desperately. But I didn't know where it was, and I didn't know how to find it.

Eventually I made my way to the new jail at the corner of Sixth and Walnut Streets. I hid my nose in my cloak against the stench that wafted from the broken windows and tried to close my ears against the cries that came from inside. But finally, as I stood there, my restlessness eased. It was then I understood what I ought to have known from the beginning.

It was Robert.

I was feeling Robert's pain. I was numb

with Robert's cold.

Waiting until the sentry marching duty in front of the jail had turned round the corner, I ran toward the iron fence that ringed the building. I shouted toward one of the broken basement windows. "Can anyone hear me?"

There was no faltering, no ceasing of the groans or cries, but there seemed to come a shifting somewhere down there in the dark.

"Is anyone there? Can anyone hear me?" I pulled my cloak up around my nose again, to stay the stench from my nostrils.

"Who've you come for?" The voice that answered was sepulchral in tone.

"I want — I needed — is there a Robert Sunderland in there?"

"What've you got?"

"I . . ." The sentry had not yet reappeared, but I feared he would soon round the corner and see me.

"Any food? Have you a blanket?"

I hadn't anything at all. "I can bring one."

"You've nothing? Nothing at all? Then what did you come for?"

"To see my brother." With those words that desperate need inside me eased again.

"What's his name, then?"

"Robert Sunderland."

"You'll have to wait . . ."

Wait. I wished I could have, but the sentry didn't grant me that luxury. I fled across the street and pretended an interest in the cobbler's wares. When he finally turned once more, when I could return to the window, no one answered my call.

But I knew now what I had felt. It was the same thing that had woken me in the night. It was my brother. He needed me.

4
JEREMIAH

I had tried my best to forget about the tailor's desertion and the general's demand, but morning's light proved me unsuccessful: I'd dreamed of the two gentlemen all night. Leaving the windows curtained, I stirred the fire and held a taper out to the coals. Once the wick flared I returned the candle to its holder on the table. Pulling the tailor's crumpled message from the pocket of my waistcoat, I set a weight upon one corner and then smoothed it out with my hand.

It was written upon a scrap of paper in script so miniscule I had to squint to read it.

Consisting of a series of words and numbers, the message could only be decoded with a key. And that, the tailor had said, could be found in a book. Thomas Paine's *Common Sense.* I had to admire the fellow who had figured that out. Nearly every

household was bound to have a copy —
even in occupied Philadelphia. The patriots
revered it and the Tories mocked it.

I took a piece of foolscap from the desk
drawer, then readied my ink and a quill.

Consulting the book, I managed to decode
the message, but it was tricky work, made
trickier by a guttering candle and the lack
of fingers on a second hand by which to
mark my place in Paine's work. After an
hour's labor the message lay before me,
transcribed.

Sergeant William Addison to undertake
escape from new jail. A tunnel started at
southwest corner and dug west for 53
feet will allow escape opposite Southeast
Square.

Southeast Square! And if they failed to
dig due west? They'd find themselves exca-
vating a cemetery.

Advise how long will take.

This message required an answer, which
in turn required coordination and repeated
communication with the prisoners. Didn't
General Washington know the trouble the
last escape had caused them? Now they
couldn't even be visited by family members.

Not unless General Howe himself granted permission. Who could wonder that the tailor didn't want any part in it? And more, who could blame him?

I crumpled both messages and threw them into the fire. The flames teased at them — curling the ends, poking at their middles — before devouring them. I closed Paine's book and put it back on the shelf, then pushed back the curtains at the windows.

Outside, snowflakes were being driven sideways by the wind. I knew what it was like to be exposed to such weather. A garrisoned soldier has little to distinguish himself from an imprisoned soldier. Perhaps he is free to go where he wants within the garrison, but who would choose to wander far in conditions such as these?

Poor, miserable prisoners. I couldn't assume they had any food, any fire, or any blankets. Though surely they had straw, and walls to keep out the wind. There had to be some way to aid in their escape.

But there wasn't.

It was no use trying to pass a message in from outside the jail. No letters tied about stones and thrown at the windows. Sentries guarded the jail at all hours. Nor was there any use trying to shout a message to the prisoners. It was rumored there were traitors among the prisoners, placed there to recruit spies to the Loyalist cause. There was no way around it: the only way to pass a message was from the inside. And that was someplace no presumed Loyalist like me would ever go. Even if I could think up some reason, Howe's orders were to let no one in without a pass. And passes were only issued by him.

Poor wretches.

The longer they stayed in that jail, the more likely they were to die there. A sad fact of army life. It wasn't the bullets and cannons that killed a man. It was the illness, the damp, and the cold. Death by prolonged misery.

I took myself downstairs and tried to busy myself with the accounts of the daybook before dinner was served. But I was soon driven from the comforts of the fire and the numbing smell of liquor by foul memories. Retrieving my cloak, I went out into the storm. Leaning into the wind, I walked the four blocks to the jail. Even in this weather it looked as smug and sanctimonious as the officials who had built it. But judging from the stench borne on the wind, those righteous people hadn't thought about the practicalities of what happened when three dozen men were crammed into rooms meant for eight or ten.

Was that . . . ? I stepped closer. Peered at the window nearest me, one that provided light to the basement. It was broken. I blinked. Put my hand up to brush away the snowflakes that had collected on my lashes. Aye. It was broken. As was the one next to it. And the one above it. In fact, every window I could see through that driving snow was shattered. And walls alone could not keep a wind as stiff and pernicious as this one away from the inmates. I wished I could do something about it. I wished I could help those prisoners escape. But it could not be done.

The tailor was right.

It was getting too dangerous to meet up with egg-girls and exchange messages at the market. The militia patrolling the city was beginning to pay attention to such things. But worse, General Washington was no longer allowing farmers to slip through the lines with their goods. The army at Valley Forge needed their supplies too much.

It was impossible.

While I stood there feeling ineffectual and utterly useless, a form turned the corner from Fifth Street and made its way toward me, cloak drawn up under the chin, hood riding low across the forehead. As it neared me, a gust of wind pried off the hood. A gloved hand reached out to catch it, but finally gave up, letting it ride at her neck.

The Sunderland girl. With that self-righteous look all Quaker girls seemed to wear. She glanced up as she neared me.

I sneered at her.

She lifted her chin and looked as if she might walk right on by.

Walk right on by that deplorable, reeking jail and all those prisoners shut up inside. Walk right on by a man who had done his duty, who had *fought* for things. Things those Quakers didn't deem as worthy as their principles. Principles were fine enough, for those who had them, but what about all the colonists who had died in the French and Indian Wars? What about all those men who'd been massacred at Devil's Hole? And what about all the people who would have died had the rest of us not risen to the task those Quakers disdained?

Sunderland.

I cursed that name. Her grandfather had been among the worst of the peacemongers in government during the wars that had savaged the countryside. I had no arm, thanks to him. Thanks to *them* I'd been left with a ghost of a hand that ached abominably even though it was no longer there.

"Hey! Did you know there are people in there? Prisoners? — *men?* — rotting in that jail right beside you?" I felt a perverse and overwhelming desire to provoke her into speaking. To make her say something, anything. As if that could make up for what had been taken from me. I snorted, though I hadn't meant to.

She stopped.

Turning, she took a step back toward me. Though she couldn't have struck me in the nose if she'd leaped at me, she looked as if she wanted to do that very thing. If I wasn't much mistaken, the girl had a temper. But while there was anger glittering in her eyes, teardrops had frozen to her lashes.

"Aye, I do know! Thee needn't be so surly about it. My brother is there among them. At least . . . I hope he still is." Her glance swept beyond me, toward the jail, then came back. She looked as if she wanted to say something more, but then she closed up that prim little mouth of hers and walked away, leaving me standing there feeling heartless. And cruel.

There had to be a way.

I took to walking about the city, ostensibly to visit the market. What little there was of it. But truly to walk around that jail, to try to figure out a way to get inside.

Over time I began to observe a pattern. Whenever I was heading toward the jail, the Sunderland girl seemed always to be walking away from it. We were both of us drawn to that place of despair. I had no doubt that she, like me, wanted nothing more than to get inside. She would have been scandalized to know what I might have done had I been granted access.

When I walked into the tavern Saturday evening, supper was already being served. Among the soldiers gathered to eat was John Lindley. "Jonesy!" he cried as he spied me. Holding up his bowl, he lurched toward me. "One more drink."

"You've already had about three more drinks by the look of you." Which wasn't a bad thing at all for my accounts.

"Congratulate me. I've been promoted." He placed an elbow on the bar as I took the bowl from him. "At least that's what they say. But *I* say I've been gulled. It's a staff job."

Staff job. I saluted him. "It's the War Office for you now, for certain."

"But it's not in Howe's office. I'm to sit one floor below."

I tried to hide a smile. He'd always been so keen on glory. It gave me the bitterest of pleasure to see him win a promotion to a staff job. No battlefield awards for bravery could be earned by sitting in an office administering the general's papers. "You'll use it to your benefit. You've always been good at that."

He leaned back with an angelic smile. "I *am* good at that, aren't I? Know what I did while I was back in England?"

Probably caught the clap. "I've no idea."

"I found myself an heiress."

I raised a brow as I filled his bowl with brandy. Passed it back.

"Daughter of Mr. Arthur Spotsworth, merchant prince. She's plain as a board and pink as a pig, but she's got ever so much lovely money to make up for it."

"Words said at leisure have a way of coming back to bite those who so misuse them."

He dismissed my warning with a florid wave, swaying as he tried to keep his feet. "Doesn't matter." He took a swig from the bowl. Swallowed. "We're to marry just as soon as I return."

I took the bowl from him and added some more. "Felicitations."

"Can you envision me, a married man?"

"You'll be as grand as the bride is rich."

"Aye. And that's the point of it all, isn't it?"

The point of it all. Perhaps it was — for people like him. I thanked God that I didn't have to worry about things like marriage and dowries. What girl with any sense would settle upon a crippled man? It seemed God had saved me from worse fates than I had known.

5
HANNAH

I was sitting in the Meeting House on the women's side, facing the presiding and recording clerks. I used to think that I might one day join their number. I used to strain to listen with my inner ear to hear the voice of God. But I did not know anything anymore, at least not with any sort of certainty.

I could not — *must not* — speak of the thoughts that daily passed through my mind. That was why I was sitting, lips pressed together, in the middle of the assembly. Even if the Spirit of God himself should move me, I dared not speak. To speak of my thoughts and to advocate for visiting the prisoners might bring disownment.

No Friend would shun me; my family would not abandon me. It was not those things that I feared. It was not the way of Friends to refuse to acknowledge each other, but it *was* their way to stand apart from one they considered too worldly. And they would point out to any who wondered that though I came from a Quaker family, though I might be beloved by many Friends, they did not consider me one of their own. And what would I be without my faith? Where could I turn in these perilous days if not to those who believed as I did?

In the hush of the silence I uncurled the fists on my lap, stretched out my fingers, and then curled them up once more. To my right, Betsy Evans' eyes were closed, her lips moving in soundless prayer. To my left, old Anne Clifton had fallen asleep again. And from the men's side came the sonorous sounds of a snore.

Falling asleep hadn't used to be a problem in the early days of the rebellion. Back then, Meetings had gone on for hours. There had been no end to the words from God. But our Meeting had been silent for months now. Not even God himself had anything to say about the occupation. About the fences that had been torn down for firewood or the andirons that had been stolen from citizens' hearths. God seemed not to care about the families who had been turned out of their homes by the British, nor for the city's maidens that sacrificed their morality nightly for the gift of a soldier's shillings.

Everywhere I looked, everything I learned only added to the sense that there were grave injustices being heaped upon our land. And that Friends, too easily persuaded to silence, allowed them to continue. What if we were not only called to maintain peace but also to defend it?

What if we'd all been wrong? What if men were called to fight for what they believed in? "If —"

Beside me old Anne started and woke. On the other side of me, Betsy's eyes had flown open. And now they were both staring at me.

Had I . . . had I spoken aloud? I clapped a hand to my mouth.

"Friend Sunderland?" The presiding clerk was looking at me with much interest.

I shook my head.

He frowned. Raised a brow. *If . . . ?*

When I stood, it was only because I did not wish to embarrass myself any further. "I only wish that God would send a word. If God would only say a word . . ." I sat down just as fast as I could. That's what came from daydreaming: a testimony that was no testimony, a word without meaning. A wish.

From behind me there was a shifting among the pews. From the men's side came a cough and then the telltale shuffle of feet against the floor. Miracle of miracles, someone was standing to speak!

Old Andrew Chandler looked round at all of us. "God speaks to His children in diverse ways all the time. If we do not hear, it is because we do not listen."

The words struck me like a slap to the face.

I *was* listening. I was doing nothing *but* listening! I was trying to ignore all those outrageous thoughts that swirled inside my head and instead listen to the voice of God.

The rest of the Meeting passed in silence. I woke old Anne when it was over. Then I took Betsy's arm as we walked out the door, thinking that if she saw me leave Meeting with my friend, Mother would not worry if I took a bit longer to return home. In that case I could use the extra minutes to pass by the jail. And a few minutes more to stop and call on one of our invalid Friends. That way if Mother asked, I would not be lying if I told her I had been making calls. In the plural.

I stopped to warn her, pulling up my cloak to shelter my face from the rain. "I should like to call on Elizabeth Dynham before dinner."

"Then perhaps thee can pass on this letter from our dear Friends in Virginia. I know she'll want news of them."

I took the letter from her and put it into my pocket.

"When she's done with it, then thee can return it to the Hopkinses on thy way past."

Nodding, I tied my cloak beneath my chin.

"Maybe thee should take Sally with thee."

My ten-year-old sister looked up at me, sending silent pleas my way through gray eyes that looked so much like my beloved brother's. Normally I would have welcomed the company, but if I took my sister into my care, then I couldn't stop by the jail. "In this cold? She's so meager! She'll catch her death."

As Sally's eyes began to tear and her chin to tremble, I regretted my choice of words. I wanted nothing more than to assure her of my affection, but I could not do it. If she came, it would ruin everything. Mother nodded slowly. "I suppose thee have reason. Only do not linger."

Do not linger.

I could do nothing but linger after I left Betsy at her house and continued on to press the letter into Elizabeth Dynham's hands. She read it — aloud — from her bed, then passed it to the others who had called and were now standing in her bedroom beside me. Each of them read it in turn and then everyone discussed it and reread it. By the time I left Friend Dynham's and returned the letter to the Hopkinses, the time for dinner had long passed. Raindrops had been swept away by a relentless wind, and the sun had begun its winter-precipitated decline in the sky.

Up ahead was the King's Arms Tavern. Its windows spilled light; from its door came raucous laughter. I decided to pass to the other side of the street, fearing to come upon any of the soldiers who frequented the place. I had not wanted company to hinder my calls during the day, but I would not have minded some at that moment. I hurried up the four blocks to the jail, knowing I ought not be walking unescorted. But as I arrived at the corner, I realized I was not alone.

Standing there in the darkest shadow cast by the building was Jeremiah Jones. I could tell by the odd way he held himself, as if he was trying to balance for his missing arm.

As I passed, he stepped away from the shadow, moving toward me.

When I hastened my step, he did the same.

I had no love for the man. Nor for any of those who spoke of Friends with derision and mockery in their voices. All those soldiers from the French and Indian troubles seemed to blame the Friends for it. It was people like him who had fanned the emotions of the mob that had killed my grandfather. And people like him who catered to the vices of those who had arrested my father. It was because of people like Jeremiah Jones that I understood what it meant to be a Friend. I had always associated the discovery of being something other than what everyone else was, with him or those like him. Those prosecutors of war and of hate.

He must have once been handsome, but the hostility and the sullenness that hung about him had hardened his features. I cast one last look at the jail and closed my lips around a sigh. It seemed indeed as if he was intent upon me. If only he could be pleasant.

"Miss Sunderland."

"Jeremiah Jones." I stopped and looked up at him. His eyes, reflecting the sun's setting rays, were remarkably clear and disturbingly blue. Though the wind was cutting, he seemed impervious to the chill. His cravat was tied so loosely that it left his throat bared, and the worn brown coat he wore was unbuttoned. The wind teased hairs from his queue and tossed them about his head as we stood there.

"You'll never be able to get in to see your brother without a pass from General Howe."

"Aye, I know it. And I've already submitted my request." That jail loomed before me so ominous. And it was so . . . wretched. If only I could free Robert from it! "I hope it will not take long to get one."

"You might as well hope for the British to leave. And thank us on their way."

It's as I had thought, although it didn't please me to hear it.

"But I might be able to help you."

I felt my brow lift.

He bowed. "Aye. Me. Jeremiah Jones."

I blushed. I could not help it. " 'Tis not that I don't believe thee."

He straightened, cocked his head as he looked at me. "No. 'Tis more that you don't like me."

Gathering my skirts, I continued on my way.

"Wait. Stop. Please . . . I can help you. I know a major on Howe's staff. He can get you a pass."

"And why would thee help me?"

"Because I think that you might be able to help me in return." He attempted to take me by the arm, just like those soldiers had attempted to take Father, and just like they had tried to take me. I wrested it from him, fear gripping my heart. I would go nowhere with any man!

He took a step back from me as he held up his hand. "I only thought it might not do to attract attention to ourselves."

I glanced over at the sentry, who was staring back at me. Staring back at us. Against my better judgment I closed the distance between Jeremiah Jones and myself. "Perhaps we should keep walking. Thee were saying that thee might be able to help me?"

"I can get you permission to visit if you can pass a message to one of the prisoners while you're inside."

"A message."

"Aye."

"Communication with the prisoners is not allowed." General's Howe's proclamation had made that quite clear. If I were caught . . . nausea rose to my throat as I remembered those rebel soldiers coming for Father. I trembled beneath the folds of my cloak as I remembered how they'd mistreated him. And then how they'd mistreated me.

"Perhaps it's not, but have you always done as you're told?"

I had, although in truth I had not always wanted to. But Father's brief imprisonment had cured me of any temptation toward disobedience. The best course was to do what Friends had always done — to stay quiet and to stand back. "I must not do it. I'm disregarding my Meeting's wishes even now. I'm to leave my brother, Robert, to learn from his choices. If I visit him, I could be disowned."

"Ah. I see. You're willing to risk something, but not everything."

I felt my mouth drop open. Such a horrid man he was!

"How do you think your brother is faring? Do you think he's hale and hearty? Do you think he sleeps well at night?"

A shiver came over me. And an aching, bone-chilling cold.

"Do you think he's well fed?"

"No." I knew that he was not. I felt his hunger just as keenly as I felt my own.

"I can help you. I can help you help him. All you have to do is deliver a message for me."

Help him do something completely forbidden? As I looked at him, I saw such zeal, such determination in his eyes, it occurred to me that I might be mistaken. His intentions could be completely harmless. Perhaps he only wished to succor a relative or a friend . . . though there did not seem to be very many of those in this city. "What would the message say?"

His eyes darted down to his shoes before coming back to meet my gaze. " 'Tis nothing but a simple greeting. To a friend."

He was lying. I knew it as plainly as I knew anything. " 'Tis a lie that thee speak."

His lips crimped as he glared at me.

"If thee wish me to carry a message, I must know what it will say."

He leveled a look at me. "It would be better — safer for you — if you did not know."

"Do thee care so little for me that thee would ask me to risk everything for thy sake? 'Tis the very definition of selfishness."

"There are over a hundred men in that jail, Miss Sunderland. Men just like your brother."

"Hannah."

He blinked. "Hannah?"

"Hannah. There is no need to 'Miss' me as if thee hope to gain some sort of favor by doing so. In the eyes of God all persons are equal."

"Fine, *Hannah*. There are over a hundred men in that jail. Every day they linger, they risk death in dozens of ways. Camp fever, typhoid, smallpox . . . starvation."

My heart faltered within me.

"My message suggests a way of escape."

69

Hope took flight in my stomach. "From the jail?"

"Aye."

Isn't that what I'd just wished for? Although, if I were caught . . . ? The memory of the soldiers arresting my father returned. And with it the nausea that always accompanied it. I feared another encounter with men, no matter their political persuasions. Besides, what was it the Yearly Meeting had decided? "An escape would free those soldiers from the consequences of taking up arms against the king."

He shrugged a shoulder. "I suppose, if successful, that it would."

"I would not be helping any man's soul by allowing him to escape the consequences of his rebellion." Isn't that the way the pronouncement had been phrased?

His face had grown dangerously hard. "I'm not asking you to save anyone's soul. I'm simply asking you to deliver a message."

"I cannot do it."

"You mean you won't."

"I mean I can't." Not for the benefit of some sanctimonious rebel soldiers. I wanted no involvement in things that did not concern me. I just wanted to see Robert and provide him with the things he needed. Father had trusted the rebels to understand

70

his peaceful ways just as he now counted on the king's soldiers to protect his property. Both had failed him. I could allow neither side to consider me a friend to their cause.

He sent me a piercing glance. "It's because you're afraid, isn't it? I don't know why I expected anything else from a Quaker. You're so afraid of breaking the rules that you won't even risk delivering a message in exchange for a pass to visit your brother. Why don't you just say what you mean?"

"I always mean what I say!"

The corner of his mouth twitched up in what I would have called a smile on any other man. "That's not the same as saying what you mean, though, is it? Meaning what you say is much easier."

"Why can thee not understand?" I wasn't afraid of breaking the rules. Friends seemed able to do nothing else these days. What I feared was the punishment for breaking the rules. "I just —" He was right: I was afraid. But I wasn't about to admit it to him. And besides, he'd already walked away.

I conspired to go calling with Betsy that week. It wasn't difficult, as Mother had taken to bed with a catarrh. I was able, after returning Betsy to her house, to spend a few minutes at the jail before returning to my own. On third day, as I spoke into the basement window of the prison, I finally received news of my brother. "Aye, he's here. Over down across the other side."

"Can't he come speak to me himself?"

"It's a jail, miss!"

"I'm sorry. It's just —"

"Said, 'Could you get him a blanket.' And some food. We all need food."

"I'm so sorry. I've been trying. He's well, though?"

"As well as anyone can be in this hellhole filled with lice and vermin."

"Can thee tell him — ?"

"Hey! You there!" The sentry had already changed directions and was headed back my way.

I turned, pulled my hood low over my head, and walked away just as quickly as I could. It took three blocks for me to catch my breath and by then I was home.

Mother was sitting in the parlor, the pierced-tin foot warmer at her feet, a cap pulled down over her ears. "Out again? In this weather? Thee will catch thy death!"

I felt my cheeks color with guilt. "I just needed some air. And Betsy wanted to go calling. I can't stand . . ." I indicated the front rooms with a lift of my chin. The front rooms the colonel and his staff had taken over.

"I know it. I just don't . . ." Mother was wringing her hands. "Sometimes I wish. . . . If he weren't quite so . . ."

"Abominably and unspeakably selfish."

"Hannah!"

I wished I could learn to keep my thoughts to myself. It was true what I'd said to Jeremiah Jones: I meant the words I said. "That's what he is. He's selfish."

"And so are we all in our own secret ways."

Why did she have to be so infuriatingly . . . right? I took a generous breath of air in through my nostrils. As I pressed my lips together to keep from speaking, I realized I was doing that often of late.

"Hannah? Hannah!" The words invaded my dreams. They sounded as if they were spoken from a great distance. "Hannah?" Sally's words seemed to grip me, pulling me from the night's imaginings. "Hannah!"

"What is it?" I was used to the little ones waking me, though it never failed to vex. But Sally usually slept quietly beside me, in the bed we shared.

"I can't sleep."

I sighed. Neither could I. Not anymore.

Not for the hour it would take now to find my dreams once more. "Why not?"

"There's too much noise."

My senses came to the alert. "Where? In the alley?" Our neighbors had had their andirons stolen just the other night.

She shook her head. "Out there." She nodded toward the door.

"In the hall?" I slipped from bed and took up a candlestick. The weight of it would provide a deterrent to any thief. "Thee stay here in bed. Pull the covers right up over thy head. Stay warm." And safe. I drew the blanket up over her as I spoke. "I'll go see what it is." I hoped I would reach Father before I ran into whoever was out there. I prayed God would see me safe.

6

JEREMIAH

John Lindley, a married man.

That thought had taunted me for the better part of a week. I had once assumed I would be a married man by now. With a wife to keep me warm at night and children to look after me in my dotage. I'd never set my cap for an heiress. Not like John. I'd just wanted someone to spend my life with. And I'd never thought that dream too grand, that goal too lofty. Not until the massacre. 'Twas then I realized what great things I'd demanded of destiny. And only then I realized destiny would not bow to my demands.

For want of an arm I'd had to give up my ambition of a commission as a regular in the British army. I'd returned to my childhood home when I ought to have been establishing my own. For want of that same arm I'd been unable to stop a careening carriage that had tipped itself over and killed my father. My mother slid into a decline soon after and died of what she called a lonesome heart.

But how ironic was fate!

Had my youthful wishes been granted, I would this moment be fighting with the British against the patriots. As it was, I would give nearly anything for the chance to take up arms against them.

I turned the last drunk out of the tavern. Redistributed the chairs. Scattered the ashes in the hearth. I put the cook's girl to work with a broom and then went back into the kitchen where her mother, Mrs. Phippen, was supervising the putting away of the pewter.

She glanced at me. "It's over there." She gestured toward a pot that still hung over a mostly dead fire.

I walked over and peered inside. The remains of the night's offerings. Boiled mutton. I scraped the bottom of the pot with a ladle and emptied what came up onto a plate. I set it on the sideboard. Taking a few crackers from a box, I put them into my pocket, then chose several apples from a basket and put them into the other. I picked up the plate and took myself toward the back door.

"It's cold enough to kill a bear. Don't

know why any man would want to eat outside."

I had no intention of doing so, having had
my supper hours earlier. But what the cook
didn't know would only vex her. I stepped
out into the puddle-pocked backyard. Most
of those puddles had frozen over from the
cold, and twice I nearly slipped as I walked
over toward the well. Once I reached it I set
the plate on the well's wooden frame along
with the crackers and the apples. And then
I sat down.

It didn't take but a moment for a lad to
appear.

Clad in a ridiculously large coat and a pair
of indecently short breeches, he limped
toward me on bare feet. He sent me a sullen look before he inspected the feast I'd
laid out before him. Put the crackers into
one of his own pockets, the apples into the
other. "Fanny'll thank you."

I hoped she'd do more than thank me. I
hoped she'd eat them. "How's the babe?"

Bartholomew shrugged. "It eats and cries
and sleeps."

"And your mother?"

He shrugged again but he didn't say anything.

That couldn't be good. Mrs. Pruitt had
been lingering at death's door for weeks.

77

Her presence was the only thing that had allowed her children the luxury of the hovel they called home. Bartholomew took up the plate and sniffed at it. "It's burnt. That cook of yours must be in a mood."

Mrs. Phippen, moral arbiter that she was, always seemed to be in a mood. I suspected she'd chased Bartholomew away from the yard more times than I wanted to know. "We'd more mouths to feed than normal. It's cold, but there's no weather to keep them away. I had to scrape the bottom of the pot to find anything at all."

If Bartholomew was grateful for the favor, he didn't say so. He never said so. "Them redcoats is a fair-weathered lot."

I couldn't disagree.

Apparently he'd decided the mutton was fit enough to eat, for he finally sat down beside me and tucked into it with relish.

"You ever go up by the new jail? The one on Walnut Street?"

"No. The poor beggars don't have food enough for themselves. No hope in finding any there for us."

If anyone could figure out a way into that jail, it was an urchin like him.

"You passed the request I gave you to the commissary?"

He nodded.

"Did he say anything?"

"What was there to say? You promised him coin, didn't you? For the flour?"

I had.

He threw a shrewd glance at me. "I suppose the army's already paid him for it."

I looked at him with newfound appreciation. That's what I had supposed as well.

"And you're offering him coin for it just the same as they did. That's twice he's been paid for the same flour."

I didn't mind encouraging graft where I could. Not if it placed the redcoats at a disadvantage.

"And then them soldiers come into the tavern and pay you for what ought to be theirs by rights."

Aye. That was pretty much the way of it.

"So the commissary makes his money, you make your money."

I reached into my pocket and took the coins from it that I'd promised him. "And here is yours."

It disappeared even as I placed it into his palm. But he stayed to finish the rest of the meal. Then he patted his pockets, nodded at me, and walked away into the night.

I glanced at the sky. Stars glittered back at me.

If I could say nothing else at all about my

life, at least I could say this: I could see those stars. The prisoners sitting in the Walnut Street Jail could not. If a man was condemned to sit in the cold, if he were fated to starve to death, at least he ought to be able to see the stars.

"While you've been out there gazing at the stars, some slices from my pies have gone missing. I roused the stable boy so he could tell you what I think about it." It was quite clear the cook thought the lad had taken them.

Like most of the city's population, the boy had a family that needed his wages. With flour costing ten times its worth and butter all but vanished, I didn't know how anyone who went about their business honestly could afford to eat. "The boy's got to eat while he goes about his work. It's part of his pay."

Her eyes raked his small form with suspicion.

"Haven't you been feeding him, Mrs. Phippen?"

"I've been giving him what he deserves."

Plainly that wasn't very much in her vaulted opinion. I looked him over myself.

His eyes dodged mine.

"I won't begrudge the lad a piece of pie

or two. For work well done." I only hoped he'd be smart enough not to take a whole pie. I wouldn't be able to dismiss that sort of theft so easily. I clapped the boy on the shoulder and walked up the back stair to my room.

No fire brightened the hearth, but there was no need. No reason to linger in the frigid air. Once my head found my pillow I expected sleep.

Only it did not come.

I kept thinking about Bartholomew. And the stable boy. I could not help all the ragamuffins I wanted to — God only knew how many of them there were in the city. And I could not help but feel pity for the prisoners who were probably just as hungry. If only the Sunderland girl had agreed to my plan.

Hannah.

She wouldn't have been my first choice in a ballroom filled with prospective dance partners. Back when I frequented them. Back when I had my choice of the girls. She was pretty enough, of course. There was something to be said for the fire that flashed in her eyes. If only I could convince her to throw in with my plan. But what more could I do? What more could I say? She said she was worried about souls? Maybe I should offer her mine.

I could not keep from smiling into the darkness. What a miserable and unwelcome gift that would be.

The very definition of selfishness.

Aye. That was me. I suppose the Quaker in her made her say it. That was one thing a person could depend upon: that a Quaker would say exactly what was meant.

And she meant not to like me.

Though I couldn't blame her for it.

If truth be told, I didn't much like myself.

7
HANNAH

I cracked the door and stood listening, and very soon I realized the origin of the noises. The sounds were coming from Robert's old bedroom . . . the colonel's room. It seemed as if he was entertaining. As my ears began to distinguish the sounds in the darkness, a blush swept my face.

I made my way down the hall to Father and Mother's room, pushing at Father's shoulder once I reached the bed.

He broke off snoring, and then snuffled and swallowed. But then he began snoring once more. "Father!" I shook him harder. He tried to shrug off my hand.

"Father — it's the colonel!"

"What?" He struggled against the bed-clothes for a moment and then succeeded in casting them aside. "What is it?"

"The colonel. He seems to be . . . entertaining."

"At this late hour?"

"He seems to be entertaining a woman."

Father's brows disappeared into the hem of his nightcap. He bounded from bed, jerked the door open, and went out into the hall.

I stooped to light a taper in the embers of their fire before I followed.

When I joined him in the hall, Father was already pounding on the door. "Colonel Beckwith! What is the meaning of this?"

The noises stopped for a moment, but soon there came the sound of muffled laughter.

Father pounded on the door once more. "Come out of there at once!"

Down the hall I heard the patter of feet against floorboards and soon saw a pair of towheads, Ezekiel and little Jonah, peeking out at us around the doorframe.

I frowned at them and shook my head.

They vanished behind the door, and I could hear them scuttle back to bed.

Inside the colonel's room, the bed creaked and there came the rustle of bedclothes. Footsteps sounded across the floorboards and the door cracked open. "I'm afraid I'm not really up to a social call at this hour." Behind the door someone — some female — giggled.

"I insist thee come out." Father's nightcap

trembled from the vigorous pronouncement of those words.

"Fire and damnation!" The door jerked open and the colonel appeared. He was dressed in nothing but his nightshirt and a wig, though the wig was riding his head at an odd angle. From behind him came a snigger.

"Thee have broken our terms of agreement. Thee are entertaining guests in thy room and thee've woken the household. I must insist that thee explain thyself!"

The door swung wider, revealing a rather pretty though scantily clad woman. The colonel slipped an arm about her waist. "This, my dear Mr. Sunderland, is *Mrs.* Beckwith."

"Really, Colonel!" Father believed him not at all. And neither did I.

"Oh, dash it all! Her name is Maryann." He slapped her on the bottom as he spoke. Her giggle ended in a hiccup as she wound a sinuous arm about his neck.

"In the name of all that is right and holy, I demand that woman leave. Immediately!"

The colonel belched, not bothering to cover his mouth with his hand. "Sorry, old man, but you can see that I'm not quite right." He grinned and swooped down to plant a kiss on the woman's neck. "And I'm

85

far from holy."

"Thee cannot —"

The colonel shut the door in Father's face.

Father stood in front of that door for several long moments before turning to me. "Go back to bed, Hannah. I shall speak to the colonel in the morning."

I woke near dawn with a fearsome ache in the pit of my stomach, a gnawing pain that threatened to eat right through my belly into my soul. It was all I could do not to bolt down my porridge. And even after I had finished I wanted to plead for more. But that's when I knew for certain: Robert did need me. And he needed me *now*. If I waited any longer to try and help him, it would be at his peril. As I left the dining room, I grabbed my cloak from its peg.

Intending to go directly to the jail, I was stopped by the vehemence in the voices coming from the front room.

"I must insist that thee begin to comport thyself as a gentleman." If the colonel had known Father, he would have known that this command was no suggestion. "And I require that thee stop using my house as a den of fornication."

I peered around the corner and saw the colonel pass a finger around the scalloped edge of the tea table. Since he had taken it as his own, he had commanded all meals be served to him at that table. And he conducted all of his business there as well. He sighed. "And here I was thinking that the winter season might not be so bad after all." He tossed his napkin onto his plate and then pushed back his chair and rose. "In any case, I am a colonel in the King's army and I've requisitioned your house as my quarters. What I do — or fail to do — in my private room can be no concern of yours."

"I will not condone the presence of such vice in my own home!"

He yawned. "Suit yourself. I won't require you to stay."

Father stalked from the room, nearly running into me on his way out. "And where are thee going?"

"I was just —"

"Thee are not to leave this house."

I felt my brow lift. He had insisted the colonel leave, but the man had vowed to stay. He commanded that I stay, though I wanted quite desperately to leave. "I only —"

"Stay."

"It's been decided." Mother had kept all the children home from school and now she was tossing things into her trunk.

"We can't just leave. And we can't just leave the house to *him!*"

"He's made staying here untenable, and it's required that we keep peace."

By whom? Another thought that I dared not speak. "I thought *they* were here to keep the peace."

"Hush now. And do be quick about help- ing the children pack their things."

It didn't take much time to press their clothes into the trunk and place their things atop them. Little Jonah's top for spinning and Sally's doll. Eight-year-old Ezekiel's slingshot and ninepins. The hired man car- ried it down the stair when I was done. I followed along behind him, waiting in the front hall along with the others. I could hear the colonel in the front parlor.

We all could.

"What do you think, Private?"

"I'm sure it's much fancier now, sir."

"Aye. I would have to agree. I find I like it much better."

Mother lifted Jonah and grabbed Ezekiel by the hand, taking them out to the waiting carriage. Sally followed behind, dragging her heels across the stoop and lingering on the steps. I was as reluctant to leave our house as she. As I walked toward the door,

I paused and looked into the parlor. My gasp must have been louder than I knew, for the colonel spun in my direction.

"Ah! Miss Sunderland. What do you think of my handiwork?"

He was standing in front of Father's highboy, knife in hand. He'd clearly been carving at the wood for a crude Union flag had begun to take form in relief.

"That is not thine!"

"True. It's not. But I'm the one who has to look at it day after day and I find it rather plain."

The best, but plain. That's what Friends always bought. "There's nothing wrong with it." It had come from Gostelowe's workshop and was a masterpiece of craftsmanship.

"There is when I've a taste for all things fancy. But have no fear; I'll take great care with your things while you're gone." As I watched, he gouged a furrow across the smooth varnished surface of its side. "Oh, dear." He looked not at all apologetic. Giving me a salute with the knife, he went back to his work of defiling our furnishings.

I ran from the house, passing Sally on the walk. Tears of rage pricked at my eyes.

Mother stretched out a hand to help me into the carriage and then she extended it to Sally. "We nearly left thee behind! Is anything wrong?"

Sally's hand crept into mine beneath the cover of our skirts. I shook my head in reply to Mother's question. Nothing was wrong that could be fixed, and knowledge of the colonel's abuse would only cause her pain. It wasn't long after we had turned the corner onto Third Street that I thought to ask where we were going.

Father answered with a scowl. "To Aunt Rebekah's."

Aunt Rebekah's? "I didn't think . . . they aren't . . ."

Mother shook her head. A warning to be silent.

Father's paper manufactory had provided overabundantly for our family's needs, yet even the finest wove paper in the colony could not command the wealth of my uncle Edward Pennington's fleet of merchant ships. And since the British had occupied the city, even the most ragged of linen and cotton cloths had been commandeered for use in the hospitals. There were none left for the superfluous making of paper; the manufactory had long since locked up its doors. Father had been cautioning thrift and patience, and I knew he looked on the vain pursuits of the city's wealthy Loyalists the same as I did: uncharitably.

It didn't take long for us to reach Pennington House on Front Street. For good reason it had been called the finest mansion in the city. Built of handsome red brick with double chimneys, it was pierced with a multitude of windows on each side of its central door. As the carriage rolled up the drive, Aunt Rebekah stepped out to greet us. My uncle joined her a moment later and stood beside her, an arm about her waist.

It wasn't often that Mother visited her sister. Upon her marriage to Uncle Edward, an Anglican, Aunt Rebekah had been disowned by our Meeting. It might not have had the effect of separating her from the rest of the family, only they had taken to worshipping with the Anglicans. It's not that we never saw them; I noticed their carriage often on its trips about the city. And it's not that I didn't know my cousins; I knew who they were. It's simply that they didn't move in the same circles we did. And since Friends didn't celebrate Christmas or birthdays, there wasn't much call to spend time with those who did not believe as we did.

I'd seen enough, however, of my aunt to love her. And perhaps rather too much of her daughter, Polly, to say the same. We were of an equal age, 'tis true, but I doubt any would accuse us of having the same mind or soul.

"Come in, come in!" Aunt Rebekah was kissing Sally's still-plump cheeks and caressing little Jonah's bright curls. She enfolded Mother in a loving, if fierce, embrace. "Come have tea while your things are put away." As we'd been standing on their front porch, a small army of Negro servants had begun to port our trunks from the carriage into the house.

"I'll see to those." Father tried to relieve a boy, who staggered under the weight of a trunk, but the youth somehow managed to dodge Father's outstretched hands and continued up the stair unaided. He appealed to Uncle Edward. "They shouldn't bother with our trunks. Our own man will be along in a few minutes' time."

Aunt Rebekah was looking at Father as if she didn't quite understand what he was saying. "Bother? It's no bother."

Uncle Edward was frowning. He placed a hand at my aunt's back and escorted her inside.

"I cannot allow a slave to —"

Mother laid a hand upon Father's arm and gave her head the tiniest of shakes.

He scowled but said not another word

about trunks or hired men or slaves. The Philadelphia Yearly Meeting had begun disowning those who insisted upon keeping slaves. Though our members had hoped those who were not Friends would follow their example, none had. Indeed, none seemed to have noticed.

"Thee must seek not to offend, Elias." Mother's concerns were spoken in a low, firm voice.

"If I see an injustice, must I not try to right it?"

"Aye. Of course thee must. But 'tis not our home. We are but guests here."

We followed Aunt Rebekah, Uncle Edward, and the children into the parlor, where the walls had been painted a vivid coppered green and where yellow upholstered chairs kept company with a settee done up in brilliant coral. Atop the mantel, crystal vases glimmered in the morning light.

Father paused in his entering, as did I. "Not so much guests, perhaps, but prisoners in a cage of gilt." He sounded just as miserable as I felt.

While Mother and Father were lodged in the guest room, Sally with our cousin Caroline, and the younger children in the nursery with young Edward, I was to share Polly's room. It was just as much a spectacle as the parlor downstairs. Though the soft shade of blue in which it had been decorated was more restful to the mind, the number of flower-strewn flounces which bedecked the bed's coverlet and hangings proved a remarkable distraction to the eye. And so did the amount of lace which frothed from Polly's stomacher and dripped from her sleeves.

"You're to sleep there." Polly pointed to a trundle bed, which had been made up on the floor in the corner.

I unpinned my hat and bent to place it on the mattress. "It must be an imposition to be required to take in a stranger to share thy room."

She shrugged and looked at me. Or rather, at my gown. Her gaze flipped back up to my eyes. "Just as long as you aren't set on sharing my beaux as well."

In the general confusion of our move and subsequent settling in, and despite propriety's demands, I slipped away from Aunt's house and walked up to the jail unescorted.

Once the sentry guard had passed, I walked to the basement window. "It's me!"

"Who is it?"

"Me. The one who asked after Robert

94

Sunderland."

"Oh. You."

"How is he?"

"Just a minute."

I had to leave when the sentry started back in my direction, but once he'd passed, I returned. "Are thee still there?"

"You'd asked about Robert?"

"Aye."

"Well, he's sick."

I felt as if I'd been struck in the belly. "With what?"

"I'm no physician, miss! It wasn't said. Could be dysentery or smallpox. There's putrid fever going round. Could be anything. You want me to pass a word from you?"

"Tell him . . . tell him . . . I've been given permission to visit. I'll be coming to see him soon."

"He's ill but he's not that sick. Not yet. He'll know you're speaking lies. Word is, the general doesn't let anyone visit."

" 'Tis not a lie!" It wouldn't be. Not by the time I'd finished talking to Jeremiah Jones. Though I had intended never to speak to him again, it seemed I would now have to count upon him to turn my fib into a truth.

8
JEREMIAH

I'd come upon Hannah, as always, as she was leaving the environs of the jail. She was looking at me this day as if she loathed me. But hate is a slippery sort of thing. Sometimes it can turn back on itself. Sometimes the thing people hate most is themselves; I knew all about hate and self-loathing. I bowed.

"I'll do it."

"Pardon me?"

"I will do the thing thee asked of me." She spat the words through gritted teeth.

I wished she would speak the words she was thinking. I had a feeling they would be most amusing. I smiled. "Then I shall get you a pass."

"When? I need it quickly." Ill-disguised need burned in her eyes.

"I'll get it as soon as I am able."

"And how will I know when thee have come by it?"

"I'll find you." I bowed once more and turned to continue on down the street.

"But — we're not at home. A colonel has been quartered at our house."

That stayed me. "If you're not at home, then where are you?"

"At my aunt's."

"Though you might think that I know everything about you, I don't. I only know you're one of those Quakers." And that your grandfather was one of those who provoked the Indian Wars. "It would be helpful if you would tell me the name of this aunt."

"Pennington. We're at Pennington House."

I felt my mouth drop open before I could stop it. "You've fallen into a remarkably soft bed during these hard times, then!" The Sunderlands had made a nest for themselves among the most loyal of Loyalists in the city. "On second thought, perhaps I should forget I ever asked you for anything."

"No. Please! I need the pass."

"Then I'll find you once I've obtained it." I'd not one idea about how to go about asking John for a pass, let alone delivering it to her, but it was better than the alternative. It was better than having some conspicuous Quaker girl gadding about town, asking after me.

I returned to the King's Arms in search of

my barkeeper. I scanned the customers as I looked about. It was a terrifying sight, all of those redcoats. And grounds for a riot. At least that's what it sounded like.

John Lindley hailed me from the crowd. Sauntered up to the counter. Firelight glinted off the gilded gorget that hung about his throat. He was just the type of dandy of which Hannah's Penningtons would approve. I wondered if he'd met them. If he had, that connection might prove useful. "What do you know about the Pennington family? Have you fallen in with them yet?"

"They're the pride of your fair city, didn't you know? I'm certain Mr. Pennington would kiss King George's feet if ever given the chance."

So he had met them.

"And it just so happens I've been invited to a ball at Pennington House." He was preening like a goose.

"You? What would they want with a devil like you?"

He grinned. "I've heard they have a daughter."

Indeed they did. Pretty Polly Pennington. One of those fair flowers of Philadelphia with no shame and very little sense.

Lindley grasped my good shoulder. "Come with me. What do you say?"

"I'd say I haven't been to a ball in years. And besides that, I wasn't invited."

"Who cares about invitations! This is Philadelphia. Not London."

"Things have changed since we saw each other last."

"Please. Come."

And so, not because John sounded so desperate but because it would do my plans no harm to be noticed in the company of one of Howe's staff officers, I said yes.

"I shouldn't have come." I'd known it the minute I entered Pennington House the next evening. I knew by a certain telltale wobble in Mrs. Pennington's smile. And from a look of consternation on the fair Miss Pennington's face.

I bowed. Began to apologize.

John laid a hand on my arm. "I asked my good friend to see me safely to your lovely home."

Mrs. Pennington smiled charmingly. "Thank you, Mr. Jones, for your service. Of course you should stay. Please. Won't you take some refreshment with us?"

Refreshment was the last thing I was interested in taking. Truly I shouldn't have come. I could no longer observe the expected proprieties. And I'd long since

99

dispossessed myself of niceties. "I had not meant to inconvenience you."

"Oh, but it's no indisposition at all." Even a lie sounded pleasant, coming from that gracious lady's lips.

"I'll just . . ." I put my hat back on my head, intending to leave.

But at that moment, Hannah Sunderland appeared at the top of the stair.

"You know our cousin, don't you?" Polly had followed my gaze. "Please stay. That way she'll have someone to talk to. She's a *Quaker,* you know." She'd lowered her voice as she spoke that indelicate word.

"Oh, do stay!" Mrs. Pennington too was watching Hannah's descent. "She and her family just joined us. This way she'll have someone to talk to while the others —" She broke off. But I could finish her thought. This way Hannah would have someone to talk to while the others danced. It seemed we were both unfit for polite society.

For her part, Hannah paused in her step as if she regretted descending. But she did not retreat fast enough. "Hannah, my dear, have you met Major Lindley?"

Her shoulders had hunched as if she feared some violence from him. But as we watched, they straightened. She descended and came to stand between Mrs. Pennington and her daughter. Her face was grave, her eyes wary.

"Major Lindley is on General Howe's staff."

John bowed. "A pleasure."

Hannah inclined her head, though she did not extend her hand, she did not flutter her eyelashes, nor did she flash a smile. In short, she did nothing at all that her cousin had done.

"And this is Mr. Jeremiah Jones."

It seemed she had not noticed me. To be fair, my hat had thrown my face into a shadow. She was a sight to regard as she looked at me. Her face went pale as the moon and then her gaze ricocheted between John and Mrs. Pennington and her cousin, as if she was frightened that they might discover our business. If she didn't gain possession of herself, she'd betray our plans before we'd even begun to accomplish them.

I removed my hat. Bowed.

"Oh, but we've —"

I didn't want her to divulge our acquaintanceship. People might begin asking questions. "We've had the pleasure of passing each other on the street, but have never before been introduced."

Mrs. Pennington led the way into the parlor. The family's fabled carpets had been

101

taken up and the chairs and gaming tables pushed against the walls. In the corner, a cluster of musicians tuned their instruments. The sound of strings and the glow of a room lit by candlelight made me want nothing so much as to leave. To spend the several hours here that politeness now required would be certain torture. To be expected to watch others dance and flirt was too cruel a request. Which was why I rarely frequented polite society.

The truth was that I preferred no society at all.

"Please, Jeremiah Jones, would thee like to sit?"

I turned my attentions from the dance floor to the person of Hannah Sunderland. She had decided, it seemed, to tolerate me.

"We're suffered to be here now, the both of us, until the evening ends. And while thy shoes look presentable, they cannot be any more comfortable than my own."

How I hated sensible people. They were always so . . . so . . . reasonable. And it was even worse when they happened to be right. I settled into the chair beside her.

"Why did thee say that?"

I cast a glance at her. "Say what?"

"About us never having before met."

"I didn't say we'd never met. I said we'd

102

never been introduced."

Her lips folded into a careful, if moderate, frown. "I'm still not certain how I feel about our partnership, but one thing I will not do. I will not lie."

"You didn't."

"And I won't have thee lie on my behalf."

"I didn't." It was on my own behalf that I'd lied.

She looked as if she wanted to say something more. Thankfully, she did not.

It let me put my mind to work on the jail. John was our means of entry, but I had yet to come upon a way to request the pass. It would have to be on her behalf, of course. But why should an avowed Loyalist like me care about whether some Quaker's brother languished in prison? I might as well just tell the truth: I'd like to organize a prison escape.

I finally gave up in frustration and was rather surprised to find the girl still sitting beside me in apparent ease. Most girls would have taken my silence as an insult by now.

"Would you care for some punch?" I found myself saying the words before I could think to stop them. A perfunctory courtesy — a relic from another time. A time when I'd been invited into all the most fashionable homes in the city. A time when I'd been the epitome of all that was genteel.

She looked at me as if she suspected there was some trap hidden in my offer. Finally she nodded. "Yes. Please."

I excused myself and made my way to the punch bowl, where John was laughing with a captain. "Jonesy!" He leaned close to speak into my ear. "She's quite a belle. Or she would be if it weren't for that gown."

"Who?" I turned to see who he was talking about.

"The Sunderland girl."

It wasn't difficult to make a pretense of admiration. She *was* a remarkably handsome girl. Hair the color of the ripest of barleys. Eyes the coolest shade of gray. You'd know it if she looked at you. There was no artifice in them. Just calm appraisal.

"Does she interest you, then?"

"Who — her?"

"Aye." His eyes were laughing at me. "That girl. The Quaker one."

I shrugged.

He looked at me in a keen-eyed way. "You old dog! Why you'd settle for a provincial, I've no idea." His eyes strayed to my empty sleeve and a flush overcame his features. "Though there's nothing wrong with it, of course."

"Sometimes beggars can't be choosers." I didn't know why I should correct his misconception about my interest when it was so amusing to see him flustered.

"Of course. Of course. I didn't mean to imply . . ."

He was pathetic, clearly not used to thinking before he spoke. Or thinking of others at all, in fact. I used to find that quality highly entertaining.

"Of course not."

"Of course not. I mean . . . I meant the other one. Her cousin. The *Pennington* girl is quite a belle, don't you think?"

I might have found myself enamored of Miss Pennington had circumstances been different. She was exactly the kind of society girl I used to find so attractive. "She's quite diverting."

"Very diverting. Yes! Might as well have a diversion if we're to be stuck in this place for the winter."

"You would have found Philadelphia quite pleasant last summer, before all her trees were chopped down for firewood and all her houses requisitioned for quarters."

"Shame, that." He spoke the words as if he had none at all.

"Well. I'm to deliver up some punch." I picked my way through the crowds to the relative seclusion of the chair-lined wall and then sat down and handed Miss Sunderland — *Hannah* — a bowl.

"I thank thee."

I gave a nod, then looked away . . . to find John's eyes upon me. He sent me an exuberant wink.

He did actually think . . . ? Wait. Wait just a minute. He thought . . . if he thought I nursed an affection for Hannah, then it might not be so odd, in his eyes, to advocate for a prison pass on her behalf. I slid a look in her direction. To complete the illusion, however, I would have to act the part.

I flashed her the smile that had once dazzled girls in three colonies. "Isn't this companionable."

Her lips did not return the gesture. Instead, she raised the bowl to her mouth, took a sip. Swallowed. "It might be had I wished for a companion."

"Tsk, tsk." I leaned close in what I hoped would be interpreted as a display of regard. "I have a plan. Tomorrow morning about ten of the clock, I want you to request to see Major Lindley at Howe's headquarters at the Penn House. You may have to find a way to be brought to him."

"*Brought* to him . . . I have no intention of ever requesting to see a soldier!"

I shrugged. "If a simple request to see him won't work, then you might have to make a scene."

"Thee don't understand —"

"No. *You* don't understand. Do you want to help your brother or not?"

There was something going on behind those somber gray eyes. Something that took some effort to resolve.

"I know you people are known for your peaceable ways, but if it comes to it, you may have to think of a reason to stage a fit."

She turned to look at me straight on. "In the case that being driven to treason in order to visit my brother would not be enough? Do thee think the fact that a red-coated colonel dismissed us from our own home just last morning would do?"

I felt the corners of my lips quirk. "It might."

The humor that had briefly flickered in the depths of those solemn eyes guttered and then went out. "I will do what I must."

"Once you're inside, once you've been brought to the major, then you need to ask him for a pass. No matter what happens, no matter what might be said, you *must* ask him for a pass. And remember, no one knows about our arrangement. So just act . . . as if there's nothing to act about."

Now she was frowning. "I told thee, I won't lie for thee or for anyone else."

"I'm not asking you to lie. I'm simply asking you not to reveal everything you know. To pretend you're not doing anything wrong."

"To pretend is to lie to oneself."

"Then don't say anything at all!"

Her eyes caught my own. "Thee might wish to lower thy voice."

Dash it all! I would if she didn't vex me so!

9
HANNAH

The next morning over breakfast Mother leaned close and asked me to go calling with her that morning, before dinner. Which meant I wouldn't be able to go to General Howe's headquarters as Jeremiah Jones had requested.

"But if I go, who will watch Jonah?"

"Rebekah said that Jenny can do it."

My aunt nodded, confirming Mother's words.

Jenny? Jenny was one of the enslaved. "But that isn't —"

Mother made a motion with her hand to hush.

The others — Aunt Rebekah and Polly; Sally, Caroline, Ezekiel, and young Edward — were all staring at us. Little Jonah had toddled off to the corner. He was having a visit with the parakeet that lived there in a cage. Father had already looked up from the newspaper. "That isn't right? Because she's enslaved? Is that what thee meant to say, Hannah?"

My face flushed as I nodded. I had yet to feel as if I could speak freely and in good conscience in this house that was not our own.

"I agree with thee. 'Tis sorry work to take advantage of those things we have purposely denied ourselves." He made a point not to look at Mother as he spoke.

Mother leaned around me to address him. "I'm not taking advantage, Elias. I'm simply making do for expediency's sake. I haven't made a call in two weeks. And 'tisn't safe to send Hannah out, alone, to make our calls for us. She's done too much of that lately."

I flushed a deeper shade of red, knowing that my walks about the city had been discovered.

Father frowned, eyes on me, as if he was considering her arguments. "I like neither prospect. Life has demanded too many compromises of late. Would that we were all in our own homes, safe to walk about freely in our own city, with the soldiers gone and the rebellion stifled." He sighed and turned back to his newspaper.

"So we'll go, then?" Mother posed it as a question, but there was no indecision in her eyes.

"Go. And bring back some news." Father had an insatiable craving for news. It had developed after his manufactory had closed and it had not yet been quenched. I had no doubt he would go out after us in search of news himself.

Mother very nearly pushed me up the stair in her haste to change for calling. But as the door was opened for us to leave, we saw a man advancing up the walk toward us. "Friend Elliott!" Her whisper had a note of panic in it.

Normally I would have shared that sentiment, but perhaps now I would still be able to keep my appointment at the general's headquarters. If she had to stay to greet him, she might allow me to go on by myself. As she turned, I advanced. But as I reached the top step, I felt a tug on my cloak, pulling me back into the house.

I gave my cloak up to the doorman with disappointment and joined with Mother in greeting our friend.

Father too had been readying to go. He came down the front stair, dismay on his face. "Friend Elliott."

The man nodded. "I've come because there's news to be had from Virginia."

And too bad Samuel Elliott had been entrusted with that news. It would be an hour at least before he would get to the telling of it. Though short in stature, he was overlong in speech. Father often said that if he had been just a bit more strident, he might have been mistaken for a Presbyterian and saved our Meeting half its trouble. As it was, he settled into an offered chair as if he planned to stay a while.

But one could not long begrudge him his news. Everyone yearned for word of our Friends being held in exile. They'd been arrested along with Father by the patriot Supreme Council back in September without due process or any explanation at all. And when officials had appealed to the Continental Congress on their behalf, Congress appealed to the Supreme Council and the Supreme Council had washed their hands of the whole affair. Once they had been exiled to Virginia, there was no one who claimed the authority to release them.

We waited for over an hour, only to hear that all the Friends were doing well and none of them was ill. Samuel Elliott left soon thereafter.

Father minced no words. "The only benefit of lodging here, with thy sister, is being saved the prospect of having to ask people to stay for dinner."

Mother didn't scold him the way she

might have done had we been back at Chestnut Street. There, our house had been renowned for its board. And we could count on upwards of twenty guests dining with us during the several-day Yearly Meetings that were held in the city.

As they stood talking, I slipped from the parlor, grabbed my cloak, and made for the door. My plan was to leave and be back before any had noticed that I'd gone. But I had not counted on the enslaved.

"The carriage for you, Miss Sunderland?" A man had stepped from the shadows as my hand reached for the door.

I cast a glance at the parlor. How long would it be until my parents appeared? "Hannah."

"Pardon me, miss?"

"Hannah. That's my name. And what is thy name?"

"My name be Davy, Miss Hannah."

"No. No 'miss.' Hannah will do."

"It may do for you, miss, but it surely won't do for me."

I might have told him all people were equal to each other in God's eyes, but I hadn't the time. I hoped God would forgive me. "No carriage, thank thee. I'm walking."

"You'll want Doll, then."

"I want no one. I'm perfectly fine by

myself."

"Miss Polly always takes Doll. She's not to leave the house without her. You're of an age, if you don't mind my saying, and Mrs. Pennington will tan my hide if I send you out into the city alone."

"Thee are not sending me anywhere. I am simply going by myself."

He shook his head. "No, miss. Not without Doll."

As if she'd been summoned by the conversation, a woman appeared at his elbow. I recognized her fine, dark features. Earlier that morning she'd served us breakfast.

He turned an admonishing eye on her. "You'll go with Miss Hannah wherever she go."

Clearly there was no way to deter him, and if I dallied any longer, I would risk being seen by my parents. *And* I'd be late. I'd just have to let her come along. "Fine then. Let's be going."

When we reached the gate, I moved to open it, but Doll reached it first. She was clearly my elder, so it didn't seem right for me to pass through first. "Please." I gestured her forward.

"No, miss."

"Please, I insist."

She shook her head, slowly but with

114

definite conviction. "No, miss. 'Tisn't right for the likes of me to pass before you."

"I'm expected at General Howe's headquarters at ten o'clock, and if thee do not pass through first, I shall feel obliged to stand here until thee do. And that will make me late."

She shook her head gravely. "No, miss. I know my place and it sure ain't to go ahead of you."

We stood there for a moment, she, I supposed, wanting desperately to stay within the constraints that she'd been given, and me desperately wishing that she didn't have any constraints at all. Would that she could know the truth that I did: There was that of God in everyone. And no man should bow to any but Him.

"What if thee went first and held the gate open for me?"

Doll pursed her lips, lifted her chin. "If that's what you want me to do."

That was not what I wanted her to do, but as Mother had said just that morning, sometimes we had to settle for expediency.

She opened the gate and held it for me. I went through it with a sigh of relief. If we walked quickly, I could still make it to headquarters on time.

"Hannah!"

I turned to see Mother coming down the steps, tying her hat beneath her chin as she came. "Wait for me!"

I only had several blocks to settle on a plan.

When we reached Third Street, I moved to the right as Mother began to turn left. Poor Doll, caught in confusion, was nearly knocked over by a cart that rumbled past.

"Hannah — this way! We're off to the Gilberts'. I've a mind to read the letter of which Friend Elliot spoke."

I wanted to read it as well, only not right then. Right then I had to figure out how to get to Major Lindley's office unaccompanied. A gust of wind sliced between us, pushing our skirts against our knees. "But the Gilberts are in the Northern Liberties. We'll be chilled to the bone before we reach them. Hadn't we better stop at the New-lands' first, to warm ourselves?" It was the only ploy I could think of to keep her in the city, myself along with her.

"Perhaps . . . I suppose the letter will still be there when we arrive."

My knees nearly buckled in relief. At least now I could walk in the right direction, though I still had to absent myself before we walked too much farther. I could not just state that I wanted to visit the general's

116

headquarters, could I? I ventured a look at Mother beneath the brim of my hat. No, I could not. For if I did, then I would have to explain my purpose. I was quite sure she had never contemplated disregarding — not once in her forty years — a pronouncement of the Meeting.

Not like I had.

And had she ever dared to contemplate it, I knew she would never have done it.

Not like I was going to.

Only two blocks left. I did not know how people managed a life of deceit. It was much too taxing, in my opinion. I'd already had to insist upon changing Mother's order of calls, and for no good reason save the cold. What could I possibly say that would convince Mother and Doll to go on their way and leave me behind?

"I haven't had the chance to call on the Evans in a while . . ." Mother was looking off toward Spruce Street, where Betsy lived with her family.

"Why don't I call on her?" I could do it after I'd stopped at Major Lindley's office.

Mother looked up the street toward the Northern Liberties, then back toward Spruce Street. "I'll leave thee with Doll then. Once thee are done, thee are to come on to the Gilberts directly."

117

"Why don't thee take Doll with thee?"

"And leave thee unescorted? In this city filled with soldiers! Now that I've been blessed with good health again, there will be no more of that!"

"It isn't necessary —"

"Thee must not forget that there are reputations to be defended and discarded in a city occupied by an army. I'll see thee at the Gilberts."

I watched her walk, stiff with resolution, up Fourth Street. My situation, however, was no better than it had been. "Thee don't have to stay with me, Doll."

"I just do what I'm told."

"Surely there's somewhere else thee would rather be."

"If I left you here alone, Davy'd have my hide."

I might have tried to coax her to change her opinion, but after the navigation of the front gate at Pennington House, I had no hope for success. There was nothing to be done for it then; I started off toward the general's headquarters, Doll following behind. Once we reached the building I was obliged to tell her the truth. "I have an appointment I must keep inside this building. Thee are free to return to Pennington House if thee wish."

"No, miss. If it's the same to you, I'll just wait right here."

I looked into her luminous brown eyes.

They looked right back at me.

"I suppose there's no way to make thee leave."

"No, miss. I wish I could do what you seem to want me to, but I take my orders from Davy. And he say stick with Miss Hannah, so stick I'm going to have to do."

"I shall return as soon as I am able."

"Yes, miss."

"Hannah."

"Yes, Miss Hannah."

Holding back a sigh, I turned from Doll and climbed the steps.

10
JEREMIAH

How difficult was it for a person to present herself at a particular place at a particular time? Hadn't I told that girl to have herself shown to John's office? At ten o'clock? Late enough to have opened up the tavern, but too early to think too hard yet about the service of dinner. I watched the minute hand of the clock that sat above John's fireplace round the face once more.

". . . in any case," John was saying, "we were told to expect a great uprising of Loyalist support once we occupied the city. And to the general's surprise, no great numbers have volunteered for the militia."

"I'm sure they'll become much more interested once spring begins to melt the snows." Where was she?

"You've lived here long enough. What do you think? Where are all these Loyalists we were promised?"

"Who told Howe to expect them?"

"That fellow who fled this city for New York. What was his name? Gilford? Galliard?"

"Galloway?" Joseph Galloway, Superintendent General of the city.

"That's the one."

"Galloway's entire fortune is linked with this city. He would have promised General Washington's head if he thought it would make Howe liberate Philadelphia from the rebels."

John's eyes went wide. "Are you saying that he lied, then?"

"I'm saying that he might not exactly have been telling the truth. Or if he was, then it was the kind of truth that a man wishes were true . . ."

"As opposed to the kind of truth that is, in fact, true?" John's face was growing red.

I shrugged.

"These infernal colonists! It's the way it's always been with them. Say one thing and do the other entirely."

Not, of course, like it had been with the Parliament: say one thing and do the other thing instead. Colonials in the army? Why not? Every man just as good as the next, except when it came to commissions. But as much as I wished to say it, as much as I wished to speak of what was unfair and unjust, I did not do it. I could not do it. Not if I wanted to maintain my position as the owner of one of the taverns most friendly to Tories.

Not that I'd had to work very hard to earn that reputation. I was known as the man who had lost his arm in Pontiac's War. Who would have thought that a veteran would have turned against his old master? Certainly not the hundreds of soldiers who frequented that veteran's tavern.

I could not afford to have my loyalties questioned, and I didn't care a fig what the patriots thought of me. Those who had meekly looked on as Howe marched into the city. At least I was doing something about my convictions. "Colonials. Who can trust them?"

John grinned. "Who exactly! Remember Devil's Hole? And how many of them turned and ran?"

I remembered.

"It was only you and I who held the platoons together."

It was only me, if I remembered correctly. When the volley had started and the smoke had swirled, I had been the only one left. John had been long gone.

"I've always thought fate dealt you a bad hand, Jonesy. You ought to have been born

British."

That was the whole problem: I had been. I'd been born a British citizen on colonial soil. And the British considered me a less desirable kind of citizen for it. If there was any reason Loyalists in the countryside hadn't risen to Howe's call, it was that. They'd learned the bitter truth. They were acceptable but only to a point. The point at which they could take a bullet meant for a British officer. "And I'd always thought fate dealt you a bad hand, John. You ought to have been born with a handsomer nose."

He put a hand up to the nose that projected from his face like a beak.

It gave me immense pleasure to know that I'd reminded him of what he considered to be his only weakness.

"I've been tempted to pay one of the boys to break it for me, only I don't know that I'd end up with anything better."

"I'd do it for you. For no payment at all."

"I've always said you were the best of fellows!"

And the worst of fools.

The door swung open and a private appeared. Bowed. "A Miss Sunderland to see you, sir."

John looked toward me and raised a brow as he straightened his queue.

I shrugged.

He stood. "Miss Sunderland. Should I know her?"

I saw Hannah appear in the doorway. Leaned forward while I still had the chance. "The Penningtons' dance. Last night."

His brow puckered. Cleared. "The Pennington girl's cousin. The one you had your eye on!"

He'd said it. Not me. And it served my purposes admirably for him to be reminded of it. I couldn't have planned the encounter any better than it was unfolding. He glanced at me as he greeted her. "Miss Sunderland. To what do I owe the honor of your presence?"

Hannah glanced at me.

I pointedly turned in the direction of the clock on the mantel. "My. Look at the time."

A flush lit the tops of her cheeks. "I've requested a pass from General Howe to visit my brother, and I wanted to know if my request will be granted."

John sat. "Your brother?"

"He's a prisoner in the new jail. On Walnut Street."

"Well . . . it's a pity he doesn't have an equal share of your good sense. He's a younger brother, I suppose."

"He's my twin."

John eyed me. Looked back at the girl. "A prison is no place for a young woman of your obviously genteel upbringing. And I don't know that the jailer is used to receiving visitors."

"He will find me as unobtrusive as a mouse. I only wish to know that my brother is well. And to care for him if need be."

"You know that there was a prison break in December . . ."

Hannah nodded.

"General Howe has a great fear of visitors being used to pass intelligence. So tell me, Miss Sunderland —"

"Hannah."

"— Miss Hannah, are you a spy?" Mirth danced in his eyes. He was mocking her. How I wished he knew the truth. It would knock that smirk right off his face. But — she was going to tell the truth. I could see it in her eyes! She opened her mouth. "I cannot —"

"Come, John. The girl's a Quaker. She's not used to such games. Her people speak forthrightly and plainly. Please. Be the gentleman that I know you to be. Respond in kind." I tried to sound as if I was advocating on her behalf. As if she held some interest for me.

"I apologize, Miss Hannah. I have not

125

been gallant." He slid a glance in my direction. "Not nearly as gallant as Mr. Jones. I believe you had the pleasure of his acquaintance last night."

She nodded.

"But I wager he did not tell you how he lost his arm."

"She doesn't need to know —"

"Did you know that Mr. Jones is a veritable hero?"

The girl's eyes were growing wide.

"John! You don't need to —"

"The hero of Devil's Hole. But I suppose he did not speak of it."

"I had heard." And clearly she didn't thank John for reminding her. Those Quakers could be so stuffy about things they didn't believe in.

I bowed. "I am so sorry to offend your sensibilities, Miss Sunderland, although the battles fought with the Indians saved our colonists from certain slaughter."

"Perhaps. Although I might not find myself indebted to thy sacrifice had more sensible heads been allowed to prevail."

Just like a Quaker. Hang her and all of her kind!

John's gaze was bouncing between the two of us. "I must apologize for my friend, Miss Hannah. He's usually not so churlish. In

126

any case, regarding your request." He sat down behind his desk, pulled a leaf of paper from a drawer, dipped his quill into an inkwell. Scrawled several lines across the page. "I cannot see how General Howe would begrudge a pass for a gentlewoman like yourself." He took up a tin pounce box, shook some sand onto the letter. Let it rest for a moment before shaking it back into the box. He rose and presented it to her with a flourish.

"I thank thee."

"And I thank you. For taking such kind interest in this boorish friend of mine."

She turned her eyes toward me. Her gaze was tempered with frank suspicion.

I didn't much blame her.

"I must . . . I must leave. Good day." She turned and walked through the door.

"Thank you ever so much." I clapped my hat onto my head.

"What? What did I do wrong?"

"It's Devil's Hole, you simpleton. They don't believe in arms!"

"Don't believe in — ?"

I sighed. Pretended myself to be hopelessly set back in my suit by his careless words. "The Quakers. They don't believe in war. Of any kind."

"But you were a hero. And I thought I was

doing you a favor."

"Then I beg you: Please, favor me not at all."

"Well." He looked at the door, consternation in his eyes. "I suppose . . ." He turned toward me. "I suppose you ought to go after her, then. To smooth over my failings. It seems that I've been the boorish one."

I didn't need an invitation. I left him without apology and swept out the door.

I caught the girl on the stair between the first and second floors. Took hold of her arm as though I was her escort. Leaned close to hiss into her ear, "Hadn't I said ten o'clock?"

She tried to wrest her arm from mine. "Aye. Thee did."

"So why did you choose to appear at half past?"

"I did not choose it. 'Twas chosen for me. I had both my mother and an enslaved woman in my train. And I had to figure out what to do about them. It doesn't do for a girl to go about the city unescorted."

I had not considered that. If only there was a different way to undertake the planning of the escape. A different method of passing messages. A different person to deliver them. But Miss Hannah Sunderland,

Quaker, was all that I had. "Just . . . see to it that it doesn't happen again."

She raised her chin and tried to slip past me.

I stopped her by refusing to let go of her arm. By forcing her to turn around and face me.

"You have the pass. Tomorrow I will meet you on Walnut Street between Third and Fourth. At four o'clock. In passing I will hand you the message. After that, you must visit the jail and deliver it to a William Addison as soon as you possibly can."

"Why William Addison?"

"He's a sergeant."

She looked at me as if I had said, He's a turnip.

"He's a *sergeant*. He has charge of the men — least those in the cell with him. The British have housed all the officers over at the hospital. The non-commissioned have been left to look after themselves."

She nodded, though it was not so certain a nod as I would have liked. "William Addison." She nodded once more. "But thee will make certain that Robert is included in this plan."

"I will." I'd tried to. I had made the request in the message, though I doubted the sergeant would be able to do anything about it. If Robert was not in William's cell, then nothing could be done for him. But Hannah Sunderland didn't need to know that. All she had to do was deliver the message.

11
HANNAH

I found Doll at the corner, waiting for me just as she had promised. "I hope thee had no trouble."

"None but what I could expect."

I looked to her for further information, but her features revealed nothing but the fact that she wasn't about to reveal anything to me. I turned in the direction of Spruce Street and began the walk to the Evanses'. Though I didn't want to spare the time, I'd told Mother I would visit Betsy, so visit I must.

After having stayed there just long enough for warmth to return to my fingers, we started off for the Gilberts'. It did not take more than twenty minutes to reach the Northern Liberties. Once there, Anna Gilbert herself answered my knock.

"Come in, come in! Your mother is still here." She stepped closer. "And still waiting to read the letter from Virginia."

I moved aside to let Doll enter, but she did not step up to the invitation. Knowing from prior experience how futile it would be to insist, I sighed and entered first.

The Gilbert girl took my cloak and gestured for Doll's as well, but she would not surrender it.

"It's so warm in the parlor, with all the callers." The Gilbert girl gestured for it once more.

Doll addressed herself to me. "I'll wait right here, miss, if it's all the same to you."

" 'Tis not the same to me. There's a fire in the hearth in the parlor and there's nothing but a chill draft here. Thee will come in with me before the cold makes thee ill."

Doll cast a leery gaze toward the parlor. We couldn't see into the room, but we could hear the sounds of many voices coming from it.

I tilted my head in that direction. "Come."

"Nothing good come from mixing with you people." She entered the room behind me. "I heard about you. Treating all folks the same as each other."

" 'Tis as our Lord said: 'In Christ there is no Jew or Greek, slave or free.' "

"Our Lord must not have lived in Philadelphia or He would've knowed what's true. But I can pass a tray as well as anybody."

As we walked into the room, she moved toward a table, picked up the tray that sat upon it, and held it out to Friend Milligan.

That woman looked at it, shook her head, and tried to take it from Doll, to offer it right back the same way she would have done to any of the other guests.

Doll wouldn't let go of it.

Friend Milligan took hold of it and pulled it from Doll's hand. "Thee do not want any? Perhaps then some tea?"

Doll shook her head.

"Then, please, take a seat."

Looking distinctly uncomfortable, Doll sat.

The letter from Virginia eventually made its way to me. I quickly parsed it, trying to find some hope that our Friends there would be soon released, some hidden message behind the innocuous words. Our Friends knew their letters were subject to confiscation. At the very least they expected the letters to be read by guards on both sides of the lines. We knew there would be no protests, no criticism of the jailers in their messages. John Pemberton was ill. John Hunt was recovered. They hoped they might be sent more blankets. Such were the misfortunes of war. Our needs so very great, our hopes so very small.

We left soon after, the three of us.

Mother tried to pull Doll into walking beside us, but she would have none of it. "You can pretend anything you want while you're among your own kind, but out here on the streets, we in my world. And in my world, we aren't friends no more than we're kin." Giving us a sullen look, Doll dropped back behind us and stayed there until we had reached Pennington House. And then she disappeared around the corner as we walked up the front steps.

That evening Major Lindley came to call on Polly. I happened to be crossing from the parlor to the dining room at the time. As he shed his cloak into Davy's hands, the major saw me. "Miss Hannah!"

"Major Lindley."

"How does it go with your brother? Did you find him well?"

Davy did not seem to be listening, and no one else was present in the front hall, but I could not keep myself from flinching just the same. I drew near the major, looking up past his rather large nose and into his eyes. "I must ask thee to keep news of the pass between ourselves. My parents must not know that I plan to visit him. They are not . . . pleased with his politics."

134

Polly came down the stair at that moment, resplendent in a gown of many colors.

"Ah! So you *are* a spy, then. Of sorts. Have no fear; I shall keep the secret between us." With a merry wink he took up Polly's hand as she stepped down into the hall and gave it a kiss.

Secret? I hadn't meant to ask him to keep a secret. I had only wanted to tell him the truth.

The major did not overstay his visit that evening. Polly came into her bedroom just as I was slipping into my bed. The slave named Jenny accompanied her and helped her from her gown. "Major Lindley said you obtained a pass to see your brother."

I closed my eyes against the news of his perfidy. Had he not told me he would keep the pass a secret? "I had asked him to keep that knowledge to himself, as I must now ask thee to do."

"Of course I will. But . . . have you been there? Have you seen him?"

"I hope to go tomorrow."

"How exciting! You must tell me what it's like. I want to know everything about it!" She made it sound as if I was going to visit General Howe or some other personage she considered just as august.

Jenny helped her into a new shift, brushed out her hair, and warmed her sheets. Then she turned them so Polly could climb into bed.

How exciting!

On that happy thought she soon drifted off to sleep.

On that happy thought I worried through half the night.

The next afternoon I tried to leave the house without anyone taking notice. I had not counted on Davy. He sent Doll out to me before I could even protest. She came, grasping her cloak about the throat with one hand and pulling it close about her waist with the other. "Since you consider yourself decent folk, you might consider going out next time at a decent time of day."

The shadows had grown long and the cold more pronounced. "I'm sorry. I'm expected somewhere. Otherwise . . ." Otherwise I would not have found myself in such a predicament, dependent upon the presence of an enslaved woman. Not for the first time I wondered how exactly it was that I had been caught up in such deception. But that ache of hunger and a bone-chilling cold swept over me and I remembered.

Robert.

He was the reason.

We walked up Walnut Street in silence. Had I tried to speak, the wind would have stolen the words from my lips. It was better to trod, head down, one foot in front of the other. Quite soon we came to Third Street. A look at the way ahead showed Jeremiah Jones walking toward me. I stopped.

Doll ran into me.

This business did not sit well with me. I'd completely forgotten about Doll and I didn't know what to do with her now. I couldn't imagine that Jeremiah Jones would want her with me when he passed by with the message. But neither could I imagine what else she would willingly do.

I put my hand on Doll's arm. "Thee must stand over there, at the corner, for a moment."

She shook her head as she sighed. "Davy told me to stay with you no matter what you say."

I looked up toward Jeremiah Jones. I could tell he was frowning beneath the folds of his muffler. He was glaring.

"I have to speak to that man and my words need to be my own."

Doll shrugged, refused to meet my eyes. "If Davy ever asks, I don't know nothing about no man."

137

"If Davy ever asks, thee may tell him the truth. I would expect no less."

"The truth." She nearly spat the words.

"Why would thee ever say anything other?"

"Why? Because there's the truth and then there's the *truth*. Ain't no Negro ever gained nothing by telling the truth. The truth is something I want no part of. You couldn't make me tell the truth if you whipped me for it."

I had a mind to stay there and determine exactly what it was that Doll meant, but Jeremiah Jones was still glaring, and I had no desire to further incur his wrath. "Thee can watch me all thee want, only please: do it from the corner." I did not stay to know what she would do, but stepped out away from her toward Jeremiah Jones.

As I approached him, he put a hand up to his hat. "Hannah."

I nodded.

He drew even with me, slowing a bit and extending his hand. As he did so, a piece of paper fluttered from it.

I bent to retrieve it before the wind could carry it away, and I offered it out to him.

He took a quick step back, glanced about and then stepped forward, quite close. "That's for you. To keep."

"Oh." Oh! It must be the message of which he spoke.

"Deliver it tomorrow. Remember, it's for Sergeant William Addison. I'll meet you in the street after." He was looking at me as if he wanted to say more, but then he moved away, tipping his hat once more. "Godspeed, Hannah."

I watched him walk away, wanting to stop him. Cry out to him. I didn't even know William Addison. How was I to learn who he was? How was I to know what to do? And what did I know about being a spy?

12
JEREMIAH

I shook my head as I walked away. She'd tried to hand the note right back to me — in plain sight where any could see it! How could one teach the art of deception when the student denied its very utility? It was like trying to teach an angel to be a devil. But I had to hope for her success. Otherwise it would be both our necks together. At the gallows.

John Lindley came in for supper that night. He was wearing a look so long he might have tripped over it as he came through the door. "You need a drink?"

He nodded.

"Rum?"

"Brandy."

I pulled the cork from a bottle with my teeth and then poured him a bowl.

"Might need two. Howe's gone and asked to be recalled."

Recalled? That was news. "To where?"

"England."

A recall was long overdue in my opinion. He'd been given time enough to quench the rebellion and hadn't done it. "You think they will?"

John shrugged and took a drink. Planting his forearm on the bar, he turned to look around. Then he leaned in close. "Word is, the prime minister is none too happy with him."

I could see why. General Washington was only a few scant miles down the road with half his troops laid low by illness. Yet Howe hadn't managed to roust himself from his mistress's bed for the two days it would take him to defeat the ragtag army. If I were the prime minister, I would have called for his head long before now. "Who's to replace him?"

John picked up his bowl and eyed the bottom of it and held it out toward me. I pulled the cork once more and filled it. "Does it matter? General Howe's a true gentleman."

"When is it to happen?"

"Before the spring campaign, I suppose." He was tapping his fingers against the counter now, looking as if he'd rather be talking to someone else. "I just wish something could be done."

"You can't very well recall the request."

"No. But . . . blast it all! There ought to be something that can be done to fete the finest officer in the army. Something memorable."

I recorked the bottle and stowed it on the shelf behind me. "Write him a play." The army might have been a den of play-actors for all the masterpieces that were being practiced and planned for production down at the theater.

"A play."

"Or some sort of ode in his honor." An idea was growing in my mind. General Washington was looking for a way for his prisoners to escape. John was looking for a way to fete his general. What if the same diversion could be used to meet both ends?

"Everyone has written some sort of play. Or other."

I'd forgotten: The officer corps seemed to attract nothing but frustrated playwrights. "How about a ball?"

"We've been dancing all winter."

All winter. It needed to be something different, then. Something novel. Something . . . that could be looked forward to all spring. "What about —"

"There he is!" John muttered the words under his breath as he turned from the counter and held out a hand to a major,

142

who was swiftly approaching.

"Jonesy? Major John André. John, this is Jeremiah Jones. He was invalided out after Devil's Hole."

"Oh? Tough luck, then."

I saved my smile.

"Jonesy and I were talking about General Howe's departure. How we ought to fete him."

The major flashed me a look. "I'll have a brandy as well."

I took another bowl down from the shelf as he leaned on the counter next to John. "It's got to be something extraordinary. Something more than another play or a ball." The major accepted the bowl from me and took a drink. "Something different."

General Howe's brother, Admiral Howe, was due to return to the city soon. "What about the boats?" I asked.

André looked up at me. "What about them?"

"Couldn't you do something on the river?"

"A regatta?" He flashed a smile that was stunning in its brilliance. "A regatta on the river! Splendid idea. And we could do everything else as well. It could be a regatta-theater-ball. A regatta-*pageant*-ball — even better! A whole day filled with celebrations. It would be a medley of events. A veritable

Meschianza!"

I shrugged as if it didn't matter much to me, one way or the other. But a day filled with festivities would provide multiple opportunities for a diversion. I only hoped it would fall late in the season. The tunnel might take a while to dig. "Let me know how I can help." I'd do whatever I had to in order to keep abreast of the event. On the night of the festivities I wanted every officer within ten miles of the city to be completely and utterly drunk. Unfit to respond to the prisoners' escape.

"We will." With a clap on the back and a wink, John left with André. But they would be back. If I played them right, they would plan the whole event right here at my counter. And I would be informed of every detail.

Once they were well gone I gave over control of the drink to my barkeeper and went upstairs to my room. Locking the door, I drew the curtain and took *Common Sense* down from its shelf. Then I worked for the next two hours to find just the right words.

By the time the watchman called out eleven o'clock, I had completed my message.

Howe expected to be recalled in spring. Officers to have a gala upon his departure. Suggest that night for escape.

I uncoded it once just to make sure it said what was meant. Satisfied, I hid it in a finger of a glove. Now I just had to find a way to get it to General Washington.

The next morning I braved the rain and returned to the tailor's. Two visits within a week's time. More times than I'd visited in the previous two years. He eyed me with no little suspicion. "I didn't expect to see you back so soon." He shot a glance toward his apprentice. "Did you want something altered?"

I cursed my lack of thought. I should have brought my other coat. "I thought . . . perhaps . . . it could be I'll need another."

"Another?"

"Coat?"

He sighed and tossed a look at his apprentice. "Go and take those new shirts over to Howe's headquarters for Colonel Hillman." He nodded toward the corner where a package sat tied up with string.

When the boy had sauntered off, the tailor sent me a look over the rims of his spectacles. "Another coat?"

145

"Not really."

"Then what is it? I already told you everything I know."

"I have to pass a message to the general."

He shook his head. "To headquarters. That's what we say. To *headquarters*."

"Fine. I have to get a message to headquarters."

"Then you're going to have to do like I told you and find the egg-girl."

"Which one? And how will she know to trust me?"

"She's the one with the blue cart. And you'll have to wear a purple-colored feather in your hat."

"A feather in my hat."

"To signal you've something to pass. And she'll have a scarlet-colored ribbon on her cap if she's something to give you. Here. Let me lend you mine." He pulled out a drawer behind the counter. Bent down and reached an arm into it. "Just stick it right into the brim where it's been cocked."

A feather in my hat. That could be a problem.

I wasn't one to walk around with things sticking out of my hat, though the tailor did it all the time. But he was a dandy. And he cared so much about the smallest of details

146

that he could be expected to wander about the market looking for delicacies like quails' eggs.

I, on the other hand, was not.

It was difficult enough to tie my cravat in a respectable knot, let alone match the clocks on my hose to my waistcoat and the embroidery on my coat to my gloves. Glove. What did it matter? Whose eye was I hoping to catch? I didn't even bother with waistcoats anymore. Nor did I button my coat.

I couldn't.

And now here I was, parading down High Street with a purple feather stuck into my hat in the middle of a rainy afternoon. If I didn't hate the British so much, I would have never willingly suffered such indignities. As I approached Fifth Street, I saw John come around the corner. I sped my walk, but he caught up to me with a jog.

"My! Aren't you looking dapper. One might think you've set your eye on some fair girl."

I didn't return his grin.

"Is it the Quaker one?"

"Is what the Quaker one?"

"The girl. Is she the reason for that handsome feather?"

I wanted to wrench the wretched thing from my hat and stomp it into the mud.

"The reason for this silly feather is that . . ."
Is that what? What reason could I give him?
That wasn't the truth?

"No need to explain."

"It's not — I mean —"

"Love makes fools of us all."

"Why should you be so interested in my
thoughts of Hannah?"

"Hannah?" He shook some raindrops
from his cloak. "So things are progressing
quickly, then?"

"Miss Sunderland." And curse her for
insisting that I use her Christian name. She
wasn't a Christian. She was a devil in
disguise. "And she's not . . . I'm not . . ."

He punched me in my arm. The missing
one. "Forgive me. I take such interest in
others' affairs because I have so little interest in my own. All that awaits me in England
is a pile of lovely money. And very little
charm. She's quite delightful really. And
very frank."

"Who? Your heiress?"

"No. Miss Sunderland. Your beloved Hannah."

"She is not my Hannah."

As we came abreast of the market, he took
himself off with a wink.

She was not my beloved anything. A
nuisance was what she was. But if she

148

explained the presence of this ridiculous feather, then I suppose she'd made herself useful. For a change.

I began to scan the brick-buttressed market booths at Fifth Street. If market it could be called. Last spring there had been vendors here by the dozens. Now, at this time of day, the market was nearly deserted. I could hear the echoes of my own shoes striking the cobbles. I counted only seven booths occupied. And it felt as if each one of those vendors was watching me.

I made a point of looking over all of the wares. In truth, there was no way around it. I had to go to each booth in order to find the blue cart. One of the vendors had three meager-looking parsnips for sale. Another had a slim wedge of cheese. A third had brought a small sack of flour. And finally there was the egg-girl with her blue cart.

She wasn't a girl really, more of a haggard, careworn woman. But the tailor had always been rather over-romantic in his sentiments. There were four baskets of eggs sitting in her cart. Apparently those were all she had to offer, but they were quite a bit more than most Philadelphians were used to seeing these days.

Her cap was trimmed with a scarlet ribbon. She seemed to be . . . waiting. For something. For me. "How much?"

"Ten shillings the egg. Coin. Not paper."

Then it was a good thing I kept my own clutch of hens. They were down in the cellar so no one could steal them from me.

"I'll buy one."

She raised a brow as if I'd said the wrong thing.

If I had, I didn't know it. She expected me to buy more than one egg at that price? Is that what people with purple feathers in their hats were supposed to do? Pour out their coin as if it were water?

"If you're interested in something special, I have some quail eggs in my cart. I know they're your favorites."

My favorites. That must mean she had a message as well. Of course she had a message for me! She was wearing a red-colored advertisement on her cap. I nodded. "I had a taste of them once at my tailor's and I've never forgotten it. Thank you for keeping it."

She looked at me sharply.

"Them. The eggs. Thank you for keeping them."

"There's not many I'd go to this trouble for." She reached back into the cart beneath the straw, pulled out a handful of diminutive eggs, and offered them to me.

But . . . I didn't have anything to put them in. Another false move. Shopping at the market without a basket. Had those guards been paying any attention, they might have arrested me as a spy right then. As it was, the other vendors had noticed. And they were smiling.

Hopefully it was at my stupidity rather than my artlessness.

"I suppose . . . I could put them . . ." In my coat's pocket? I reached beneath my cloak to open it up. Leaned toward her so she could place them inside.

She frowned, but she did it.

As I took the money from my other pocket, I palmed my message. I tried to give it all into her hand at once, but the message fell from my palm, threatening to flutter to the ground.

She plucked it from the air between us and then glared at me.

I opened my mouth to apologize and then realized it would only succeed in drawing attention to ourselves. "Do . . . you come often? To market?"

"Not as often as I'd like. Those rebels haven't been kind in letting me through their lines."

"So . . . ?"

"You'll just have to keep an eye out. For

151

the blue cart."

The blue cart.

I walked through the streets, feeling as if the eggs were burning a hole in my pocket. When I reached the King's Arms, I went round the back and up to my rooms. Behind closed curtains I shed my cloak. After shaking the rain from it, I let my coat slide from my shoulders. I stirred the embers in the hearth and then took the eggs out one by one, setting them on my desk. Then I felt in the pocket for the message.

There was nothing there.

Moving closer to the fire, I peered inside the pocket, but my fingers had not lied. It was empty. I'd been so sure . . . she was wearing a red ribbon. I thought back on our conversation. Remembered her words, her actions. She'd had a message, and she'd delivered it. I was certain of it. But how had she done it?

I looked at the collection of eggs. Picked them up, each in turn, looking for something, anything, but there was nothing there. She'd passed me a message. She had to have. Only I couldn't find it. God rot the tailor and his cowardice! I wasn't meant for spy work. I didn't mind passing information on when I heard a thing or two, but how was I to know how to pass the messages themselves? Now I'd have to go back to the tailor's.

Perhaps . . . was anything written on the shells? I lit a taper and then held them close to the light, one by one. Nothing. They were so small that it would be hard to find the space to write anything at all.

I took another look at the egg I was holding. At one end was a hole so small I'd failed to notice it. Setting it on top of the desk, I crushed it with my fist. Pushed the fragments away to reveal a small splinter-sized note. It took me a try or two to unroll it. And another while to figure out how to keep it from rolling in on itself as I read it. There weren't many words so it didn't take long to decode the message:

Still awaiting reply. How many guests are expected? When?

How many guests? I didn't have any idea. Were they hoping to empty the whole jail? When would they arrive? It would take some time to dig beneath a prison wall and tunnel under the street, wouldn't it? But how much time? I didn't know. I didn't know anything at all. What I needed was a report on the tunnel's progress. I needed to send Hannah back into the jail with another message. And this time she would need to bring out a reply.

13
HANNAH

I did not know that hell had taken up residence on earth. I had not known there could be such a place as this, filled with filth and all manner of foul odors. I held the neck of my cloak to my nose as I waited for the guard to inspect my pass.

It was not only the smells that made my heart quake within me and assaulted my hope. It was the moans and the hacking coughs that issued from the door bolted in front of me. And it was the way the torch on the wall seemed incapable of spreading any but shadowed light.

"Robert Sunderland, eh?"

"My brother." I tried my best to remain unobtrusive, not wanting to give the guard any reason to transfer his attentions from the pass to me. I might have drawn in deep breaths to calm my racing heart, but to do so would have been to risk retching.

The guard folded up my pass and handed

it back to me. "Don't know why the general would allow a girl to go about in all this mess." He rose from the chair, hiked up his breeches at the back, and spit into the corner. "Let me see what you brought." He grabbed for the basket I held, rifling through the linens, inspecting the bread, the bottle of wine, and the wedge of cheese I'd taken from the house. As he passed the basket back to me, he kept hold of the cheese.

" 'Tis for my brother!"

"He won't miss it." He looked me in the eyes as if he dared me to say anything else.

I did not. For though Major Lindley had issued my pass on General Howe's behalf, clearly neither of them held any sway down here. If I was going to be allowed to visit Robert, it would only be in payment for pleasing this man. "Please, enjoy it."

"Oh, I will." He nipped off the end of the wedge as he tugged at the bolt on the door. A rodent ran out when he pulled it open.

I gasped and clutched at my skirts.

The guard laughed, then called through the door, "A miss here to see her brother. General's orders." He bowed and swung the door wide as though inviting me into one of the finest homes in the city.

An icy draft struck me full in the face, swept past my neck and ruffled my skirts, carrying with it all kinds of rank smells. I tried my best not to gag. The door shut behind me as a candle flared to life. The face behind it leered, as if a girl who wanted to see her brother was every bit as suspect as the prisoner.

I clutched the basket to my chest. "I'm to see Robert Sunderland. By order of General Howe."

"I don't know who the prisoners are, miss. I just keep the keys to the place. Robert Sunderland, you say?"

I nodded.

"An officer is he?"

"No." At least I didn't think he was. He hadn't ever said.

"I'll ask round." He lurched down the hall, taking that small haven of light with him, stopping to bang upon each door. "Robert Sunderland in there? Robert Sunderland?"

Finally there came a feeble response. I didn't wait for the guard to come back down the hall to escort me. I flew toward the taper. "He's in there?"

"So they say." He jammed a key into the lock, wrestled with it, and then pulled the door open. "Robert Sunderland?"

Looking over the guard's shoulder, I could discern nothing beyond the reaches of the candle's poor light. But I could hear plenty. I heard sniffs and coughs, the sounds of swatting and scratching. The patter of raindrops, high up, against the broken windowpane. And a dismal drip-dropping of water beneath as the torrents found the floor. "Robert?"

"Hannah?"

I nudged past the guard toward my brother's voice.

The guard caught me by the arm. "Can't go in. Not allowed."

"But I've things for him."

"Hannah! Is that thee?"

He forced me back behind him. "No mixing with the prisoners."

"Then let him come out." I needed to see him!

He pushed me back into the hall and disappeared inside, reappearing a moment later, dragging Robert by the elbow. My brother collapsed into my arms.

"But — he's sick!"

"Not so bad as some of the others. I'll give you two minutes." He retreated down the hall, taking the light with him. Robert was here, yet those feelings of gnawing hunger and bitter cold had not yet abated. I took up one of his hands in mine. His flesh was chill; to clasp his fingers felt like grasping at bones.

"Thee came."

I helped him to the wall where he sunk to the floor. I knelt beside him. "Of course I came. Just as soon as I could. I had to get a pass first." I held the bottle of wine to his lips.

He swallowed and then he took another drink.

"I brought bread. And some linens."

He didn't take any of them. Instead, he took up my hand in his. "Do they know I'm here?"

I didn't have to ask of whom he spoke. "Yes."

"Do they know thee are here?"

"No."

"It was the right thing to do, joining the army. Thee know that, don't thee?" He squeezed my hand so hard I feared he'd crush it.

"Yes." It had been the right thing; I'd never doubted it. "But . . . I worry for thee." And even more now than before. How could anyone survive such deprivation?

"It's the same here as it was in camp. No blankets. No wood." He'd let his head fall back against the wall.

No blankets? "But are they feeding thee?"

"Never enough. Twice, three times a week."

What? "But General Washington isn't letting any food come into the city. Most of the farmers haven't been to the market in months. It's because the general's keeping it all for thee! Thee were supposed to be the fortunate ones!"

Robert began to laugh, but it ended in a spasm of coughing. "If he's taken it all, one thing's for certain: He's not sharing."

I didn't understand. How could the soldiers in the rebels' camp be in such dire straits if they were keeping all the food for themselves?

He put a hand out toward the linens. "For me?"

"Aye! All of it is for thee." If only I'd known he had nothing. I'd been worried about whether he had linens to wash himself when I ought to have wondered if he had a blanket or shoes.

"Two minutes!" I heard the guard start for us and could see the specter of the candle as he approached.

Robert squeezed my hand once more. "Tell Betsy . . . tell her . . ."

I bent to embrace him. "Thee must —" What? Take care of himself in this foul and odious place? It was plain he could do noth-

160

ing on behalf of himself.

"Time's up." The guard grabbed Robert by the elbow and pulled him to standing, unlocked the door, and tossed him inside. Then he held up his ring of keys and gave it a jingle. "I've food for any who will change sides and fight for the King."

Was the guard trying to bribe them into discarding their loyalties?

I heard my brother groan and then cough. Heard others join in coughing along with him. How many of them were there in that cell?

None replied to the guard's offer. He shook his head as he locked the door. I followed him down the hall, passing ten doors before we reached the end. Just how many prisoners were they keeping in this jail?

When we gained the end of the hall, the guard knocked on the door. The bolt shrieked as it slid through its casing, and then the door swung open. The first guard greeted me, licking his fingers. "So you saw him, then."

"I did. I shall come again, soon." I said it more as a promise to myself than to warn the man.

He shrugged. "It's nothing to me. But bring more of that cheese with you next time. I liked it."

■ ■ ■ ■

I met Doll at the bottom of the jail's steps. We were not two paces from the place before I retched. I retched until my stomach had no more to offer and then I retched some more. The guard marching sentry duty saw me, and he turned before he had walked the length of his circuit.

Doll sighed as she unfastened the apron beneath her cloak. She handed it to me. "Don't know what good comes from going into a place like that. Just look at the hem of your gown. And your shoes. Mercy, but you stink!"

I took one deep shuddering breath, trying hard not to think of the things that I had heard and seen. But it was no use. "They keep prisoners down there in the basement like . . . like animals!"

"We got to clean you up before you go back into the house. Davy finds out I let you go someplace like that, it'd be my head along with yours. That's for certain."

"They've no food. No fires."

"We'll clean you up in the stables."

"Who knows how many of them there are!"

"I can fetch another of your gowns, and if

we do it quick, ain't no one going to see us."

"Aren't thee listening? Don't thee hear what I'm saying?"

"I'm hearing that you good and mad. And plenty scared. But this is a war, not one of you folks' tea parties. People's dying. You don't know cruel until your family be taken to live ten miles away from where you are. So when you're ready to start talking 'bout things I can do something about, then I'll start to listen."

When you're ready to start talking about things I can do something about . . .

I had been charged to do something for someone. I'd gone down into that pit of misery to see Robert. But with the sheer horror of the place, with the slim margin of time I'd been allowed, and with the dreadful condition of my brother . . . I'd forgotten to do what I'd agreed to. The message for William Addison was still tucked away in my pocket. And I dared not think what Jeremiah Jones would have to say about it.

14
JEREMIAH

"What do you mean you couldn't deliver the message? Was he not there?" Wouldn't it be just my luck if Sgt. Addison had already died! I drew Hannah from the street over into a shadowed alley. It wouldn't do for any to overhear our words.

She bit at her lip. "I do not know."

"You don't know." The girl was beginning to exasperate me. Even more than she had in the past. "Because . . . ?"

"Because the men are separated into rooms. I asked for Robert, so they took me to his room."

"And William Addison wasn't in it." I hadn't thought of that. If I were going to be a spy, I needed to start thinking like one!

"I . . . don't know."

If I yelled at her the way I wanted to, I wasn't sure I would be able to ask her to do anything at all for me again. Something about the way she held herself demanded respect. And vast reserves of patience. "All right. Fine. Let's come at this from a different tack. What *do* you know?"

"I know that the guard who keeps the keys is a bully. I know that there are many more men in each room than there should be. They have little in the way of food, wood, or blankets."

"The guard is a bully." That I could have told her without ever setting foot inside the jail.

"The one who keeps the keys. And the other, the one who keeps the door, demanded that I give him the cheese I'd brought for Robert!" The flush that rode her cheeks had deepened with each word.

A man who was amenable to graft. Perhaps he could be bribed. A good thing to know, though it didn't help at the moment. "So you don't know if Sgt. Addison is in the same room as Robert?"

She shook her head.

"And you also don't know where else he might — or might not — be?"

She shook her head.

"You don't know, in fact, if he's there at all."

A bit of fight had come into her eyes. "And how was I to discover it? Did thee want me to ask?"

"No. Yes." Blast it! There was a prison break being planned that the prisoners knew nothing about. And the whole of it depended upon them digging a tunnel. I closed my eyes against a worsening ache in my head. "Fine. Fine." Everything was fine. "You'll just have to wait a week until —"

"A week! But Robert is ill. I have to visit again tomorrow."

"No one has visited that jail since November. How is it going to look if you suddenly begin visiting every day? And what would your parents say?"

"Do thee know what it's like in there?"

I could guess. "Next Saturday. That's when you should return."

"That's a whole —"

"Seven days. Yes. I know. You'll go on Saturday, you'll find out which room Sgt. Addison is in, and you'll contrive to deliver the message."

"Or . . . ?" The word rang with challenge.

"Or you might as well buy your brother a coffin. Unless he's in on the escape, chances are he won't come out of that jail alive."

The following Saturday I walked up Walnut Street at half past four as Hannah walked down. We met at Fourth Street.

She paused just a moment as we passed.

166

"William Addison wasn't in Robert's room, but I asked my brother to find out where he is. The next time I visit I will try to pass the message. But it would be easier if they were in the same room."

And it would certainly be easier if I didn't have to depend upon a girl to carry my messages.

"The escape will happen soon, won't it?"

"As soon as it can." As soon as they dug that infernal tunnel. They were already behind schedule.

"I think . . ."

"What?" Soon someone was bound to notice that we had paused.

"They don't have much food."

Much food? "How much is not much?"

"They're only being fed two or three times each week."

"Sometimes prisoners complain —"

"And sometimes they die from starvation!" Her eyes were blazing with fire.

Starving prisoners weren't likely to be able to dig their way to freedom. "I'll have a bag of grain delivered to Pennington House. Can you smuggle in five pounds?"

"I can smuggle in ten."

I rather doubted it. "I'll have it delivered to . . . ?"

"To the stables. At half past three. Every

seventh day."

"Every Saturday, then."

I watched her as she continued on down Walnut Street. If she weren't so completely irritating, there might be something to admire in the lift of her chin. And in the determination that burned in her eyes.

"How is the courtship progressing?"

I started at the sound of John's voice. "Courtship! What? Of her?"

"Come, Jonesy! Any man can see that you fancy her."

"I don't —" I bit back my words. If I was too convincing in my argument, then I would talk myself right out of my best ally.

"Tell Johnny what's the matter, then."

"Nothing's the matter."

"Then why are you staring at her as if she's gone and dashed all your plans?"

Because she had.

"I've a way with the girls. I'm sure I could fix whatever's gone wrong between you."

I eyed him, wondering if perhaps he was right. Maybe he could fix everything. I let him lead me into my own tavern and then I let him order me up a drink.

"Now. Tell me the whole story."

I shrugged as I tried to figure out how best to put him to use. Took a drink. Then another.

"Just say it, man!" Patience had never been his long suit.

"It's her brother."

"The rebel one?"

"The same."

A furrow etched his brow. "She visited him, didn't she?"

"Aye."

"So she ought to be happy."

"He's complaining about this thing and that." I tried to sound as if his complaints had no merit.

"He *is* in prison."

"Which is what I told her. It's not as if a man should expect to be treated as a gentleman when he betrays his King. General Howe might want to feed them now and then, though. Wouldn't do to have the prison population die of starvation."

"They'll die soon enough of putrid fever or dysentery."

My brow rose of its own volition.

"It's going around. Again. So what has this to do with Miss Sunderland?"

"She thinks I ought to ask you to have him moved."

"Moved? As if I were the general himself!" He smiled, seemingly bemused at the thought. I knew him well enough to know that he dreamed of being one someday.

"That's what I told her." I shook my head as if trying to rid myself of a disagreeable conversation. Then took another drink.

"To where?"

"To where, what?"

"Where did she want him moved?"

"Oh! Well, now. It's rather complicated. I don't know if I quite remember. There's a cousin in the jail as well. Third or fourth. William something or other . . . Addison. That's it: William Addison. Some distant relation. In any case, that's where she'd want him to be. In this Addison's room."

"Why?"

"He's a sergeant. She thinks her brother will get better treatment. But I told her . . ." I shrugged. "What can you expect if you take up arms against your King? What can any of them expect?"

"Traitors. They should all be hanged."

"Exactly. I don't see why she ought to have gone all peevish when I only told her the truth." I tried to look exceedingly glum.

"That's the problem with women. They refuse to see the truth, though it bite them on the nose."

I shrugged. "That's that, then."

He eyed me over the rim of his mug. "She means that much to you?"

I held up my empty sleeve. "I don't have

many prospects."

"Then I'll see what I can do."

"You don't have to —"

"What's the good of working for a general if you can't intervene for a friend?" He was looking as if he might just do what I had asked. Rather, what he thought Hannah had asked.

"Just make certain — I mean — he's not *my* brother."

"Don't worry. The general understands the affairs of the heart."

Of course he did. Wasn't he being bedded this winter by the delectable Mrs. Loring? As her husband counted the coin the arrangement had brought him? Another of the British army's commendable traditions. Rewarding the married woman's husband with favors. It was all so . . . respectable.

So respectably repugnant.

One more reason to despise them. Their officers and everything they stood for had gone rotten at the core.

John had fallen into the habit of supping at the King's Arms, drinking heavily with his meal. The next Friday evening he rose from his table uncharacteristically early. "Time to be off." He stumbled as he pushed from the table. Put a hand to it for support.

171

I crossed the room to steady him. "Aren't you eating here tonight?"

"Can't. I promised the lovely Miss Pennington that I would attend her party."

Hannah's cousin? Again? She didn't need to get caught up in John's vices. "What harm would it do to sober up a bit before you go?"

"And remember why I can't make love to her in earnest?" He put a hand up to his wig, searching for the ribbon that bound his queue. Squared his shoulders. "Right then. Let's be off."

I handed him his hat.

He set it atop his curls. Glanced at me. "Where's yours?"

"My what?"

"Your hat. We mustn't be late. It's not like England."

"You're the one who's been invited, not I."

"I told her we'd both come."

"Then you told her in error and you can apologize for yourself when you see her." If he was sober enough to remember.

"No, no. I always did best you in etiquette."

"Though I beat you in charm."

"Pity, 'tis true. Ah well." He jammed his hand into the small of my back and nearly

172

pitched me over with the gesture. "Where are your rooms, then?"

"They're up the stair in the back. Why?"

"I've taken it upon myself as a challenge to see if I can't bring the old Jeremiah Jones back to life." He stiff-armed me toward the stair as he spoke.

"The old Jeremiah Jones is gone."

"Bah! He's just gone into hiding. I'm going to coax him out with some dancing and flirting. We'll have Miss Sunderland blushing at your every glance before long."

I had to take his arm to keep him upright. "You're in no condition for dancing."

"Then perhaps I shall just lure Miss Pennington into a dark corner and kiss her."

"Her father is one of the pillars of this city."

"Isn't a fellow allowed to dream now and then?"

I stopped in front of my door but kept him pinned to the wall with my shoulder so he wouldn't slide down onto his face.

"Is this it?"

"This is it." I put my key in the lock and shoved open the door.

He pushed me aside and threw his hat on my writing table, then lurched into the middle of the room and surveyed the place, hands at his hips.

173

I went to the hearth and stirred up the fire. Taking a taper from its holder, I lit it.

John snatched it from me and went to examine the coats that were hanging on pegs.

"Haven't you got anything in yellow? Or English blue?"

Yellow? Blue? I turned to look at him. "Why should I?"

"Because what you've got is ten seasons old. Brown? And what do you call this?" He turned so the light from the taper would fall on the fabric. "Goose-dropping green? My granny used to wear a gown this color."

I grabbed the brown-colored coat from its peg and pulled it on.

"You've a wig, haven't you?"

"I do."

"At least you've not gone into a decline that steep. Well. Where is it?"

"It's in the trunk somewhere."

He threw the lid open and rummaged through it for a moment. "Ah. Found it!" He walked it over to the fireplace and held it up to the light. Poked at it here and there. Held it out in my direction. "I suppose it will have to do. Though you really ought to have it redone. If it's not too late. Have it made into a cadogan, with the queue looped back upon itself."

It was fine just the way it was. Especially after having not been worn for more years than I cared to admit. I snatched it from him and pulled it down atop my head.

"Tsk, tsk. That will never do. Your own hair is much too long. Have you a razor? I'll cut it for you myself."

"And slit my throat in the process. No." I pulled the wig from my head and threw it back into the trunk. Knocked the lid down with a nudge from my foot. "My own hairs will have to do."

"*Have to do!* You shouldn't 'have to do.' You're owner of the King's Arms! You must have money laid by. You ought to do better than this." His indictment included my wig, my clothes, my room. My very life.

I ignored him, turning to put on my better pair of shoes. Clamping one of them between my knees, I pulled off the plain steel buckle and replaced it with the carved German silver. "And what is the point of all of that? When it doesn't really matter? What girl would want me?"

The only reply to my brutally forthright question was a snore. Straightening, I saw John sprawled across my bed. I tossed his hat onto his chest.

He woke with a snort. "Ah . . . yes. Well, then. What was I saying?"

"You were remarking upon what a sorry life I had constructed for myself."

"I rather bungled things, didn't I?"

There was a moment of awkward silence between us.

"Well . . . there's still Miss Sunderland." He said it as if she were some second-rate prize. As if a girl worth ten Polly Penningtons should somehow be considered less. For some reason, a great seething rage threatened to explode from within me.

I took a moment to caution myself. What did John's opinions truly matter? The important thing was the prison escape. And to arrange it I needed the help of both he and Hannah. "Yes. There's still Miss Sunderland."

By the time we reached Pennington House I was sure the invitation was better refused than honored. "I really don't think I ought to go in."

"And why shouldn't you?"

I eyed the grand door that stood closed, above us. "Why should I?"

John took the stairs with sprightly steps. "She's cowed you!"

"She has not."

"She has!" He laughed. "I never thought I'd see the day when Jeremiah Jones was afraid of a girl. Too good!" When he finally finished laughing, he came back down, grabbed me by the elbow, and dragged me to the door. "If her family has installed themselves here at the Penningtons', she'll have a whole line of men paraded before her nightly if I'm not much mistaken. It wouldn't do to absent yourself from her for too long."

"She'll make a mincemeat of me over her brother."

"Just tell her you've talked me into granting her the favor."

"I'll not."

"You've too much pride."

I'd not enough as far as I was concerned. If I did, I wouldn't be walking around like some altar boy in my best clothes. But I couldn't deny that it felt good to wear a waistcoat again. And my pair of silver buckles.

"You're far too handsome to absent yourself from the female population." There was a note of wistfulness in his words.

"Nothing a new suit and a fistfight couldn't do for you."

"Women do love a man in uniform. At least that's what I've noticed about these Philadelphia belles. The girls in England couldn't care a fig. They're after what's in a man's pocket, not what he wears on his back."

"Good thing your heiress kept her hands where they belong, then. What's her name again?"

"I call her my Brunhilda. She thinks it's a compliment. In any case, don't remind me of her. I plan to enjoy myself this evening to the hilt."

"Ah, yes. Before the sword of matrimony severs you from your pleasurable pursuits forever."

As a servant opened the front door and ushered us into the front hall, I was smiling. John was looking decidedly morose.

15
HANNAH

"I don't see why I must attend." Mother was helping me into my gown so that I wouldn't require the services of Jenny, the enslaved woman. I dressed each day in my parents' room to avoid her unwanted help.

"This house is not our own. We must be peaceable . . . and thee were invited."

"Only so that I could entertain Jeremiah Jones." He was so embittered that I doubted any person could accomplish that task.

"Thee must be kind to that man."

He wasn't very kind to me. But Mother didn't know of our intrigues and she must never learn of them. And so I nodded and tried to smile.

She put out a hand to straighten the modest ruffle that issued from my sleeve, then kissed me on the cheek and whispered into my ear, "Go see if thee can aid thy cousin."

Polly was already being aided by hands much more able than mine. As I walked into her bedroom, Jenny was helping her into her stays while Doll was waiting with a gown.

"Hannah! You must change for supper. My guests will be here any moment."

"We are not in the habit of changing." Friends valued simplicity more than propriety. Polly changed for dinner every day and then again for evening entertainments, but I was as dressed as ever I would be. My gown may have been dark plum in color, but it was made of the finest silk.

"Oh. I thought — I mean, for a party, would you like to borrow something of mine? I've a light striped silk in a pale green that would do quite admirably. It is almost spring, after all."

"No. But I thank thee for thy generosity."

Irritation and something much like pity shone from her eyes. She turned to allow Jenny to lace her stays. "Oh! Mr. Jones is coming. Was I wrong to have him invited? To provide you with some company?"

Aunt Rebekah had already warned me of that fact. "It was kind of thee to think of me."

Her smile shone like a beacon. "I *knew* you fancied him!"

"I — I don't — I mean —"

"He's a very handsome man beneath that

mess of hair. Even despite his manner of dress. Which is very singular, if you'll pardon my saying. And I'm quite certain he returns your interest."

"I can't think why he should —"

"Because you're lovely. You really are. With your fair hair and gray eyes. Any man would find you pleasing. Except . . . you mustn't mind if I ask you to leave me Major Lindley."

"Of course not. I mean I *am* a Friend."

"Your body may be, but your heart is not."

She had inverted it; the reverse was true. It should be true, in any case, though I was beginning to suspect that perhaps it was not. It was in this state of confusion that I descended the stair in the wake of my cousin. That she had put such thoughts of Jeremiah Jones and hearts into my head!

I looked up from my thoughts to find him watching my descent.

Consternation did the queerest thing to my stomach, and I found myself hardly able to look away from him. By the time I reached the bottom stair I could tell that a flush had colored my cheeks.

He bowed. "Miss Hannah."

"Hannah." Did he choose to disregard the simplest of requests?

He bent over my hand before I could

remember to snatch it from him. I did not need such pretenses of courtesy. No one did. And especially not from someone who welcomed wicked men into his tavern.

"I know that you do not require such shows of propriety, but others seem to find scandal in their absence. Please believe me when I say that I wish nothing other than to honor your person."

"Thee would honor me most by treating me as the least." And if he left me alone altogether, that would be even better.

Major Lindley had offered his arm to Polly and was escorting her into the parlor.

"It would behoove us both if you would draw less attention to us." Jeremiah Jones's blue eyes had turned the color of a stormy sky.

I found it odd that he was so changeable in his moods. It did not recommend him as a man of peace. "Then perhaps thee would do me the kindness of treating me as I request to be treated."

"If I do that, if I call you by your Christian name, then some might assume there is an agreement between us."

"There is, is there not?" Despite every modicum of good sense that cried out for me to disassociate myself from him.

"An agreement of *marriage*."

Oh!

"Have no fear. No one with their wits about them would think that a girl like you would favor a man like me." He was scowling by the time he finished speaking.

A man who was not a Friend? Of course none should think I would marry a man who was not a Friend. In any case, he did not seem to expect a reply, so I walked toward the parlor to join the rest of the party and Jeremiah Jones followed behind.

I spent the better part of the evening trying to decide why it was that people wasted so much of their time on vain pursuits like music and dance. Jeremiah Jones spent the better part of the evening studying the dancers with a yearning that made me think he wished to be among them.

"Do not feel as if thee must remain by my side, Jeremiah Jones. Thee may dance if thee would like to."

He shifted in his chair to face me. "I can't. Not anymore." He'd said it as if it was the worst of pronouncements.

" 'Tis not so terrible a thing, not to be able to dance." I'd not danced for my entire life.

"Then you must never have done it."

I was startled by the ferocity in his vehemence.

"I was once considered the best dancer in the colony. You cannot know how it feels to be held up as the epitome of a gentleman, to be the coveted guest of a ball, and then be cast from polite society. To be considered no one at all."

He was right: I did not. And I might not ever understand how it might make a man feel, but I understood that he suffered still from what had befallen him. "I am sorry, Jeremiah Jones, for all of the pain that it has caused you."

"You? *Sorry?*" His brows came together and he began to say something, but then he must have thought the better of it, for he closed up his mouth. Jaw working, he rose and left the room.

I might have been humiliated, but no one seemed to notice. Everyone was dancing. No one was paying any attention to a Quaker maid, dressed in a simple fashion, sitting in the corner. With all of the noise and with everyone's attention given to dancing, I decided I would not be observed if I slipped away. And if God allowed, perhaps I would be well into sleep before Polly retired for the night.

I had just rounded the corner into the hall when I walked straight into the sturdy chest of Jeremiah Jones.

"Forgive me, Miss — Hannah."

"The fault is entirely my own." Had I not been so eager to flee, then he would not this moment be clutching at my arm with his hand, struggling to keep his balance. I cupped my own hand beneath his elbow and righted him.

His temper seemed not to have improved, for he wrested his arm from me.

"I apologize for what I said to thee earlier —"

"You've no right to speak of things that don't concern you."

Perhaps I should have left then, but even among Friends it would not have been polite. Following Christ's example, when there is enmity between us, we seek to remove it, not flee from it. "Perhaps thee are right. And if that is the case, then again, I must apologize."

He looked me over for one long moment, his face finally relaxing. "Would you care to return to the parlor?"

No, I did not. But I had been bid to attend and I did care to do as I had been instructed.

"I promise not to snap at you." He bowed. "We are supposed, in fact, to have an interest in one another."

We were? I knew Polly had amused herself

with such fancies, but I hadn't counted intelligence among her strongest attributes. "But . . ." My hand was plucking at my sleeve ruffles before I realized and my cheeks, once more, were stained with a blush.

"It works quite well to disguise our association."

"It . . . does?"

"And it would also explain — to any who are watching — why we happen to be in each other's company so often."

"I will not lie to thee, Jeremiah Jones. I can have no interest in thee other than the salvation of thy soul."

His smile disappeared. "I would never have imagined otherwise. I assure you." He had seemed almost warm an instant before, but now the glower had come back into his eyes.

"My Meeting would not hesitate to disown me."

The color of his eyes lightened and the corners of his lips turned as if preparing for a smile. "And my own friends would surely demand if I had my wits still about me. Had I any friends, that is."

When he offered his arm to me, I accepted it and we went back into the parlor together — the girl who could hope for no understanding among Friends and the man who, apparently, had none.

16
JEREMIAH

I left Pennington House with John and the other soldiers. We walked up Spruce Street together. One of the officers whistled a merry tune while another danced a jig. As we passed by an alley, their steps slowed, then came to stop entirely in front of one of the city's numerous brothels.

I kept on walking.

"Jonesy! Off to bed so soon? Stay. Come in with us."

In with them. To the brothel. I paused in my steps.

John left his comrades and walked toward me. "Just because you're war-scarred doesn't mean you have to be a monk."

I turned from him and began to walk away once more.

"There's nothing to worry about. I've heard one of the girls has a soft spot for the lame and the crippled."

"Thank you, but no."

"Hey!" He stopped me with a hand to my shoulder. But still I wouldn't turn to face him. "You didn't . . . I mean . . . you weren't injured *there* too, were you?"

As if that could be any worse than what had happened. "Don't be a blockhead."

His hand left my shoulder. "I'm sorry."

I looked past him for a moment into the building. It was filled with soldiers and scantily clad women. I longed — in that brief instant — for a simple touch. For a girl's soft hand and delicious scent. I longed to think that I mattered to anyone at all.

"No." I shook my head, pushed into the dark of the night, and walked on. The pain of being alone would only be doubly compounded were I to pay for the pleasure of being bedded.

"Don't be . . ." The rest of John's words were lost to the wind.

And so I went back to the King's Arms alone. Undressed myself alone. Fell into bed alone. Yet still I was not alone in that spartan room, in that big bed. A small, quiet voice haunted my thoughts.

I am sorry, Jeremiah Jones, for all of the pain that it has caused you.

I wished her voice would leave my head. What would a Quaker know about flirting

189

and dancing and courting? How could a Quaker know how much everything depended on how agilely, how gracefully you comported yourself on a dance floor?

Dash her eyes! Those cool, dispassionate, all-seeing eyes.

She had no right to speak to me of dancing. Not when she didn't even know the steps to the simplest of country dances.

I am sorry, Jeremiah Jones.

I am sorry.

She hadn't spoken the words in pity. She'd spoken them in sorrow. The words had been weighted with the same grief that I felt. As if she also mourned what I had lost. The moment she had spoken, I had felt like weeping. I felt the press of years of unshed tears in my chest. At my throat. In my eyes.

She was sorry.

No one had ever said that they were sorry. No one had ever acknowledged that the man I used to be existed no more. That it was a pitiful shame something like that had been allowed to happen. Mostly, people just pretended that I wasn't there; life went on around me. And mostly I pretended I didn't care. But no one had ever, not once, said what she had. And for that I felt a terrible, dreadful rage build inside me.

No one. Not one.

Not ever.

A single ragged sob escaped my throat. So I clawed at my arm. At the stump where the ache was near constant. The pain attacked with such vengeance that when tears came, it was on account of the arm and not the other.

It wasn't on account of her words.

I woke early, before dawn on Saturday. I always woke early. What reason did I have to linger abed? But that morning I was awakened for cause of a sensation. I reveled in the feeling for a moment before I looked with dread at what my eyes could not deny. I could have sworn my hand was back. If I closed my eyes, I could even feel pain pulsing back and forth between its fingers. But when I opened my eyes, I could not deny its absence. It was not there. It had not been there for many years.

I did not believe in it, but I could feel it.

It did not happen often, but neither did pain ever fully leave me. It was as if the ghost of my former self were mocking the miserable reality of my present self.

It was best just ignored. In time it would go away. It always did. But it hurt like the devil while it lasted.

Go away!

191

I dashed some water on my face, then threw some at my hand that was not there, wondering if it might quench the pain. It only dropped straight to the floor.

Cursing myself as a fool, I tugged on my breeches and pulled on my coat.

I arranged with Bartholomew to deliver the bag of grain for Hannah to Pennington House. I took myself out, as was my habit, in between the service of dinner and the preparation for supper. My steps were listless, my direction aimless. My phantom of a hand was still with me. It surprised me still that when I looked down, I could not see it hanging out from beneath my cuff. Though had I seen it, I might have cut it off to spare myself such torture.

When Hannah Sunderland approached, I was immune to her finer qualities. 'Tis possible that I might have even glared at her.

She gave the impression of smiling, though she wasn't. It had to do with her eyes and the way they glowed. "I've news!"

"Then spill it quickly. I haven't much time."

The glow in her eyes turned into a bright, hot flame. And it was directed straight at me. "Thee needn't be so cross. I've done nothing thee cannot approve of. And they moved Robert to a different room; he's with

192

William Addison now."

I found myself waiting for an expression of gratitude, which she did not know to offer. I'd confused my twisted lie with the truth. Feeling foolish made me churlish. "Excellent. And you delivered the message."

"I did."

I nodded. At least she'd finally got one thing right. "Next time you visit, ask how far they've dug that tunnel."

She put a hand to my arm. "I thank thee."

I shook it off. "For what?"

"For the grain. And for including Robert in the plan."

That, I could take some credit for. But I didn't. I turned on my heel and walked away. My armless arm was throbbing and stopping to talk to Hannah had only increased the pain.

Walking down the street, I paused in front of the tailor's shop and surveyed his wares. John was right. Yellow was in fashion. And apparently so was blue. I used to care about such things.

The tailor spied me in the window. Waved at me to come in.

When I did not do his bidding, he opened the door for me himself.

"I've come to a decision, Mr. Jones. If

you're going to continue to frequent this place, then you're going to have to order a new suit of clothes. Or two. I can't have you standing about in coats ten years old. You'll scare my clients away."

He pulled me into the shop, took out a measure, and started to work. Grunting, he assessed the span of my shoulders.

I struggled to hold myself straight.

"Nothing like a suit of new clothes to improve the man. I'm surprised those you wear haven't fallen apart."

"It doesn't matter what I wear at the King's Arms. No one can see through all that smoke in the dim light."

"But they can see you when you walk the streets . . . a certain girl best of all." He winked as he said it.

I batted his hand away from my waist. "She's Quaker."

He shrugged. "And so were the Chews and the Shippens. But they aren't now."

"Just between you and me . . ." Should I tell him? He'd gotten out of the spying business, hadn't he? But why should there not be one person besides me who knew the truth of it? He'd put his measure away and was intent upon making notations in a book.

"You'll need a new waistcoat, a new coat,

and new breeches. And some new shirts as well."

"The old ones do just fine."

He pulled at my arm and revealed the worn edge at the turn of my cuff. "Just fine for a beggar. Which you decidedly are not."

The tavern was doing a brisk business. It was frequented by soldiers who paid for their drink with gold. Doing well? I was doing spectacularly. "There's no reason for extravagance."

"What's your hesitation, man? Most men in your situation would be proclaiming their status all over town! And if you did, you'd soon be invited to the finest tables and the best parties."

"They don't interest me."

"They used to."

Aye. They had. Back when I was intent upon amassing money and status. But now I had what I needed. I didn't want anything from society anymore.

His face softened, and he looked at me from beneath his brow, lips pursed. "I can make you a coat that won't keep sliding from your shoulder."

"To remind people of all that I have lost?"

"You do your best to remind them anyway." He straightened my collar as he spoke and put me all back together. "I would suggest something in yellow."

"Please. By all means, so I'll stand out among this crowd like some canary bird. Then they can all look on as I go about my spying business."

"Ah. 'Tis what a man might think. But the British are funny that way. They'll never expect treachery of a man who dresses himself in the latest of modes. They can bring themselves to do nothing but admire him. Whereas a man wearing a suit of clothes a decade old . . . well, the best to be expected of him is treason. They mock us colonials, you know."

I knew.

"I'm not talking about clothes, Mr. Jones. I am speaking of strategies."

He was wise, even if he was a peacock. I let him talk me into three new suits. One of a color he kept calling English blue, one of some sort of green, and one of bright yellow. He sent me on my way many pounds poorer and with the suggestion of seeing a wigmaker.

17
HANNAH

It was my third visit to the jail in as many weeks. I was wearing an extra pair of hose and had a bag of barley suspended, in a sling that Doll had fashioned, beneath my petticoats. Within my basket were nestled a wedge of cheese *and* a small pot of butter. I was hoping to buy some extra time from the guards.

The first of them took the cheese. The second, the butter. I waited, with as much patience as I could muster, outside the cell door in the hall.

"Robert Sunderland." The guard cracked the door.

A rustling came from inside, but no reply.

"Robert Sunderland!"

A faint, piteous cry rose up.

"Let me go in."

The guard shook his head and then spit into the room. "I can't do that."

"Let me in!"

"Can't. No mixing with the prisoners allowed."

Far more concerned about Robert than my own safety, I pushed past the guard into the room. Stepped right over men lying on the floor until I reached the safety of the far wall. I doubted the guard would want to come in after me. But as I exulted in evading the British guard, I realized I had landed myself in the middle of a den of rebels. I shivered.

"Come out!"

"I will not."

He looked around, the same as I did, and he must have come to the same conclusion. None of the men seemed to pose any threat. Of the ten . . . twenty . . . that I counted, more than half were prostrate. The others sat hunched against the walls with seemingly very little inclination to do anything at all but try to keep themselves warm.

The guard swore and then drew the door shut, locking it behind him.

"Robert?" I could not see well enough to make out features in that dingy, gloomy place.

"Hannah?" A spindly arm reached out toward me from the floor.

I knelt beside him and put my hand to his forehead. He was hot and his hair was dampened with sweat. "Robert?" I could not keep the fear from my voice.

"It's the putrid fever." The voice came from over against the wall. "That's what they all have."

"All?"

"All the men lying on the floor."

"It's my head, Hannah. It hurts so badly."

I pulled at the knot of my cloak. Removing it from my shoulders, I rolled it into a pillow and then eased it beneath his head.

". . . so thirsty."

"Is there no ale?" I could hardly see in the dim light.

"No." That same voice again.

"Water?"

"None."

"Then thee should ask for some!" Weren't these the same sort of people that had arrested my father? What had become of their boldness? I reached out a hand to the man lying beside Robert. I felt his forehead and then that of the man beside him. "They're all burning with fever. They need broth. And some bread." I appealed to that faceless voice by the wall.

"You can ask, but you won't receive."

Why wasn't anyone doing anything? "Is there a jug?"

"By the door."

199

I rose, stepping over the men as I made my way to the door. When I found the jug, it was empty. "Keeper!"

I heard the scrape of a chair down at the far end of the hall.

"Keeper!"

"I'm coming." He didn't come quickly and he seemed to take great pleasure in stopping to pound upon all the other doors along the way. At last I heard the jingle of a key and the rasping of the bolt against its hasp.

"So you're done, then. Didn't last long. What did I tell ye?"

"Bring me some ale or some water."

"Water! And who do you think you are? Queen Charlotte? If those rebels want water, then they'll have to get it themselves. That's what the agreement is. Each army provides for its own."

I pushed him aside, stalked down the hall, and shoved aside the chair he'd been sitting on. When the other guard pulled the door open, I exchanged the prisoners' empty jug for his own.

"Wait — what? Stop there! You can't — that's mine!"

"There are twenty prisoners down that hall who don't have a drop of anything to drink and they're burning with fever. They can't go fetch what they need. Thee can."

"But —"

I didn't wait for his reply but marched back down the hall.

"Hey! That's me jug!"

The second guard stumbled to keep up with me. "You can't go in there."

"I just did."

"I'm not supposed to let you."

"Thee already did."

"You can't be with the prisoners."

"Open the door." I might have considered breaking the jug over his head, but Robert needed the water more than the guard needed sense.

He fumbled with the keys, glaring at me as he opened it, but open it he did.

I set the jug on the ground and knelt beside Robert. "I've some drink for thee." There was nothing in that cesspool of a room to use to cool his face, so I pulled a handkerchief from my pocket, wet the hem, and daubed the sweat from his forehead.

I moved around the room, helping the sick prisoners to drink before I offered water to those sitting along the wall. By then there was little left. And by the time I had washed the faces of the ill, my handkerchief was warm from their heat and plenty soiled.

With Robert resting easier, I turned my

attentions to the escape. "Where is William Addison?"

One of the men at the wall made a feeble movement. "I'm here." The owner of the voice that had been answering me from the shadows. His red-rimmed eyes squinting, he winced as he stepped into meager light that filtered down from the window. He was paler than he ought to have been and he favored one of his legs as he stepped toward me. The tattered tails of his shirt hung low.

He straightened as he approached, though the effort seemed to cause no little pain. "Forgive me, miss. I would've liked to have dressed for entertaining."

"Thee mustn't —"

"But we ate the last of my breeches on Thursday."

"Ate — ?"

"Don't worry yourself. They were buckskin. You could close your eyes and almost imagine it for salt pork. Except we didn't have no salt."

Another man laughed, though I had found no humor in William Addison's words.

"And it wasn't pork either."

I lowered my voice as I gathered my skirts and stepped close. Tried not to react to the foul odor that had rolled from his mouth. "How does work go on the tunnel?"

"The tunnel!" He snorted. "Look around you, miss. Over half my men are down with the fever. The other half are near to dead of hunger."

"Thee mean to say that . . . ?"

"We have not begun."

They had not even begun! But . . . "Thee are already nearly a month behind!"

"A month behind. What do you think it's like in here? There are no days or weeks or months. There's only eternity. And we live it one agony at a time. This is forever."

"No." No. I would not let it be forever. Robert had to escape, and he needed these men in order to do it. "What do thee need? If thee had the men, what else would thee need to accomplish the work?"

"What do . . . ?" He looked at me as if my language were incomprehensible.

"What do thee need? I can try to get it for thee." What would men have to have in order to dig? "A shovel? Or a pick?"

He laughed outright. The light slicing through the shards of the window made a grid of his face. "We need food. And some blankets. We need wood for a fire. If you want us to pick up a shovel, you're going to have to keep us alive long enough to do it."

"Time's up!" I could hear the jangle of the guard's keys as he neared the door.

I pressed the handkerchief into William Addison's hand and took one last look at Robert. *Stay thee alive.* Before the door clanged shut, I looked back and had one last glimpse of those piteous, miserable faces.

I'd thought I had saved Robert when I'd agreed to carry messages into the jail. I hadn't counted on him getting sick. I needed to find a way to keep him alive until the tunnel was finished, and in order to do that I had to make sure it got started.

Doll was waiting for me at the corner. She stepped from the shadows at my approach, making a face that I soon realized had to do with the filth that ringed the hem of my skirts, and the number of things that I no longer had in my possession.

"Where's your cloak?"

My cloak could not matter. "They've next to nothing to eat in there. Still!" How had they survived this long?

"You surprised at that?"

"How can General Howe incarcerate prisoners and then not feed them?"

"The same way you people make folks work and then not pay them."

"What?"

"Nothing. I didn't say nothing." She fell

into step just behind my elbow with a dour twist to her lips.

"My family doesn't own any slaves."

"And yet you still manage to use one."

I blushed at her accusation, for it was nothing but the truth. I might not own Doll, but I was the beneficiary of her aid. Without her I could do none of what I had done. But the truth demanded an accounting. If our Meeting had chosen to take a stand against slavery, then I must attempt to hold with it in the letter as well as in the spirit. "Thee are right. This should not be. I will not require thy service any longer."

"Davy sure do. And so do Mrs. Pennington."

Even if I were to use Doll, what I was asking her to do was far beyond the bounds of what my aunt would condone. Far beyond what I would ever ask of any free woman or any friend. "But they would not require thee to aid me in these endeavors. In fact, they would insist, and quite rightly, that thee not. I must honor my beliefs and theirs as well. When I leave the house to come here on seventh days, I insist that thee not come with me."

"Well, now." She cocked her head as she looked at me. "What you going to do when your mama find out what you're about?"

"I shall tell her the truth."

She smiled. "I like to see that."

"I will." I knew I would have to sooner if not later, for the truth was always bound to come out. "And I shall tell thee too, right now. I am helping my brother, and several of the other prisoners, to escape."

She began to laugh. And then she began to howl. "I never heard nothing funnier than that!" she said at last, swiping at her tears with the corner of her apron.

"I am."

She put a hand to her waist. "How?"

We had not yet got so far from the jail that I felt safe in talking. "I would rather tell thee later."

"Well, this slave has had enough of your foolishness. You can tell me now or you can tell Davy later. It make no matter to me."

"I'm carrying messages —"

"How?"

"How what?"

"How you carrying those messages?"

"In my pocket." I put a hand to it as I spoke.

"In your pocket! Just waiting for someone to take them out and read them?"

"I pass them to the person in the jail."

She muttered something under her breath. Shook her head. "You need me to make you some secret place to put those. Someplace they ain't never going to find it. And how are they going to get out of that jail? With those guards walking all around?"

"They're going to dig a tunnel."

"A tunnel! With what? A teaspoon?" I heard what she muttered that time. "Lord have mercy! You folks is madder than Moses!"

It *was* mad. As well as terrifyingly dangerous. And Doll was entirely right not to want any part in it. "So thee see why I have to keep on visiting. It's the only way to ensure that my brother escapes."

"Oh, I can see why. I can see things getting a lot more worse before they start to get any better. That's for sure."

"But I don't want thee to help me. I can choose whether to place myself in danger, but thee cannot."

"Oh, I'll help you. It's the funniest thing I ever heard, you being a spy an' all."

"Hush!"

"Don't you worry none. No one would believe me if I told them!"

"Thee can't tell —"

"I won't. You with your proper ways and your strange ideas. And besides, you don't know the difference between what's true and what's truth. I'll help you. Someone

207

gots to. If you want to keep alive."

I didn't know whether I should be insulted or encouraged at her words. But I put aside my feelings for more important matters. "I need to get them more food."

"More than you been carrying beneath those skirts?"

I nodded.

"Now you talking crazy! How many people in there?"

"Not for everyone in the jail. Enough for everyone in the room. There are twenty of them." Even as I spoke the words, I knew that I would never be able to deliver enough food for twenty people, at least not on any regular basis. But I could deliver some. Anything would be more than they had now.

We walked down the street, Doll and I. Me trying to figure out how to come by enough food and her muttering about some people having a good case of the crazies.

18
JEREMIAH

Evenings at Pennington House had become a weekly ritual. But this night an invitation to supper had been extended for Saturday evening as well. The meal was interminable. I much preferred to eat where none could see me. That way I didn't have to worry about cutting meat with a knife or trying to keep peas from rolling off a fork.

The courses dragged on, one after the other, as I tried to avoid eating the food. But the sights and the scents were making my stomach beg for recourse. I could not be ungrateful. At least the Penningtons begrudged their guests no good thing. Indeed, I did not know how they could keep such a large table and host so many guests. But while there was no lack of food, there did seem to be a regrettable lack of manners.

All John and his compatriots could talk about was the war and how the army planned to crush the patriots in the spring. Mr. Pennington seemed rather pleased by the prospect, though his wife kept decrying talk of such violence. Hannah's father and mother were distinctly uncomfortable.

Hannah herself was decidedly cool.

She wanted nothing to do with me. She did not look at me. She did not talk to me. She seemed, in fact, to try to keep as far from me as our two chairs would allow. But why would she do that? When she knew that our plan depended upon people assuming that we fancied each other? I already knew she did not have the ability to lie, so it was quite apparent how she felt about me.

She despised me.

After supper we repaired to the parlor, where pretty Polly was to give us a concert.

Hannah was seated next to me. I disgusted her so much that she did not even want her skirts to touch me. She kept pulling them back over her knees whenever they began to slide in my direction. And then, quite politely but unmistakably, she turned from me entirely.

After the concert, the evening was given over once again to dance. All these people did was dance. I discovered something then that I had not known about myself: I had begun depending upon Hannah Sunderland

210

to be my companion at these functions. I had, dare I say, almost come to enjoy our time together.

It seemed that she, however, had not.

And suddenly I could take no more of being poor Jeremiah Jones who nobody wanted to be with and everybody pitied. I walked to where Hannah sat in a chair along the wall. Bowed and sat down beside her. "If my arm distresses you overmuch, then please, do not feel as if you have to suffer my presence any longer."

"Thy . . . arm?"

"You've done nothing this evening but try to place yourself as far from me as possible. It's quite plain that I disgust you." I didn't know why I had hoped for — or expected — anything else.

"Disgust me!"

"I can reach no other conclusion."

Her mouth dropped open, her eyes began to blaze. She rose, one hand outstretched as if to beseech me, but then she let it drop to her side and stepped back. "Follow me." She hissed the words before she walked past me toward the front hall.

I fully expected to meet her at the door where she would show me out, but she took us in the opposite direction altogether. After purloining a taper and a lantern, we went

211

out the back door, into the garden, and then down into the depths of a root cellar.

I was three or four stairs behind, my steps slowing as I leaned against the side of the cellar wall for support in descending.

She stood against the far wall, the fury in her face magnified by the lantern she held beneath her chin. "Thee must cease thy pigheaded foolishness!"

"*My* pigheaded foolishness?"

"Not everything has to do with thy arm!"

"No. It doesn't. It has to do with those men in Walnut Street Jail and how to get them out!"

"I can't worry that every time I see thee, I will say something that might offend thee."

"Me? Offended by you?" If my voice had risen, it was only because hers had as well. "I'm trying to pretend to court you, but you rebuff me at every turn. All I require — all your brother's escape requires — is that you play along in this charade. But if you find me so offensive that —"

"Nothing about thee offends me!" It was good that we were in the root cellar, otherwise her words would have been quite clear to all and sundry.

"So it's just my imagination that you cringe at my every approach? That you turn from every advance? Scowl at every joke? I

212

didn't have such bitter lovers' quarrels even when I had lovers."

"It's the *putrid fever!*"

I blinked. It was — it was . . . what?

"It's Robert. He has the putrid fever. I tended him today. I tended many of the men. And I don't want that any more should fall ill on account of me."

All my pride and vanity poured out of my depths as if from a sieve. "What a dolt I've been."

Her chin crumbled. She began to cry.

"I —" Across the expanse of the room I could only watch as all composure left her.

"They're so hungry and so cold and so . . . so. . . . wretched! They haven't even started digging. And now there's the fever."

"Wait. What?"

"The fever!" She wailed the words.

"No. The other. The part about them not having started." How could they be expected to finish their tunnel before the British left in spring? "What are they doing down there?"

At this she began to cry even harder as she clutched the lantern's handle in her fists. She looked so angry, so alone, and . . . so scared.

I knew exactly how she felt. I closed the distance between us, even as she retreated, trying to wave me off. "Don't. Thee must not. Please. I don't want thee to fall ill."

"Just — if you turn." I put a hand to her shoulder and turned her to face the wall. "And if you don't touch me . . ." With her not facing me or touching me, my intent was to pat her on the shoulder. But all my precautions were for nothing. She turned back around, burrowing into my shoulder as if it could provide some comfort.

I took the lantern and held it out from us. "You are the yellingest Quaker I have ever had the displeasure to meet."

She pulled away from me and wiped at the tears still streaming down her face. "I know it. My temper has always been my weakness." She stilled. Looked up at me. "Thank thee for that word. 'Tis true. I had forgotten my testimony. God sent thee to remind me of it."

"I have nothing at all to do with Him."

That coaxed a smile from her, even though tears still glistened on her cheeks. "There is that of God in everyone, Jeremiah Jones. Even in thee."

I strongly doubted it. I stalked to the stair. Held the lantern high, gesturing her forward.

As she passed me, I saw the trails tears had left on her face. This would never do.

Not unless we wanted the whole party to wonder what we'd been up to. "Hold this." I passed the lantern to her, then fished a handkerchief from my pocket. I dabbed at the streaks on her cheeks.

She was of a height with me, having stepped up onto the first stair. As I attended to her, she looked at me, unblinking. "Thee are not the unfeeling man thee would like people to believe thee are."

"You know nothing at all about me."

"I know enough. Only . . . why are thee doing this? With the prisoners?"

"Because there is no one else. And because I can't *do* anything else." And it irritated the devil out of me! "I should be out there fighting with them this minute! But I can't hold a musket. I can do nothing at all."

She laid a hand on my arm. "Thy nothing is going to save twenty men. I doubt that thy presence on a battlefield would guarantee anything other than someone's death. This is not some second-rate service that thee are doing. It is noble, Jeremiah Jones. It is the right thing to do."

How desperately I wanted to believe her.

As I came down the stair Monday morning, my barkeeper motioned me over into the

215

office. "There's a man out there waiting for you."

This was it. I'd been found out. "Where is he?" Maybe I could sneak out the back through the stables.

"Out in the public room. He's one of those Quaker fellows."

A Quaker? "Out . . . ?"

"There. In front of the fire."

I didn't know if I wanted to speak to one of those people so early in the morning. But if he was anything like Hannah, he wouldn't leave until he was done saying whatever it was he had to say.

In fact, it was Mr. Sunderland himself, standing by the fire in a dark-colored, impeccably tailored coat, an uncocked hat on his head.

I nodded. "Mr. Sunderland."

"Elias. Sunderland."

I didn't understand why these people got so upset whenever anyone tried to be polite. It just made me want to be . . . impolite.

"I am here to speak to thee about my daughter."

"Your daughter."

"My daughter, Hannah Sunderland. Thee are not of our faith. And even if thee were . . ." He tried, but failed, to keep his gaze from drifting toward my arm. "I am

216

here to tell thee to keep thyself away from her."

"I assure you, Mr. Sunderland —"

"Elias."

"I assure you, my intentions are nothing but honorable." After all the girls and all the affairs, the one father that warned me away is the one that had nothing to fear. At least not in that way.

He looked at me as if he could not bring himself to believe me. "Be that as it may, a relationship with those who are not Friends can only bring Hannah dishonor."

"Frankly, I'm not —" I was about to say that I had no intentions regarding Hannah at all. But that would make me seem even more disreputable than before. Before I was merely misguided. If I admitted to a complete lack of interest in her, I'd be nothing but a rake.

"Do thee understand what I have asked?"

"I do." I couldn't honor his wishes, of course. But I understood them.

"Then I expect thee to abide by my wishes."

Another thing about people who were so scrupulously honest: they left so little room in which to be dishonest. But what could I say? I could plead no suit; I did not want to. And I could not admit to my true intentions. Having a daughter marry out of the faith was one thing. Having a daughter hang on the gallows for treason was another thing entirely.

He was still looking at me. Waiting, I suppose, for some sign of agreement.

I nodded. After all, *I* had no prohibition against lying, though I wished I could be telling the truth. It would be safer for Hannah not to associate with a man like me. But I couldn't just quit all contact with her, nor could I write her out of our plans. I needed her too much.

19
HANNAH

As I walked down Walnut Street with Doll on fifth day, Jeremiah Jones tipped his hat at me. I slowed. Stopped. "Good afternoon, Jeremiah Jones."

There was a strange hesitation in his manner. And he stood far enough away from me that I was worried we might be overheard. "Good afternoon." He frowned at Doll, who had come to stand behind me.

"Doll is enslaved at Pennington House."

He raised an eyebrow. "Enslaved. Such a quaint way you have with words, Hannah Sunderland."

"The way I have with words is nothing more or less than the truth."

His lips lifted for a moment. "Be that as it may . . ."

He seemed to be waiting for — oh! "I've come by some lovely apples." Doll had helped me take some from the pantry. "Would thee like one?" I drew back the

219

cloth as I spoke.

He flashed a tight smile. "How kind." His hand slipped into my basket. I saw him tuck a message between the bottom of the basket and the cloth. I would secret it in a small pouch sewn into the skirts that had been gathered up at my sides in a polonaise. He saluted with the apple. "Good day." And then he turned on his heel and left so quickly that I might have been offended had I any reason to be so.

I let my gaze travel the street, trying to determine if any had seen us. As we walked on, I came to the conclusion that only one person had noticed that we had stopped and talked. But that person could place at great peril our plans. For that one person was my father.

When we returned to Pennington House, once Davy had relieved me of my cloak and basket, he told me my father awaited me in the parlor.

I offered a quick prayer for courage, reassured myself that he could not know of my visits to the jail, and then fixed what I hoped was a look of pleasant inquiry upon my face.

That I should have had to fix a look upon myself at all was the measure of just how far I had fallen from a life of simplicity and honesty. I knew I was useless in the ways of prevarication, for I had been trained up in truth. It was the only thing I could do well: speak plainly. I would just have to pray that the truth would not be demanded of me.

"He look none too happy, if you don't mind my saying." Davy mumbled the words as he passed me on the way out to the kitchen.

No. He would be none too happy to have seen me speaking with Jeremiah Jones, a man of war, a man of violence. A man who was not one of us.

As I walked into the room, I saw Mother sitting on the settee beside Father. Her hands were resting in her lap, but they were clenched about each other, the knuckles gone white with tension.

"I was told thee wanted to see me."

"I saw thee speaking with Jeremiah Jones this afternoon. This has gone too far, daughter. He is not a Friend."

And what could I reply with any sort of honesty? " 'Tis not what thee think."

"Well, then 'tis certainly how it must look. Thy mother had several Friends demand of her if she knew that thee were acquainted with him."

My heart lay heavy within me. We had not

been so discreet, then, as we had hoped. If our relationship had provided cover for our meetings in the eyes of his friends, it had done nothing but provoke distress in the eyes of mine. "I have no interest in him, Father." None aside from his ability to help Robert escape from jail.

Mother looked as if she would rise to come implore me, but she did not. "I know thee have always had a soft spot for the weak and the wounded. But he is a man, not some docile beast."

Weak and wounded. Most of the time those two words were a pair, but I could not reconcile them in the case of Jeremiah Jones. Wounded beast, that was the picture of him. "I would never fix my sights upon such a man." That was the truth. But what I wanted to say next . . . that was rather tricky. "Most of the time our meetings are the doing of Polly's major. He insists that the man has a fancy for me. And as Polly fancies him . . ."

Mother turned to Father. " 'Tis difficult, Elias, living in a home not our own."

He took up her hand in his. "I do not know what to do." He directed his attentions back to me. "Thee think thee are being kind to the man, but thee do not understand."

"I do understand." I did. Truly, I did.

"I have already spoken to Jeremiah Jones about this matter."

He'd spoken to Jeremiah Jones? I felt a flush creep up my neck to my face.

"I asked him to have nothing more to do with thee."

I bowed my head at his words.

"And I must ask the same of thee. Let there be no more meetings arranged between thee."

"I cannot control the things that Polly does. Nor the major's actions."

"Then I shall explain to thy aunt that thee are not to partake in these endless evenings of frivolity. We can be grateful for their generosity in providing shelter without succumbing to their inveterate ways. Do I make myself understood?"

Oh yes. Quite plainly, just as always.

It was one thing to warn me away from further meetings with Jeremiah Jones, but I did not think that one last conversation would be that great an indiscretion. Though Father had spoken to him, I suspected that he might not fully understand the import of my Father's request since he had been bold enough to greet me in the street. I kept our plan to walk out the next afternoon. Only when I saw him I turned quick into an alley, hoping he would follow me.

He did.

I did not waste any time in repeating my father's request.

"Aye, he did tell me that."

"Then thee must not speak to me again."

He threw up his hand. "You can't be — ! You know that your father's concerns are unfounded! He would have no worries at all if he knew what was really happening."

"No worries? He would be even more distressed!"

"It's not that I want you to tell him. It's just that we have to keep meeting. And I don't see any reason not to since there's no danger to your virtue."

"But he *has* asked, and I must honor his request."

"No, you don't. Are you a spy or some sniveling child?"

"Thee cannot bait me with thy silvered tongue. I am simply a girl who wants to see her brother freed from prison."

"You seem to suffer under the misconception that you're involved in some polite undertaking, which requires only half-hearted commitments. If the British catch you, they won't be swayed by the fact that you took pains to obey your father. They'll hang you for a spy whether you've obeyed his rules or not!"

I knew that. I had pondered that terrible fate every night since I'd agreed to his plans. I had nightmares of being taken by the same kind of men who had arrested my father. The fact that I had to associate myself with one who had invited them into his tavern still rankled. "Lower thy voice. Someone might hear thee."

"What do you think we're about here?"

"Freeing prisoners from jail."

"Aye. Through devious means."

"Just because I've agreed to such deception does not mean that I have to lie or cheat or attempt to deceive everyone."

"Everything about you is deceptive! You look like some — some charming, respectable, noble, decent woman, but here you are being cantankerous and obdurate. And exceedingly mulish!"

"If thee want my help, then thee will have to honor my ways."

He stared at me for one long moment, anger snapping in his eyes. "Fine."

"Thee understand, then, that I must not see thee anymore."

"That's not what your father said."

"He did too!"

"He said that you must not *arrange* to

225

meet me anymore. I understand the words, but I don't understand why you insist on observing them."

Now it was he who was being exceedingly stubborn. "He told me not to see thee. What do thee expect me to do?"

"Expect you — ! I expect you to keep your part of our agreement."

"I will."

"I need you to keep delivering the messages." His tone suggested that he was threatening me.

"I shall."

"Then . . . ?"

"I will deliver thy messages, but there can be no meetings arranged between us."

"If you don't want to be part of this, just say so." The words came out in a snarl.

"I do. But I can't — *I won't* — if it requires me to violate my beliefs."

"Do you believe your brother has any chance at life at all if he stays in that jail?"

"There must be no meetings arranged." I bobbed my head, gathered up my skirts, and walked on. But I was quaking with the knowledge that though I'd been faithful to my father's demands, Jeremiah Jones was right. I might have just guaranteed the failure of the escape. If we could not speak and could not meet, then there was no way to conduct our business. Robert was as good as dead.

Polly had another party that evening. She nattered on about it all afternoon. I told her I would not be attending, but she only scoffed at me.

"Of course you will. Mr. Jones will be there. Major Lindley practically promised."

"I have a presentiment that he won't be attending."

"A presentiment." She put her hand mirror down and turned to look at me. "Are you? . . . oh!" Her eyes grew wide. "You've had an argument, haven't you? A lovers' quarrel. Do tell me what it was about!"

"We've had no quarrel and we are not lovers."

She rose from her chair and pattered over to me, the hem of her caraco jacket flapping around her knees. "Only those who are quarreling protest that they are not."

"I'm not protesting. I'm simply stating a fact." Although in truth we had rather quarreled, hadn't we? Yet it had nothing to do with being lovers.

"But you did. I can tell."

"How?"

"By the way you're holding that book. As if you'd like to tear it in two."

I relaxed my grip and watched as the color seeped back into my knuckles.

"Do tell. It will make you feel better about the whole thing. I promise I will agree that you were right. We shall both curse the stubborn foolishness of the man and then you can help me get dressed without all that dreadful scowling."

I'd been scowling? Well. I fixed a smile upon my lips, thinking that perhaps I would feel better in the telling of it. "My father forbid me to see him —"

Polly's hands flew to her breast. "So you're star-crossed lovers!"

"We're not —" I sighed. "In any case, I saw him one last time to tell him, and he insisted that I disregard my father's wishes."

"But of course you must!"

Hadn't she just promised to agree with me? And to curse Jeremiah Jones's stubborn foolishness? "I don't see why I should —"

"Because the course of true love never did run smooth. Don't you see? It just proves that you were meant to be together!"

"All it proves is that the man is pigheaded, and that he won't listen to reason!" And besides, there was no true love. "I can't fancy him, Polly. He isn't even a Friend."

She waved aside my words as if they didn't even matter. "How utterly romantic!"

" 'Tis not romantic. 'Tis —"

"Oh, but it is." She returned to her chair and picked up her mirror again. "Don't worry. I'll help you find some way around it all."

"I don't want a way around it. I mean to honor my father's wishes."

"Then you go about honoring them, and I'll go about finding some way around them."

"But I don't want thee to!"

"Of course you do. If you didn't, you would never have told me about it."

I was certain Friends weren't meant to feel as if they wanted to strangle their cousins. "I only told thee because thee insisted upon it. And thee promised that thee would agree with me and then thee didn't."

"Because you were wrong. But don't worry. I shall make it all come right."

I gave up speaking about it. Polly had a memory like a sieve. The less I spoke of the incident, the sooner it would be forgotten.

20

JEREMIAH

What a waste! I rolled from my side to my back and stared into the dark. A delightful evening spent in the company of Miss Pennington and her many friends, watching them all dance, dispensing comments I didn't mean and pretending to sentiments I didn't feel. I don't know why I'd gone. Hannah had been quite clear about her intentions to obey her father. I hadn't really expected her to be there, though perhaps I'd hoped. Her presence made the evenings at Pennington House tolerable.

I'd have to tell John to stop scheming invitations for me. But I had discovered, through overheard conversation, the date when the army intended to fete General Howe. May eighteenth. Generally I heard enough soldiers' gossip at the King's Arms during the day that I didn't need to go looking for it at night. And certainly not at a dancing party.

I'd missed Hannah, though.

I'd had conversations now and then throughout the evening, most of them fueled by compliments. Just like in the old days. The insincere kind were always the easiest to offer. What had I said to the Pennington girl? Something about her gown being a shining vision of all that was right in the world. In fact, the satin had been much too gaudy and covered with far too many fripperies for my taste. And the height of her wig had been ridiculously extreme.

Used to be that my taste, like hers, had been dictated by the latest modes from London. But I'd come to appreciate a simpler aesthetic. Come to value fine fabrics rather than an abundance of trimmings and lace. If I was to pay a compliment to any one at all, I would give one to Hannah. The problem was I hadn't yet come by the way to say it. How did you tell someone that being with her soothed your soul and made you feel as if you wanted to be a better person? There were no words to put to such thoughts. Besides, she wouldn't be interested in pretty compliments. The plain and honest truth. Those were the only kind of words that seemed to matter to her.

I don't know why I bothered to think of her at all.

It was that thought that finally pushed me on toward sleep — thinking about why I ought to stop thinking about her. And it didn't really work. I dreamt about her all night. I awoke to feelings of comfort and a cozy warmth that I remembered from years past. I don't know why I should have. If I'd dreamt of Hannah Sunderland, then surely she must have been yelling at me for some reason or other.

I tried to put away all thoughts of her, but the night's fancies had brought my missing hand back to life. And so I blamed her for it. As many times as it had happened, I had never become accustomed to that phantom pain.

As a result, my words had more bite than was normal. I'm afraid I yelled at my barkeeper and at the stable hand. I even yelled at the cook herself. But it had the satisfactory effect of keeping the staff away from me. I was able to nurse my morning ale in private.

And plan for the day's intrigues.

Today I needed to find the egg-girl. There'd been no sign of her the last time I'd gone to the market. I also needed to figure out some way to pass Hannah messages that wouldn't require arranging a meeting.

Returning to my room, I locked the door and secured the curtains. And then I sat down to encode a message to General Washington.

Though I had learned to do many things with my left hand, dexterity at the finer things still eluded me. As I wrote out my message, I paused once. Twice. Swiping at the sweat that damped my forehead.

My elegant script, gained from long hours of practice at the hand of a demanding schoolmaster, had been taken from me along with my arm. He would surely have caned me if he had seen the scrawl of a script to which my penmanship had been reduced. I could only hope it would fall into the hands of someone with enough patience to interpret it.

I crossed out a particularly illegible word and began once more.

My quill broke in the middle of the word. Blast it all!

I plunged the quill into my water basin to release the ink from the tip, then gnawed on it with my teeth to bring back the point. A splinter of the bone poked into my gum in the process.

Sitting down once more, I dipped it back into the ink and completed the word. Dabbed at my forehead.

I finished not long after the clock down-stairs struck eleven.

General Howe to be feted night of 18 May at Joseph Wharton's Walnut Grove. Fine night to meet our friends. Advise of meeting place.

But I was not yet done with my work. It was one thing to write a message, but another thing entirely to pass it on.

I folded it into the smallest square that I could. The difficult part would be to pass it to the egg-girl without being seen to do it. I'd almost dropped the message I'd passed before. I didn't want to tempt fate a second time. With the weather improving, the market was busier that it had been, which meant there were more eyes watching the goings-on.

At one point I'd had a looking glass for shaving. I stood in the middle of my room, trying to think where I might have put it. I rifled through my highboy chest of drawers with no success. Considered my trunk. At the very bottom, my hand fell upon the smooth wood of its turned frame. I drug it up through stacks of clothes that I never planned to wear again. Pairs of gloves. Embroidered waistcoats. Detritus of a life I

234

no longer lived.

Propping the looking glass up against my water pitcher, I set it at an angle so that I could see my pocket. Placing my basin atop my writing desk, I pretended it to be the recipient of my endeavors.

I dropped the note into my pocket and then set about getting it to the basin, undetected.

The first attempt ended in miserable failure. I dropped the note just as soon as I pulled it from my pocket. The second try went no better. I ought to have succeeded at the third, but the glass showed me the reflection of the note as I pulled it from my pocket. The trick of it was to keep it hidden within the hollow of my palm while somehow maintaining a natural ease of movement.

If only I didn't have such a large hand!

One might have thought that a perfect blessing for work such as this. But my fingers were too inclined to clumsiness and my palm both too large and too shallow at the same time.

I took a bottle of rum from the mantel and poured myself a drink, downing it as I paced the floor. What a poor excuse I was for a spy. It might be easier to convince the tailor to take up his old position than to train my hand for a task for which it was so ill-suited.

But this message was important, and I was the only person who could start it on its way to General Washington. I stood in front of the looking glass once more. Took a deep breath. Let it out in a sigh. I would practice all day if I had to. In fact, I ought to have done so long before. I had been treating my hand as if it were its fault the other had been cut off. What I should have done was train it to take the other's place.

Now I was paying for my lack of foresight.

I worked at passing the message for over an hour. Accomplished it three times in succession without revealing even a corner of the paper. Finally I left it atop the overturned basin, satisfied with my mastery of the task.

I sighed with relief.

And then I picked it up once more, pretending to be the egg-girl who would receive it. Opened it to admire my handiwork . . . only to discover that the sweat of my labors had smeared the words beyond recognition.

I could hear the cook's daughter serving dinner by the time I finished with my labors and descended by the back stair. I left by way of the public room, unwilling for her mother to catch me and start in on complaining.

It occurred to me as I approached the market that the egg-girl might not be there. That I might not be able to pass on my message. In that case, there would be no remedy and no passing of messages this day. She was my only contact with General Washington.

It was with great relief that I spotted her blue cart. And with great anxiety that I saw John walking right toward me. I couldn't pretend not to have seen him.

He'd already seen me. "Just the man I need!"

"You've been looking for me?" Had he seen me leave the tavern? To come straight here? I'd have to do a better job at hiding my destination.

"No. I've been looking for a present for Miss Pennington."

A present? "Then you need some sort of bauble or trinket." She was that kind of girl. "Go on up to Mulberry or Sassafras Street. Try one of the shops along there." And do it now!

"Anyone can buy a fan or a length of ribbon. I thought, perhaps, that food would be a more appreciated gift."

I might have applauded his noble turn of

thoughts had it been any day but today. In a city lacking most things, food was a luxury indeed. But . . . "Why do you want to buy her a gift? It's not as if you're courting her."

His gaze dropped, became fixed on his shoes. "A man has to do something to pass his time in this miserable town."

"If you give her a gift, she will think you're courting her."

"Let's just say that I wish I were courting her."

"She can't tell wishes from your Brunhilda in London. John! You can't make promises you don't intend to keep."

"We'll be gone this spring. It's all in fun. She knows it's all in fun."

I doubted very much that she did. "What if she were your sister?"

"Then I'd very much regret the dreams I've been having about her of late!"

When I spoke, it was through my teeth. "What I mean to say is, what would you think of some soldier who made love to your sister in this manner, even though his affections were pledged elsewhere?"

"His affections? There you err. My affections are mine to keep. 'Tis my life that is pledged to the heiress in London. In any case, the only appealing thing about your question is that I have no sister. Hence I really couldn't say what I would think. Or not."

"You're an abomination."

"And your morals are becoming rather tiresome. You're such a colonial! And I mean it in the worst of ways. I would never have imagined it of you."

And neither would I have. Not from the perspective that a dozen years earlier had provided. At that moment I had been just like John. And it was for that reason, I suppose, that I couldn't entirely abandon him to his folly. "I just wish you to be the gentleman I know you are capable of being."

"A gentleman! Even my own mother never sounded so prim. You've become positively proper." He said the words with an air of good cheer, but as I walked into the market he followed me.

I considered delaying my visit to the egg-girl, but my hours of practice — and the prospect of wearing that ghastly feather — had delayed my departure from the tavern too long. If I risked waiting much longer, the girl might leave.

As I approached the cart, John continued his chatter. My palms grew sweaty at the thought of what I was about to do in front of the keen-eyed gaze of a British major. Within the cover of my coat's pocket, I

239

flexed my fingers, found the message, and closed it up within my palm. I could not bobble this pass. Not today.

The egg-girl nodded a greeting as she cast a leery-eyed glance toward John. "Can I get you something, then?"

"I was wondering . . . do you have any more of those quail eggs?"

"Quail eggs!" John was peering behind her, at the cart. "Those would do."

I tried to shoulder him away. "She brings them for me. As a special request."

"I might have some . . ." She slid a glance toward John again and then raised her brow at me.

I shrugged.

Pressing her lips into a firm thin line, she brushed aside some straw and pulled out a small basket. "A half dozen."

I slipped her a coin, along with my message. She quickly plunged her hand into the depths of her pocket. And kept it there as she eyed John.

I nodded. As I was turning to leave, John grabbed my arm to halt me. Had he noticed? Had he seen?

"I say, can I get some of those as well?"

The egg-girl looked at me, unease making her eyes grow wary. "The gentleman bought all I had, sir."

240

"Then we cannot call him a gentleman, can we?"

"Come along, John, you've more to do than harass poor country girls." I didn't wait for him to follow, but turned and walked away.

He did as I had hoped and followed at my heels.

"Can I have one of those?"

"One of what?"

"One of those eggs. I've a passion for them." He was looking at me as if I was bound to say yes.

"No."

He blinked. "I'm only asking for one."

"And I can't give you even one."

"When did you become such a disagreeable cur?"

"Look, I've my own affairs to worry about. I'm trying to get back in with Miss Sunderland's family."

"Oh! Say no more. Miss Pennington told me all about her disagreeable uncle." He winked as he turned off toward Fourth Street. "I think I'll take your suggestion and look for something on Mulberry Street."

I walked back to the tavern with quaking legs and a pull in my gut. Passing that message in John's presence had been much too dangerous.

21
HANNAH

Breakfast had been served on seventh day and eaten with no help from any of the slaves. At least not for us. Father had insisted that Mother do our serving. And when Doll moved to take away our plates, Father gathered them himself and broke two of them in the process. It was one thing not to wish to encourage the practice of enslavement. But another thing entirely to try to avoid it in a place such as Pennington House.

I hesitated in dressing that afternoon. My gown could not be too fine, for my calls would include a visit to Robert at the jail. I had already explained away my sudden insistence upon wearing my best cloak. I simply told Mother I had given my other one to someone in greater need of it than I. It was nothing more than the truth. Sighing, I pulled a gown from my trunk, shook out the skirt, and examined the hem. Somehow Doll had managed to remove every sign of last week's visit. Not a speck, not a smudge, not a smell lingered.

I took off my gown and wound one of my sheets around my middle. I planned to stow my extra night cap beneath my hat. But then I was left in a quandary. William Addison had requested a shovel.

Doll had scavenged a rusted-through shovel head from the rubbish pile. It was up to me now to figure out how to smuggle it into the jail. I pulled it from its hiding place within my trunk. It was much too big to fit into my pocket and it was too bulky to secure with my garter. The rust had eaten a hole through its neck . . . perhaps . . . I pulled a leather thong from my trunk and threaded it through the hole. Lifting my petticoats and skirt, I tied the thong about my waist, letting the shovel head dangle between my legs. It was heavy and I would have to forgo the bag of grain this week, but if it would hold, it might just do. I practiced walking, promptly banging the inside of my knee against its edge. I tried again, more slowly and with my legs further apart.

It felt odd.

And it probably looked odd as well.

But as long as the thong stayed fast about my waist and hidden beneath the fullness of my skirts, no one should suspect anything. I met Doll out back and we walked around to the front gate together. As we walked, I began to fall into an awkward, if regular, rhythm of walking.

"What you got under there?"

I glanced at her. "Thee don't want to know."

"I do too want to know. If you going to be walking the streets like some kind of rheumy old goose, I ought to know what's going on."

"It's the shovel. I've got it beneath my skirts."

"The shovel? You got that under there!" She looked the length of me as if wondering where, exactly, it was hiding. "If those men don't manage to escape, it won't be because you didn't help them none!"

We had come out onto Walnut Street, joining the throngs of citizens and soldiers. "Let's not talk about that." I hissed the words over my shoulder at her. She still had the annoying habit of walking one step behind me.

When we reached the jail, I left her on the corner and mounted the steps. After showing my pass to a guard, I was led to the door to the basement. As I walked down the stair, hand on the rail, I felt a loosening of the thong around my waist.

Just one minute more.

If it would hold until I made it to the cell, then all would be fine. But when I reached the bottom of the stair, there was no guard in sight.

"Keeper?" My call echoed in no one's ears but my own, and the door to the guard keeper's room had been padlocked. The thong gave once more, leaving the shovel to hang at my ankles. Perhaps it was a blessing that no one was there. I set my basket on the stair, meaning to lift my skirts and draw the thong tight, but the door above me opened at that moment and the lumpen form of the guard appeared.

"You again?"

He eased his bulk down the stair, a hand to the rail. At the bottom he paused beside me, straining for breath.

Hurry!

He hitched his belt up over his wide girth and then ambled over to the door, taking a long moment to find the key in his pocket. Once we gained entrance, he shuffled behind his table and then hefted his bulk into his chair. "I don't mind saying that I was hoping you'd visit today. I was feeling a bit peckish."

I pulled a wedge of cheese from my basket and set it before him.

He broke off a hunk right then and shoved it into his mouth. "I don't suppose you have any bread for me? To go with it?"

I shook my head. I did have bread, but it wasn't for him. It was for Robert.

"Shame. Haven't had any in months. Least none that's good enough to mention."

"May I see my brother now?"

"Hmm? Oh. Of course." He rose with a sigh and then knocked on the door.

As I moved toward it, I felt the thong give way altogether. The shovel landed between my feet, biting into the bone at my ankle. I swallowed a cry. At least it had only fallen on packed earth. Had it been paved with stone, my secret would have been discovered for certain.

"You going in or did you change your mind?"

"I . . . just . . ."

He was waving a hand in front of his face against the stench that had blown into the room through the door.

The moment I moved, the shovel would be exposed, and there was no good reason to offer for having hidden one beneath my skirts.

He shrugged and began to shut the door. "Don't blame you for changing your mind. Their own mothers wouldn't recognize the sorry wretches." He gestured toward the basket. "You can just leave the rest of what's in there for me. With me. I'll make sure he gets it."

I was quite sure that he wouldn't. In any case, I had no intention of abandoning my basket. "No. I do want to see him. It's just that . . ." If I couldn't advance toward the door, neither could I retreat and go back up the stair. Either movement would reveal what I had tried so hard to hide. "I don't . . . I wonder, could you go see . . . are they — I mean is he still in the same cell?"

"The same cell? I suppose he would be!" He called to the guard, who sat on the other side of the door. "You haven't changed anybody round, have you?"

"No."

If only I could get him to leave the room! It wouldn't take but a moment to pull the thong tight once more. He turned toward me. "No. So are you staying or going?"

Could I pray to God for help with a deception? "I'm . . . going." My glance fell to my basket. "I'm going to offer thee some bread to go with that cheese." If food would take him back to his table and make him turn around for just one moment, then it was worth the giving of it. I pulled the loaf from the basket and offered it to him, mourning the fact that I was taking it from Robert's own mouth.

A smile lit his face. "Cheese with bread." He held the loaf up to his nose, sniffing at it. "Better than what the army feeds us." He turned toward his table.

I had just one chance. I slipped my hand beneath my cloak, into the slit in my skirts and jerked hard on the thong where it had given way. Keeping my hand there, hidden, I walked through the door.

Robert was none better, though he was sitting by the wall instead of lying on the ground. My cloak had been passed to another man. William Addison shielded me and ordered the others to look away while I untied the shovel and pulled the sheet from my middle. Robert saw my basket, lifted the cloth out entirely, and shook bread crumbs into his hand.

"I'm sorry. Next time I'll try for a blanket." I didn't know that I would be able to find one, however. The army had forcibly requisitioned all they could find — and all they could steal — from the citizenry. "But . . ." I removed my hat and handed him the nightcap. "I brought this. I had to give the bread to the guard in order to bring the shovel in. And I had to leave behind the

grain in favor of the shovel . . . I'm sorry."
Sorrier than he could know that I'd had to
choose the general welfare of the soldiers in
that room over his own. I couldn't keep
tears from leaking into the corners of my
eyes. It wasn't fair. I didn't care about the
rest of them. I mean . . . I did. I had to in
order that they could save my brother. But
they were the kind of people who had always
despised Quakers. Who probably, if truth be
known, despised us still.

When I came out, I expected to find Doll
waiting for me at the corner. She wasn't
there. I walked past Fifth Street and still
found no sign of her. I turned around and
started back the way I'd come. That's when
I saw her. She was a flurry of blue- and red-
colored skirts, beating her hands against a
soldier who had her pinned up against a
wall in the shadows. My legs began to shake
and I fought nausea as I remembered one
of Father's captors trying to do the same to
me.

Doll cried out, wrenching me to my
senses.

"Let go of her!"

The soldier looked at me with a sneer.
"What's it to you?"

Rage overcame my shaking. "She belongs

to me. Now take thy hands off!"

He planted an indecent kiss on her lips before releasing her. Doll smoothed down her skirts and put a trembling hand up to her head scarf.

"Did he — ?"

"He didn't do nothing nobody ain't done before."

"He didn't hurt thee?"

She glowered at his back with narrowed eyes. Spit into the dirt in his direction.

"Has that . . . happened before? While thee have been waiting for me?"

"Some of them soldiers think any Negro standing around at corners got nothing to do but please them."

I took her words as a yes. "Thee ought to have told me!"

"He the only one been so shameless about it."

Guilt at having subjected her to such indignities mixed with the shame I felt at saying what I had and for the lie I had spoken. "I didn't mean it, Doll, about thee belonging to me."

"I certainly don't belong to him."

"This is too dangerous, leaving thee on the corner standing about. There are too many soldiers here."

"They not all as bold as that one. And I'd

of bit his nose right off in another minute."

It wasn't right that my decision to help Robert should place any in danger other than myself. "Thee mustn't aid me anymore."

"Who's going to walk with you? And who's going to clean you up after?"

"I'll care for myself."

"Who's going to know whether you come back out of that place if nobody know you go in?"

"Thee know where I go on these afternoons. If ever I shouldn't return, thee must tell my father where I am."

"Davy says I gots to go with you."

"Davy doesn't know what I do."

"You need someone to help you and that's the truth. That Mr. Jones can tell you what to do all he want, but he don't know, do he? He don't know what it is he asking you to do."

It had become a common occurrence: people asking me to do things without knowing the import of their requests. The next day, on first day, Betsy Evans pulled me aside on my way into the Meeting House.

"I know thee have been visiting the jail."

I pushed the hood of my cloak from my

head, releasing a cascade of snowflakes as I did it. Why should I not speak truth to Betsy? "Aye."

"I have to know: Is he well?"

He was not well. None of the men were. But what was the point in telling her? In telling any of the Friends? What would they have done about it? "He asked me to pass on his greetings." Or he would have had there been any time. I knew he would have.

Her eyes grew shiny as she blinked back tears. "When thee see him next . . . could thee tell him . . ." There was something going on behind her eyes, something happening in her soul. "Could thee tell him that I . . ."

Be courageous, Betsy!

"Could thee tell him I wish him the best?"

My spirits fell as if those words were meant for me. They were trite, insipid words, words that could be spoken to any man or woman, but words that would never be whispered to a heart's beloved. She might as well have asked me to bid him farewell.

22

JEREMIAH

It was dinnertime on Thursday and the soldiers weren't quiet as they went about their eating. After being confined to the barracks with the foot of snow Sunday's storm had left behind, and after watching it dissolve and then flood the streets during the previous day's rain and fog, they were more restive than normal. A group of them had brought their piper along and ordered him to play. Unfortunately he was too young yet to be any good at it. And he was much too loud. I hadn't quite caught what John had said to me.

"You want me to go to the wharves with you? Why?"

"Because I command you to do so. In the name of the King."

"You couldn't command a whore to give you a smile."

He sniggered. Raised his mug in my direction.

"And if the King knew you at all, he would have you drummed out of the army in a thrice."

"Perhaps. But don't tell General Howe that. He thinks me a wonder. But do come."

"I've business to tend to. Books to keep. Soldiers to feed."

"Even God himself took a day off."

I eyed him as I closed up the daybook. If truth be told, I was rather touched by his concern. And the weather was fine; the rain and fog had disappeared and the sun was making promises of the spring to come. "All right, then."

He downed the last of his ale and grinned. "You won't regret it!"

As we got to the wharf, I could see why he'd been so eager to enlist me. Miss Pennington awaited us, looking pretty as a portrait in a green striped gown with the skirts caught up at the sides. One hand grasped a parasol while the other was clapped atop a straw hat. She wore no cloak. Wishful thinking for the month of February, but who could begrudge anyone their wishes this fine day? She was the very picture of spring. And accompanying her was Hannah.

Her eyes widened as she saw me.

I doffed my hat and grinned.

She had turned to Miss Pennington and was whispering in her ear. Her cousin took her hand in her own, seemed to tug on it. The wind blew their words to us as we approached. "Nonsense! You knew nothing about it. And if anyone should say anything, I will go to Uncle myself and tell him he's being a brute. Besides, I invited you. To accompany me."

"Clearly thee knew that *he* would be here."

"And what is that to you or me? Though now that they are here, we might as well enjoy their company." She fluttered a handkerchief at us, smiling gaily.

John saluted back. Whispered under his breath, "You can thank me later."

I would indeed. Right after the prisoners had escaped from jail. I would have bowed to Hannah, but I knew it would only incur her displeasure. And on this day of unfettered sun and warm breezes, when we could meet in public instead of some dark alley, I was willing to do almost anything but endure her scowl. I nodded instead.

She hesitated for a moment before returning the gesture.

I took a step closer as John pulled Miss Pennington away toward the end of the wharf. "We might as well take advantage of this opportunity. To talk."

She looked at me as if I had spoken a blasphemy.

I offered up the arm I had. When she would not take it, I bent down to speak into her ear and I seized her arm as I did it. "They think we're lovers. We might as well act like it. At least then they'll afford us some privacy."

"My father —"

"Said no arranged meetings. This one may have been arranged, but it was not arranged by us. I am just as astonished as you are."

"I don't know . . ."

I steered her away toward John and Miss Pennington. "If you looked at me as if you weren't going to strike me, it might not make them suspect that we are any other than what they think we are."

Her lips curved in a demure smile. I only wished it were a smile of true pleasure.

"Since they think that they are doing us a favor, may I suggest that we use this opportunity to arrange a place to leave messages?"

"But 'tis so deceitful. Allowing them to think . . ."

"That we are lovers? It is not our fault. And knowing you, I'll wager you've protested the idea once or twice."

She flushed.

"People will believe what they want to. So you might look at me as if you've found something in me to admire."

She turned to look straight at me. "There is much to admire about thee."

That was better. She looked as if she actually meant it this time.

"Thee are resolute and brave and kind."

"Kind! You don't have to sound so persuasive. They can't hear you."

"I am not given to flattery. I am simply stating the truth."

Well, that was something. "I've a plan for the messages. We must continue the habit of walking in the afternoons. Only, when I have a message to pass, I will stop at Peterson's Bookstore and leave it between the leaves of a blue-covered volume of *Aeneid*. If you time your walk to mine, then it shouldn't be but several minutes before you can go into the shop and retrieve it."

"Thee want me to recover it in plain sight?"

"If you cannot do it, then we can arrange to meet as we did before."

She looked at me. I could not interpret the struggle taking place behind her eyes. Finally she spoke. "I will do it. But I would be rude indeed if I kept asking to see a particular volume and did not ever buy it. The man runs a business concern, not a lending library."

She had a point. "Then at the end of each message we shall name a new book to ask for the next time."

She nodded after a moment, though the gesture lacked somewhat in confidence. "And how will I know that thee have a message to pass?"

"You will see me outside the tavern as you walk past."

She nodded. "And what if I have a message for thee?"

"Then . . ." Then what? "You must carry a basket in your hand."

"I usually carry a basket in my hand."

"Then you must not carry a basket in your hand."

She took her time in replying, but eventually she nodded. "Does the bookseller know of this arrangement?"

"No one knows of our arrangement. And we must keep it that way."

She opened her mouth as if she was going to say something, but then she shut it. A frown furrowed her brow.

I eyed John, who was looking at us. "Please try to look as if this is diverting."

"I would if I didn't know that my very life

depended upon their ignorance of our plans."

"The only way they would suspect anything at all is if we didn't act like the lovers they think us to be. If nothing else, we should be glad to be about in this fine weather."

A shade of something passed through her eyes. "Then we must enjoy this delightful walk."

It turned out that John had more on his mind than a walk. There was a pinnace waiting at the end of the wharf. "To take us out to the flagship!"

Hannah Sunderland, Quaker that she was, would not be impressed by any warship, but Miss Pennington might. My estimation of John Lindley slipped several pegs. He may have been worried about the state of my lonely heart, but not nearly as worried as he was about his.

John helped Miss Pennington onto the pinnace, then held his hand out for Hannah. She looked askance, at me.

I nodded. We might as well go along for the excursion. Because I was more than certain that if we stayed behind, she would turn tail and run back to Pennington House.

A crew of sailors rowed us out past the

dozens of merchant ships that crowded the now ice-free port. And then out farther still toward a ship that was anchored by itself on the river.

As we neared, I realized why.

Polly put a handkerchief to her nose. "They really ought to do something about the smell! Are those . . . ? Why — they're staring at us!"

"What's that?" John had turned in the direction of her outflung finger. "Oh. It's a prison ship."

I heard Hannah gasp as our proximity revealed the silhouettes of prisoners crowding the decks and the windows.

"What poor manners they have — to stare at us that way!"

Hannah's face had drained white, but now it had flushed red. "They're not staring. They're dying! They're trapped on that deplorable ship and they've nothing to do but wait to die." Hannah was looking at Miss Pennington with something akin to hatred in her eyes. I could not blame her. But I could try to restrain her words. I laid my hand on her arm.

She jerked toward me.

I shook my head.

She ignored me. "I suppose thy king condones such treatment."

John had taken Miss Pennington's arm and turned her from the unpleasant sight. Now he took it upon himself to respond. "*My* King? He's your king too."

I closed my eyes against her indiscretion, trying to think of something to say. "You know how it is with Quakers. They don't hold with any authority but God's."

John smiled a tight smile. "Yes. Of course. I'm sure that must be why you find her company so charming." He looked at me as if he was certain I'd gone mad.

John slipped a hand around the back of Miss Pennington's waist and drew her off to the side.

I looked down at Hannah. "There's no need to make so public your loyalties."

"I had not meant to. I hadn't known I had any. But he's just so . . ."

Arrogant? Conceited? Haughty?

". . . so cruel."

"To people like him we're just colonials. We have never been, nor will we ever be, quite so good as those English born and bred." I knew it from bitter experience.

"Had they bothered to treat their prisoners with anything other than cruelty and disdain, had they thought to treat us like equals rather than intractable children . . ." Her gaze still rested on that hulk of a ship.

"If they had done, they might have already won this war."

"Why do they have to be so condescending?"

"From their absolute conviction that we're so much less than they are."

She pressed her lips together and spoke not another word, though a flush continued to ride the tops of her cheeks.

"We're going to have to rejoin our friends. And I'm going to have to ask you to keep your politics to yourself."

For a moment she looked like she might cry. "I should not even have any. But . . . I'll try."

"If you don't, if you can't, then you're likely to end up on one of those." I nodded at the prison ship that floated listlessly beside us. I nudged her into motion. As we approached the flagship that had been anchored farther out, John pulled a bottle of Madeira from someplace, poured a glass for each of us, and raised it in the direction of the prison ship. "To the prisoners! May the rebellion and its ideals die as painful a death."

Miss Pennington echoed his words with a giggle.

He offered a glass to me.

I declined it.

"What? You aren't drinking?"

"Motion of the boat. There was a reason I joined the army and not the navy."

"Ah. Miserable sort of luck. I've never been affected myself. Miss Sunderland?"

To my surprise she did not insist upon his calling her Hannah. She simply declined his offer.

He shrugged. "More for us, then."

Once the pinnace reached the flagship we were assisted aboard. Captain Hamond himself greeted the women. Miss Pennington bloomed with the attention bestowed upon her. Hannah shrank against me. When John introduced her to the captain, she did not even give him the honor of blushing at his compliments.

It was a mistake to have come. But once on the ship we could not leave until the entertainments had been concluded. And they were many: a concert by the admiral's band, a tour of the top deck, and refreshments afterward.

At last, as the others sipped at port, we were afforded a few moments of peace.

"Thee call him thy friend." It was quite clear that Hannah questioned my judgment in terms of John.

"I *called* him my friend, but that was many

years ago. And I was a different man."

She peered up at me with puzzlement etched on her brow. But then it cleared. "I see. Thee hope for him. Thee hope for change."

I snorted. "I despise him."

"Then why are thee so often in his company?"

"Because he's useful to our endeavor, and I find it fascinating to observe firsthand the object of my abhorrence." I did. Truly. I saw in him the man I might have become. It was perhaps more than a simple fascination. If I could be honest with myself, I wobbled at the edge of obsession.

When she looked up at me, there was sadness in her gaze. "Then it is a hard path thee have carved out for thyself. For I think, despite thy words, thee care about him still."

23
HANNAH

What was happening to me?

Somehow, at some point, my heart had decided to take sides in this rebellion. If I could not support the king, did that mean I supported the king's enemies? Did that mean I had become a patriot?

And what of Jeremiah Jones?

I'd felt safe in his presence, even on board that horrible ship. I had pretended to be enamored of him just as he'd requested. Only . . . I hadn't thought to enjoy it so much. It was to have been a pretense, but I had never known how to lie. And now my heart had decided to create its own truth.

I was sorely in need of redemption and peace. I awaited the coming of first day in great expectation of all the peace that it would bring. But going to Meeting didn't help. There was a restlessness and turbulence inside me that only grew as I sat there. I had turned traitor to my faith and I knew my heart had grown dull because of it. Peace would only come with confession. And that confession must be made in front of the Meeting.

But what then?

The knowledge that I had gone against the expressed testimony of the Yearly Meeting by visiting the jail would cause the Meeting no little distress. For certain I would be labored with by the elders. But the knowledge that I was conspiring to help the prisoners escape? That would be grounds for disownment. Worse, some might feel it their bounden duty to report my activities. And then I would be hanged as a spy. There could be no other judgment.

I must confess in order to save my soul.

But I could not confess in order to save my life. And Robert's life as well.

I had wandered from my faith and now it threatened to betray me. Was there no escape from this web in which I had been caught?

I walked with Mother from the Meeting House, offering her my arm as an aid down the steps, but she did not release it at the bottom. "Thee have been heavy of heart of late."

"The winter has been long."

"Aye. But spring is here and summer is coming. We must look ahead with expectation to those things we cannot yet see."

Look ahead with expectation? I had done that! I had expected great things of this first-day Meeting, but it had only led to disappointment.

Mother patted my arm and then set me free so she could talk with Rachel Evans.

Though I knew I ought not, I used that freedom to make my way to the King's Arms Tavern. I went around back and asked one of the servants for Jeremiah Jones. There was something I needed to say to him and the opportunity to do it was worth more to me than my father's ire.

He greeted me with a raised brow and a searching glance. "I suppose this wouldn't be considered arranged since I didn't know about it?" Clearly he was confused by my presence.

"Thee have taken my faith and thee have stolen my peace and now I have nothing left at all!" To my horror, tears began to prick my eyes.

His brows lifted another inch higher. But they sunk as he approached me. Annoyance flashed in his eyes. "You're the one who agreed to do it. I didn't hold a pistol to your head. You agreed to do it of your own free will."

"But I didn't know how much it would cost me." It had taken from me everything I valued.

"Cost you? It's cost you practically nothing! Think about those poor —"

"Nothing? It's cost me everything! I don't know what to believe in anymore. Tell me what to believe."

"You're asking *me* what to believe? I couldn't lead a blind man into a church. But I do know this: You have to come to faith on your own. Otherwise it's just words and rules."

Words and rules. I blinked. Words and rules. It was true, wasn't it? In a sense? "Then . . . what do thee believe?"

He took my hand in his. "I believe all men are created equal. And I believe that man's cruelty toward man must be answered by justice. No matter what side of the rebellion he is on."

He sounded more Quaker than I felt. "But there has to be something more. Something beyond us . . . beyond the rebellion."

He laid a finger across my lips. "You didn't let me finish. The problem with you people is your politics."

"But we're not wed to any —"

"Refusal to bear arms isn't a religion, it's a *position*. You can't base your faith on a position. You can't live your life as a protest. Sooner or later positions resolve themselves, and then what's left? They're temporary. And subject to things like kings and rebellions more than your sanctimonious, self-righteous leaders would like to think."

Sooner or later positions resolve themselves. That's what had happened: I'd changed my position. I hadn't set out to, but that's what I'd done and now there was no place for me at the Meeting House. Tears began to fall from my eyes. I might have made a swipe at them, to try to stem them, but I felt the pressure of hundreds more.

Jeremiah Jones reached out his hand and pulled me close. Pressed my head against his chest. "There will be justice. Whether it happens in this world or the next, I have to believe that there will be justice."

Justice.

I thought about it all the way back to Pennington House, and it gave me the strength to face the deception that my life had become. We had dinner, all of us together, after Aunt and Uncle had returned from their church service. Boiled goose, chicken pudding, and pickled oysters were brought to the table in turn. It was after the last course, some jumbals served with a very fine cottage cheese pie, that Father spoke.

"I would like to offer payment to those who have cared for us during our time here."

The Pennington children stared at Father through wide eyes. My own brothers and sister seemed more interested in examining the table. Uncle's face bloomed red. "Payment? For pity's sake, why?"

"For the work they do on our behalf."

"They would do the same work whether you were here or not."

"But we add to their labors."

Polly was looking at me as if she did not quite understand what my father was about. Aunt Rebekah was looking at Mother in just the same way.

Uncle cleared his throat. "In any case, what do they need with money? I feed them. I clothe them."

The servers of the meal, Davy and Doll, seemed acutely uncomfortable.

"It isn't right to enslave people." Father's voice was respectful though insistent.

"They aren't people. They're Negroes. And it goes a lot better under my roof for them than it does under many others. I'd like to see them complain." He sent a glance

270

toward Doll and Davy as if daring them to do the same. "I'd send them on down to one of those plantations in Virginia. Let this be the end of such foolish notions!"

"I only want to —"

"You only want to meddle in other people's affairs. Why are none of us ever good enough for you? When I accepted you as a guest, I didn't expect that you would pack up your morals and bring them with you." Uncle shoved his chair away from the table and stalked from the room. After offering an apologetic look at Mother, Aunt did the same.

"I'm only trying to do what's right." Father said it to himself more than to any of us.

Mother placed a hand on his arm. "I know thee are. And God will reward thee for it."

But what was the difference between his trying to do right and my trying to do right? Why should his actions be applauded by the Meeting when mine would see me disowned?

That afternoon a group collecting money for the poor came soliciting. Aunt invited them in, and she and Mother hosted them in the parlor. Mother bid me sit with them as they talked over tea.

It galled me that so much trouble be taken for the poor, to whom one of the Friends' Meeting Houses had been given over, when the prisoners suffered from conditions much worse.

"Just this January past, Hannah gave up her own cloak to one in need."

To *prisoners* in need!

They all smiled at me and then began to speak in earnest of the effort to help the poor. Finally I could not help but interject. "I've heard the prisoners in the new jail are also in need of food and clothing." And medicines and blankets and wood.

Aunt Rebekah smiled. "I'm quite sure you're mistaken. In any case, General Howe says Mr. Washington is charged with their upkeep. If they're short those supplies, then the blame falls to the rebels."

"But what if they're not receiving those supplies? It isn't right that the prisoners become victims of the politics of war."

Mother was raising her brows at me, a certain sign of her disfavor. "If they're in the jail, then I'm sure it's their own fault for taking up arms against the king. Really, Hannah, thee sound as if thee support their cause."

"I'm only suggesting that perhaps some of the money from the collection be diverted to their needs."

One of the visitors clucked in dismay. "But the poor don't choose to be so. They have no other help but this."

"The prisoners didn't choose their lot either!"

Aunt Rekebah had begun refilling teacups. "It can't be so bad as you've heard, Hannah. If I know nothing else about General Howe, 'tis that he's an honorable man."

If I heard one more word about General Howe's supposed honor, I might have to bring up the fact that he was known to be carrying on with his Commissary of Prisoners' wife! As it was, I rose from my chair, bobbed my head, and took myself up the stair to the sanctuary of Polly's bedroom.

Unfortunately she had sought retreat there as well.

"Have they gone yet?"

"No."

She wrinkled her nose. "I despise all those do-gooders."

"They're only trying to aid the poor."

"Well, they don't have to make everyone else feel so shabby about it. They can be so tedious about such things. It's all they ever speak of." She yawned as she put down her embroidery. "They always make me feel so lazy. As if they expect me to try and right all the world's wrongs."

"Shouldn't thee?"

"Why, I haven't the time! There are gowns to be fitted and dances to be attended. And besides, if I went about with such a dour look on my face, I might well see the bloom of my youth vanish without ever having been married. And that would be tragic."

Indeed. "Do thee ever wonder what it's like on the other side?"

"The other side of what?"

"Of the war."

"You mean the rebel side?" She sounded quite shocked at the idea.

I nodded.

"Well . . . it must be dreadfully dreary. They can't be having half the fun in Valley Forge as we are here in the city."

"But do thee ever wonder if they're right?"

"About what?"

"About their ideas. Their cause."

"I've never given it one thought. Besides, when they were here, they closed the theaters and cancelled the horse races. Life would be ever so dull if they occupied us again."

"So it doesn't matter to thee who's right or who's wrong?"

"Why should it matter as long as things go on the way they always have? Regattas in the spring and fox hunts in the fall, with parties enough to last all year." She looked up as a clock downstairs struck three. "Bother! Now we have to go back to church. There's some special lecture that's been arranged." She rose from her chair, placed her hat on her head, and stuck a pin into it. After giving herself a long look in the wall glass, she sashayed out of the room.

I picked up my own embroidery and turned my chair toward the window's light. Why should it matter who was right and who was wrong? Because it did. It mattered for a very many people.

Mother came up to me after Polly had gone. I'd known I would have to pay for my carelessly spoken words; I'd only hoped it wouldn't be quite so soon.

"Thee feel everything so keenly, Hannah. Thee must pray to God for help in moderating thy words and thy sentiments."

"I can't see why no one takes up a collection for the prisoners."

"Truly? In a city controlled by the British? Do thee think that very wise?"

I knew she was waiting for me to shake my head, but I would not do it.

"Thee know the Yearly Meeting addressed that very question. We are not to involve ourselves in the rebellion. Not in any way."

"But they're starving, Mother. They have . . . hardly anything!"

"And how do thee know this?" She was watching me through narrowed eyes.

I said nothing. Jeremiah Jones was right. Sooner or later my indiscretion was going to cost me more than I could afford to pay.

"Thee mustn't believe everything everyone says. We've all got too much time on our hands with this occupation. And gossip often sounds like truth." She bent to kiss me on the forehead. "If the prisoners aren't being supplied, then it's their own fault for rebelling against the king. But I'm certain things can't be as dire as thee say."

They weren't. They were far worse.

24
JEREMIAH

John was lounging at one of the tables near the fire, staring glumly into his bowl of brandy. I shared his mood. Business had been slow due to the number of troops being sent down the river for foraging.

"You look as if you've married your heiress already."

When he looked up, not one sign of a smile creased his face. "I've no money left. I'm completely dead-flat broke."

"Too many presents for Miss Pennington?"

"Presents for the players of pharo, more like! I've had a dastardly string of bad luck. Can't seem to win at anything."

Now that was an interesting piece of news. "There's a pharo bank? Here?"

"Haven't you heard? A Hessian runs one out of City Tavern. And then there's a cockpit over in one of the alleys."

Gambling? Cock fighting? "The simple

solution would be to stop playing."

"I can't. Don't think I wouldn't like to. But at this point I have to find some way to make back all I've lost."

"What is it you're playing with, if you've lost all your money?"

"My commission."

His commission! I'd heard of soldiers doing such things, but I'd always figured them for the desperate, frantic type. Not the gentlemanly, sophisticated and arrogant type. "And what will you do if someone finally wins it?"

"I suppose I shall have to go home and marry my Brunhilda. Become disgustingly domesticated and respectably corpulent. You'll have to come some night. To pharo. Take pity on an old friend and let me win a pound or two off you."

Pharo.

John's invitation kept flitting through my thoughts. I'd always had more than my share of luck at the gaming tables. And the ability to know when to quit. I never let winning go to my head; never let losing rob me of good sense. Pharo could provide the very opportunity for revenge for which I'd been searching. The chance to play presented itself on Saturday, two evenings later. John had no invitation to supper that evening.

"What? You've had a falling-out with Miss Pennington?"

"They've fallen ill over there with the grippe."

I felt the blood drain from my face. I hoped Hannah hadn't caught it. The grippe was a miserable sort of sickness. I'd known grown men who had succumbed to it. I'd have to send the stable boy over to see if he could find out who was ill.

"Pity, that. I meant to pass a message to Miss Sunderland about her brother."

I felt my heart pause in its beating. "What about him?"

"Just that he, and all the others, will probably be transferred to ships soon."

"*Prison* ships?"

"You don't think we'd give them the pleasure of a yacht!" He chuckled at the thought.

Prison ships. A death sentence. It would be kinder to let him die of neglect in the jail. To let all of them die in the jail. I would have to tell them to dig as fast as they could. Faster even!

When we arrived at City Tavern, we had to elbow aside a few captains and lieutenants in order to make ourselves room at one of the tables. John purchased his checks on the strength of his commission. I purchased my own — far fewer than he — with coin. The game started pleasantly enough. By the time an hour had passed, we were both still at the game. I cocked my card, risking both my stake and my gains.

John only ventured his gains.

I won; he did not.

Eying the abacus that kept track of the cards played, I decided to bend my card a second time, hoping to double my gains without risking my stake.

John had only his stake to venture, and so he did.

We both won.

We won and lost at the game for another hour. By that time I had won several times in succession by risking both my stake and my gains. John had been playing more conservatively, betting his gains only. But caution prodded me with an urgency I couldn't ignore and so I decided to bet only my gains.

John did the same.

We both lost. I looked at him and shrugged. He dabbed at the sweat that dotted his forehead. He looked scared. Terrified, in fact. I might have gone home, but a perversity inside made me wonder what he would do if I risked my stakes.

He risked half of his.

I won; he lost.

What would happen, I wondered, if I bet everything I had? Would he do the same?

He did.

The punters sitting around the table had gone silent. Only one of us could afford to lose.

John dabbed at a trickle of sweat that trailed down from his temple.

The banker exposed the cards.

John shouted in relief. I let the banker collect my checks and rose from the table, trembling at the thought of what I had almost done. I had almost forced John into losing his commission. Perhaps I should have. It would have been one sure way to keep him from Miss Pennington — sending him back to London.

But had I done it, I would have rid myself of my only ally at the general's headquarters. With John by my side I would never be accused of being what I was. Who would suspect a spy in the company of a staff officer?

Daft, daft, daft!

I'd almost allowed vengeance to trump the escape.

I needed to pass the information about the

prison ships, but the next day was a Sunday. The bookseller wouldn't be open, and I couldn't wait even a week for Sgt. Addison to receive the message. They needed to dig faster. If Hannah's father refused to let his daughter speak to a man who was not a Friend, then I would do what I had to do.

After rising the next morning, I put on the plainest of my new suits and walked over to the Meeting House.

I lingered at the corner until I saw good number of people filing into the building. The men all seemed to go in one door, the women in another. I joined the men, trying to enter as unobtrusively as possible, though the light blue color of my coat advertised itself among the dark colors and subtle patterns of the rest of the men. Inside, the plain, unadorned white walls and humble benches did not cast any shadows in which to hide.

As I settled myself on a bench, many heads turned in my direction and then just as quickly turned away. I saw Hannah and nodded. Watched her flush bright red.

The service started with some discussion of the care of the poor, who had been ensconced in one of the other Meeting Houses in the city. It continued with the reading of a letter from some congregation up in New York. A man got up to confess to having owned a slave, whom he asked to come up and stand beside him. With much weeping he described in detail how he had gone about setting the man free. A few more people stood up to say one thing or another. Then someone confessed to having a concern about treating too freely with the British.

It seemed like a more polite, more refined version of what was said at King's Arms Tavern every night of the week.

But then there descended a terrific silence. It was ominous in its abruptness. Terrible in its complexity. The first few minutes I did not understand what it was about. I kept waiting for someone to speak.

Only no one did.

I snuck a look about me. Many had their eyes closed, lips moving. But just as many had theirs open, fixed upon some point in the distance, though there was not much worthy of attention in that sparsely furnished place.

The man next to me fell asleep. I thought about elbowing him, but decided that if he made a cry upon waking, it would be too costly a gesture.

Twenty minutes, half an hour must have passed.

And then a person stood. She quoted some verse of Scripture I vaguely remembered from my youth about a lion lying down with a lamb. She sat.

The silence continued.

So . . . these people were waiting for someone to speak their mind? Is that what it was all about? I glanced around. No one else came to their feet. If no one else was going to speak . . . I looked round again, but no one appeared to want to take the floor. So I stood, figuring if a few more people spoke, then we could all go home.

I cleared my throat. "I think that if any of us had any sense at all, we would realize that this rebellion is doing nothing but ruining our city and destroying the lives of some of the best of our people."

Hannah flashed me a look of horror, then directed her gaze to the front of the room.

I sat down, expecting that at any moment someone would give a benediction. But no one did. We all sat there for another hour. I had a crick in my neck by the time I shuffled out the door. I tried to time my exit with Hannah's. When we finally met in the crowd that mixed in front of the building, I was hoping we were not much noticed.

She was looking at me as if she had been scandalized. "Thee cannot be interested in becoming a Friend!"

"I never said I was."

"Thee make a mockery of us just by being here." She stepped closer, eyes snapping. "Thee may not use my faith as one of thy weapons."

"I'm not. Lower your voice. People are beginning to look. Smile."

"Like this?" Her lips curved, though the anger in her eyes did not lessen. "As if thee were saying something nice?"

"I'm not saying anything mean. I'm just wondering if this is all your church is about. People speaking what's on their mind."

"No! 'Tis not about speaking *thy* mind. 'Tis about speaking God's."

"Well, whether it's my mind or His, I felt the need to say something. Weren't you tiring of being there?"

"We wait, in silence, to see if God has something to say to us. Sometimes we end up leaving in silence as well."

I pulled her away from the crowd. "God isn't speaking to you people; He's yelling at you. Shouting at you. No wonder He falls silent at your meetings. You keep pretending that you can't hear Him."

"Thee cannot know the first thing about it, Jeremiah Jones!"

I ought to have said *Thank Goodness!* and

285

walked away. But a man I'd never met came up just then and invited me to dinner. Along with Hannah and her family. I should have declined the invitation, but Hannah was looking at me with so much venom that I found myself accepting. And tipping my hat at him as he left.

"What are thee playing at?"

"Nothing. I'm simply trying to have the chance to talk to you without having to arrange it. Your requirement, not mine."

"Then speak and be done with it."

"Listen: We both want the same thing. And it's in both our interests to pretend a certain regard for each other."

"I don't mind pretense in the parlor, but I will not abide it in my house of worship."

"I wish I could be as steadfast in my convictions as you people are." Why couldn't she just be nice! I was trying to do her brother — and all the other prisoners — a favor.

"It comes from so many of us having been forced to endure shame, and beatings, and imprisonment."

"Which is why it's such important work we're doing now. In any case, I beg your pardon for any offense I may have caused. But until we settle on another way to meet, you might just have to endure me as a convert." I extended my hand.

She looked at it for a moment before doing me the honor of extending her own.

As we gripped hands, I dropped the message into her palm. Bowed . . . and then left.

25

Hannah

I could not credit it. The Evanses had invited Jeremiah Jones to dinner and then treated him as an honored guest. They labored over his contribution to the Meeting as if he had said something worth saying. As if it had been from the mouth of God.

Mouth of God!

If only they knew he believed in nothing at all and that he was scheming that very moment to do exactly the opposite of what the Yearly Meeting had commanded. If I was to tell them that he was working to free the prisoners, they would cast him out of their home. Perhaps even turn him over to the authorities for treason.

Mother took me by the arm as we left. "Thee were quite rude to Jeremiah Jones this afternoon, Daughter."

"It angered me that he had the gall to speak in Meeting."

"But there is that of God in everyone. Thee know that."

That of God in everyone. It's what the founder of our faith had believed and what I believed as well. The Creator of our souls had left a part of Him inside us, and the more we responded to and came to resemble Him, the more our inner lights increased.

"Perhaps he was led to our Meeting to speak the wisdom of God into our midst."

Led to our Meeting? To speak *wisdom*?

"I think thee should soften thy heart a little. So as to encourage his fledgling faith."

Fledgling faith! "If his heart truly seeks God, then he does not need my encouragement."

"Tsk. We all need encouragement. Especially during these dark days."

Well . . . that was true. And perhaps I was being a bit churlish. He'd only come to deliver a message. And he had been encouraging. He'd helped the widow Smythe into her seat at the table. He'd spoken to the Evanses' children — to my own brothers and sister even — as if they might have something interesting to say. Had I not known his true motives, I would have been deceived as well.

I went to Meeting the next week with no

little satisfaction, knowing from my visit to the jail that work on the tunnel was quickly progressing. I also went with a measure of relief, knowing Jeremiah Jones would not be there. But he was. He did not speak in Meeting, though he did pass me a message afterward. It was he who had devised the scheme with the bookseller, so I did not see why he would not use it. I was beginning to think that his only purpose was to vex me.

"What is wrong with thee, Hannah?" Mother took my hand in hers as we walked out of the Meeting House. "All I felt at Meeting was thy bitter spirit. And all I saw was thy sour expression."

"Everyone thinks Jeremiah Jones is so honorable, but he's not!"

"And how would thee know this?"

Once again my words threatened to land me in trouble. "He was a soldier during the Indian Wars."

"People change, Daughter."

That's what I had once thought as well. But now . . . I didn't know what to think. Meeting used to be the one place where I could be free from the specter of Jeremiah Jones. The one place where I could lay aside my deception. But now there was no place in this city where he was not. Somehow he had managed to prosecute a wholesale invasion of my life. If it weren't for Robert's sake, I could not have borne it.

She patted my cheek. "There's a good girl. The Hamiltons have invited us to dine with them and several others as well. Jeremiah Jones will be among us. See that thee are kind to him."

I would have done so if he had been kind to me.

He fell into step beside me as I walked behind the children, passing me his message as I bumped against him in walking.

"I wish I could tell you that you're rid of me. You can hardly stand to look at me."

It was true. I could not deny it. "I hate thee, I loathe thee, and I despise thee."

He fell back as if I'd struck him.

I fell back as well, letting the others continue on. "If it was not for thee, I could be . . . I could be *happy* right now." Or at least not quite so confused or nearly as angry.

"Happy — ?"

"If not for thee, I would be fine. *Everything* would be fine. I wouldn't have to worry about delivering messages or trying to keep my neck from the gallows. I wouldn't have to lie to my parents or deceive my Meeting. I wouldn't have had to choose sides!" I would have yelled those words if I wasn't so concerned about others hearing them.

"It's not my fault that —"

"It is too thy fault. Everything is thy fault! Every bad thing that has happened to my family started with thee."

"I hardly think that's fair!"

"My father was arrested last September."

"And I had something to do with that?" His voice had gone hoarse from the strain of whispering his objections at me.

"The men who came for him came straight from thy tavern. They were drunk from the liquor thee sold them."

"I didn't make them drink it."

"But thee made them welcome in thy place of business."

"I welcomed their *coin* into my business."

"And they accosted me!" It was the first time I had ever spoken those words aloud. It had happened as my mother and the children had followed my father's captors out into the street. No one had known. And now my soul felt dirty with shame.

"I —" The exasperation was swept from his face by shock, only to be replaced a moment later by a dark and terrible rage. "Did they . . . ?"

"They put their hands all over me." I didn't want to tell him, but some strange compulsion to speak had overcome me. "And they . . . they made themselves free with me." It made me tremble to remember it. Afraid I might start to heave, I put a hand to my mouth.

He put his hand to my shoulder, trying to turn me toward him. "But they didn't — they didn't use you?"

"No." No, they had not. I had been saved that final indignity when Mother had sent the children back into the house. I could not bear to look at him now. I was used to Jeremiah Jones towering over me, but I had never felt so small beside him. "They did not. But they made me feel as if they had. And now — thee've asked me to — I must —"

"I've asked you to save men just like them."

I looked up at him then and saw such compassion in his eyes that I began to weep. "I don't want to do it." I drew my hood further over my head as Friends from Meeting approached. I longed to throw myself into his arms, but pride — and propriety — would not allow it.

Jeremiah Jones must have understood, for he made no move toward me. But after a moment he did speak. "Those men in the jail are not the men who misused you."

"Aren't they?"

"They aren't the same."

"I just want to help Robert. That's all I want to do."

"You are."

"I don't believe in war." I didn't believe in much of anything anymore. I chanced a look up at him. "I wish thee had not served them."

"I wish I had not either. And if I have my way, they'll never drink again." As he looked down at me, the hard lines around his mouth softened. "Can we be friends, Hannah Sunderland?" He actually looked sincere.

I was a Friend by persuasion. Now he was asking me to be a friend by predilection. And I discovered that I wanted to. I swallowed back a sob, turning it into a hiccough instead. "Aye. Perhaps. I think we can."

His lips turned up in a cautious smile. "Nothing would please me more."

It was a courteous and gracious reply. A reply I might have expected him to give to one of the city's Tory belles in the candlelit glow of Aunt Rebekah's parlor. Not to a plainly dressed Friend in the middle of Second Street, who had just revealed to him the darkest secret of her soul. So when he held out his arm to me, I put my own around it.

"You will always be safe with me."

I nodded, though still I was reticent to look at him. But I knew that what he said was true. Somehow I had always known it. I had always felt safe with him.

As I sat in a chair on fourth day, embroidering, Polly sighed from the luxurious confines of her bed as she turned a page in *The Magazine a la Mode, or Fashionable Miscellany.* Sighed again as she shut it up. Then she threw it across the room toward her dressing table. "There's no use in looking at new fashions if one isn't allowed to go out anywhere to display them!"

A soft rapping came at her door and then it opened. Sally peeked in. When she saw me, she stepped into the room and addressed herself to Polly. "Caroline said to ask, Can we borrow thy dolls?"

Polly pushed herself away from her pillows. "Why didn't Caroline come to ask me herself?"

"She said that thee would say no."

"Did she now." Polly scowled for a moment. Then she brightened and pushed from her bed. Kneeling in front of her trunk, she opened the lid, removed three dolls, and then handed them to Sally. They

295

had painted china faces and were wearing costumes more elaborate even than those Polly generally wore. "I'll give these to you, but on the condition that only you can use them."

Sally agreed so readily to that injustice that it made me wonder what they were doing. "What are thee playing at that thee need so many?"

"We're having funerals. For all the children who have died of measles. Caroline will pronounce the rites for the Episcopalians and I shall do for the Friends."

I had trouble hiding my smile. "Thee must be feeling better, then."

She nodded and cradled the dolls in her arms as she left.

Polly pouted as she resumed her pose on the bed. "I can't believe they all had to get sick. And then fall sick again!"

And I was afraid to believe that they might actually be growing better. The grippe had been bad, but the measles were a frightening and dreaded plague. "I'm sure no one ever asks to become ill."

"It's ruined everything! No dancing parties, no dinners. It's just not fair." She rolled to sitting and faced me. "Help me escape."

Escape! That word brought a sudden chill to my spine. I reminded myself that she could not possibly know of the plans for the prisoners at the jail. "Escape from what?"

"This house. Mother won't let me go anywhere. Not as long as young Edward is still feeling poorly. I'll go mad if I have to spend another day shut up here inside."

"I can't do that. Not if thy mother has expressly prohibited it."

"But *you* do it."

"Whatever can thee mean?" I tried to keep my eyes on my needle, but my fingers were shaking so badly that I soon gave it up.

"You and Doll."

"She goes calling with me."

"And she also goes with you to the jail."

"Thee already know that I go to visit my brother. And thee also know that my parents must not learn of it."

"Why? Because they've *expressly prohibited it?*" She challenged me with a look of defiance.

Could I truly claim that her reasons were not as valid as mine? I suspected, of course, that they were not, but how could I prove that to her without explaining about the escape?

"You're escaping. You can't call it anything but. And that means you can help me do it too."

"I'm not certain it's worth the risk."

"It is for you."

But the life of my brother, the lives of the other prisoners, were at stake. Of course it was worth the risk.

"I don't think it's fair that you get to go while I have to stay. So . . . how do you do it?"

The next day, Polly put a hand to her hat as we walked down the front steps and then glanced back at Davy over her shoulder. "We just leave? Like this? With everyone watching?"

"We told him we're going out and what can he say? We're leaving together."

"I suppose you're escort enough." She didn't sound happy about the prospect, and when we got to Third Street she bid me farewell.

"But where are thee going?"

"I've an appointment to keep."

"Thee can't just leave!"

She frowned at me as she tapped her foot. "That was the whole point. To escape."

"But thee are leaving *me* without an escort. I can't go home without thee or we'll both be in trouble."

"So go find your Mr. Jones. I won't tell."

"I . . . can't."

She shrugged as if my concerns had noth-

298

ing to do with her. "Do as you wish. And I'll do the same."

"But what will I say if someone asks me about thee?"

"Why should anyone ask after me? Be back here in an hour and then we can walk home together."

"I wish thee wouldn't leave."

"I'll be fine. And so will you be. Besides, what can go wrong?"

What can go wrong?

Whatever could have gone wrong had, because over an hour later she had not yet returned. I'd already looked over every volume at the bookseller's and I'd considered every good at the grocer's. I had occupied myself in every way that I could think of and still she was absent! There was nothing to be done but enlist the aid of the one person who might know where she had gone. I promised a coin to an urchin on the condition that he go to the King's Arms and bring out Jeremiah Jones.

26
JEREMIAH

Three days it had been since I'd seen Hannah Sunderland. And all that time I had nursed a growing rage for the men that had misused her. I knew who they were. They'd all fled town as the British army had approached. Otherwise I would have beat their heads together. Just the memory of her, pale-faced and trembling, so wounded and yet so brave, made me want to strike someone. Those cowards ought to have been made to pay for what they'd done.

I don't know what had possessed me to promise I would keep her safe. I had the desire, it was true. 'Twas the means I lacked. But ever since I'd met her, I'd been saying and doing and feeling things against my better judgment.

Restless, I walked out toward the kitchen to consult with the cook about supper. Before I could reach her, Bartholomew Pruitt came slinking into the tavern saying something about having a message.

"A what?"

"There's a miss out there says she needs to see you. Quick."

"A miss?"

"A lady."

And she was asking for me? I followed him out the public room through the door. Hannah emerged from the shadows as soon as I stepped outside. She was wringing her hands. Her eyes were distraught.

I seized her arm. "What's happened? Are you — ?"

"I'm fine." A flush swept her cheeks as her gaze fled from mine. "It's not me; it's Polly. She's gone missing."

"She . . . what?"

"She noticed me going out with Doll so she asked me to help her escape from the house."

"Escape?"

"That's what she called it. Her mother hasn't let her out for over a week. Not since the little ones came down with a fever again. So we left the house together, but then she deserted me in the streets. I think she must be with thy John Lindley. At least I think she must be. I can't go back without her, unescorted, and she can't go back without me."

301

It sounded like something John would arrange. The scoundrel. It wasn't as if he had business enough at headquarters to conduct! "How long has she been gone?"

"Nearly two hours."

Two hours. Where could they go in two hours? In a city that was lined with pickets and defended by barricades? "Why did you agree to do it?"

"Because I didn't want her to ask more questions about my visits to the jail."

More questions? "She knows?"

"About the visits? Aye."

I felt exasperation spark in my veins, but there wasn't time to press her about it. Where had they gone? Where would I go if I wanted to dodge an escort? And relish a few hours alone with a girl?

They were observing the footrace that had been set up between two battalions of light infantry. What other activity would allow a man to become *lost* with a maid along the river?

When we caught up with them, they were wrapped in an embrace near the northern defensive line, on the banks of the Schuylkill River. Hannah's eyes widened as a blush enflamed her features. Fury firing my steps, I stalked toward them, grabbed a fistful of

302

John's coat and spun him away from the Pennington girl. "You stupid whoreson!"

"What are you doing?"

"What are *you* doing? Out here — alone — with one of the flowers — one of the most *recognizable* flowers — of our fair city?"

He gazed off beyond my shoulder. Toward Miss Pennington. "She's a colonial! It's not as if she's some earl's daughter."

"No. It's as if she's Edward Pennington's daughter, who is one of the colony's most vocal . . . most *loyal* Loyalists. Officers have been made to marry girls for less than you have done."

He paled.

"Aye: Marry!"

"I don't . . . I mean . . . I didn't think —"

"No. You didn't. And it's going to take the ingenuity of all of us to keep you from dire consequences."

"Can no one believe that I didn't mean any harm?"

"Not when it looks as if you did. Would you be out here like this with one of your English misses? With your own heiress?"

"Blazes no! And risk — ?" He stopped speaking as shame colored his eyes.

"And risk having to marry one? Why should our colonial maidens be any less

303

valued than your own?"

A flush lit the tops of his cheeks.

"Are they not worthy of the same respect you pay your English maidens?"

"You make me sound as if I'm a rake."

He was. "You're going to apologize to Miss Pennington, we're going to go back into the city, and you are never going to do this again."

We walked back, allowing John to return to headquarters as we passed it. Hannah and Miss Pennington accompanied me down to the King's Arms. We were parting ways when a shout went up at the corner and a horse-drawn cart barreled toward us.

I pushed the girls out of the way but was struck by the animal as it passed. I fell to my knees, my hand plunging into one of the puddled ruts that scarred the streets before my arm collapsed and I rolled into it.

Hannah offered an arm to help me up, but I waved her off. "Go home. Back to Pennington House. I'm fine." I suspected my ribs were bruised and my shoulder strained, but the biggest damage had been to my ego. I hadn't had the balance to keep myself from falling. And now I was covered with filth.

"Thee've soiled thy hand!" Hannah informed me of the obvious while Miss Pennington covered her nose with a handkerchief. Of course I had soiled my hand. What man could fall on these streets and not soil his hand? But worse, I suspected that the slime had soaked through my coat to dirty my stump as well.

Any normal man would have been able to wash his hand. I could not. So I did the next best thing. Entering the King's Arms, I grabbed up a cloth and, clamping it against my body, tried to rid my hand of the muck. It only succeeded in smearing the foul mess onto what was left of my bad arm.

"Let me help thee." Hannah had followed me. She grabbed at the cloth, but I managed to hang on to it.

"I can do it."

She looked at me directly for the first time since Sunday. "No. Thee can't."

I might have expected to find pity in her eyes, but there was only empathy. And stubborn determination. "There's no shame in asking for help from others."

"I don't need anyone's help."

She continued as if I had not spoken at all. "The only shame is that thee have not asked before." She took hold of my stump and tugged. The cloth dropped to the floor.

"Now look what you've done!"

She turned toward the cook's daughter, who was standing there, gawking. "I need a pitcher of water, please. A clean cloth and a basin."

The girl did as she was asked while I protested Hannah's attentions. "Don't bother yourself with me."

"If I don't, then who will?" She didn't seem to care what I thought about the matter. She'd already stripped me of my coat and was working at the button on my cuff. I could see Miss Pennington lurking at a window near the door. "Your cousin's waiting for you. Shouldn't you — ?" I tried to pull my arm away from her.

She caught it in the vise of her grip before I could wrench it away. Cuff unbuttoned, she rolled up my sleeve. Then she poured water from the pitcher into the basin and motioned me over. "Come here."

Did she want me to wash myself? Wasn't it obvious that I couldn't? It takes two hands to wash one. The ultimate of cruelties.

When I didn't come, she took hold of my fouled hand and tugged me toward the basin. Plunging my hand into it with both of hers, she began to clean me. She delved into the intimate spaces between my fingers and then moved with her thumbs up toward my wrist. When she was done, she spread the new cloth out on the counter and wrapped it around my hand. Then she took up the basin, walked over to the window, and dumped out the filthy water.

Bringing the basin back, she poured more water into it from the pitcher. "Now then. The other."

"The other what?"

She gestured toward my other side.

"My other . . . ?"

Lips pressed into a firm straight line, she bullied my stump from my shirtsleeve by doing the same thing she'd done before — unbuttoning my cuff and pushing up my soiled sleeve. But this time she had to roll it all the way up to near my shoulder.

She dipped a cloth into the basin, wrung it out, and moved toward me.

I jerked away from her. "Don't!" I didn't want her to see it. I didn't want anyone to see it. I tried hard not to look at it, myself. Not more than was necessary. Once in a great while I poured a full basin of water and swished the remnants of my arm through it. Seemed to do well enough.

She wasn't listening. She never listened. She was looking at my stump through narrowed eyes. "There's a wound here that would do well with an unguent."

"An unguent?"

"Aye. To soften the scar."

Soft or hard, it didn't matter.

"Right here." She placed a finger on my stump and softly stroked it.

It felt like the touch of a thousand angels. Gentle. Cool. It stilled, for once, that terrible ache that ricocheted back and forth between my fingers that were no longer there. Sweet relief, sweet reprieve. I wanted to beg her to continue, but I jerked my arm from her instead. "What does it matter?"

"It matters, Jeremiah Jones, because it would bring relief. Why would thee keep thyself in pain? It must distress thee."

Miss Pennington ventured to set a foot inside the tavern. Squinted at us through the gloom. "Hannah? If we don't get home soon . . ."

Though she looked up from her task, Hannah tightened her grip on me. "If we're late, 'tis only because of thy foolishness, cousin. I'll accompany thee home when I'm done." With that she recaptured my stump and then she bathed it, a firm hand on my shoulder to keep me from shrinking away.

A hand on my shoulder. A touch on my arm. When was the last time someone — a woman — had touched me?

A memory teased at the edges of my mind. There had been a ball somewhere. A dance. A girl's hand reaching out in flirtation. A light touch on my shoulder. A hand I'd captured in my own. I'd planted a kiss on that palm. I was certain of it. That's what I would have done. That's what I'd always done.

"A man ought to be able to do for himself." It shamed me that I could not clean up my own messes.

"And a man can, admirably, when he acknowledges his own limits and asks those who know him to help him when needed. It seems to me the strength of a man is in knowing his weaknesses."

"Weaknesses!"

"There is weakness in all of us, Jeremiah Jones. 'Tis only in denying, in despising it, that we succumb to it."

27

HANNAH

Seventh day had come once more. The children were all well and the weather fine, so Polly and her mother had gone out calling. Mother had done the same. I had barricaded myself in Polly's room in order to fill my basket for the afternoon's visit to the jail.

I pulled a knotted cloth from the bottom of my trunk and counted once again the number of rolls I'd collected from the dinner table that week: eight. My pocket was still filled with their crumbs. I'd slipped down into the kitchen earlier and asked the cook for a bit of cheese. The jailer expected it now, and Aunt Rebekah's cook seemed not to mind my asking for an extra bit of food every now and then. I wished we were still at our home on Chestnut Street. Then I could have taken freely from the pantry and cellar. At Pennington House I could only take to hand what was available when no one was looking.

Eight rolls were all I had for the men, one onion not yet gone too mushy, and a turnip of average size. Taken together with Jeremiah Jones's bag of grain, they would have to do.

I went down the back stair and found Doll outside waiting for me.

She helped me fit the grain into the sling and then she reached for the basket.

I clutched it to my chest as I turned from her. "I'll carry it." I didn't want Jeremiah Jones to think I had a message to pass.

"Just wanted to contribute something of my own." Her hand snaked beneath the cloth.

"Thank —"

"Don't you go thanking me. Weren't for you anyways. Was for those prisoners. Don't suppose it would hurt them none to have a bit more to eat." She refused to meet my eyes.

I gave her a swift embrace before I led out through the back and into the alley.

Robert had been ailing last week when I had visited. I prayed, as we walked up Walnut Street, that he would be much strengthened. I slid a glance toward the King's Arms as we passed.

No Jeremiah Jones; no message.

I heaved a sigh of relief. It was bad enough

to walk into the lion's den every seventh day. I didn't want to have to worry about passing messages as well.

The guard didn't hesitate in taking his cheese when I offered it. "You haven't got any bread there, have you?" He was eyeing my basket with a hopeful gaze.

"No." I did not. What I had was for the men and I was planning on keeping it for them. Only a bully would insist upon taking it from me.

"You early today?"

" 'Tis four o'clock, the same time as always." Was he going to deny me entrance? Could he do that? And if he did, what could I say?

"Well, let me just see . . ." He hiked his belly up over the rim of the table and then lurched around his chair toward the door. Drawing it open, he poked his head through. "That lady's here again. The one to see her brother. Is Captain Cunningham done?"

"Don't see no reason to keep her waiting."

The guard waved me through. As we approached Robert's cell, I began to discern the smell of broth over the stench of refuse. Perhaps General Washington had been able to get supplies delivered!

The door to the room stood ajar, so I pushed it open. I was astonished to find I was not their only visitor. A man stood there among them, a kettle swinging from his hand. He was grinning. "Smells good, don't it?" He dipped a ladle into the kettle and then brought it out and waved it around the room. That wholesome smell, in the midst of that foul place, set even my own stomach to growling.

"Want some?"

None of the men moved. I could not understand it. Why did they not move to partake?

"It's from that headquarters of yours. And . . . what's his name? *Mister* Washington?"

"That's *General* Washington to you." William Addison was glaring at the man through red-rimmed eyes.

"Come and get it. While it's nice and hot."

One of the men who'd been lying on the floor rolled from his side to his belly and crawled toward the man. Kneeling, he stretched out cupped hands.

"That's it. Right here. There you go." The man swung the ladle in the prisoner's direction, but then quite deliberately stopped short and let it spill out onto the filthy straw.

The prisoner didn't seem to care. He bent

to the straw and lapped at the quickly disappearing soup.

William Addison lunged from the wall toward the man.

The man dropped the ladle and pulled a pistol from his waistband, pointing it at the kneeling prisoner. "I've been wanting to shoot me a rebel."

My fear had turned to trembling rage. "Stop!" I wrenched the kettle from the man's hand and swung it toward William Addison. He latched onto the handle and slowly stepped back with it toward the wall.

I addressed myself to the man with the pistol. "What is the meaning of this! Have thee no shame?"

The man swung the pistol in my direction. "Who are you?" His gaze went out past my shoulder to the door. "Guard! There are to be *no visitors!*"

There came a scrabbling at the door. "She has a pass from the general, Captain Cunningham, sir."

"There are to be *no visitors* to my jail."

"It's the general himself what gave her permission, sir."

He looked at me, malice glinting in his eyes. And then he lowered the pistol.

I found that I could breathe once more.

314

"Thee have no right to deny them their own food!"

"Not denying it." He pushed back his coat and shoved his pistol into his belt. "They're welcome to it. Just so long as they salute me properly."

"As long as they grovel. Is that what thee mean to say?"

"They're rebels. It's their proper attitude."

"I'll have thee dismissed for this." Or whatever it was the army could do to its officers.

"For treating the rebels as they deserve?" He gave me a long malevolent look. "I don't think so." He stalked from the cell.

The prisoners had already gathered around the kettle. William Addison was passing around the ladle.

I knelt by Robert and gave him my basket, noting that he took nothing from it before he passed it on.

"Who is that man?"

"Captain Cunningham. He's the provost of the jail. The general brought him in special, from New York City. He comes down every day just to taunt us."

"Every day?"

"That's why we aren't fed. He wastes it all. Or sells it for his own purse."

"But that food is meant for thee!"

He gripped my hand. "Which is why we're trying so hard to get that tunnel done. Without thee we would have succumbed long ago. All of us would have."

I glanced around the room. The prisoner who had lapped at the broth lay where he had fallen. "Will no one help him?"

"He'll be dead before the week ends. Nothing should be eaten once it mixes with that muck. There's two who did it died of the runs last week. Better not to eat at all."

Tears pricked at my eyes. Of all the rebellion's indignities, this man and his cruelties somehow seemed the worst.

"Hannah?" He squeezed my hand. "How is Betsy?"

I placed my hand atop his own. "She's fine. The British daren't quarter troops in their house; Mr. Evans is too important to their cause. She's fine."

My answer seemed to put him at ease.

"Won't thee eat anything?" If I took back my basket, I might still be able to salvage half a roll for him.

"Can't."

Panic clawed at my stomach. Was he that ill? "Not even one bite?"

"Only the prisoners who dig get to eat."

"But —"

"It's only fair."

"It's not fair! The food I bring is for thee."

He pushed himself up to his elbow. "I'm starting to feel better. And once I start digging, then I'll start eating. I promise."

"I'll have a word with William Addison."

"No! Don't. Thee don't — thy food might sustain us, but 'tis the diggers who will free us."

"I don't bring it for them. I bring it for thee."

"But it must go to them. We're all brothers here."

"No." No, they were not all brothers. I had but one brother. The rest were nothing like him.

The dreams began on second night. A slow disintegration of the earth, the sky, of everything around me. An abrupt and stifling absence of air. And then . . . nothing. A complete absence of everything.

As I woke, my mouth stretched into a soundless scream.

I sat, hand on my chest. My heart ought to have been pounding, I was that terrified, but its beat was slow and steady. Then as suddenly as that terror had come, it lifted. And it was replaced with a perfect, calming peace.

I had the dream again on fourth night and

on sixth night. It was then that I began to suspect it meant something dreadful.

On seventh day, as I descended the steps into the madness of the jail, I feared that I might discover that Robert was dying, that his illness had left him choking and gasping. But I did no such thing. In fact, as I circled that pitiful room, I could not find him at all. A panic began twisting through my stomach that carried my heart up to my mouth. A peculiar smell in that place had already made the hairs at the back of my neck stand on end. For the first time in many visits I feared that I might gag. Stepping over the men that lay ill on the floor, I went and tugged at William Addison's sleeve. "Where is Robert?"

He put a finger to his lips, nodded toward the corner where the tunnel was being dug.

Robert had barely had the strength to speak to me last week. He couldn't have recovered in such a short amount of time. Which meant . . . he must have needed food. An indecent rage rose within me that he'd had to choose between his hunger and his health. It was followed by a wave of helplessness and then a trickle of despair. Why had I ever thought I could do anything

318

at all for him? "He's well enough to dig then?"

". . . well as he'll ever be."

"What's that?" Addison hadn't spoken clearly, and it was difficult to understand him when he wouldn't meet my eyes.

"He's fine."

He lies.

I heard the voice as clearly — more clearly even — than William Addison's.

How could he be fine when just last week he was lying on the ground? I could, perhaps, believe that he was better. But to think he'd recovered enough to dig? "He's in there?" I eyed the place in the floor where I knew the gaping mouth of the tunnel to be concealed. A whip of fear lashed at my stomach.

William Addison spit into the straw. "He's certainly not out here. Now. Be off with you before any suspect what we're about."

I emptied my basket. Holding back one of the rolls, I placed it into his hands. "For Robert."

He nodded, eyes sliding away from mine.

28
JEREMIAH

I'd seen Hannah pass by on her way back from the jail and she was not carrying her basket. The slave woman was. I waited until she had passed by and then went out to the bookseller's.

"*Aeneid.* If you please."

He gave me a keen once-over before moving to take the book from the shelf. He set it down on the sun-splashed counter in front of me and then crossed his arms and stood there. Waiting.

I glanced up at him and then I opened the book, flipped through the pages. Tried to be discreet. There was . . . nothing. I went through it once more, but came to no different conclusion. There was no message. Shutting up the book, I slid it toward the bookseller. Put my hat on my head and left. Why had Hannah — ?

"Jeremiah Jones!" A breathless voice made me turn.

Hannah was gesturing to me from the side of the building.

Casting a glance behind to see if any had noticed, I joined her. She took my hand and pulled me back into the far reaches of the afternoon's shadows.

"An arranged meeting? Isn't this against your beliefs?"

"The prisoners are deliberately being starved."

Prisoners weren't known to have the best of luck or the most genteel of treatment. "How do you know?"

"Because I saw the provost dump a ladle filled with broth onto the floor. He might have wasted it all if I hadn't been there. If I hadn't taken the kettle from him, I'm sure he would have left the cell with it."

She'd taken it from him? I couldn't quite imagine . . . I frowned as I tried to conjure up the sight. Gave up. "Can you prove it?"

"I saw it. The prisoners saw it. Anyone in that jail will tell thee what goes on. It's no secret!"

"No one will believe the prisoners. And the guards won't talk for cause of their jobs. That means it's your word against theirs. And you aren't a reliable witness because your brother's a rebel."

"What are thee trying to say? That nothing can be done?"

"I'm only saying that there's no proof."

Her eyes spit sparks at me. "Then what about this? What he doesn't waste, he sells."

"Sells?"

"Aye. He sells the prisoners' food for his own gain."

"I might just be able to do something about that."

But what? What could I do about the jail's provost selling food for gain? The British wouldn't care. It wasn't their food to begin with. They hadn't bought it; the patriots had supplied it. They'd probably shake the provost's hand and give him a medal for a job well done. There were more ways than bullets to kill someone; starving the men took less effort than feeding them.

I nearly rubbed a hole through the counter as I cleaned it, so fixed was I on the prisoners' plight. It wasn't just. But in a time of war, who cared about justice?

I did.

And so did Hannah.

But we were only two in a city filled with pleasure-loving officers and the Loyalist families who were trying to impress them.

They didn't care about justice.

What did they care about? They cared

about . . . diversion. Amusement. They cared about themselves. The provost was a perfect example. Too many people in this city were set on taking advantage of everyone else. Where there was war, there was corruption and bribery and vice of every kind.

So to fix a problem of graft, I must look not for the honest man but for the dishonest man. I wanted a selfish man. A man that would view the situation at the jail as an opportunity to enrich himself. I didn't want that man to take the food for himself, of course. I just wanted him to have self-interest enough to stop the provost.

That meant I needed the general . . . or someone on his staff.

I went to speak to John Lindley that very afternoon. I'd decided if I approached him at his office at headquarters, he might be more inclined to take the information seriously.

"The prisoners? Who cares about the prisoners? If they were dim-witted enough to get captured, then who should care how much they suffer? I don't have to tell you what war's like."

"But the provost is deliberately starving them. I'm not talking about unintentional

323

neglect; I'm speaking of undeserved cruelty."

"And how do you know this?"

"Miss Sunderland. She observed the provost when she visited her brother."

"She's still going to visit him? After all this time?"

I shrugged, though what I really wanted to do was knock that smug, pompous look off his face.

"So, she says she saw Captain Cunningham doing what?"

"Spoiling a kettle filled with broth. In a room filled with hungry prisoners."

"But her brother's one of them. You know she'd say anything in order to help him."

"If truth be told, it's not the cruelty that concerns me. It's her claim that the provost is selling the jail's food. At a profit."

"Selling it, eh?"

"I don't care whether you believe it or not. I care that Miss Sunderland actually thinks I can do something about it."

"You're truly besotted by her, aren't you?" He examined me as if I were some lesser species of man.

"Please. You've got to give me something to say to her. Something that will make her think I've mentioned her concerns to the right person."

"If you think so highly of her . . ." He shot a glance up at me before taking up his quill. "I'll mention it. I don't care what the provost is doing with their food, but if he's selling it to line his own pockets, that should come to the attention of General Howe. Might even be he'd reward a staff officer for information like that."

I had to fight to keep from smiling. Because that's what I had counted on: John's finely tuned sense of self-aggrandizement.

29
HANNAH

I had the dream every night the next week. So on seventh day I approached the jail with fear and trembling. Though I desperately hoped that I would see Robert sitting against the wall, I did not see him at all.

"Where is he?" I asked the question of William Addison as I knelt beside him to unpack my basket. I hid my nose in my shoulder as I did so, trying to keep that dreadful smell from my nostrils. Spring's warmth had done more than just melt the snow; it had released new and noxious odors in the jail.

His eyes slid away from mine as he inclined his chin, same as before, toward the tunnel.

"But can thee not get him? Can I not speak to him?"

He shook his head. "Not now. 'Tisn't safe. Not with the guard walking about. Night is when we change out men."

"But I cannot come at night."

"Leave a message. I'll give it to him."

I could have, but I didn't want to leave a message with this rebel. I didn't trust him. I wanted to speak with Robert. I wanted to look him in the eyes and know how he was feeling, understand what he was thinking. "When I come next week, could thee arrange it so I can see him?"

He looked at me with such an odd expression. "I'll try. Do you have a message for me?"

For him? I'd been so worried about Robert that I had forgotten my reason for being there. I shook my head.

"Nothing? They're so set on us escaping, you'd think they'd bother to keep us informed now and then."

"Do thee have any messages for them?" I'd never passed a message back the other way, to Jeremiah Jones, but he must have some way to get information to General Washington.

Indecision was etched into William Addison's frown. "It'd be nice to know what's out there, above the tunnel. And nice to know which way we're digging."

"Thee would have to dig west, wouldn't thee? Or thee might end up in the cemetery."

"And we might end there still, in spite of all this work. Two more died during the week. In any case, perhaps you *could* pass a message. It's fine to tell us to dig west for fifty-three feet, but I've no way to tell which direction we're headed."

I held out an arm toward the west. It did not seem that difficult.

"Aye. But you've no idea what it's like down there. How a man can get turned around. We could be digging toward the provost's own house and I'd never know it."

I'd thought nothing at all of the actual digging of the tunnel. "How far have thee dug?"

"Twenty feet." He said it as if it was a great accomplishment.

"But thee've not yet accomplished the half!"

He shrugged. "You think you could do better?"

"What's taking so long?"

"*You* want to try to dig through clay? Fifty-some feet of it? And then scoop the dirt into a hat and drag it back through the tunnel into the room?"

"They bring the dirt back here?"

"What else is there to do with it? It has to go somewhere."

"But . . . where is it?" I hadn't noticed

any kind of pile.

"You're standing on it."

"I'm — but —"

"I figure we've raised the floor over two inches since we started."

"And they bring it out in a hat?"

"Nothing else here to use."

"Take this." I thrust the basket at him.

He pushed it right back at me. "They're sure to notice you've left it."

"They won't." At least . . . I didn't think they would. I hoped they wouldn't. Anything that would ensure Robert's escape was worth the risk.

When the guard came to get me, I walked behind him, trying to keep from him the fact that I had left my basket behind. And when I passed through the door, I went as swiftly as I could up the stair.

"Hey!"

I stopped, not daring to move.

"Hey, you. Miss!"

This is what had happened when Father was arrested. I'd been called back from following the others into the street. I'd almost been safe. My gorge rose in my throat as I turned, gripping the rail with a hand gone suddenly cold. "Aye?"

"About the basket you always come carrying."

I was afraid even to breathe.

"I was thinking, when you come next time, could you put a roll in it for me? I've a hankering for some good bread."

"A roll?"

"Along with the cheese."

A roll and some cheese. I nearly sunk to the floor in relief.

I left the jail, collected Doll, and walked with her round the block, paying careful attention to the space around the southwest corner. What would happen if the tunnel didn't come up at the right spot?

They might crawl up into the cemetery.

In the other direction?

They might find themselves in the middle of a stream.

If they managed to dig straight in the westerly direction, they would reach the other side of Sixth Street, and would end up in the fenced yard of a wheelwright. Well. That was quite clever. And it made me wonder who it was that lived there. I walked past the door, listening for any clues as to the inhabitants, but there was nothing. And the windows were too covered with grime to peer inside.

■ ■ ■ ■

I spent the rest of the day trying to fix upon a way to help William Addison. There must be some way to determine whether they were digging in the right direction. I wondered if they could hear the rattle of carts and the clomping of horses on Sixth Street as they dug. That might be a help . . . but then it might sound just the same as Walnut Street. If they'd mistakenly turned in that direction, there would be no cover once they emerged. There had to be some other method of guidance. They needed something straight that would not bend itself to their efforts. A kind of inviolable guide.

But what could be placed at one end of the tunnel and remain unbending at the other end, across a distance of fifty-three feet? What else could I smuggle into the jail that would help to solve such a puzzle?

The question still pressed on my mind as I sat in Meeting the next day. My pondering had not provided me with any solution. The problem remained: A tunnel of fifty-three feet could be dug, but there was no way to guarantee where it might end. The effort might not produce the desired result, and if it did not, then all the work would be for naught. Robert could be arrested just as he came to escape.

Several points of business were conducted. A marriage was approved. A concern was put forth about the Friends in Virginia. Then worship began, and along with it the waiting and the silence.

I was glad that Jeremiah Jones no longer came to Meeting. I'd spent my time those two first days wondering what he must think of us. It changed things, made me look at our Meetings differently as I tried to see them through his eyes.

Please, God. There must be some way. Please show me how to help them dig straight.

I don't know why I prayed. I expected no answer. Indeed, I had not received any answers to my petitions in many months.

Several minutes later, Betsy's mother stood. I could feel a flare of expectation as heads turned in her direction. God was going to speak!

"Go ye therefore and be Children of Light, whose flame never fades, whose light always goes forth, shining in the darkness. Be Children of Light whose courage never wavers, whose light always goes straight from its source." She stopped speaking for a moment as a look of befuddlement crossed her face. Opened her mouth. Closed it. Opened it once more. "Unbending." She sat down.

Children of Light.

What was God saying? Of course we were to be Children of Light. That's what Friends had always been. It's what George Fox had called us from the start.

No one else spoke. The Meeting ended some time later. But by that time I realized I'd been given an answer to my prayer.

I emptied my basket on my next visit to the jail, of onions and rolls and half of a chicken. And then I took from it one thing more. "This is for thee." I held it out to William Addison.

He took it from me. "A candle." Looked up at me. "So I can see more clearly this squalid mess we're living in?"

"So thee can tell if the tunnel is straight."

He looked a question at me.

"If thee set it at the entrance to the tunnel and thee can see it still at the end, then it must be straight. And if thee cannot see it, then thee will know the tunnel deviates in direction."

"Ah. Very clever." He held it up, rolling it between his fingers. "Though it might help, of course, if there were some way to light it.

And relight it."

"Why, thee just —" Oh. One of the luxuries of wealth was having a fire that rarely went out and servants to relight it if it did. "I'll bring a char cloth and a flint next week." I scratched at an itch on my arm and then scratched at it again as I looked around the room. Just standing there in the filth and the mire made everything within me start to itch. I'd been hoping Robert would appear as we were talking, but he had not, even though William Addison had promised his presence the week before. There were several men sitting against the wall who could have taken his place in the tunnel. I didn't understand why my brother need always be absent. "I want to see Robert."

He nodded toward the wall.

"I thought thee were going to keep him out this once. That's what thee told me last week."

He looked at me again, with that same odd sadness in his eyes. It was then my heart understood what my mind had refused to comprehend. "Is he . . . has he . . . ?"

William Addison put the candle down and took up my hand. "He died."

I sank to my knees in that filth and squalor. A slow disintegration of the earth, the sky, of everything around me. An abrupt

and stifling absence of air. And then . . .
nothing. A complete absence of everything.
I lowered my head to my knees as the damp
soaked through my stockings to my skin and
the stench seeped into my skirts. But I
didn't care. I couldn't care. Robert was
dead. "How — ?"

"He was digging. The tunnel collapsed.
We couldn't pull him out in time."

A howl escaped my lips.

"Hush! No one's noticed. Not anyone
outside this cell. And if his death is discovered, then they're going to start asking questions."

He was right. Of course he was right, but
I could not keep silent. A keening moan
escaped my lips. "I want to see him."

"You don't. You don't want to see him.
It's already been three weeks."

I pushed from my knees to standing. "I
want to see him."

The men had been watching me; I knew
it from the way they turned their heads as I
glanced around the room. Robert was there,
he had to be there, but I could not discern
where they had hidden him.

William Addison nodded toward one of
the men, who was sitting in the corner opposite the tunnel. That man moved aside,
exposing a pile of straw. He swept some of

it away. As I approached, I discovered it was from there that the peculiar smell had emanated. It had come from my brother.

I would not have known it was him, but for his clothes and the cowlick at the center of his forehead. It was the twin of my own. His body was bloated beyond recognition, his neck crawling with maggots, but it was plain to see how he had died: He'd been buried alive. His hands were stained with earth, his fingernails packed with dirt. But what made me weep was his mouth. It was ringed with a dirty froth.

I always woke from my dream with a soundless scream.

No wonder I'd felt such great terror. *He* had felt great terror. I was comforted knowing that it had been assuaged by such great peace. I knelt beside him and put a hand out to smooth his hair, pulling bits of straw from it. I wiped the dirt from his brow and then took the hem of my skirt to wipe the froth from his mouth. When I could do nothing more to improve his condition, I swept the straw back over his body.

The prisoner resumed his position.

William Addison cleared his throat. "We mean no disrespect, miss. We're just trying to keep the rats away."

"Why did thee not tell me?"

When he looked at me, I saw shame in the depths of his eyes. "I was afraid you would stop coming. We all knew you were only coming to see him. But the rest of us need you too. They say the British are leaving soon. If they evacuate the city, they'll have to put us on ships. This jail is bad, but those ships are worse. Wouldn't none of us survive them."

"Thee shouldn't have kept this from me."

"I know it and I'm begging your pardon, but if you don't come the guards will wonder why. They don't know Robert died. So . . . will you do it? For us? Will you keep coming?"

30
JEREMIAH

The tailor had finished the rest of my new suits several weeks ago. I'd hung them up on pegs and had gotten in the habit of eyeing them as I was getting dressed of a morning.

English blue.

Myrtle green.

Yellow.

I don't know why I'd let him talk me into them, though I suspected it had to do with Hannah Sunderland. I didn't really want to work out what, exactly. I needed her to deliver messages to the jail more than I needed . . . what I wanted. And going to her church had provided quite an education. Those people actually sat around waiting to hear from God.

As if He weren't busy enough attending to other matters.

It was fine and good to pray and hope for some sort of answer, but some things you didn't need someone to tell you. When the world had been turned upside down, and right was being treated as wrong, any Christian person would try to do something about it. What were those people waiting for? Were they so afraid they might do the wrong thing that they failed to do anything at all?

English blue and bright yellow.

Decidedly not for Quakers.

I grabbed the yellow coat from its peg and put it on. The tailor had been true to his word. As I descended the back stair, the coat remained fixed to my shoulder.

Dinner wasn't as busy as normal so I had time to talk to my barkeeper about the hosting of the coming night's ball. I had him write up an order for new cloths. Went into the kitchen and asked the cook to undertake an inventory of pewter.

"What? Today?"

I shrugged. "Or tomorrow."

"If I had some decent help, I might be able to accomplish something around here!" She glared at her daughter as she spoke.

I left before she could turn her sights on me. As I walked back into the public room, John and his comrades came through the door. He ordered bowls of punch for them all. I called for the cook's daughter to serve them and then pulled a chair up to their table.

John glanced up from his conversation. Cocked his head. "Love suits you, Jonesy. Haven't seen you looking this good since we were lieutenants together."

The line between compliment and criticism must have been a very thin one in John Lindley's mind. I smiled anyway. "And how are your plans coming for the general's fete?"

John shrugged, pulling a face. "We've talked of plays, but we've performed nearly a dozen already this season. If we do another, it has to be something more. Something . . . different."

Something more. Something different. Something completely extravagant and wholly inappropriate to fete a general whose victories were dubious at best. It was ridiculous to send him sailing home as if he deserved all the adoration that his officers had lavished upon him. It was almost as if he were some medieval sovereign surrounded by chieftains who were pledged to fealty, no matter the truth of who or what he was. "You ought to have a joust."

"A what?" John was looking at me with some interest.

"A joust."

He scratched at his jaw. "A joust. Knights and their ladies, horses and spears. That would be a spectacle."

Indeed it would.

"How many officers are we?" John asked the question of André, who had become his shadow of late.

"Twenty-one."

"Twenty-one knights, so there must be twenty-one ladies."

André's smile matched John's. "A tournament held in honor of General Howe's honor. Perfect!"

Perfectly absurd. "You ought to have the jousters compete for the ladies' honor in honor of the general's honor."

"How cunning — yes!" John and André toasted each other. "For the ladies' honor. And they *have* been delightful, these Philadelphia belles."

"Though they couldn't hold a candle to London's society." There was general agreement with André's sentiment.

But of course they couldn't. For the most part, colonial girls were meek, kind creatures who expected truth where they encountered lies and virtue where there was only vice. They'd adopted British fashion with the enthusiasm of converts. And yet they'd been secretly scorned as provincial the entire

341

season, though they hadn't even noticed. They were pretty in their way. They were exotic. But they weren't quite suitable.

"We can't pretend they're genuine ladies." John was only saying what they were all thinking.

"That's true. They're not. Not really."

It seemed as if they were ready to discard the whole idea. The Crusaders hadn't been so quickly defeated. And heaven knew they'd collected nearly as many girls for their harems, leaving them all behind when they'd sailed for home. "You ought to style them as Turks."

André's eyes lit with a gleam others might have called inspiration. "Turks."

Why not? It was better than styling them as savages or Orientals.

"Have you a leaf of paper you could spare?"

I went over to the counter, grabbed my daybook, and ripped a page from the back. Finding that he had followed me, I gave it to him.

"And a quill?"

I passed one to him. And then the ink-well.

He spent a few minutes sketching at something. I watched as a female form took shape. It was swathed in sashes topped with a turban and sprouting all kinds of tassels, feathers, and veils. He showed it to me and then went over to show it to the others.

"Do you think that would do?" he asked John.

"Perfectly splendid!"

And perfectly conceived to create outrage in the heart of each one of Philadelphia's good citizens. It was perfect.

"It will be a spectacle such as the empire has never seen." André was speaking with the enthusiasm of a zealot. "I wonder . . . perhaps I should make some accounting of the event. To send to the newspapers in London . . ."

I stepped forward to stack up the bowls. "I'm certain that you should." Then he could be the laughingstock of England as well.

The fete — the Meschianza, they were calling it — seemed to consume the attentions of all the officers in John's group. They were in and out of the tavern several times a day, holding conferences at the table by the fire.

I included myself in their discussions, ostensibly to help in their endeavors, but mostly to marvel at the foolishness that seemed to have prevailed over good sense.

"What do you think, Jonesy? Are flags

decoration enough for the barges?"

Flags. On barges? "No. Heavens no! You don't want to send the general off with anything so pedestrian. Those barges should be festooned with all the trimmings and bunting you can find." Which wouldn't be very much. Not in this occupation-weary city. It would give the citizenry one more reason to despise them. What's more, looking for such things would provide a distraction. And keep John from dogging my steps. I couldn't afford another encounter like the one we'd had with the egg-girl.

But I encountered him out in the city anyway. He seemed to be everywhere and nowhere at once. I touched a finger to my hat. "How are the festivities progressing?"

"We've nearly everything needed for the regatta and the joust. But there's still the interior of the house to be improved upon."

"Wharton's house? It's rather grand, as I recall. Or it was."

"For a family perhaps, but not for a tournament. Changes need to be made."

A tournament. General Howe had left them with too much time on their hands. They ought to have been gainfully employed — planning battles and scavenging the countryside for food. Any respectable army would have been readied for a move from

winter quarters long before now. But the
delay did have the advantage of showing
Philadelphians the army's true colors. "I
would think that, given the opportunity, the
citizens would be happy to contribute to
such a worthy cause."

"Do you think so?"

I winked at him. "It's all in the asking."

"We'd need . . ."

"Only the best of things. You ought to ask
for mirrors and candelabras and crystal
vases. All the luxuries these people have collected. They oughtn't mind if you explain
you're only borrowing them. You are, after
all, defending their city from rebel attack.
They'll offer them to you gladly. And even
if they don't, the army ought to be allowed
such liberties."

"That was my way of thinking as well.
Only these colonials can be so . . . *provincial*
about such things."

"When they're raised in the wilderness,
dressed in buckskins and forced to eat gruel
twice a day, it's a wonder they know how to
dance at all."

"I'm sure. But did you really eat . . . ?"
John shuddered. He'd already nearly convinced himself I was telling the truth. I
could see it in his eyes.

"Some of us did." No colonists that I

knew, of course, but somewhere in the wilds of the Ohio Valley, someone probably had.

31
HANNAH

Robert had died and there was no one I could tell. If I did, everyone would want to know how I had found out. And what could I say? That I visited the jail every week? That Robert had died digging a tunnel? That I was involved in a plan to help the prisoners escape? Perhaps I ought to have told Mother, but how could she have kept that terrible knowledge to herself? Once she shared it with Father, my visits to the jail would be forbidden.

I kept the information to myself. I had to.

Observing a private vigil of grief, I swallowed sobs as I ate my breakfast and stifled tears as I pushed food around my plate at supper. The early hours of the morning found me weeping into my pillow.

Robert was gone.

I was angry. I was furious. I wanted to march right over to Penn House and box General Howe's ears. How dare he? How *dare* he take upon himself the welfare of hundreds of prisoners only to let them die? A pitiful choice those men had been given: starve to death or dig their own grave.

That rage was the most sensible, reasonable feeling I'd ever felt. Everything about me was a lie now. I was no Friend. It had all been an illusion. I was no pacifist — I wanted to hurt someone. I wanted someone to pay for what had been taken from me.

I kept mostly to the house that week. Polly and Aunt Rebekah were constantly out making unending rounds of calls while Mother made her own. It was rumored that the Friends from Virginia would finally be freed and there was a frenzy of visiting that accompanied the welcome news. I stayed in Polly's bedroom, unnoticed and unsought, and worked at one thing or another as I blotted the tears that fell from my eyes. But sixth day afternoon, Polly invaded the space with new wigs and gowns and other finery.

"Look!" She stood across the room, examining her image in the wall glass. She had adorned herself in a wig two feet tall and skirts twice as wide as they were long. Her gown glittered as she stood there, with silver embroidery and cascades of ruffles and lace with ribbons and pearls and spangles tucked among them.

"I hardly look myself!" She beamed with apparent delight.

It was true. I hardly knew her from any of the other dozen Philadelphia belles that sashayed in and out of Pennington House's parlors.

"Here." She picked up the gown she had just discarded and held it out to me. "Try it on. I think the color will suit you."

I looked away from the dazzling spectacle she'd become to the amaranth-colored gown she was offering. I had so little energy and no desire to do anything much at all since I'd been told of Robert's death.

She picked up my hands and pulled at them. "Please. You've been poor company this week. So dull and drear."

I tried to tug my hands away.

She only grasped them tighter and drew me to standing as my handiwork tumbled from my lap.

"My embroidery!"

"You can dust it off later. After you try this on."

Jenny was already doing Polly's bidding, having loosened the laces of my sleeved waistcoat. I did not have the spirit to resist her, so I let her remove it and then fasten the open robe gown to my stomacher. It had a nice hand. I stroked the length of the skirts as Jenny laced it.

Polly clapped her hands as she watched. "You look so much better!"

Jenny pointed toward the gilt-framed wall glass.

I put a hand to the bodice as my double in the looking glass did the same. Better? With lace frothing from my bosom like milkweed and so many ruffles bunched about my elbows that I doubted I could do anything useful?

"Don't you like it?"

The color was so bright that it was almost cheerful. For a sliver of a moment I wished I could feel that way and that Jeremiah Jones could see me in it. "It's lovely. Truly lovely."

Polly grinned. "I knew you would like it."

"Aye." There was no reason to pretend otherwise. The fripperies and the flounces I could do without, but the color . . . there was something about it that cheered my heart. It had done me some good to look at myself in it. "Help me from it."

"Keep it on — you can wear it. I insist upon it."

"It would give my mother apoplexy."

She didn't even try to smother her laughter.

I shook my head. "Such gowns are not for me."

"But they could be. The Brookingdale girls wear gowns like these. And they're Quakers, aren't they?"

They did and they were. But they were not me. "I cannot be other than who I am." But who was I truly? A Friend who was working on behalf of the rebels? A daughter who was disobeying her father? A woman who found her heart bent in the direction of a man who was not at all like her? I was not who I once was. But who was I in the process of becoming?

As I worked at embroidery on seventh day, William Addison's words kept echoing in my head. *Will you keep coming? The rest of us need you too.* Should I return to the jail or not? They had a candle now, but they lacked the means to light it and I had told them I would bring a char cloth and a flint. I had given my word.

But that was before I'd found out about Robert.

They'd killed my brother. They'd made him work for the food I'd brought for him alone. Anyone could see that he'd been sick.

They are my brothers.

They were *not* his brothers. Why should I

351

do anything else for them at all?

Inasmuch as you did not do it to one of
the least of these, you did not do it to Me.

They were in prison because of their own
stiff necks and their willful rebellion. Isn't
that what the Yearly Meeting had decided?
They are my brothers.
How could Robert have thought of them
as brothers? Why had he joined them at all?
Even before I asked myself the question, I
knew the answer. I knew it just as surely as
Robert had whispered it into my ear. He'd
joined them because of Fanny Pruitt. He
was no supporter of causes; he'd been a
supporter of justice.
Justice.
If I did not go back, then the rest of the
men would die. And if I did not go back,
then I would have to tell Jeremiah Jones
why. At that thought my spirit cowered
within me, not from the rage that would
most certainly overtake him and not from
the way I knew he would yell at me. It was
for the disappointment, the resignation that
I was sure I would see in his eyes. He had
come to rely upon me, to respect me. I
could tell it by the way his lips softened at
the corners — just a little — when he

looked at me. I had earned that trust and I . . . I cherished that hard-won respect.

At that moment I realized I had to return. I had to preserve the lie that Robert was still alive. I had to help the men make the tunnel straight, and I had to keep Jeremiah Jones's regard. Though the beneficiaries of my efforts did not deserve them, though my neck be bound for the gallows, there was injustice here that I could right. A life to be paid for. And a man's regard that I did not wish to lose.

There was no choice in the matter. There never had been. That too had been a lie.

I felt no little satisfaction at the surprise that flared in William Addison's eyes when he saw me that day. I delivered the flint, steel, and char cloths, along with some food and a bag of grain. But I left the prison, scratching at an itch on my arm. It put me in mind of the previous week's visit when I'd found a louse crawling on my skin. As I walked up the street, I brought out my arm from the confines of my cloak and . . . just there! I killed another one with a squash from my thumb and then gave the itch another scratch for good measure.

Doll clucked as she saw me. "Not enough to drag your skirts through all that muck and filth? You got to bring them creatures home with you too?" She shook her head. "I know you got to help them poor souls, but do you have to get right down and wallow in their mess in order to do it?"

"I don't wallow on purpose."

I shed my gown and skirts in the stables while Doll made sure no one entered. She used her hand to try to fan the stench away from her nose as I handed her my clothes for boiling. I went up the back stair and returned to the embroidery I'd been doing. As I worked on my piece, the room grew warmer. I shifted my legs and rolled my shoulders. Aches seemed to have sprung up all over my body. I dabbed at my forehead with a handkerchief. Though the day was warm, I had not thought it unseasonably so.

Polly burst into the room near supper, wasted no time in flinging her hat upon the bed, and then began to pull gowns from her trunk. "Do you think I should wear my amber or my salmon-colored gown to the ball tonight?"

They were both far too vivid for my taste. "Which one pleases thee the most?"

She viewed them with an appraising eye. "What I'd truly like is a gown made of that new ribbon silk that the mercer got from the latest ship." She looked at first the amber and then at the salmon-colored gown. Sighed. "But one of these will have to do."

"Choose the salmon." It made her look far less like a fashion doll and more like a woman. At least . . . as I looked upon them, the gowns wavered and then blurred together. I blinked — hard — to clear my vision. Perhaps yesterday's headache had affected my sight.

"The which?"

"The . . ." I wasn't quite certain anymore, and I felt a sudden longing to lie down. "Pardon me. I don't think . . ." I let my work drop from my lap and pushed away from my chair. I had meant to go to my bed, but it seemed such a very great distance away. "I don't think . . ." Why had it become so bone-chillingly, frighteningly cold?

"Hannah?"

I tried to turn my head toward Polly, but I couldn't do it. My legs wouldn't move, my arms wouldn't bend, and I could hardly hear anything at all. "I don't think . . ." What was it I didn't think? I couldn't remember anymore. I just needed . . . I needed . . .

"Hannah!"

I heard Polly shriek, but I couldn't imagine

what for. Everything had gone so cold. And
so. . . . white.

32

JEREMIAH

"They say it's the putrid fever."

I felt the color drain from my face as Miss Pennington kept speaking. I tried to make sense of her words, but I couldn't do it. Perhaps I'd misunderstood. Though myriad candles glowed about the room, I still had trouble making out her face. And the noise of the instruments didn't much help either. "She has what?"

Miss Pennington leaned closer. "The putrid fever. That's what the doctor says."

Putrid fever? I glanced up at John.

He frowned. Shook his head.

"How would she get putrid fever?" I don't know why I asked the question. I knew the answer of course. Just as John did. She'd got it from the prisoners.

"She got it from the jail, didn't she?" Miss Pennington fairly shouted the words.

John laid a hand on her arm. "Please! Don't speak so loudly. Visits to the prison

357

have been forbidden."

I reached out and gripped her arm. "Is it bad?"

She pressed her lips together and nodded.

Hannah Sunderland was lying abed with putrid fever, and I was trapped at an abominable Saturday evening ball. A ball I hadn't even wanted to attend.

"I was going to try to get her to come tonight. I had her try on the most delicious gown the other day! In amaranth, that lovely reddish purple. The style was not so outmoded as her own . . ."

Miss Pennington babbled on as I excused myself and went to collect my hat. I pushed out into a night mild and drenched in moonlight.

Putrid fever. Not many survived it. She'd caught it from the jail — she had to have. And it was all my fault. I started out through the night at a run toward Pennington House. I was halfway there before I realized the futility in going. The hour was late. They would never let me in. And even if they did, what reason could I give to persuade them to let me see her? The fact that I was the one who arranged for her visits to the jail? That I was the one who insisted that she keep going?

They wouldn't welcome me. They would

probably turn me in as a spy.

But what if I gave them the other reason? The one that really mattered? I loved their daughter. If she were going to leave this earth, I wanted the chance to be with her one last time. To see in her eyes once more the man I wanted to become.

I raised my fist toward heaven. *What have I ever done to you?*

That was a feeble argument if I'd ever heard one. I'd done plenty. And we both knew it.

What has she *ever done to you?*

There. That was better. Much better. I hadn't a chance arguing on my own merits, but I could expound upon hers forever.

What has she ever done to you?

I dropped my fist. It was pointless. There was no use arguing with someone who wouldn't argue back. I'd never gotten much satisfaction from a God who didn't seem to speak or see or hear. I had to see Hannah, but I knew better than to trust God to help me. I had better contacts than He did anyway. I had friends in high places.

Miss Pennington's eyes sparked with mischief the following Tuesday night. "So Major Lindley will invite all the parents out for the review of the troops. They won't be able to refuse!"

That was the idea.

"You'll be waiting at the corner. And when they leave . . ." She looked at me with great expectation.

"I'll come in."

She clasped her hands to her chest. "This is the most romantic thing I've ever been party to."

John, however, didn't look quite so enraptured. He took Miss Pennington's hand up in his. "Has there been any talk about how she caught it?"

"Caught what?"

"The putrid fever."

She frowned. "No."

"If there is, just say . . . that it's going around." He eyed me. "No one knows I wrote that pass. I want to keep it that way."

I certainly wasn't going to tell anyone.

Miss Pennington pouted. "Don't you trust me?"

He smiled. "Not for a moment." He pulled her hand up around his arm. "Shall we dance?"

They walked off and left me in my chair against the wall, planning what I was going to tell Hannah when I saw her the next afternoon.

■ ■ ■ ■

Whatever words I'd had failed me as Miss Pennington left me alone in that bedroom. Hannah was so very ill. Why had no one warned me! Her face was pallid. Dark circles had made ashen hollows where her eyes had once been. Maybe this hadn't been such a good idea. She was sleeping. And peacefully, by the sound of it. She didn't need me to interrupt her. I turned toward the door.

"Jeremiah." Her whisper reached out and touched my heart.

I turned back toward the bed.

She reached out a hand to me.

I took it up as I sat in a chair beside her bed. "They told me you have the fever."

She tried to smile. "It doesn't feel like it. I'm so cold." She was quivering beneath her blanket. I looked around for another one, but there were none. I took off my blue-colored coat and laid it atop her.

Tears began to seep from her eyes.

"No. Don't! Don't cry." I hadn't planned on her crying. I didn't know what to say now. She'd always been one to berate me. If only she'd yell at me, I'd know exactly what to do.

361

"Thee are such a gentleman."

Her small hand was so cold. I wished I had another to cup it in. "Not such a gentleman as you'd think." I had too many thoughts in my head to be accused of that particular vice. They mostly had to do with her soft, lovely eyes. And her mouth.

"I mean . . . thee are not a Friend."

I'd been accused of that before and I had tired of it. "And neither are thee!"

She smiled. Or tried to.

"I mean: neither are *you*."

She frowned, making me want nothing so much as to smooth her cares away. "I meant to say, there is no peace about thee."

"There will be once the British leave." I had tried to make her smile, but I failed.

" 'Tis not a lack of opportunity. 'Tis a lack of . . . of . . . serenity."

"But we're the same, you and I. Outcasts. You don't have your faith anymore, and I . . ." Well. Enough said about me.

Tears had made a trail from her cheek to her neck. "We are not the same at all. A woman of peace persuaded to join a rebellion, and a man of war frustrated because he must use less violent means."

"But —"

"I feel nothing but confusion when thee are near." She said it as if she wished it weren't so. And those pitiable tears kept coming. If her hand weren't so cold, I might have let go of it to fish for my handkerchief.

"Truly? I'd thought . . . I mean . . . since I've known you . . . I feel much less troubled."

"Then I am glad." She glanced away. Sighed and closed her eyes.

This was it? This was all the time there was? But there was so much more to be said! Only . . . what should I say first? Should I tell her how much I depended upon her? How proud I was of her? How she was the finest woman I'd ever had the chance to meet? Should I thank her for making me feel like I could be more instead of less? For making me think I could be a man again? Perhaps . . . I should just start with the truth. "I love you, Hannah Sunderland."

Her only response was a dainty snore. Then a soft sigh.

"I love you." I'd spoken those words but once and now the only thing I wanted to do was repeat them forever. I watched her sleep, keeping her hand warm until Miss Pennington came for me.

That night, for the first time in a long time, I prayed. I even knelt beside my bed to do it. I was hoping God might tolerate a prayer from me if it was on behalf of someone like Hannah Sunderland.

Please help no harm come to her. On account of me.

Because that wouldn't be fair. Of all the injustices in the world, that would be the worst. That a woman like her would pay the price for a wretch like me.

We are not the same at all.

She was right. We weren't. But she was only looking at the places we'd come from. I was more interested in the place we'd gotten to. It's not that she didn't love me. Not necessarily. And it's not that she didn't want me. It's that she wanted her religion more. But, dash it! Couldn't she see she didn't have it anyway? She may have been a Quaker once, but she wasn't a Quaker anymore. I sighed, thinking of her small, cold hand in mine. Thinking of how I'd wished I could do more than just sit beside her bed and hold it.

Who did I think I was, hoping for some kind of ordinary life? I was no longer an ordinary man. But dash it again! She'd made me hope. Made me believe. If she'd been a man, I'd have made her answer for it. But she was just a small, pretty, indescribably infuriating . . . possibly dying . . .

woman. And she held my heart between those small, chill hands.

33
HANNAH

I was ill with the putrid fever for a week. Even when I was awake, I had the impression that I was dreaming. I kept catching the scent of Jeremiah at the oddest of times, and I could not seem to shake the impression that he was holding my hand. Seventh day came far too quickly.

When I tried to rise from bed that afternoon, a sweat broke out behind my ears and my legs threatened to collapse beneath me. It took most of my strength to creep down the back stair. The little left me was nearly used up in my search for Doll.

As soon as I found her, she put an arm about my waist and turned me right around. "It's not my place to tell you no, miss, but that's what I'm telling you. You can't be going back to that jail. Not after you just got done with the fever."

"I have to go, Doll."

"You don't got to do anything."

"I want to go." I truly did, but my body didn't seem to understand what my head wanted it to do.

"What happens if you catch that fever again?"

"If I don't go, then who will?" What if the men needed something? Or what if General Washington wanted to pass them a message? Worse, if I didn't go, the guards might discover that Robert had died. I took a cautious step forward. I should go; the men needed the food. But I was so terribly tired.

"You don't look well."

"I don't feel well."

Doll stepped back toward the house and tried to take me with her. "The only place you going is back to bed."

"I have to go." I tried to wrest my arm from her, but I didn't have the strength. "Please!"

She gave me a long look and then she sighed as she threaded her arm through my own. "If you going down in there, then I'm going too."

I might have argued with her, but I couldn't find the words. When we got to the jail, I showed my pass to the guard. But this time, instead of waiting, Doll walked up the steps with me. I tried to free my arm. "I don't think —"

"*I* don't think you should be doing this at all, and look where all that thinking got me."

I showed the pass to the guard stationed in the hallway and he opened the door to the basement stair. I started down, Doll holding on to my arm, but he stopped her.

"The pass is only for Miss Sunderland."

"Who is sick as a dog and ought to be in bed right now, only she think her brother is going to starve to death unless she feed him. So if you're going to let her go down there, you might as well let me, because sure enough it'll be me carrying her all the way back home. You want to do that?"

He frowned as he scratched at his jaw. Finally he nodded toward the stair and let us both go down.

The guard at the bottom brightened when he saw me. "You're late. I thought you weren't coming today."

"She shouldn't have, she's that sick." Though Doll was muttering, she made sure I heard her well enough.

I removed the cloth that covered my basket and held out a wedge of cheese, but when the guard moved to take it, Doll slapped his hand away. "You ought to be ashamed of yourself, taking food from the mouths of those poor souls! Either you about to have a child or you been eating somebody else's food atop your own."

The guard stood there, mouth flapping open. I might have enjoyed the sight if I hadn't been so bone-achingly weary.

"You going to let her see her brother or would you rather watch her faint right here?"

"I —"

"Go on!" She gestured toward the door even as she supported me with her arm.

The guard let us through, and the second guard took us down to Robert's room.

"Lord have mercy." Doll clung to me as if afraid she might be left behind.

William Addison came right up to me as we entered. "You look . . . are you all right?"

"I've had the putrid fever." And if the lightness in my head were any indication, I had it still. I'd forgotten just how terrible the stench and the squalor were at the jail. Now that I knew about Robert, I could discern the smell of death as well. Over in the corner, where none of the men sat, I heard a scrabbling in the straw. Doll must have heard it too, for she stepped even closer to me.

I handed my basket to William Addison and whispered into his ear as he took it. "Is the tunnel almost done?"

He sighed. "We thought so. But that

candle of yours showed us we were digging in the wrong direction. We'd turned ourselves around and headed back for the jail. Tunnel caved in twice more. We lost two men and we've twenty-five feet still to dig."

Twenty-five! "But thee have only five more weeks."

"We're digging as fast as we can."

"That night is thy best chance at escape." It was perhaps their only chance at escape.

"Don't you think I know that!"

I began to frown, but then winced at the headache it induced.

"They sent that provost away. Gave us a new one."

"Is he . . . ?"

"He's better than the other."

God be praised.

He glanced away over my shoulder at Doll and then leaned closer still. "Do you think you could pass a message for me?"

Today? I could barely manage to keep myself standing.

"If they could give us even a couple more days . . ."

I didn't know how they could, but there could be no harm in asking.

"That's some evil place!" Doll paused as we left the building and spit on the steps twice.

"Which is why I have to help them escape."

"They's death down there. I could smell it. And you've been going there every week!" She shook her head as if such a thing were unthinkable.

"Could thee . . . ?" I held out the basket toward her. That was the sign for Jeremiah. I had to leave the message today; I didn't know if I would be well enough to do it tomorrow.

She took the basket from me as she took my arm. "We got to get you right home and back to your bed."

"I have to go by the bookseller's." Though it was just down the street, it seemed as if it were ten miles away.

"Don't make me say what I'm not allowed to say. You know I'll say it! You don't have to do nothing but sleep."

"I don't — I mean —" I let her trundle me down the street. Halfway to the bookseller's I realized I had nothing to write a message on or with. So we walked by both the bookseller's and the King's Arms, Doll carrying my basket and me hanging on to her arm.

Once we got back to Pennington House, she helped me out of my soiled gown and then into a clean one. Somehow she pushed me into the house and pulled me up the back stair. And then — finally — I was able to collapse onto my bed.

I did not leave it for two days.

Life went on around me. I heard the children patter up and down the hall. I heard Polly come and go. One night I even heard shouting from the dining room, but I could not bring myself to care what it was about. Later, Aunt and Uncle stopped in the hall outside the bedroom door.

"If it weren't for you, I would toss him out into the street!" Uncle sounded more angry than I had ever before heard him. "If he landed on his head and it knocked some gratitude into him, so much the better!"

Aunt made some soothing sounds.

"A man ought not be proselytized in his own home!"

"Of course not."

"It's not to be borne. And not by those self-satisfied Quakers. They've never liked me, and Sunderland is the worst of them all!"

"They couldn't see what I did. They didn't know you like I did."

There was a long pause in which nothing was said at all. And then finally: "I was never good enough for him. I own more ships than anyone in the colonies, and I'm still not good enough for him . . . for them."

"You're good enough for me. Come."

Their footsteps continued on down the hall, but I must have fallen asleep, for I never heard them come back.

On the fifth day I awoke to the spatter of raindrops on the window. I rose without any ache in my head and dressed without any pain in my limbs. I felt as if the power to live had been granted me once more.

After breakfasting with the others, I caught Doll in the hall. "I need to go out this afternoon."

"Only place you're going is back to your bed."

"I have to leave a message for Jeremiah Jones."

She frowned. "This about those prisoners?"

"Yes. Can thee meet me at quarter until four?"

She didn't answer one way or another, but she did meet me out in the garden. She took my basket from me without my even asking and she took up my arm in hers.

"I'm fine." I tried to free myself from her.

"You not fine until I say you fine." She screwed up her mouth in that obstinate way of hers and didn't say another word as we walked to the bookseller's.

I had feared that Jeremiah might not see us, but he was outside the tavern when we passed. He even touched his hand to his hat. A smile might have betrayed me and I know for certain that a flush lit my cheeks.

There were several customers at the store when we entered. I tried to be as unobtrusive as I could, but when I asked for *Aeneid,* I felt as if I had shouted my request.

"*Aeneid*?" Did he have to repeat it? "Let me see . . ." I watched as he tapped several books on the spine. "Ah! Here it is."

Pretending to admire its cover, I turned it over to look at its back. When the bookseller returned to help one of his other customers, I slipped my message inside the leaves. When I felt enough time had passed, I laid it on the counter and smiled my thanks at the man.

Doll lit into me the moment I joined her on the street. "Now. We going right back to the house and you going back to your bed. But the next time you get up, you gots to get your father to stop doing all those things he been doing."

"What's he been doing?"

Her eyes flashed. "Only trying to help Davy and I do our jobs. He tried to serve

374

the mister and missus their dinners the other night. Only he broke Mrs. Pennington's good china — *again* — while he did it. And then Mister shouted at him that if he going to live in the house, he got to respect the way of the house."

"He's only doing what he does because he believes that thee — and all the others — should be freed."

"He entitled to his opinion, but he got no right to make life harder for us."

"He's not trying to make it harder! He's trying to make it easier." I put a hand up to my head as I spoke. That throbbing pain was returning.

"He's no servant, that's for sure. We had to re-do everything he been doing. It made the work twice as hard."

"I'm sure he didn't mean to."

"Don't matter what he mean. What matters is what is. You remember when he want to pay us all?"

I nodded.

"What do you think Mister did after that?"

It must have been something terrible from the way Doll was looking at me. "He did something?"

"He get after us about who it was complained to your father that we ought to get paid."

"But that was Father's own idea!"

"That's right. But that's not what Mister think. You tell your father to stop meddling in other people's work." She was shaking her finger at me. "It's not right."

"He didn't mean to meddle. He was only trying to do his fair share. Everybody's work increased when we moved in." I knew Father's ways were wearing on Uncle Edward's nerves, but I didn't understand why Doll seemed so set against him. He was only trying to help them.

"We don't need no more slaves. We got enough slaves already. He got to mind his own work while we mind ours."

"I didn't realize —"

"That's how you folks always are. You look at us and you think we poor Negroes. That we don't know what we want. Well, we people too! And it don't help to have you folks pretend to be something you not. You be who you are and we be who we are. Sometimes you can't do for others. They got to figure out how to do for themselves."

We walked on in silence while I considered her words. I came to the conclusion that she didn't know what she was talking about. How could any slave not want help? How could any person not want to be freed?

34

JEREMIAH

Thank you, God!

I'd seen Hannah pass on the street three days before. Though the Negro woman had carried her basket, she'd left no message at the bookseller's. If truth be known, I'd almost forgotten to go to the bookseller's altogether, so pleased was I to see her out walking. Polly had told me she'd recovered, but I hadn't dared to believe it until that moment.

And now she had passed again. And smiled. At me.

I waited until she had gone and then returned to the bookseller's. Asked for *Aeneid.*

"Don't know why it should be so popular today." He took it down from a shelf and slid it across the counter toward me.

"I've always been partial to the Greeks."

He watched me as I turned the pages. I could feel the message, but I couldn't take it while he stood there. I flipped past it.

"It's a very fine volume."

"Indeed, it is. You wouldn't happen to have the *Iliad*?"

"No. Sold my copy the day before yesterday."

"How about . . . how about . . ." What? What could I possibly ask for? "Do you have anything by Homer?"

"I do, in fact. I just . . ."

As he turned around to look, I plucked Hannah's message from the pages. Dropped it into my pocket.

The bookseller laid a volume by Homer on the counter.

I picked it up and admired it long enough not to be rude. Set it down beside *Aeneid*.

"Not to your liking?"

"Perhaps another day. For now, I'll just take the *Aeneid*."

As soon as I gained the privacy of my room, I took the message from my pocket. Read it once. Then again.

Is there any possibility to delay the escape?
The Pilgrim's Progress

If the prisoners wanted to be captured!

Or be placed on a prison ship instead. The British would not evacuate the city before the Meschianza. That much was certain. But I did not know how long they would stay after the new general took command.

I sighed as I took up a piece of paper. Tore a corner off the sheet. Wrote a message back.

No.
Pamela, or Virtue Rewarded

I did not have to pass the message up to headquarters. There was only one answer to give. And he would have said it just the same as me. The men would simply have to dig faster.

As I came down the back stair, I heard a commotion in the kitchen. I veered toward the public room to avoid it, but the cook's voice made me stop. "I've had about enough of you as I'm prepared to take!"

She was probably yelling at her daughter again. She wasn't the hardest working server I'd ever hired, but she certainly wasn't the worst.

"Weren't you I came to talk to anyway!"

But — That wasn't the girl's voice. It was Bartholomew Pruitt's. I reversed my steps and went toward the kitchen. The cook had the boy by the ear and she was giving him a good shake.

"Here now!" I'm afraid I was none too kind in my tone.

As she let go the boy's ear, he ran toward me. "It's Ma. She's gone and died and now they're turning Fanny and me out of the place."

"Who is?"

"Those redcoats. They say they're going to tear it down to burn."

That's about all it was fit for. "Where's Fanny?"

The cook closed the distance between us, threatening Bartholomew with her spoon. "She's out in the back with that brat of hers. Like no good girl should be!" Her pronouncement on the matter was punctuated by the shake of her spoon.

I leveled a look at her. "The Pruitts are family friends, and their misfortunes need no comment from you."

"I'll not have my kitchen dirtied by the likes of them."

"Mrs. Phippen, your food is abominable and your daughter is lazy. If you don't find things to your liking here, then please don't feel obligated to stay."

"If you don't like my cooking, you might

of said so before now." She pulled her apron off, stepped to the door, and yelled for her daughter.

The girls came slinking through the door from the hall.

"If we're not appreciated here, I'll take us off. I won't stay where I'm not wanted." But she did not actually leave. I suppose she thought I might change my mind if I had a chance to think things over. All her delay brought was time for me to calculate her pay. And her daughter's as well.

I showed them out the back door and then ushered Fanny in once they had gone.

Bartholomew took her by the hand and led her over to a stool. "He fired the cook for you. I told you he would help us!"

Fanny settled the babe on her lap as she looked at her brother in horror. "He fired — but —" She looked at me. "I didn't mean any harm. Bartholomew told me you would help us, but I didn't mean — I didn't know . . ."

The baby began to cry.

"I didn't mean to cause any trouble." She looked as if she was going to cry herself.

I hated it when girls cried. "The cook had been working herself out of a job for a while." That's why City Tavern had been doing such brisk business. Though I hadn't really much cared until I saw her scolding the boy. But now I was a tavern owner with no cook to run my kitchen. And no daughter to wait on the customers.

"You need to feed it." Bartholomew directed the pronouncement toward his sister as if he was knowledgeable about such things. "She needs to feed it." He was looking at me now as if he expected me to do something about it.

"Fine."

"She needs a place to do it."

"To . . ." Oh. Oh! I strode toward the office to grab my ring of keys. Gave them over to the boy. "Show her up the stair. To the fourth room on the right."

It wasn't long before Bartholomew came right back down. "Fanny told me to ask you what I can do."

"What you can do . . . with what?"

"She says the cook probably left before she'd made supper. So she told me to let you put me to use."

"Well . . ." I surveyed the mess that had been left behind. Most certainly Mrs. Phippen had been in the process of making something, but I had no way of saying what it was. "I suppose there's something to be made here."

We were still staring at the pots and pans

and sundry ingredients when Fanny joined us. The babe was all smiles now. "Is there something to be seen here or is there supper to be made?" Fanny handed the baby to her brother and tied on the apron that Mrs. Phippen had discarded. "Looks to me like she was going to make a stew, though she's a bit thin on the meat. Bartholomew? Put that baby down in that basket over there. Then chop me up these onions."

Fanny bossed her brother around with such aplomb that I didn't see any need to stay. I took the daybook from the barkeeper and had a look. Asked him to write up the bill of fare for the night on the slate. Helped pour some drinks when he got busy. And after a while, John arrived with his coterie of Meschianza organizers. He came up to order a round of drinks. Planted an elbow on the bar and leaned close when the barkeeper went to deliver it.

"I need to beg a favor. And I wouldn't ask if it weren't absolutely necessary."

I raised a brow.

"We've spent all of the money brought in from our subscribers. And all the money raised through tickets. Those buntings and flags and costumes cost a small fortune!"

Just as I had imagined they would.

"The problem is, we're only half done

planning the banquet."

"And?"

"And I'm in desperate need of a supplier for the wine."

How kind of him to provide me with exactly the entrée I had been looking for. "I'm pleased you thought to ask."

"You . . . are?"

"Indeed I am."

"I've nothing to pay you with. That's the other problem."

Ah, but that's where he was wrong! There was one thing he had which I desperately needed. "I think we can come to terms."

I wrote up an order for the fete's wine. *And* secured an invitation for myself and a guest. No one could accuse Jeremiah Jones or Hannah Sunderland of having anything to do with a prison escape if we were attending the party of the year the night that it happened.

I didn't think to check back with the kitchen until after business had slowed. I hadn't heard any complaints about the food and I was starting to hunger for some myself. As I stepped through the door, Bartholomew gave me a fierce look and jerked his head toward the basket where the baby was sleeping.

Fanny dished me up a plate.

I took it out into the back even though I was more than certain both Bartholomew and Fanny had eaten their fill tonight. It wasn't half bad. In fact, I could honestly say that it was quite good! I needed a cook. They needed . . . everything. Maybe we could come to an agreement.

As I was working over what that might be, I heard the door open. Heard the padding of feet against the earth. Bartholomew soon sidled up to me. "Fanny told me to ask, did you want us to come back tomorrow."

I put my plate down. Looked at him. "When was it that your mother died?"

"Back a week ago. Or so."

"And you didn't tell me? I might have been able to do something about your place."

He shrugged.

"Did you have her buried?"

"The rector did. At potter's field, in Southeast Square." He kicked at a stone. "Did you want us back then? In the morning maybe?"

"Back? Are you going somewhere?"

He shrugged.

"You can stay up in that room I showed you earlier. If you want." I was making more money than I had a right to be. And the Pruitts — what was left of them — had

385

nothing at all.

"I suppose I could ask Fanny if she wants to."

"I'm stuck without a cook. I could pay her what I paid Mrs. Phippen. And I could pay you what I paid her daughter."

"You paid her daughter? But she hardly —"

I ignored him. "And you could take that room upstairs, the two of you, as your own."

He thought on it for a minute or two. "You'd have to give us board as well."

"I suppose I could do that."

"And I won't chop onions and such forever."

"No. You probably wouldn't."

"Just so we're agreed."

"I think we're agreed. Why don't you go tell your sister?" I could see her peering out at us through the doorway. I let Bartholomew go ahead, lingering to collect my plate and my spoon. As I neared the door, I could hear them.

"He says he'll let us stay!"

"Truly?"

"As long as you cook and I help. And we can have that room upstairs."

The silence that followed was so long that I began to worry, but as I stepped up onto the stair, I could hear Bartholomew speaking. "It's fine. Everything's going to be fine now."

And I could hear Fanny weeping.

35
HANNAH

It was sixth day, the sky was clear, and there was a pleasant breeze. It was a fine giving day and yet Polly was crying as she entered the bedroom.

"What's wrong?"

"It's General Howe. He's decided to send men out into the countryside. And Major Lindley's to go with them."

I wondered if Jeremiah had heard about this. "I'm sure he's not leaving for good."

"It's just that Father finally agreed to let me attend a play. There aren't many more left this season, and Major Lindley was going to take me. But now we can't go!"

"I'm sure it wasn't meant for thy inconvenience."

"No. But given the chance, Father might change his mind. I hope they kill all those rebels! They're ruining all the fun."

That was a sentiment with which I could do nothing but disagree. "Kill all those rebels? My brother among them?" Someone ought to feel sorry for his death. Someone ought to be shamed by it.

A flush lit her cheeks. "Not him. I meant . . . the others. I don't see why they don't just give up."

"Because they'll be treated the same way as the prisoners at the new jail. Mocked for being colonials. Despised for having dared to resist the king. They can't give up." And I knew it now more than ever.

"They won't win. They can't. Not against the King's army."

To that I had nothing to say, because I feared the very same thing. I didn't see how they could win, but could quite vividly imagine many ways for them to lose. "I just wish . . ." There were no words for what I wished. I wished for a new earth, a place where people did not destroy themselves through violence. And I wished for a new heaven, one from which God would deign to speak.

"Anyone can see how this will end. And I wish it just would!" She slid a glance toward me. "Without any more people having to suffer."

Without any more people having to suffer.

All of the prisoners in Walnut Street Jail

suffered, though not all of them had died. Why had Robert had to die? And why hadn't I told Jeremiah? I'd almost done it. I'd almost written it on the note I'd placed in *Aeneid*.

So why hadn't I?

That was the puzzle.

The memory of Jeremiah's comfort that night down in the cellar had kept me calm through many a storm. The thought of his presence made me feel safe in this world where I feared I would never feel safe again. So why had I not told him?

Perhaps because of exactly those things.

I'd woken from the fever quite certain that he was sitting right beside me. When I'd discovered he was not there, when I'd cried, Mother and Father had assumed it had been for joy at being alive. I hadn't told them it was out of distress. I'd been so sure of his presence that his absence felt like being . . . abandoned.

The fever had changed everything.

If he knew Robert were dead, he might force me from the plan altogether. The prisoners knew the date and time. There wasn't anything complicated about it. They would either be finished with the tunnel on the night of the Meschianza and they would escape . . . or they would not.

But I could not allow Jeremiah to dismiss me. There was too much left undone and too much that was still unresolved in my heart. And until I arrived at some sort of solution, I would not be set aside.

During dinner that afternoon, Davy came into the dining room, walked up to Uncle, and held out a silver tray. Uncle took an envelope from it and then set it on the table beside his plate and continued eating.

Polly's face was a tempest of emotions. Finally she put down her fork and her knife and pushed away her plate. "Aren't you going to open it, Father?"

He looked at her over the rim of his goblet. "Later. After we're done with dinner."

"But it might be something important."

"Even important things can wait for cook's pudding."

Polly began to say more but was silenced by a look from her mother. She poked at her food in a desultory manner for the rest of the meal, sliding dark looks at her father as she did so.

After the dessert had been served — and eaten — and after the table had been cleared, Uncle took up the envelope. He bowed it back and forth between his hands.

Polly watched with impatience clearly written upon her face.

Finally he asked Davy to bring him a knife. After prying off the wax seal and opening the envelope, he pulled a card from it. He read it and then frowned, turning it over and then back again.

"What does it say?" Polly nearly shrieked the question.

"It's an invitation."

"To what?"

"Tsk." Aunt Rebekah admonished her with a glance. " 'Tis none of your business, Daughter, I'm sure. And in any case, 'tisn't proper to conduct business at dinner."

"It's not business. Papa said it was an invitation."

"Which is none of your business." She said the words with a smile that brooked no reply.

"I don't see why Papa wouldn't speak of it." Polly was complaining as we climbed the stair that night to bed. She'd been disagreeable all afternoon.

"If it wasn't meant for thee . . . ?"

"It was." She was both definite and firm in her opinion.

"How can thee know it?"

"It was from Major Lindley. An invitation

to his Meschianza. That fete for General Howe."

"But how can thee be so certain?"

"He told me he was going to send it. And Peggy Shippen received her invitation this morning. If Papa didn't tell me, it's because he hasn't decided yet whether I should go. I'm going to have to make him understand that it's imperative."

Polly launched her campaign the next morning as we were all sitting in the parlor with our handiwork. "Did you know that Major Lindley is the third cousin to the Earl of Warwick?"

Aunt Rebekah looked up from her work. "Is he, dear?"

"His family has a country seat in Wiltshire."

"Do they?" Aunt embroidered on for several minutes while Polly fairly boiled with impatience. Finally, Aunt looked over at Polly and smiled. "I'm sure it can't be nearly as lovely as the Fairmonts' country home down near Germantown. Or the Mortons'."

The Fairmont and Morton sons had joined the Queen's Rangers just that autumn.

"It's an *ancestral* home." Polly spoke the words through her teeth.

"Perhaps when the major retires out of

the military, he'll finally be able to return to it. Life as an officer is not as genteel as it might seem." She set down her work, directing her full attention to her daughter. "It's not all picnics and plays and dancing."

"Of course it isn't."

"I don't want you to get the wrong impression of military men."

"I haven't."

Aunt took her work back up. "Good."

It was plain to me that neither of them believed the other. Polly suddenly uttered a cry and popped her finger into her mouth.

"What's come over you, child? Where's your thimble?"

She shrugged.

"If your head is in the clouds now, how am I ever going to get any work out of you once I tell you that you've been invited to that fete the officers are all carrying on about?" Her eyes were on her handiwork, though she shot a glance at her daughter in between stitches.

"And . . . ?"

"And . . . your father and I have decided that you may go."

Polly leaped to her feet with a cry, letting her embroidery go flying. "Oh! Oh! I must . . . I must . . . go to the mantua-maker! For a new gown!"

"That's the best part about it. And the thing which convinced your father to accept. The gown is to be provided."

Mother and I exchanged a look. It sounded strange in the way of customs to accept such a gift from a man to whom one was not wed.

36
JEREMIAH

I sat in my bedroom Monday morning, staring at the message the egg-girl had passed me.

Army expected to leave soon. All prisoners to be placed on ships. Expand plans to include more men.

So . . . John hadn't been lying. The British were planning to leave and they were going to place the prisoners on ships. Poor wretched souls. If jail meant risk of life, prison ships were an immediate death sentence. No one ever left them except in shrouds. Of course General Washington wanted to expand the escape plans. But the prisoners were confined to cells; it wasn't as if we could just invite more people to come along. It wasn't worth risking the integrity of the plan in order to include more men. At this point it was doubtful whether any would escape at all.

The more I thought about it, the more only one solution seemed possible. I could not, in good conscience, reply in the negative without at least trying, though I was not even sure, in fact, that I wanted my idea to work. If it did, then I would be risking everything I had come to hold dear.

I surprised Hannah on Saturday by meeting her in the middle of the street and walking alongside her as if we had chanced upon each other while walking in the same direction. The slave that accompanied her fell back to trail us.

She looked at me askance. "Is there something wrong?"

"I have to ask you something, and I want you to say no."

"Do thee fear that I will say yes?"

Yes. I did fear it. But duty required me to ask in spite of my personal sentiments. "I need you to bribe the guard at the jail."

Her eyes widened. Her face paled. "No."

I closed my eyes in relief. Now I could say that I asked, could say that I tried. And in truth, it could not be accomplished. Though why I was worrying so much about telling the truth, I had no idea.

"Why?"

My eyes snapped open. "Why what?"

"Why do thee want me to bribe the guard?"

"We've heard the men are to be placed on ships. Soon. General Washington wants more of them to be able to escape. The only way to do that is to convince the guard to open up the cells. Let more men than just Robert's escape."

"But it's not clear yet that any *will* be able to escape."

"I know it."

She was silent for several steps. "They're to be placed on ships?"

"Aye." I did not like the things I saw taking shape behind her eyes. "But —"

"And thee think the guard can be bribed."

"It's very dangerous. Too dangerous! Because if he can't . . ." If he couldn't, then he would turn Hannah over to General Howe. And if Hannah was betrayed, then it was only a matter of time before she'd tell them the whole entire truth. I knew her; she could not — would not — lie. "Forget I asked."

"I'll do it." Her eyes had gone so dark that I could not see into the depths of them, and her face had nearly gone white.

Dash it all! "I told you to say no!"

"I'm saying yes."

"You can't say yes. I wouldn't have asked you if I thought you'd say yes."

"Thee asked me because thee could not bear to tell the general no. And thee knew it was the right thing to do. If thee are going to start telling the truth, thee must start with thyself."

"Say no."

"I can say nothing other than yes. And thee would do the same, Jeremiah. For those men, thee would do the same."

I reached out toward her but then stopped myself. I had no right. I had no right to ask of her any of the things that I had. "I don't want you to do it."

"I have to."

"God help us, Hannah, I never meant to get you killed."

"Thee wish me to do it this day?"

I wished her to do it not at all.

"We are very nearly there."

She was right. She was always right. I'd brought along some coin just in case. I slipped a purse into her basket along with a message. "There's ten shillings in there. Promise him ten more."

"And when he asks for the rest?"

"Tell him that he'll not get it until after the escape."

She nodded. Squared her shoulders. "I

must go." She turned and walked away, head held high. And it was all I could do not to call her back to me.

I could hardly sleep the next days for want of news. It was Monday again before I saw her walking down Walnut Street the same way she had dozens of Mondays before. As she passed by, I saw her head turn, the slightest of movements. Caught her gaze.

She stopped. And at the same time, I started toward her.

She began to walk once more.

I lengthened my stride in order to reach her. "Wait. Stop!"

A wiser man — a smarter one, in any case — wouldn't have said anything. Wouldn't have given any sign of notice at all. But I could not keep myself from reaching out toward her. I needed to know that she was truly well. That she hadn't been betrayed to Howe. And there was something I needed to say to her as well.

She stopped, though she gave the impression of wanting to hop away, like some bird sitting on the thinnest of branches.

The Negro woman who always accompanied her had stopped as well. And she was giving me no little warning from her wrath-filled dark eyes.

"If it's about thy message, I delivered it. And I secured an arrangement about the other matter." She stepped closer. Close enough that I could smell her scents of lavender and lemon balm. And read the anxiety in her eyes. "The guard is in agreement."

"It's not about the message." It was about . . . me.

"Then what is it?" She was looking past me, down the street. And then she turned and looked up it, toward the jail. "I must not be seen speaking with thee."

"You're right." I took her by the elbow and pulled her toward the tavern.

"But I can't just — !"

"The easier you come, the less people will notice."

"I'm forbidden to —"

"Who gives a horse feather about your father and his proprieties! He's left his son to rot in that jail, and you're worried about disobeying him?"

She'd gone so pale I was frightened she would swoon. Apparently the slave woman was too, for she took hold of Hannah's other elbow. "Let's . . ." I couldn't take her into the tavern, much as she needed a restorative of whiskey. "Help me take her around to the kitchen."

By the time we reached it, color had

begun to come back into her face. But still she leaned on me.

"Fanny!"

Bartholomew's sister turned from the fire where she was stirring a kettle. "Mr. Jones?"

"Bring me a bottle of whiskey!"

The slave woman had pulled a stool away from the heat of the fire, but even as she pushed her down into it, Hannah was brushing her hands away, trying to stand up.

Fanny had returned. "Is it for — ?" She held it out in the direction of Hannah.

I nodded, gesturing for her to serve it.

At Fanny's approach, Hannah looked up, ceasing her struggles with the slave woman. Her eyes grew wide as she looked at Fanny and then she dropped to the floor in a dead faint.

"Was that . . . Fanny Pruitt?"

The slave woman wrung out a cloth and laid it across Hannah's forehead. I'd had Bartholomew help me take Hannah upstairs, where we'd placed her in my bed. The boy was standing, even now, over by the door, biting at his lip.

"Is it the fever?" I asked the slave woman because she was the only person who seemed to know what to do with her. Hannah had been pale before she'd fainted, but now she looked flushed. "Has it returned?"

Hannah's eyes sought mine. "Was that Fanny?"

I nodded.

She closed her eyes. Though she made no sound, tears began to slide down her cheeks. "You know Fanny?"

She nodded as her chin crumpled.

"But how do you know her?"

"My —" Her words broke off into a wail.

The slave woman knelt down and gathered Hannah to her chest.

"How does she know her?" The Pruitts weren't Quakers and they hadn't been nearly grand enough to mix with people like the Sunderlands. "Where did they meet?"

The slave woman glared at me. "Why does it matter where she know her? Don't you know how the heart sound when it breaks?" She patted Hannah's head as it lay against her shoulder.

"I didn't — I mean —" I didn't understand anything. At all.

Eventually Hannah stopped crying and the woman stopped clucking. Sometime during all the turmoil, Bartholomew had fled. I wished I could follow him. But it was my fault Hannah was here in the first place. And there was still a mystery to be solved.

Hannah sat up, used the cloth to clean away the remnants of her tears, and then pushed away from the bed. "Thank thee, Jeremiah. Thee have been very kind to me." She nodded, not quite meeting my eyes as she walked toward the door.

Wait just a — ! "But how do you know her?"

She cast a glance in my direction which promptly fell toward the floor. "My father used to employ her."

Her father . . . used to . . . "And then, when she was discovered to be with child, he turned her out."

Her gaze crept up to meet mine. "Yes."

"Did you know her mother was dying?"

"No."

"Do you know how she and her brother have survived these past months?"

"No."

"Do you have any idea at all what it's like to live in squalor, at the pleasure of the British Army? And be turned out of your hovel of a home simply because your mother has died? Because someone needs your house for firewood?"

"No! But I know that my brother —" She bit the end off her sentence. Seemed to swallow it.

"Your brother what?"

404

She didn't want to answer me. I could tell by the fury that clouded her eyes. But finally, she did. "Fanny was the reason my brother joined the patriots. And Fanny . . ." Her chin had begun to tremble once more. *"Fanny . . ."* She stopped speaking. Took in a deep breath. "Fanny is the reason I supported him."

"The same Fanny that your father deemed too dissolute to employ?"

"I would have kept her, but it wasn't my decision to make."

"What I can't understand is why you're so set on obeying a man you seem to disagree with as a matter of course."

"What does it matter if I — ! Thee just don't —"

"Don't even think of telling me that I don't understand."

"Thee don't. I am not my father!"

"And I am not —" The man I wished I was.

The slave woman waded into the middle of our discussion and stood there, hands at her hips. "If you don't stop all this cater-fussing, I'm going to take you both by the ear! Now. You be nice." She admonished Hannah with a shake of her finger. Then she turned to me. "And *you:* You be good! I

405

going to be standing right out there. In that hall."

Hannah gasped and started toward her. "But thee can't — don't go! Thee are supposed to stay with me."

"Sometimes people gots to say things to each other that ain't for nobody else to hear." She speared me with a look as she said it. "So you just get on with the getting on with it so we can get on with the doing of something else. I got work to do. And you . . ." She turned and leveled a look at Hannah. "You got places to visit."

We stared at each other, across the expanse of my room, as the slave marched out the door. And then I started to work on closing the distance between us. "For a Quaker, you sure have a lot to say."

"It's because thee have a lot to learn, Jeremiah!" She didn't back away, but she didn't move toward me either.

"I thought you people were supposed to be kindhearted and gentle-minded."

"And I thought thee were supposed to be —"

I took one more step closer.

"I thought . . ."

"Yes?"

"I thought thee were the enemy."

"I'm a friend. The only one you have."

406

"But there's no . . . there's no peace when I'm with thee. Thee bring turmoil like a cloud brings rain. And I can't think. I can't hear. I can't —"

"Hannah."

"Yes?" It sounded like a sob.

"Hush. Be still."

"I — can't!" It *was* a sob. A sob of pure frustration. And she passed it on to me as she grabbed hold of my coat with one hand and wrapped her other arm about my waist.

I kissed her temple. Inhaled her heady scent of lavender and lemon balm. "You've the heart of a patriot inside you. You know there's great injustice here. And isn't your God the God of justice and mercy?"

"It feels —"

"It feels like rage. It feels like anger."

"It feels *wrong*."

I pressed her head against my good shoulder. Mostly so I wouldn't be tempted to shake her. "It's everyone else in that blasted Meeting of yours that's wrong. You're the one who's right!"

"But how do thee know? How can thee be sure?" She pushed away from me just enough to be able to look at me.

"Because I know you." I took up her hand. If she would only believe the truth of what I had just told her.

She didn't want to believe me. I could see it. And I also witnessed the moment when she changed her mind. "There's only the two of us then against the entire British army."

"In my mind, that's just enough."

She smiled. A small smile that quivered as it curved across her face. It made me want to kiss her.

Kisses.

Why was it that my body remembered so many things that I longed to forget? Fingers that dug furrows through my hair. The scorch of stolen kisses. Sighs that had risen, unbidden, at my touch. There were some things a man could never forget. And it was useless to try. It just gave the memories life. So I tried to talk myself out of the scent of lavender and the feel of Hannah in particular.

She was not meant for me.

She was probably already promised to some broad-brimmed, peace-minded Friend. Someone who never raised his voice and would never think to shake sense into anyone. Someone who would probably never know just what a treasure he had married.

Which was all the better for me.

I didn't need a woman telling me what to do. Or how to act. Or what to believe about God. I didn't need a woman looking me straight in the eyes or poking at my arm or telling me I was wrong about nearly everything I'd ever thought was true. I didn't need a woman. And I definitely didn't want one touching me.

The only problem was, I didn't believe myself.

I knew I was lying.

37
HANNAH

I sat in Polly's room on seventh day, drenching myself in the bright sunlight, feeling as if the world might one day right itself. And then Polly came clattering through the door, trailing exuberance behind her.

"It's arrived!"

"I'm not quite certain I —"

"My costume — for the Meschianza! You really must see it." She turned toward Jenny, her constant shadow, gesturing for help with removing her gown. "It's a polonaise with sashes and bows and fringe and spangles!"

Jenny placed the costume on the bed with great care and then helped Polly from her gown. As soon as she was freed, my cousin tore the string from the package and ripped open the paper.

"Help me put it on!" She nearly flung it into the enslaved woman's hands in her haste.

I rose and helped Jenny sort out how it

was meant to be worn. We each took one side and helped Polly into it. She danced across the room and then stood looking at herself in the wall glass, twisting and turning, trying to see all parts of herself at once. "What do you think of it?"

"I can't quite say . . ."

"I know — I don't have the words either!"

It wasn't that I didn't have the words; I just didn't want to say them. The costume was so spectacularly extravagant that it was almost indecent. At its most basic layer, it was made of white satin. But there were sashes tied up at the waist, which hung quite low and dripped with tassels, and there was fringe . . . and everything else she had promised. And the whole was topped with an incredible gauze turban of the worst taste, decorated with even more tassels and feathers and a veil which could not even begin to hope to hide it all.

That afternoon I visited the jail as was my custom, but there was a woman sitting on the guard's lap when I arrived. She seemed in no hurry to leave it.

The guard didn't even have the grace to be shamed. "This is my . . ."

"Cousin." She looked at me with a brazen stare.

411

I set a wedge of cheese on the table. He grabbed at it and took a bite. And then he passed it to his . . . cousin . . . rather reluctantly.

"The cell?"

"Hmph?"

"I would like to be shown to the cell."

He rose, spilling the woman from his lap. But instead of walking to the door the way he usually did, he pushed her toward me. "Why don't you search her?"

She eyed me and then looked at him. "You want me to do what?"

"Search her. You know. For forbidden things." He was looking at me, a smile playing at his lips. "Maybe she's a spy."

The woman looked just as aghast at the idea as I was. She turned around to face him. "You didn't pay me for that!"

"It's something we're ordered to do. Everyone visiting the prisoners is to be searched. Although, now that I think on it, I've just remembered that no one is supposed to be visiting the jail."

I tried to smile and I tried not to think about the bag of grain and the other things that I was hiding beneath my skirts. "After all this time? Surely if I were going to smuggle something in, I would have done it by now."

"Everyone is to be searched."

I couldn't very well argue that I wouldn't be visiting much longer. There was nothing to do but comply . . . and pray. I held out my basket.

The woman lifted the cloth. Pushed her hand into it and felt around. When she pulled it out, her fist was closed around a roll. She smiled and then bit into it. "I searched. She isn't taking anything in."

"I meant a search of her person."

"Here?" She plopped down onto his lap and wound an arm about his neck. He succumbed to her kisses for a moment. But then his eyes popped open and he saw me watching them. He pushed the woman from his lap again. "A real search."

She frowned, put a hand to his chest, and pushed away from him. Then after casting a look back at him, she walked over to me. "Take off the cloak, then."

I set the basket on the ground, pulled at the ribbons which bound the cloak at my throat, and offered it to her. She pointed to my pocket, so I offered it to her as well. As she felt about inside of it, I blessed Doll for her foresight in making me a secret pouch. Throwing my pocket back at me, the woman gave me a scornful glance from head to toe. "She's one of them Quakers. Doesn't even wear a hoop. She can't hide anything under those skirts. There's no room." She gestured toward my hat, holding a hand out for it.

I pulled the pin from it and then removed it and placed it into her hands.

She turned it over and poked around inside, feeling beneath the brim. "Nothing there neither."

"Try her shoes."

I bent to pull them from my feet, hoping the outline of the blade of a hoe wouldn't show through the folds of my gown. I handed them to her, waiting as the cold of the bare earth pressed through my stockings, into the soles of my feet.

She ran a hand around inside them. She turned them over, pulling at my plain silver buckles. "Nothing there." She tugged at the buckles once more.

I held out a hand. "May I . . . ?"

She gave the shoes back to me.

The guard was looking at me, confusion crimping his brow. "There has to be something."

There was of course something. There were several things. There was a note beneath the folds of my polonaise and some char cloths tucked underneath my garter. There was a bag of grain. I'd pulled a pair of breeches on beneath my hose and another pair was wrapped around my waist. There was also a hoe dangling beneath the skirts she had declared too modest to hide anything at all.

"There's nothing." The woman had given up the search and flounced back to the guard's lap. He frowned as he caught her about the waist, but he gestured toward the door.

I knocked upon it and sent up a swift prayer of thanks as it opened.

Once I gained admittance to the cell, my heart quailed within me. More than half the men were lying prostrate on the floor.

"Another bout of the putrid fever." William Addison said it with no little regret coloring his voice.

Again! And with so little time left. "The tunnel . . . ?"

He shrugged. "We're trying. If only we could put it off another day or two."

"Thee can't. If thee cannot get out that night, then thee must not go at all. General Washington's men would not know to expect thee at the lines."

"We're trying." He was looking around at his stricken men.

I reached out and gripped his hand. "Thee must succeed. There will be no other chance." I unfastened my cloak and handed it to him. He used it to shield me from sight as I divested myself of all I had smuggled in. I handed the message to him.

He read it and then held it out to me. "Do you know what it says?"

"I do not."

"Read it."

Once escaped, proceed directly to lines. No sick or lame.

"He would have me leave my men here?" He'd taken a step closer as he whispered.

"If thee take them, then thee are sure to be caught. And it will go worse for thee than if thee had stayed."

"But if I don't take them, then it will go worse for them than if they had been caught. And most of those men have been working on the tunnel."

He had forgotten to whom he was speaking. He was talking to me, who had taken their cause as my own and sacrificed my brother to them. I understood the cruel irony and the tragedy of General Washington's orders, but was it worth the lives of a handful of men to keep several dozen others from escaping? "General Washington has planned a disruption after midnight. He will keep the British busy as long as he can, but thee must make haste to cross the lines. Once the disruption is silenced, it may well be too late to make it through."

"If we make it out of the city, then what are we to do in between our lines and theirs?"

I shrugged uncertainly. "Every measure has been taken in order to help thee, but it will up to thee to succeed."

"You want me to send my men through that tunnel not knowing what awaits us on the other side?"

"Thee would rather take thy chances and stay here?"

We could hear the guard begin his walk toward us, keys clanking against his thigh.

William Addison looked once more at his men. Cringed as one sat up and hacked into the straw. Closed his eyes and sighed. "No. I'd rather die as one free."

When I was shown back into the guard's room, it was to find the woman gone and the man staring at me, an avaricious gleam in his eye.

"I thought we had an arrangement."

He shrugged. "We did. We do. But why can't I look for a safer means of investment?"

"Thee took the money. I expected thee to be honest in the doing of it."

"That's the thing about dealing with a cheat, miss. We aren't known for our honesty."

"It's a shameful trick thee tried to play."

He looked abashed, but only for a moment. "Can't blame a man for trying."

I threaded my arm through Doll's as we walked away from the jail. I wanted to be able to talk to her without anyone overhearing. "They're going to escape soon. On the night of the eighteenth."

"During that big party everyone talking about?"

I nodded. "After midnight the patriots are going to create a disturbance to give the prisoners a chance to get through the city. Thee should join them. If thee can make it to the lines, thee can be free."

She looked at me with such disappointment that shame began to creep over me. "And what would I do then?"

What would she do? "Anything thee wanted."

"And where would I go?"

"Any place thee wanted to."

"And what would all those folks on the other side of the lines do with me? A Negro woman with no work to do and no master?"

"Thee could find work."

"Not anywhere around here. And Mister Pennington, he'd bring me back as soon as he found me. He'd have me whipped for sure. And what's a woman my age want with freedom? Why you want me to leave everything behind? I got my husband here and my children. They ten miles away, but at least I can see them now and then. If I go, I can't never come back. Why you want me to give them all up?"

"Thee are married? Thee have children?"

She laughed, but there was no mirth in it. "You think I'm just the person that you see?" She eyed me. "You did! That's what you thought. You thought I just the person you needed me to be. Good ol' Doll. Always there when I need her. Don't give her no mind when I don't. Well, that's just fine. That's what I got to be. That's what kept me my position at Pennington House. Being the Doll that everyone want me to be. Even after Mister sold my family up to Germantown."

"I just — thee don't want to be free?"

"Free to do what? Wander about the colony, begging food and scraps, aching for the folks I left behind? Don't sound like no freedom to me."

419

"But God made thee just the same as me. And thee deserve freedom just the same as me."

"I believe that. I surely do. I am free. I free to do what you say: free to escape. And I free not to. You just as bad as all the other folks, telling me what I got to do. The only thing Doll got to do is find a way to live in this world. Just the same as you. You talk so much about making everybody free, but you don't understand. There's no use setting me free into a world where there is no freedom. You got to do more than help me escape. You got to make a world for me to escape to."

38

JEREMIAH

"The Penningtons are having a supper tomorrow and I've been invited."

I saluted John with my bowl of punch on Monday as we sat in front of an open window in the public room, enjoying the breeze blowing up from the river.

"And so have you."

"Me? I've been warned away from Miss Sunderland if you remember."

"I remember, but it seems as if Miss Pennington has forgotten. Or doesn't care. I'm sure you'll receive the invitation today. And really, it doesn't matter one way or another, because if the Penningtons have invited you, then the Sunderlands have nothing to say about it."

I didn't want to distress Hannah, but I did wish to see her. And I didn't care a whit about what that priggish father of hers would allow. And besides, it would be a great pleasure to inform him about what had happened to the Pruitts after he'd dismissed Fanny from his service.

John was watching me as I deliberated over the news. Suddenly his face split into a grin. "So you'll go, then."

"I'll go." Though the devil might hang me for it.

"And how is the tavern business, Mr. Jones?" Mrs. Pennington asked the question in between the first and second courses from her place at the foot of the table. She couldn't have offered a better opportunity for me to say what was on my mind. I inclined my head. Smiled.

"There's no finer tavern in the city!" John raised his glass in my direction.

I returned the favor. "Business has picked up considerably under the occupation, though I found myself short-staffed several weeks ago."

Mr. Pennington frowned. "Is the slave market not in operation?"

"I don't favor the use of the enslaved."

Mr. Sunderland cast a sharp glance in my direction.

Mr. Pennington scowled. "Another do-gooder, are you?"

"Everyone is entitled to their own beliefs." Mrs. Pennington frowned down the table at her husband.

"I've always thought that a person works harder when they're working of their own volition."

Mr. Sunderland was nodding strenuously. "Exactly so. There is that of God in everyone and no one should have the right to enslave any man."

"Or throw any woman out of service and into destitution when the cause is not her fault."

To my right, Hannah gasped. A cloud seemed to pass over Mr. Sunderland's face.

"In any case, I found myself without a cook and was happy to hire a pair — a brother and sister — who had been turned out of their home when their mother had died."

"Shame." Mrs. Pennington was too good to steer me in such useful directions.

"It was a shame. The sister had been in service elsewhere but was poorly used by a passing soldier."

Mrs. Pennington's smile seemed to wither as she glanced over at Polly and at Hannah. "I'm not sure that —"

"Her employer shoved her out the door, though her mother was dying and her brother could only find work as a messenger. A very great shame, don't you think,

Mr. Sunderland? Surely you agree with me. As a man who purports to see God in everyone. Or perhaps . . . perhaps there are people God favors a bit more than others. Perhaps He's more like us than one would think."

"I don't think —" He cleared his throat. "It's not normal, under the circumstances, to keep a girl like that in service."

"If you can't, then I can. She was pleased to find gainful employment once more. Fanny is her name. Fanny Pruitt, though I wouldn't expect you to be acquainted with her situation. No more than her former employer had been." I would never be invited back to Pennington House. I would never be granted permission to speak to Hannah again. But somehow that prospect did not bother me. I felt . . . free. And vindicated. And right.

As we passed from the dining room to the parlor after supper, John drew near. "What was all that talk about? I have to tell you, conversation on topics such as yours would be considered woefully impolite back in London."

"Here as well."

"What are you — ?" He broke off his inquiry as Miss Pennington came up and threaded her arm through his.

She smiled at me. "You're very wicked, you know."

I winked at her. I knew.

"Hannah is just over there." She nodded toward the corner. "And if you aren't careful, she may just slip up the stair before the dancing starts."

John sent me a quizzical glance, then allowed himself to be led into the parlor. I thought about excusing myself from the dance that would soon follow, but then decided it would greatly increase Mr. Sunderland's displeasure if I stayed. And especially if I kept myself close to fair Hannah's side. So I walked over to her and offered my arm.

"Was that necessary?"

"Are you asking as a scandalized guest or as a woman who told me not a week ago that she was not her father?"

She looked at me for a long moment and then placed her hand about my extended arm.

I could not help but grin at her. "I didn't arrange this meeting."

Her chin lifted. "Neither did I."

"Just so we're agreed on everything."

"I hardly think —"

"Good. Please don't. I doubt that your cousin's tricks will work after this. And I'd like to enjoy the evening without being browbeaten, berated, or otherwise scolded."

"I have never done any of those things to thee."

I raised a brow.

"I have, perhaps, strenuously . . . *encouraged* thee as unto righteousness. On occasion."

I offered her a chair and then sat in one beside hers. As the first dance began, I leaned toward her. "How close is the tunnel to being done?"

She pressed her lips together and shook her head as her gaze swept the room.

"None can hear us."

" 'Tis not that I fear being overheard. Not anymore. 'Tis that William Addison fears the tunnel may not be completed in time."

"Does he not understand the urgency?"

"Half his men linger at death's door from the fever." She moved to lay a hand on my arm, but then seemed to think the better of it. "He's doing all that he can."

"They've three weeks left. We must hope that they succeed. They have no other choice."

She laid a hand upon my arm at last. "Thee are troubled."

"Of course I'm troubled! It's one thing to have them escape the jail through a tunnel, but another thing entirely to help them escape the city. How am I going to get four dozen men through the lines unnoticed?"

Her gaze held mine for a long moment. "How *do* thee plan to do it?"

"I was going to have them pretend to be the militia. For surely the real militiamen will be called up at the first sign of the general's diversion."

She frowned.

"Do you have a better plan?"

"It's just . . . they have no shoes. And most of them don't even have breeches."

I raised a brow. No breeches? And she was visiting them? Weekly? "We'll just have to . . . clothe them."

"With what?"

What, indeed? How many men could we hope would escape? Three dozen? Four? Who had forty-eight pairs of breeches and forty-eight pairs of shoes to spare? The only people who suffered from abundance in this city were those with gold to spend. We sat there for some moments. She must have been contemplating the same gloomy thoughts as I, for a pallor had crept over her cheeks and her lips seemed to dip at the corners.

Something she had said earlier began to bother me. "What was it you meant about

427

not fearing to be overheard anymore?"

She started at my words. "I only meant that everyone who ought to know already does."

"And who *exactly* is that?"

"Well . . . Polly knows, of course. About my visits to the jail at least. And there's Doll. Thee have met her already. Whenever I leave the house, she's been told she has to go with me. So I had to tell her. And there's Betsy. She was practically promised to Robert before he left to join the patriots. And I needed her help one day to escape my mother. I had to tell her. And there's the guard at the jail."

"So you're telling me that half the city knows what we're about."

"Half the city? I did not say half the city. I said three people. Four . . . maybe five."

I was trying, with all that was in me, not to yell at her. I gritted my teeth. Took a deep breath in through my nostrils. I had clenched my hand so hard the one that was missing had begun to ache. "Spying is a very serious business. And the spies that are most successful are those who only reveal themselves to those who need to know. No one is actually supposed to be visiting the jail."

"As I told thee: They truly did need to know."

"Spies reveal themselves only to other spies. And I'm quite sure that Doll and Betsy and Polly are not spies."

"No."

"And you were compelled to tell them of your visits . . . why?"

"Are thee saying that thee had rather I lied to them?"

"What is so terrible about lying!"

She cringed as some of the guests on the dance floor turned in our direction.

I tried to smile. God help me, I tried. "You're already committing sedition and treason. You could be hanged three times over if any of the men are caught during the escape. I don't see any danger in a simple lie. Or half-truth even."

"The danger is that it's wrong. 'Tis a sin to lie."

"You seem to think that I'm quibbling. But your . . . your . . . *principles* have placed not only your life, not even my life, but the lives of all those prisoners in danger. When the men are found to have escaped, they'll remember that you visited. What if they betray you?"

"Doll and Betsy would never betray me."

"And how do you know that?"

"I just do."

"Dash it all! I don't want to hang from a

429

noose just because you're too pious to lie!"

"Thee must stop thy bullying!"

"I am not — !" I stopped. Took a deep breath. "I am not bullying. I am merely trying to convince you to be reasonable."

"When I look at the world we live in, Jeremiah, I see violence and hate and corruption. I see poverty and larceny and all manner of evil, but I do not see reason. Doll will keep quiet because no one would believe her if she tried to tell them. And Betsy will keep quiet because she loved Robert . . . loves him still."

Her eyes had suddenly gone sad, awash in unshed tears. But I could not let her sentiments sway me from my argument. "Love."

"Aye. *Love.*"

"If I could count the times women have told me they loved me and then decided to have nothing more to do with me —"

"I am not speaking of affection or flirtation. I am speaking of . . . of a love that means something. A love that means everything."

How I longed to believe in such a love. "So half the city knows of our plans and you say I must trust them because . . . because you trust them. Why, I ask, should I believe you?"

"Because thee need me, Jeremiah. Thee

430

must. Thee must believe me because thee have no other choice. We are both of us imprisoned to the other."

Hang the woman, she was right. I had no other choice. If the prisoners were to escape, it would be in spite of all the truth that was being told. And it would be orchestrated by the sorriest pair of spies that history had ever assembled.

"I will not lie for thee. Or for anyone else."

"Not even for that brother you so desperately wish to see freed?"

Her lips trembled. "Not even for him."

I felt myself then to be the bully that she had called me. "Just . . . try harder not to tell so much truth."

She was so infuriating!

And I still hadn't managed to purge her from my thoughts by the time I'd walked home from Pennington House and taken myself to bed. How could Hannah Sunderland be so brave and courageous and . . . and *pretty* . . . and not realize how astoundingly dim-witted she was being? So now there were Doll and Betsy and Polly to keep from being interrogated. As well as the prisoners at Walnut Street Jail.

Three more people. No. No, she'd said *four* more people. Or *five*.

It was no use. I got up and splashed water on my face by the dying fire's light, certain I wouldn't be able to sleep now. Not even if I'd wanted to. How could I when there were so many cursed people on which my fate — and the lives of the prisoners — depended?

What was wrong with Hannah that she couldn't understand the danger? I had tied myself to a maddening, exasperating, infuriating woman who would never learn how to be a spy.

But what if fortune smiled upon us and the prisoners did escape? What would the men do once they left the tunnel? The jail was at the wrong end of the city. They'd have to not only get past the British but walk five miles toward Germantown before they could be assured of encountering any allies. It was no good to tell them to construct the tunnel and then wash my hands of them once they'd escaped. Forty-eight people couldn't walk through the city without being noticed. Even in the dead of night.

I had to make a plan.

Perhaps I could persuade one of the night watchmen to our side. Especially since it was all but certain now that the British were going to leave. If the prisoners could disguise themselves as a citizen's militia . . .

perhaps.

There might just be a way.

I made it a point to look out for the watch-man. Began to give him drinks without marking them down to his account. When I thought him sufficiently amenable to per-suasion Thursday evening, I engaged him in conversation.

"So what are you going to do when the British leave?"

He sighed. "You don't think that's a rumor, then?"

"I think the army's ready to take up the fight again. They've been resting up all winter. And they can't fight the rebels from Howe's headquarters."

"No. I suppose not." He said it as if he was none too happy about the prospect. "Any word on if they plan to take along those that are loyal?"

"They've done it before." They did it when they'd been forced to leave Boston for Halifax.

"My wife has been after me to find room for us on one of those ships. I keep putting her off, but if you say they're planning to leave . . . ?"

"Come now. You think it will be as bad as that once they've gone?"

"Don't want to be here if those rebels take back the city again. They might not look too kindly on those who worked for the British while they were gone."

I frowned. He didn't sound as if he was cheering the return of the patriots. In fact, he sounded decidedly hostile toward them. I'd guessed wrong, and now I'd have to find another man. Another plan. And I'd less than two weeks' time to do it.

39
HANNAH

As the Meeting sat in silence on first day, waiting for God to speak, I slid my hands beneath my thighs so that I would not forget myself and draw attention where attention was not wanted. And I pressed my lips together so that I would not speak.

Remember those in prison.

Remember those in prison.

Remember those in prison.

I closed my eyes to try to stop the words, but still they resounded in my head. And when I opened my eyes, they fastened upon Jeremiah. To the great delight of some Friends, he had apparently decided to return to Meeting.

Between trying to ignore God and trying to ignore Jeremiah, my nerves were worn thin by the time Meeting ended. I tried to keep the whole of the women's side between myself and him as the Meeting emptied, but

435

soon there were just the two of us left in the room.

He nodded. "Another silent meeting."

"Yes."

"Surely you people must be thinking something while you're sitting here."

"We are."

"And what would that be?"

"Some of us pray. Some of us bring to mind the Scriptures. Some of us listen to our thoughts to try to discern if they're from the Spirit."

"And if you decide you've been given something to say, what would you do about it?"

"It depends on what that word is."

"So even if you think you've heard from God, you're not obligated to share it? If, as an example, it's not what the others want to hear? Or if you don't agree with it yourself?"

"It's not a debate, Jeremiah. 'Tis a Meeting. A Meeting to discern the will of God. How irresponsible I would be if I simply spoke every word that came into my mind!"

"No more irresponsible I suppose than if you did not speak those words that came into your mind. The ones you know that God has given you to speak."

How did he know my secret thoughts?

He leaned close. "What is it that you're

trying so desperately not to say?"

"How do thee — ?"

"Only a person who doesn't know you could fail to understand the look on your face."

I could not lie. I had never been able to lie. "Remember those in prison. Those were the words that I heard."

"That's it?"

I nodded.

"Remember those in prison. They hardly sound subversive."

"It is when the Yearly Meeting specifically prohibited ministering to the prisoners."

"Maybe the Yearly Meeting is wrong. Cunningham certainly couldn't have harassed the prisoners like he did if more people had remembered those in prison."

That was true. If more people had visited, then Cunningham's actions might not have been tolerated. "But thee don't understand how it is."

"Then explain it to me." There was no annoyance, no impatience in his voice.

I shook my head. It was no use.

"I want to understand."

"The prisoners in the jail are only there because of their rebellion against the king." I waited for him to interrupt with some vexatious tirade about the king's abuses, but he did not. "What moral purpose does it serve to allow them to escape the consequences of their choices?"

"Does the King have the right to starve them to death? To leave them for dead?"

"The Meeting refuses to believe that they aren't being fed." That was part of the problem. If only they would listen to the truth!

"But how would the Meeting look upon Captain Cunningham stealing the prisoners' food for profit? Or deliberately spoiling that which was intended for their mouths?"

"They would condemn it, normally."

"Normally."

"If the prisoners weren't rebels." That was the other part of the problem.

"So they condone the King's practices, but should the Continental Congress render British soldiers the same treatment, they would condemn it?"

"They would have to."

"I don't see anything very friendly about that, and it does not sound like justice to me. What's right ought to be right for any man. For every man."

I agreed. Though I did not want to, I agreed!

He looked at me, with something very much like compassion in his eyes. "Now what is it again that you don't want to be responsible for saying?"

"Remember the prisoners." Though it was a message that burdened my heart, it was a message not one of the Friends in Meeting would want to hear.

"Is it reasonable?"

I nodded.

"Is it honorable?"

"Yes."

"Then why won't you say it?"

I would not say it because I was afraid to.

What would happen if I said it?

I couldn't sleep that night for the questions that filled my head. I *could* say it. Of course I could say it. The thought was only three words long and people had said contrary things in Meeting before. They had been words that had changed everyone's mind on how things should be. And if the message was truly from God, then wouldn't people somehow realize it? What was so terrible about remembering prisoners?

Only the prospect that I might be disowned by the Meeting altogether.

In a religion that had little to do with politics, things had become very political indeed. I had been given a message I could no longer ignore. But it was a message no one wanted to hear.

As I lay there listening to Polly's deep breaths and soft snores, I considered whether I truly wanted to be part of a Meeting that turned its back on injustice. Whether I wanted to be part of a group that did not want to be reminded of the truth. I had a chance to do what was right, and I had no doubts about the message I had been given. But if the worst happened, if I were no longer allowed to be called a Friend, then what would I be?

By the next first day, my heart was no longer divided. I pushed to my feet at the earliest opportunity. I did not wish to wait even one moment longer. If God had given me a word, then there must be no delay in sharing it. As I stood on trembling legs, I found courage in Jeremiah's steady gaze. "Remember the prisoners." I sat.

There was silence for quite a while, but then there came a rustling from the men's side as someone stood. I closed my eyes as I waited to hear the voice speak.

"I fail to see the meaning of Friend Sunderland's words. Remember the prisoners? What is it that we're being asked to do?" The man sat.

A woman took his place. "God always

urges us to remember those in chains."

As she sat, Betsy's mother stood. "Those in chains for *His* cause, not the rebel's cause."

The man rose once more. "But isn't that verse from Hebrews? Doesn't it go on to say, 'Share the sorrows of those who are being mistreated'?"

From the facing bench, the recording clerk was nodding. "I agree with our Friend's statement. Share the sorrows."

The first man spoke again. "Perhaps that's what Friend Sunderland's words were meant to do: Spur us on to remembering to share each other's sorrows."

Though there were words being spoken at Meeting again, they were the wrong ones! I debated, while they talked, whether I ought to clarify my words. I closed my eyes and prayed for forgiveness and guidance. I ought to have spoken much sooner. Had I said the words when I had been given them, perhaps the Meeting might have accepted them without such confusion. By not giving them a chance to do so, I was a party to their sin. I closed my eyes and finally felt the quietness and peace that I knew was of God.

I was sick and in prison and you didn't visit me.

No. Please don't make me say those words. But how could I repent with one breath and then ask to be spared the work of repentance in the next?

Inasmuch as you did not do it to one of the least of these, you did not do it to Me.

Resigned to my duty, I opened my eyes with a sigh and then stood once more. " 'I was sick and in prison and you didn't visit me.' 'Inasmuch as you did not do it to one of the least of these, you did not do it to me.' What I said before: I meant that there were those who were sick and in jail in the city and not one of thee ever visited them. The captain charged with supervision of the jail sold some of the food meant for the prisoners and deliberately spoiled what was left. Had Friends been there, we might have prevented many deaths. 'Remember the prisoners' meant exactly that. Worse than forgetting them, we failed to remember them. I ought to have spoken this word sooner, but I did not do it. I was afraid to. And for that I beg thy forgiveness." I sat.

As words were spoken and opinions exchanged, I caressed the soft, worn wood of the pew. I gazed at the stark, plain walls. I looked at every beloved inch of that space, trying to engrave it in my memories, because I knew that I would never be coming back.

Father drew me into the parlor once we reached Pennington House. "I've been placed in a rather delicate situation. The elders want to know if thee have taken up the rebel cause."

"No." I was done with causes. I much preferred people to political positions.

"Then I must know what it was that thee meant to say this morning in Meeting."

"I said exactly what was meant."

"But then . . . it must not have sounded as thee meant it to." His voice was pleading.

"It sounded exactly as I meant it. I said what I meant to say."

"Thee know the position the Yearly Meeting took on the prisoners."

"I do. And I don't believe it was right."

"We couldn't just abolish the consequences of the prisoners' rebellion." He had come as close to arguing with me as he had ever done. And yet that same beseeching look was still resident in his eyes.

"The consequence of the Yearly Meeting's pronouncement was that the prisoners were thrown into a jail with no food, no blankets, and no fire. Another consequence was that the captain who was to have given them these things sold them all before they could ever reach the prisoners, and then placed the money into his own pocket. Most of the men inside that jail will die by illness or through starvation."

"How do thee know this?"

"I have visited them. Every week I have visited them."

"But thee must know that it was not right to help them. The consequence of their actions was that they committed themselves to the rebels' care. What else was to be done?" He sounded as if he truly wanted to know. "I thought . . . I thought they all needed to learn a lesson. I thought that . . . surely I didn't know . . ."

"I said what I meant. I'm sure the elders will have no choice but to counsel the Meeting to disown me. Especially when thee tell them I've been visiting the jail every week for five months now."

"But if they had been told what was happening . . . If thee tell them. Explain, maybe . . ." Beads of sweat were forming on his forehead.

"I'm leaving the Meeting. They don't even have to disown me."

"Thee can't just leave. Not over this. They didn't understand. No one understood."

"It's not because of the Yearly Meeting.

It's not because no one would visit. It's because none of thee truly wanted to know."

Polly was waiting for me at the top of the stair. She handed me a handkerchief.

I dabbed at my tears.

"Did you . . . leave your church?"

"I suppose I did."

"Don't worry. He'll see the error of his ways soon. My own papa always does."

I feared my father wasn't much like hers.

Her face had brightened. "If you aren't going to that church of yours anymore, does that mean you don't have to obey all those rules?"

"I . . . don't know." I hadn't thought that far ahead. The thought of not belonging to the Meeting was still so strange and new.

"Here. Come with me." She drew me down the hall and into her room. She flung up the lid of her trunk and pulled out the amaranth-colored gown, thrusting it into my arms. "You can have it."

"I don't . . . I can't . . ."

"Truly. Take it. It's last year's color anyway. I don't want it anymore."

"I don't know that I can —"

"Oh! I just realized. You can go to the theater with me now!"

"I don't think I want to."

"And you can dance!" She clapped her hands. "This is going to be so diverting. To catch you up on all the years you've missed!"

"I thank thee for thy interest in me. But my thoughts on those things haven't changed. I'm still the same person I was. Only . . . different." I was no longer part of a Meeting. I was alone.

She patted my arm. "Don't worry. Children are supposed to rebel against their parents. It's how we get what we want. Don't feel badly about it. Enjoy it." She pushed a set of bracelets past her wrist, checked her reflection in her hand mirror, and then flitted out the door, off on one of her endless excursions.

She was so insensible. And so young. And there was so much she did not comprehend. I only hoped that one day she would. Then she would realize that there was no enjoyment in this rebellion against everything my parents knew and were. There was only sadness.

40

JEREMIAH

"I need your help, Bartholomew." He was perched beside me that Monday evening at the well. We were eating supper together.

"That's what you pay me for, isn't it?"

"This has nothing to do with our agreement." And considering all that Fanny had been through, I wasn't quite sure I should be involving him in my plans. But I didn't have any other choice. "It could be very dangerous."

He didn't look impressed.

"It has to do with the soldiers."

That caught his interest. "Those lobsterbacks? Which ones?"

"Over at the barracks."

"What do you want me to do?"

"I need you to filch forty-eight of their uniforms and forty-eight pairs of shoes."

"Without being hanged for it? What's Fanny going to do if I end up dead?"

"I told you it was dangerous. But you

447

wouldn't have to do it alone. You couldn't. You'd need some of your friends from the alley to help you."

"They think I've gotten too good for them since we came here."

"I'll pay them. I'll pay you too. Extra. Half now and half when it's done."

"They'd probably do it for nothing. Just for spite. Those lobsterbacks are mean as the devil."

"Next Monday there's going to be a big party upriver."

"That messy-chanza?"

I nodded. "All the officers are going to attend. From the afternoon when it starts until it ends the next morning."

"All the rats are going to be away from the nest."

"That's right."

"Still doesn't mean the soldiers won't be in their barracks."

"Long about one of the clock, General Washington is going to make all the soldiers in the city rush for the lines."

He smiled. "Something like an attack? Is that what you're saying? The patriots are finally coming out of their camp?"

"Not a full attack. Just a disturbance. But when that happens, what do you think those soldiers at the barracks will do?"

"They'd report to the lines. And leave those barracks wide open and empty."

"Exactly. So, do you think you can get me those coats and shoes?"

"With a bit of help."

"I'd need you to collect them that night and then run them as quickly as possible to the wheelwright's yard at the corner of Walnut and Sixth Street."

"Why?"

"There will be a group of men there waiting for you."

He sent me a sly glance. "You're going to break some of those prisoners out of the jail, aren't you?"

He was too smart for his own good. "Why would you say such a thing?"

"Because there's no one supposed to wear a uniform but those soldiers. And the only reason someone else would wear one is to pretend like they were one. So the only reason you'd need forty-eight of them is if there was a group of men that —"

"Yes. I'm going to break some of those prisoners out." Although if he had seen through my plan so easily, the whole escape might be in danger of being discovered. Especially if a group of street urchins was going to come into it.

"That will be something to see!"

"I don't expect you to stay around to see it. I expect you to deliver the uniforms and shoes and then leave. Just as fast as you can." I counted ten shillings into his palm. And then watched him disappear into the night the way he used to. I was sending him back to the very alleys I'd rescued him from.

Forty-eight uniforms. Forty-eight pairs of shoes. Were the prisoners really so destitute as that? Because if any one of them got caught, it meant the lives of three women and a handful of boys.

God help us all.

That night I sat down to write my message to William Addison.

Plans fixed. Uniforms to be issued at blacksmith's yard. Once attired, proceed directly to lines.

If he were half the soldier he was rumored to be, then he would be able to divine what he was to do. They would have to be swift. I didn't know how long the diversion would last and it was possible that it could be over-run. In that case, time would be of the essence. There would be none to spare for those who could not dress themselves; those who were too sick to walk would have to be left behind. The date was set. The plan was fixed. It would be up to them now. The prisoners' fate rested in their own hands.

The next morning I put on the hat with the reprehensible feather and took myself down to the market. But as long as I looked, and I could not circle the market forever, there was no blue cart. And no egg-girl. Least not the one I was acquainted with. I bought eggs from another girl just in case any of the guards had become familiar with my habits.

I had to let the patriots know the prisoners would be wearing the wrong uniforms. But if there was any other way to get a message to General Washington, I didn't know of it. So I did the only other thing I could think to do: I paid a visit to the tailor.

He looked up as I came through the door. "Mr. Jones." His smile wasn't quite so welcoming as it might have been. "I hadn't expected to see you so soon." His glance was darting between his apprentice and me.

"I came to ask about that blue suit. You said your suppliers for the fabric were the best, though it would have to come by cart. Through the countryside."

His brows peaked, though he quickly tugged them back down. He turned to the apprentice. "I need some of that brocade from up in the attic."

"The brocade we put up there just yesterday?"

"The very same."

The apprentice looked none too happy about the prospect, although he complied.

"What is it?" The tailor hissed the words once the apprentice had left. "And be quick about it."

"The egg-girl wasn't at market."

"Those who pass through the lines can't always be depended upon."

"Then who is your alternate? I've a message that must be passed without delay."

He shook his head. "There isn't one."

"No one? But . . . what did you expect to do if the egg-girl ever failed to show?"

He shrugged. "She never did."

"So what am I to do?"

"I've not the first idea."

"You have to do *something!*"

He took a measure from his pocket as we heard the boy clatter down the stair. "It's you, son, who has to do something. Remember, I've nothing to do with it anymore. Though if you're passing a note, you might want to include that there's been quite a bit of mention of New York City lately."

I left the tailor's shop with a desperate

need to strike at something.

I had a message but no messenger. Information that needed to be delivered but no means to deliver it. Surely Hercules had never faced a more daunting task.

Who did I know that could pass through the British lines and then come back again? And what reason would someone have for doing such a thing? The farmers did so, of course. That's why the use of the egg-girl had been ingenious. But something must have gone wrong for her. I could not assume that she would ever return. By next week this business would be done and I could go back to just being the owner of the King's Arms. But the prisoners still needed to escape.

I took deliveries of foodstuffs from the countryside all the time. And from the ships that sailed into the harbor. But my suppliers' only loyalty was to my gold coin. They were businessmen with no appreciation for politics or causes. I could ask one of them to deliver my message for a fee. But then I might become a commodity that they could sell to the British and for a much higher price.

There was no solution to my problem.

Only a message which sat in my pocket.

Undelivered.

I went back to the market the next day, hoping against hope. To my surprise and very great delight, the egg-girl was there. It was difficult to restrain myself from going straight to her cart, but I took the time to look at shallots and dandelion greens. Considered some leeks and some peas. Made arrangements to have a not too battered-looking ham hock delivered to the tavern. My circuitous wanderings finally led me to her. "Have you any quails' eggs? I have a great hunger for them."

"I've lost my quail."

"You've lost . . . ?" What was it that she was trying to tell me?

She met my gaze with great reluctance.

"You've lost your quail. How does one lose a quail?"

"Someone wrung his — *her* neck."

God help us all. "And you don't have access to another."

"No."

"Are you looking for any other to replace it?"

"No."

Then she was out of it now as well. Just like the tailor. "She didn't leave any extra eggs, did she? Before she was killed?"

"No." She whispered. "He . . . she . . . didn't."

"I deeply regret your loss."

She swiped at an onslaught of tears with the corner of her apron. I dug past the note to the coins I carried in my pocket and offered her the amount I would have paid for the eggs. And then some.

The tailor was out. The egg-girl was out. But someone still had to pass through the lines to deliver the message. Hannah and I were the only ones left.

I was going to have to send Hannah through the lines. I couldn't see any other way around it. A man alone on horseback in the countryside had every reason to be accused of spying. Even if I weren't arrested, I was certain to be interrogated. But Hannah had a chance.

Fanny said she had worked for the Sunderlands at their country home, out toward Germantown. Perhaps Hannah could make a case for going to check on it. Or she might be able to contrive to visit some friends in that direction. There had been word of a skirmish out near Bristol. If General Washington's troops were still in the vicinity, it might make for the quickest exchange.

The plan was fraught with danger, but it

was the only option I had. Hannah was the only person I could trust. Now I just had to arrange to speak to her, without of course going about actually arranging it.

I spent the afternoon trying to figure out how to be circumspect about our meeting, but it only succeeded in making me testy. Who ever heard of a spy who refused to meet with her spymaster? If I needed to speak with her, I would. Her principles be hanged!

41
HANNAH

"Jeremiah." My heart lifted when I saw him in front of Pennington House fifth day morning as I went to call on Betsy. He seemed to be . . . was he waiting for me?

"I don't have time for explanations or for one of your scoldings. I need you to deliver a message for me."

A scolding? I hadn't intended to say anything at all! "Thee might have waited until seventh day." My words came out a bit stiffer than I had meant them.

"It's not for the sergeant." He gestured for me to start walking. Doll followed along behind us. "I need you to take a message through the lines."

"Through — ?"

"And then I need you to find someone who can deliver it to General Washington."

Through the lines. He wanted me to leave the safety of the city for the danger of the battle lines? "And how do thee propose I do that?"

"Your family has a summer house. Out toward Germantown."

"We do. But I have to tell thee that —"

"You can say you're going there to visit."

Of all the insufferable — ! When I saw him, I had been going to tell him that I had left the Meeting, but it seemed he wanted to do nothing but order me about. "There's nothing there. The Hessians stole everything they could find inside it. And then the patriots tore it apart for firewood."

"Then . . . is there someone you could visit, outside the lines?"

"No one that would make any sense to go see."

"You might just have to make something up." He was watching me carefully.

"If thee want me to do something, I must do it honestly or not at all."

He choked on a laugh. "You're a spy! There's nothing honest about it."

"Hush! Someone might hear thee. I will take the message, but I will do it on my terms."

"Fine. Meet me behind the tavern, at the stables, tomorrow at ten of the clock. I'll have John sign a pass for you."

"Tomorrow, then." I only wanted this

business to be done. The messages passed, the prisoners escaped, these furtive meetings finished. I wanted to be able to talk — truly and honestly — with Jeremiah about things that had nothing to do with causes and intrigues.

His eyes seemed to soften as he looked down at me. "I've held the message for too long already. This is the only way."

I nodded. "Until tomorrow."

I waited the next morning by the corner of the stables, in the shadows. Doll waited with me. She was shaking her head and mumbling to herself. "Pure foolishness if you ask me! Leaving the city to ride out there among those soldiers."

Jeremiah soon appeared. "I wouldn't ask you if I didn't truly need someone." At least he was less surly this morning. "Usually . . . there's supposed to be an egg-girl."

"A what?"

"A girl at the market. To carry the messages. But she's not able to do it anymore."

"Why not?"

"Because she can't." The way he'd closed up his mouth precluded any questions. "And I can't. A man on horseback between the lines? I'd be arrested before I'd gone a mile. I wouldn't ask you, but there's no other way I know of to get a message out of the city."

He handed me a pass. I tucked it into my pocket as the stable boy led a horse down the aisle toward us. I didn't know I had backed away from it until I rammed right into Doll. "I'm not very fond of horses."

"This is Queenie."

Queenie.

"As in Charlotte."

I could not help but raise a brow.

"She never was very handsome, but I could never fault her for loyalty. And she's my gentlest one." The horse didn't look any more impressed to see me than I was to see her. "She may look old, and she is, but it makes it more unlikely that a soldier will want to take her from you."

My knees began to tremble. "Soldiers take horses?"

"They've been known to."

"But they won't take this one?" If his face was any indication, they just might. "I think, perhaps —" I was starting to feel a bit light-headed.

"If any of the sentries tries to make you dismount, then just let them have her. She's not worth your life."

"What?" I reached back toward Doll and she caught my hand. "Thee said thee had a plan. But thy plan involves trying to talk my way through the lines, searching through the woods for General Washington's men, and then praying that no one takes my horse. That doesn't seem like a plan to me."

"What is it that you want? You want me to tell you that nothing's going to happen to you? You want me to tell you that no one will catch you? That you'll never be detained or questioned or hanged! I wish I could. I wish I could find all those men that —" He broke off as he glanced at Doll. "I want nothing more than to see all this over and done and —" His words caught again and he took a deep breath. Reached out for my other hand. "I once promised to keep you safe, and I wish to God that I could, but you're a spy. It's an occupation not without danger."

"Do not yell at me. Thee cannot fault me for having fear."

"I don't want —" His eyes were searching my face, looking for . . . something. "I wish I did not have to ask you to do this. And I do not fault you for being afraid. I'm afraid. You once told me I ought to ask for help when I needed it. I'm asking now."

I understood then that it was frustration that fueled his anger, not I. I turned my hand in his and grasped it. "I will go. But I cannot let anyone take the horse from me. I can't go to Germantown and back in one day without one. And if I don't return by this afternoon, then my parents will start to search for me."

He led the horse out into the yard and gestured for me to step up onto a large stone. The stable boy held the stirrup for me. I stepped up onto the stone, put my foot into the stirrup, and hopped, expecting to come down on the saddle. I didn't. I slid right down the horse's side, grabbing a fistful of Queenie's mane as I did.

"Haven't you ever ridden before?"

"No." I clamped my jaw shut to trap the words I wanted to say as I stepped up into the stirrup once more.

Jeremiah ran his hand through his hair. "Just . . ." He gestured for the stable boy, who then helped to hoist me up. Once I was sitting in the saddle, Jeremiah handed me the reins. I clutched them in my hand.

The horse nickered and stamped a foot.

I heard myself gasp and grabbed for another fistful of mane.

"Hannah, I can't let you do this. Come down." Jeremiah stepped toward the horse.

I shook my head. "I have to do this."

"You can't. And I'm not trying to disparage you; it's simply plain that you don't know how to ride."

"And who else is going to do it?"

"What about one of the others? Your friend Betsy, perhaps?"

"Don't be ridiculous. There isn't time." I dug my heels into Queenie's sides the way I'd seen the dragoons soldiers do and went trotting, slightly off center, out onto Walnut Street.

It wasn't so easy to ride a horse as I had imagined. All those officers galloping in and out of the shambles on Market Street made it look easy. But it was rather too jouncy for my taste, and painful besides. I was sure to have black bruises pounded into my thighs before the day was over. The third drawback only occurred to me as I approached the first redoubt.

I didn't know how to stop.

As I came upon a small band of men, loosely gathered about an open fire, one of them stepped onto the road with his musket. "Papers, miss."

I began to tremble so badly that I was in danger of dropping the reins. And with the horse's jolting gait I couldn't have collected my wits if I'd been able to. "I can't stop."

He held up his hand. "Papers."

"I can't stop!"

"Stop!"

"Stop!" I echoed the soldier's cry to the horse, but it didn't have any effect. The soldier stepped into the middle of the road and made a lunge for the reins. The horse jerked her head, tearing the reins from my hands, and began a mad jig of a dance that took us sidewise down the road.

"Stop, miss!"

"I'm trying!" Only I couldn't. We danced right past the sentry.

"I'll have to shoot!"

As I heard the cough of a shot, I ducked, grabbing onto the horse's mane with both hands. The horse started as if the bullet had been meant for her, and then stretched out her neck and galloped off toward a bend in the road. I didn't mind the galloping so much; it was easier on the legs and the head than whatever the horse had been doing before. Only just as I had become accustomed to her gait, the horse slowed so abruptly I nearly pitched forward over her head.

As she settled into a walk, I decided to try to regain the reins. By grabbing at locks of the mane, I was able to pull myself forward. But about the time I'd worked my way up her neck, gained her head, and reached past it for the reins, the beast dropped its muzzle into the grass.

"Stop that!"

The horse raised its head for an instant, righting me, and flicked an ear in my direction. But then it went right back to grazing. If I could only . . . I released a hand to reach for the reins, but they dangled just out of reach. I pushed myself back to the saddle, wincing as it encountered my thighs. What had ever made me think I could be a spy?

Robert had.

But now he was dead.

If I'd left him where he was, if I'd never agreed to help Jeremiah with the escape, then perhaps he would still be alive. I'd failed at everything I'd tried and now I couldn't even get an old horse to move.

Be still and know that I am God.

I *do* know that you are God! That was the whole problem. The whole point! He was a God that wouldn't speak and wouldn't listen and made me say things that nobody wanted to hear! I'd tried being still. I'd been a Friend my whole life. Being still was what we were good at. But it hadn't helped. And now I was no longer a member of the Meeting.

Back behind us, in the distance, the *pop* of a cannon sounded.

The horse raised its head and turned to

465

look back over its shoulder.

I used the opportunity, while its head was near, to grab at one of the reins. Caught it!

Then the earth in front of us exploded. The horse jumped and then stood stock-still, head raised, ears twitching.

If I could just get hold of that other rein . . .

As I bent forward to grab it, a swarm of flies began to buzz about us. It seemed rather strange. But as I looked out toward the wood, I saw fireflies flashing from the gloom.

At midday?

That was more than odd.

About the time I realized we were being shot at by cannon from behind and muskets ahead, the horse realized the same thing. I felt her muscles tense and then shift.

"No! Wait!"

I left my cries behind us where I'd said them. The horse didn't even seem to remember I was on her back. With one hand grasping a rein and the other clutching her mane, I tried with all my might to hold on.

Eventually the horse slowed to that jolting jounce I so disliked. But after a while she slowed still more to a walk. By then I was ready to collapse in relief. We'd left the sounds of battle so far behind that we ought to have happened upon General Washington's men. But I was beginning to suspect that we'd left them behind as well.

I was a complete and utter failure.

Just as I had resigned myself to trying to turn the horse back toward the city, a man stepped onto the path. "What have we here?" His coat flashed buff and red. His pistol was pointed at my head.

The hairs at the back of my neck began to prickle. I dug my heels into the horse's sides; she did nothing at all but stop in her tracks. Had I been able to feel my legs, I would have jumped to the ground and fled. As it was, I felt nothing but a terrible dread.

"What are you about, missy? On this fine and frightful day?"

"I —" I didn't want to tell the truth, but I hadn't the first idea of how to tell a lie. So I said the only thing I could. "I have a message for General Washington." I winced as I said it, certain he would have no choice now but to shoot me as an enemy spy.

"For General Washington, eh?" He stared at me for a moment. Spat onto the road. Lowered his pistol. "Come by way of the battle, did you?"

"I came down Germantown Road."

"Did we trounce them?"

"I . . . couldn't really say." I didn't know which *them* he was against. He was wearing a red coat, but he wasn't acting like a redcoat. Or maybe he was just biding his time.

He walked up and grabbed hold of the reins. "Lost your way, did you?"

I did not want to place myself under the control of any man. "If thee could just point out the right direction . . ."

"You're a Friend, are you?" He looked at me in a speculative sort of way, then led the horse into the brush. "It's a tangle back here."

I didn't like the way he was being so evasive. Nor the way he was leading me farther off the road. "I must insist that thee unhand my horse. This instant."

"Can't. We've had too many spies in camp."

If only I knew where he was taking me!

He led me on a twisting, turning path through the stumps and bogs that had once been a forest. I began to smell woodsmoke. A sentry stopped us and then let us continue. Soon I could see movement in the distance, along with tents and fires.

And men in *blue* coats!

The man hailed a soldier. "Is Captain McLane about?"

The soldier nodded toward a tent that

stood off at a distance from the rest.

Once we reached the tent, the man lifted the flap. "Captain McLane, sir? There's a lady here. Says she's got a message for General Washington."

My escort stood aside as another man pushed through the flap. Quite large of nose with an excess of unruly hair, he planted himself in front of my horse and crossed his arms. "Well?"

"I *do* have a message for General Washington."

"May I see it?"

"Are thee the one who will pass it on to him?" He didn't seem to be a very trustworthy sort of person.

"Aye. And then he'll pass it back down to me."

"Can thee turn thy back, then? For just a moment?"

He scowled, though he complied.

"Thee as well." I addressed my escort.

He too frowned, but he also turned away.

I drew the message from my polonaise, and then smoothed everything down again. "Thee may both turn around."

The captain extended his hand.

I leaned down and handed him the message. He whisked it from my hand and started back for his tent. But he threw a look over his shoulder at me before he disappeared. "Stay here."

I'd like to know where he thought I might have gone.

My escort lounged by the captain's fire while I sat atop Queenie. I wished I could have dismounted, but my legs had gone numb and I knew that if I got off, I would never have the strength to get back on.

Several minutes later the captain reappeared. "I've a message of my own for you to carry back." He passed it to me.

"Can thee . . . turn again?"

He threw up his hands and vanished back into his tent.

My escort led me out of the camp and returned me to the road, then pointed back the way I'd come. "The city is that way."

"Thee couldn't . . . ?" What did I want him to do for me? Take me back to Pennington House? Promise that I would make it there safely?

"Can't give you a pass. Those lobsterbacks would know you'd been to camp for sure. Best thing to do is lie. Make something up. Your cousin was sick. Something like that."

"I have a pass."

"Aren't you the lucky one? Most everyone else has to find some way to sneak in through the lines."

I would have if I'd known where to do it and how. I didn't want to face another soldier; especially not a redcoat. Not after what I'd just done. As he passed me up the reins, I vowed to keep hold of them this time.

42

JEREMIAH

I couldn't shake the feeling that I'd done the wrong thing in sending Hannah out into the countryside. But I didn't know what I ought to have done instead; the information needed to get to General Washington, and I had no other person to send. If she rode into trouble, if she were taken by the pickets on either side, there would be no one to blame but myself.

The streets seemed quiet, the city almost somnolent. But it wasn't until dinnertime that I realized why. Only three soldiers appeared of the sixty or so who usually took their meals at the tavern. I stepped out into the street to see if there were any set on joining them, but there was only one clattery cart and a mangy dog trotting down the street. I closed the door against the breeze that had blown up from the river.

"What's wrong with the others? Did the cooking put them off?"

One of the men hoisted his tankard and took a drink before replying, "I'm sure they'd rather be here than where they are."

"And where is that?"

"Out toward Germantown, trying to roust Mr. Washington from his camp."

Out toward Germantown! "Whose company?"

"The first battalion, light infantry. The seventeenth regiment and the forty-sixth. Did the Queen's Rangers go as well?" He consulted his companion who nodded. "And the Rangers."

That was . . . seven thousand men marching down the same road Hannah was traveling. "They don't hope to see any action, do they?"

The soldier shrugged.

The door opened and John came through it. He stalked toward a table and sat down. "Blasted luck! Half the army's been called out to fight those rebels and I'm stuck here at headquarters."

"Has General Howe gone himself?"

"No. He's got business to attend to. With Mrs. Loring." He winked and smirked. "Which is why I'm here. What's for dinner?"

"Pickled tongue with green peas. Some cheese and a pie."

"I suppose I'll have to eat it, then."

I sent Bartholomew back to the kitchen for another plate.

"They weren't intending to march straight down Germantown Road, were they?" I was hoping that John would tell me the other soldiers had been mistaken.

Bartholomew set a plate down in front of John.

John snorted as he picked up a spoon. "General Howe's not so dim-witted as that. He sent some of the men up the river and some up Frankfort Road. It's the rest that went straight on to Germantown Road."

My hopes fell to the floor. I'd sent Hannah into a trap. Even if she had made it past the redcoats in leaving, she'd have found herself in between the lines, in the middle of a veritable battle. God help her, I'd sent her straight to her death.

I spent the afternoon pacing the floor from the public room back to the kitchen. Glancing out toward Walnut Street, stalking past Bartholomew and then past Fanny and the babe she cradled. Glaring out at the stables.

Where was she!

Finally about three o'clock I caught a glimpse of Hannah rounding the corner on old Queenie. By the time I'd burst through the kitchen and yelled for the stable boy, she had arrived in the backyard. Not willing to wait for the stable boy, I reached up for her myself. "Are you fine, then? Did you . . . ?"

She nodded. "I am well." She accepted my hand and leaned on it as she slid from the saddle. But as she took a step away from the horse, she stumbled.

I offered my arm.

"My legs. They feel so . . . queer."

I leaned close. "Were you . . . ?"

"I am fine."

"No one . . . ?"

"I was not stopped."

"Did you — ?"

She burst into tears. I don't know why; I was trying to be nice. I pulled her to my chest with a hand to her head. She clutched at my lapels and would not let me see her face until I put my hand under her chin and lifted it. Then I looked in her eyes.

"I was so frightened." The words were scarcely more than a whisper.

"So was I." I pulled her close once more.

She passed a message to me before she left. Once she had gone, I turned back to the tavern only to find Bartholomew beckoning me. "I've something for you to see."

I followed him toward the stables. He nodded toward the stable boy, who slipped out behind us. Then Bartholomew motioned me toward one of the corner stalls. He threw aside some hay to reveal several stacks of what looked like dark-colored clothing.

"What are those?"

"Forty-eight coats. And there's forty-eight breeches beneath them." He scrambled toward the other corner of the stall, pushing aside more hay to reveal four large, lumpy sacks.

"And what's in those?" I was afraid I already knew the answer.

"Forty-eight pairs of shoes."

"The coats and breeches and shoes that I asked to be taken on the night of the Meschianza? During the party? *Only after* General Washington begins his disturbance?"

Bartholomew shrugged. "The boys got them early."

"I didn't *want* them early. What do you think will happen when the soldiers realize forty-eight sets of uniforms have gone missing?"

"You think they'll notice?"

"How could they *not* notice? Wouldn't you notice if an entire set of clothes went missing? Wouldn't you say something about it to your friends?"

"It wasn't my idea. I didn't know what

they'd done until they brought them all here this morning. They needed the money."

"The money."

"The half that you promised once the task was done."

For want of patience our entire scheme had been compromised? "They're going to have to find a way to put them all back. And then they're going to have to steal them again."

"Put them — !"

"It didn't take you very long to guess the reason for the uniforms. How long do you think it will take the barracks sergeants to do the same?"

He was poking at the dirt with the toe of his shoe. "Not long."

"Not long enough. And once they figure out our plan, we might as well just tell them where to collect the prisoners."

That evening, as I was eating supper, Bartholomew stepped toward me from the night just as he used to do. Only this time he brought another boy with him.

"This is Ethan."

I nodded.

Bartholomew poked him in the elbow. "Tell him."

The other boy folded his arms across his

477

chest and lifted his chin. "If we're to take all the things back and then steal them again, we need to be paid again."

I'd figured they'd need to be paid something. They already knew about the plan and there was no point in involving any more people in the escape than there already were. I was in danger of becoming as bad as Hannah. "That sounds reasonable."

"Ten shillings for returning them and ten shillings for stealing them back."

"Five shillings for returning them and five for stealing them back."

"We have to do twice the work."

"Because you didn't wait to do it when I wanted it done."

He scowled. "Then keep them."

"If that's what you'd like." It's not what he wanted, of course. What he wanted — what they all wanted — was money. I lifted another spoonful of supper to my mouth.

The boy frowned. Exchanged a glance with Bartholomew. "I can't guarantee that we can put them back and steal them again without being caught."

"Couldn't guarantee it the first time either. But you did just fine." He was wavering. I could tell. "Bartholomew, why don't you ask Fanny to feed your friend while he thinks it over."

The boy's eyes grew wide as he looked toward the kitchen.

"Let me know what you decide."

43
HANNAH

After drying my eyes on Jeremiah's coat, I left King's Arms. By the time I reached Pennington House I was walking normally once more, though I was sure my legs would ache for the week to come. Davy must have been waiting for me. He opened the door before I had even stepped onto the porch. I could see Doll standing right behind him, gesturing at me.

Mother was passing through the front hall as I entered. "There thee are, Hannah! Thee look just as tired as I feel. Doll said thee'd gone in search of a letter from our Friends in London."

I shot a glance toward Doll.

She stared back at me, daring me to say anything different. I might have, had it not been guaranteed to plunge us both into deep trouble.

Mother sighed. "I spent the whole day trying to track it myself, without success.

Where did thee find it?"

"I didn't. I never saw it."

"Well. That's discouraging. A whole day wasted! Perhaps we'll find out at Meeting who has it." Her smile was bright, though it wobbled a bit at the corners.

"Perhaps thee will." I had no intention of attending.

I was not allowed to leave the Meeting as easily as that, however. The elders came to Pennington House the next afternoon to reason with me. But as much as my father tried to explain away my words, I corrected him at every opportunity. And by the end of their visit, only a very hopeful soul would have thought my words anything but sincere, my heart anything but compromised.

Upon departing, one of them lingered. "Thee must know that if this is how thee feel and what thee believe, then we must disown thee."

"I know it."

Father was looking anxiously between myself and him. "She does not know what she's saying."

"Her words have the feeling of conviction behind them. And thee must remember that those who have been persuaded from the truth may not be called Friends."

I hoped that would be the end of it, but I was mistaken. On first day, *Sunday,* my parents brought a guest home with them for dinner. My uncle was none too pleased and I was quite surprised. I nodded as he greeted me. "Jeremiah Jones. I had not expected to have the pleasure of thy company at Pennington House." A smile to rival his own played at my lips.

"I'm here to impress upon you the error of your ways."

A thing I never would have expected.

"Any sensible person such as myself — a sincere admirer of the Society of Friends — will tell you that you've been overcome by pride."

"Pride?"

He slid a glance toward my father, who was trying to explain to Uncle the reason for Jeremiah's visit. "And stubbornness." He leaned closer. "Why didn't you tell me you'd left?"

"I would have told thee on fourth day, but thee had no time to listen. And after . . . well." I shrugged.

He was close enough that I could catch the scents of leather and rum that hung about him. "At least I won't have to attend those Meetings anymore in order to see you. I've received from John two invitations to

482

the Meschianza tomorrow. You must come with me."

"I can't." And I wouldn't have wanted to after seeing what those officers expected Polly to wear.

"If you're in attendance, then no one can question your involvement."

"I cannot come. I promised my father that no meetings would be arranged between us."

"What does it matter now? All will be over tomorrow night. For better or for worse. For once, can't you just be defiant?"

I smiled. I could not help myself. " 'Tis all I've been since I met thee."

"Why can't you just —"

I laid my hand against his cheek. I did not care who saw me.

He stilled, though his eyes yet blazed.

"I gave my word. And even though I've left the Meeting, my word must be true or it becomes nothing at all."

"But it's the best way — the only way — to save yourself."

" 'Twas never about myself, Jeremiah."

"Then — dash it all!" His voice had gone hoarse with emotion. "Let it be about me. 'Tis the only way to save me. Because if they suspect you —"

"If they suspect me, then God will grant

me courage to face them. Of that I have no doubt." I had to believe that was true.

"You don't know what they do to traitors."

"I know what they do to prisoners. And it cannot be much worse."

"But —"

"Hush thee now."

"I'm not some child. And I can't just let you give yourself away."

" 'Tis not up to thee, Jeremiah."

"Then give me some hope." He eyed my father and then took my hand in his and squeezed it. "For us."

Hope. He was asking for hope in a world gone mad. What was there to hope for? Robert was dead. The tunnel might not even be finished. The prisoners were more likely to be captured than to make it to patriot lines. And yet . . . this escape was about people, not causes. And now, Jeremiah and I were just the same. We were two people unattached to causes who had only each other to care for.

"Please, Hannah. I need to know that afterward I'll still be able to see you. I do not want our partnership to end."

Partnership. There was something, some hidden place inside my heart, that thrilled to hear his words. But I did not dare to think on them too much, not before the escape was accomplished. If there had been danger in our actions before, the next evening they would increase threefold. Unless every man of the prisoners in Robert's cell and the ones next to it escaped, I had great reason to fear that my role would eventually be revealed.

The next morning, the day of the Meschianza, Polly was up with the sun. She sent Jenny in a dozen different directions at once and then began a loud lament about slaves never wanting to work.

"That is not true, cousin! Were I to give thee twelve different things to accomplish and no time in which to accomplish them, I would bemoan thy slothfulness as well."

"I did not —"

"Thee will never be ready in time if thee don't allow Jenny to complete the tasks already given her."

Polly flounced over to a chair and sulked while Jenny continued with the preparations. By dinnertime I could bear the tension in the room no longer. I stayed in the parlor to pass the time until the major came to collect Polly. It seemed every member of the household had that same idea. When Polly finally descended the stair, we were all of us attendant upon her together. And a great silence fell upon us all as we beheld her in the costume.

"I cannot be silent any longer!" I jumped as Father roared at my side. "This is an outrage! Completely decadent and immodest. I have tolerated disrespect and impertinence. I have lived in a household given over to frivolity, and I have added to the burden of those enslaved. But this cannot be borne! A daughter of this city should not be paraded around by those blackguards as if she were some infidel!"

Polly had gone white, though her eyes glittered with rage.

Uncle was looking at her as if he had never seen her before.

Aunt had put a hand to her mouth.

"I think, perhaps . . ." Uncle looked as if he did not know what to think at all.

"Father!" Polly went to him, hands clasped at her chest. "You cannot fail to send me now. Not after I accepted the invitation and was given the gown. Not on the day of the fete."

"I find I must agree, for once, with your uncle, Polly. You will take that . . . that . . . drape off at once. It will be returned to Major Lindley along with your regrets. This has gone on long enough. I will not have my daughter known across the city as a

486

strumpet."

"You can't do this to me!"

" 'Tis not me that's done anything. 'Tis that major and his whole dashed army. You've him to thank for this spectacle."

She stamped her foot. "You've ruined my life! No one will ever invite me anywhere again!"

Uncle was unmoved.

"I hate you!" She tripped up the stair, her white satin shimmering and spangles glinting, the feathers and tassels on her turban bobbing in time with her steps.

Mother patted me on the arm and then nodded toward the stair. I didn't know what I could do for Polly, what comfort I could offer, but I did as I was commanded.

She was sobbing into her pillows as I entered the bedroom.

"Thee will spoil the gown if thee keep crying so."

She turned a tear-streaked face toward me. "I can't get it off."

"Stand. I'll help thee."

As she stood, that dreadful turban slid toward her ear. I started first with that, disengaging it from her hair and then her hair from the feathers and tassels. Next, I started on the gown, or tried to. "Perhaps I should ask Jenny to come."

"No." She cast her arms about her chest as if to hide herself from view.

"Then thee must help me. How did thee get thyself into this?" I could not quite remember how Jenny and I had helped her into it before.

"I don't know. I just slipped it on. It came so easy . . ."

"I don't know how to aid thee."

"Just tear it off. I don't want it anymore!"

I couldn't bring myself to remind her that some other girl probably would. There was certain to be one; Major Lindley was not the kind of man who would attend the event of the season alone.

"Just get it off. And then send it away." She stood still and quiet for the moments it took me to relieve her of the garment. And then she sighed as she pulled on a short gown over her petticoats. "He's leaving, you know. They all are soon."

I said nothing.

"It's not as if he doesn't want me. He's been ordered to New York. To the city. And it's no place for a woman to be."

"I can't imagine it would be any better than here."

"I wanted him to fancy me."

"He did fancy thee." It had been plain enough for all to see.

"He fancied me enough to flirt with me, but not enough to marry me."

"Did he ever speak to thee of . . . ? There's a girl in London, apparently."

"He says she's an old, ugly termagant that his family is forcing him to marry."

I could not see how anyone thousands of miles away from here could force a man armed with a musket to do anything he did not want to do, but I could tell that such thoughts would not be appreciated.

She climbed up onto her bed. "Perhaps . . . if the British leave . . . do you think the rebels will come?"

"Undoubtedly."

"Maybe they'll have balls too. And keep the theater open."

"And perhaps they'll free the prisoners and put the State House and Penn House back to rights."

Polly did not hear what I had said. Eyes wide open I could tell she had already set her heart to dreaming.

Over supper that evening, with everyone seated at the table, Father announced that he would be taking our family back to our house.

Ezekiel promptly burst into tears. "I want to stay with cousin!" He and young Edward had formed a fast friendship.

Mother took him away from the table. We could hear the echoes of his cries as they went up the stair. "I don't want to go! I want to stay!"

I felt like crying as well, though for a completely different reason. I knew I had to stay — if Uncle Edward would let me — even as I truly wanted to go. I hadn't known when we left the house that I wouldn't be returning. I hadn't appreciated just how many of my hopes and dreams were tied to that place.

But old things must pass away. I only hoped that new things would not be long delayed in coming, and that they would prove even half as dear as those things I was leaving behind.

Uncle Edward cleared his throat. "You've convinced your colonel to leave, then?"

"I demanded an interview with General Howe's replacement himself. I told him how untenable the situation had become. We'll leave tomorrow morning. And we thank thee for thy generous hospitality."

Uncle lifted a glass in Father's direction.

I would have preferred to have spoken to Father in private, but he was arranging the transition in public. I needed to make my wishes known now, before everyone dispersed for the evening. "I would prefer to stay here. If Uncle Edward would have me."

Aunt Rebekah sent an eloquent look my way. "Of course you may stay. Of course she can, can't she, Edward? She and Polly are of an age."

Uncle didn't seem to know what to make of my request. Father didn't respond. Only Sally spoke. "But thee can't, Hannah!"

I wished I could return to our house just so I could share my life with her again. I had missed her these past months. My little sister of ten years had grown into a girl who seemed a stranger.

"Hannah can take the spare room." Aunt Rebekah addressed Father, making it sound as if everything had been decided. "We'll move her things in just as soon as Doll and Jenny move your things out." She turned around to address Davy. "You'll take care of everything, won't you?"

He bowed.

Aunt Rebekah beamed a radiant smile at Father. "There. It's all decided, then!" She turned toward me. "We're delighted to have you stay."

Father looked none too happy about it.

"Aren't we delighted?"

"Yes. Of course. Delighted." Uncle Edward raised his glass in my direction and then took another drink from it.

We lingered just long enough for Mother to rejoin us. As we broke up, Aunt Rebekah drew me near. "It will all be fine. Everything will work out. You will see."

I couldn't see anything at all. There seemed to be no clear way ahead. But I had thrown myself on their mercy, and she had caught me. I would just have to trust that what she said was true. I only wished she could blot that terrible, accusatory look from my Father's eyes and the pain from Sally's voice.

Mother caught my arm as I walked from the room. "Thee are staying? But . . . why?"

"I've left the Meeting. Thee know I have."

"But thee can't have meant what thee said."

"I meant every word."

Sally joined us. "Thee can't stay, Hannah!"

I took her face between my hands and kissed her cheek. My own sweet sister. "I will miss thee."

"Hannah!" Mother's voice was strident. "Why?" Her question was so pleading, so plaintive that I had no choice but to answer.

"Because of Robert. He was there, in that jail, and I was the only one who went to visit him. I was the only one who went to visit any of them."

Mother clutched my arm. "How is he?"

He's dead! Oh, how I wanted to say it. I
wanted to weep with the knowledge of it.
But I couldn't. I wouldn't. Too many lives
depended still upon my silence. So I patted
her arm, disengaged myself from them both,
and walked up the stair. When I got to Polly's room, I collapsed on my bed and wept
for all that I had given up.

44
JEREMIAH

I spent the morning of the Meschianza carting wine from the tavern. Bartholomew helped me by loading the cart and then handling the reins. Once we got to the estate, he carried the crates inside. The fine, elegant mansion of Joseph Wharton had been repainted and redecorated. One of the outer walls had also been knocked out so that a salon could be attached to house all the guests at supper.

Everything that had been begged and borrowed from the city's elite had been arranged in a display of magnificent gaudiness. Dozens of mirrors had been positioned to reflect the winking lights of hundreds of candles. Flowers and ribbons and shrubberies had been woven in suspension about the room. Several dozen slaves, adorned in costumes and fettered with silver necklaces and bracelets, milled about in preparation for service.

It was an utter disgrace.

Once the bottles had been delivered, we hastened from that place. Bartholomew amused himself among the throngs crowding the wharf while I used a glass to survey the land out toward Germantown. Somewhere over there, tonight, General Washington would create his disturbance.

I prayed that it would last long enough for the prisoners to escape.

That afternoon, three galleys festooned with pennants and filled with officers made their way downriver. They were followed by barges carrying the military bands, and cheered by spectators filling every kind of ship that had business upon the river. Bands played. Flags fluttered. When the procession reached Wharton's mansion, it was greeted by a seventeen-gun salute.

It was a veritable festival of foolishness. A carnival of idiocy.

That the British army should cavort and caper and frolic in full view of a city they had methodically destroyed! There was no growing thing left within the city's limits. No fences and very few shutters. The city smelled like a latrine and looked far worse. That they had insisted on such a celebration was a testament to their complete arrogance and total disregard. If the citizens of Philadelphia had not realized it before, I hoped they would realize it now. I suspected that once the British left, the citizens would cheer the patriots' return.

Although . . . a thought that had begun to worry at me raised its head again. What would happen once the patriots returned? They'd be set on retribution, that was certain. And they would especially target people like me. People who had seemed to embrace the Loyalist cause.

It was hardly a secret that my tavern had become a den for soldiers. And it was widely known that I was a personal friend of John Lindley. What wasn't known at all was my part in the soon-to-take-place escape. And tonight, once it was over, there would be none to vouch for my true loyalties. I could very well end up with a noose around my neck after all. And for no good reason but that I had played my part too well.

I tugged at my cravat and then stepped outside to take some air.

As the crowd disembarked at the pier, grenadiers formed two lines with a file of light horses behind them. It was through this assembly that the guests walked up from the river toward a lawn lined with troops and prepared for an exhibition of chivalry.

A herald and three trumpeters announced two different groups of knights who, after paying homage to General Howe and his brother, challenged each other to a joust. Lances were brandished. Shields were displayed. Salutes were passed around like cards. They came at each other with spears and pistols and swords and then finally called the tournament in a draw.

With great relief everyone repaired to the ballroom and there was much dancing, interrupted by an impressive display of fireworks, which was followed by more dancing. At midnight the salon was opened to cries of delight and general awe.

John was resplendent in his knight's costume of white satin with silver fringe and a pink-and-white sword belt fastened with silver lacing and large pink bows. His white satin hat was decked with red, white, and black plumes. And on his arm was . . . not Polly Pennington.

It wasn't until after the supping was over that I was able to address him. He was holding a glass of wine, staring glumly into its plum-colored depths.

"That isn't the lovely Miss Pennington you're escorting this evening."

"No. Miss Pennington's father thought the costumes far too scandalous. Apparently.

My maiden is the rather dim and chinless Miss Brewster. I am doomed to be forever surrounded by graceless women."

I couldn't help but grin.

"You needn't look so cheerful about it."

"Our colonial maidens didn't appreciate being dressed as Turks?"

"I rather thought they look like they're enjoying themselves."

I glanced around the room. In my opinion they looked as if they thought they *ought* be enjoying themselves. But there were telltale signs. Hands frequently lifted to adjust the position of a turban. Fingers tugging up sleeves made of slippery satin. Smiles that weren't quite so wide as they might have been.

"You're without your usual companion as well." He had turned a bleary eye in my direction. "Miss Sunderland."

Hannah. She ought to have been here by my side. I shrugged. "She doesn't attend parties. She doesn't dance. She only wears plain clothes."

John raised his glass. "To the colonies and their maidens."

I drunk heartily to that toast.

"You haven't changed your mind, have you?"

He squinted at me. "What's that?"

"Have you changed your mind about your wealthy Brunhilda?"

He took a long swallow. "Don't recall her to me. Some things are best not brought to mind."

"You're still going through with it, then?"

"With the marriage? Of course I am. I'd be a fool not to!"

"Even when you've fallen in love with Miss Pennington?"

At the mention of her name, his eyes had gone soft. But then he blinked. And when he turned back to me, all traces of sentiment were gone. "I must be strong. And I must not be governed by sentiment. I've got the cause to uphold."

"Cause?"

"The cause of my advancement. It takes a fortune these days to hold any position at all in the army."

"So you're choosing . . . ?"

"No choice about it. I'm a completely loyal man. Entirely devoted to my own interests."

"And Miss Pennington?"

"I told her a tale about my family forcing me into marriage. She felt quite sorry for me by the time I was done. Besides, I'm sure she'll receive dozens of proposals. From men more worthy of her hand than

I." He saluted me with his glass. Downed it in one long swallow and then lurched off to affix himself to Miss Brewster's side.

Over at one of the tables, John André was delighting the officers with his tales of capture at the hands of General Montgomery up in Canada. Of just how backward and uncivilized the colonials were. And at one of the other tables, an officer had convinced one of the Meschianza's maidens to dance for him like some Turkish girl.

I walked past and somehow managed to spill my entire glass of wine on him.

He pushed to his feet, blustering, while the girl backed away. I hoped she had the good sense to keep on going.

At the foot of a table, clenching a wineglass in his fist, sat a lone officer. A colonel. He was staring out a window into the darkness of the night. I sat down next to him.

He flicked a glance at me and then went back to staring out the window.

"Party not to your taste?"

He turned, propped an elbow on the table, and leaned toward me. "I told General Howe this was a mistake."

It was. A monumental mistake.

"If I were a rebel, this would be the perfect

night for an attack. Half these fools came up here on barges. I'll bet there's not a dozen horses for the officers, and all our infantry is back in the city. If Mr. Washington were a smart man, he could capture us all. This night. And he wouldn't need but fifty men in order to do it." He took a long swallow from his glass.

"What did the general say?"

"Said if they hadn't the courage to attack us this spring, then they wouldn't have the sense to attack us now. And besides, Washington is a gentleman. Can you imagine that? A colonial a gentleman? In any case, the party was being thrown in his honor and how could he forbid his own men to attend?"

The fool didn't even realize he'd insulted me.

Long about one o'clock there seemed to come some change in the mood of the party. A pause in the general conversation. In the distance a series of explosions could be heard. And then, several minutes later, a staccato of drums. At tables across the salon the officers were eyeing Howe, but the general seemed oblivious to pedestrian concerns. Or thoughts of war.

Voices gradually picked up and laughter began again. But several minutes later, a

501

soldier entered the room. Spying General Howe, he went over and bent to speak into his ear. The general jerked away. Turned to look out the window. Gestured violently for the soldier to come closer. As General Howe questioned the soldier, conversation began to wither around them. Officers pushed away from the table, leaving chairs upturned in their wake.

"That's musket fire, isn't it?" The officer I'd been speaking with took another sip of wine.

"Sounds like it." I left him to follow the crowds wandering out onto the lawn. They were staring off toward where I'd trained my glass that afternoon.

One of the maidens beside me shivered. Tugged at the coat of her escort. "What is it?"

"Hmmm? Oh. I'm sure it's just part of the festivities. The soldiers in the city wouldn't want General Howe to leave without adding their farewells."

The girl broke into dimples. "How kind!"

I lifted my glass and drank to the escape of the prisoners. Godspeed. To each and every one of them.

45

HANNAH

Long about one of the clock I heard explosions from the direction of Germantown. They were followed soon after by the thunder of drums. It was foolish of me, but I pushed back my blanket and crept to the window. Opening the sash, I put my head out into the night. The jail was many blocks behind me, but I scoured the shadows with my gaze just the same. Wanting, hoping, praying for my will to be done.

I wanted them all to escape.

I lay there through the night, tense with worry, waiting for the watchman to call out that prisoners had escaped. But no alarm was raised, and after a while the noise ceased. Dawn's first light somehow found me sleeping.

When I woke, it was with the thought that everything was finally finished. My part in the escape was over. There were no more visits to be paid to the jail. But even as I celebrated the end of my clandestine activity, I remembered one thing more. Today, this morning, my family would return to the house, leaving me behind. I did not know what I should do, whether I should offer to help them pack or whether it would be better if I kept myself hidden away.

Listening to the sounds of trunks being shut and footsteps treading up and down the stair, I decided to time my appearance to their leaving. I embraced my sister and my brothers as they left. I nodded at my father.

Mother kissed my cheek. "Thee are always welcome, Hannah."

"I know it."

"I will pray that sense comes back to thy heart."

Just as I would pray that it always remained attuned to God's voice.

She gave me a swift embrace and then . . . they were gone.

Aunt Rebekah took up my hand soon after, drawing me with her into the parlor. "I do not know you, Hannah, as well as I would like."

I did not know what to say. The reason we did not know each other was because she had left the Meeting when she'd married my uncle.

"I feel badly that religion has come between our families. Perhaps . . . do you have any questions? About what your life will be now? Polly has been indulged too much, to my way of thinking. But it's possible that you've been indulged too little. There is joy to be had from art and literature and music. The heart needs beauty to expand and grow. I want you to know that there is a purpose served by some of the things of which Friends disapprove."

I wasn't quite sure I was ready to believe that. But I did have a question for her. "Was it difficult? To leave?"

"It's always difficult to leave people you love. But I haven't missed the Meeting."

"Not at all?"

"Perhaps . . . just a little. I still see those plain white walls in my dreams and sometimes I find myself missing the stillness. The silence. That anticipation of hearing from God. But you can be a Friend, Hannah, even if you're not a member of the Meeting."

As I looked at Aunt Rebekah and listened to her speak, I noticed something about her that I had not seen before. Though her gown was carmine in color, and though it was ornamented with trim, it was rather . . .

505

plain. And though the furniture in the parlor was upholstered in the gayest of colors and even though it was gilded, it was not nearly as ornate as that in Polly's room.

Aunt Rebekah was smiling at me.

I smiled back. "Why did thee leave?"

"Because I met Mr. Pennington, and I realized there were good people outside the Meeting too. People who had faith and felt it just as deeply. It didn't seem right that they be condemned simply because they practiced their faith in the same God in a different manner."

"It was the injustice of it all."

"Yes. But mostly it was love. I left for love." She looked at me for a long moment. "Now then, what about your own young man?"

I felt my brow furrow.

"I'm speaking of Jeremiah Jones. Though I suppose he's not so young now, is he? He was terribly handsome as a young boy. Still is, if I'm not mistaken."

"I don't know that he's . . . I didn't think . . . I mean, he wasn't . . . isn't . . . a Friend."

"And now you aren't either."

"I don't know . . . without the Meeting. Who would approve the match?"

"Do you trust yourself to hear God's voice?"

I nodded. I did. I'd recognized His voice back when I'd first heard it, though I hadn't wanted to admit it.

"Then you don't need anyone to tell you what you know in your heart already. I've decided we're celebrating your coming to live with us tonight, and I took the liberty of inviting some guests to sup with us. Mr. Jones will be among them. If you would like to wear one of Polly's gowns, I'm sure she wouldn't mind. And Jenny can help you dress."

I thought back to the amaranth gown with fondness. But I wasn't ready to wear it yet. It wasn't a faith that I was leaving behind; it was the Meeting. Jeremiah would have to accept me as I was or not at all.

I donned my own plain gown with the help of Polly's sister, Caroline. But as I walked from the bedroom, I thought the better of it and borrowed a neck kerchief of lace to tuck into my bodice.

Jeremiah was already in the parlor by the time I came downstairs with Polly. He rose as we entered and walked into the dining room with me.

"It's kind of thee to come tonight."

His smile brought a flush to my cheeks. It was only heightened when Aunt Rebekah seated him between herself and me.

"Your numbers seem depleted this evening." His voice was low against the murmurs of other conversations.

But Aunt Rebekah was quick in her reply. "Hannah's family has moved back to their home on Chestnut Street."

We supped on turtle soup, roast duck, and boiled parsnips. And afterward, Polly played the harpsichord for us. Jeremiah was seated next to me.

When he spoke, it was in a whisper. "They escaped. At least all the men in Addison's cell did. I don't know about the others."

I could not keep from smiling.

"But I have to ask you to go back to the jail on Saturday. One last time." His eyes searched mine.

One last time? When I had hoped never to see that place again? "Why?"

"You must pretend you don't know that your brother escaped."

He hadn't. "So thee want me to . . . ?"

"Go to the jail as if nothing has happened. Just the way you usually did."

"Please don't make me go back."

The way he looked at me told me he understood. "You must. Just this one last

time. And then it will all be over. I promise."
He took my hand in his as he said it.

I gripped it with my own.

As Polly began her second song, he spoke again. "Have you truly left your family?"

"Aye. And the Meeting as well. I couldn't stay. Not after what I said."

"I'm sorry."

And the truth of it is, he was. I could see it in his eyes.

"I know what it means to be cast away from something you love."

There was a look in his eyes that caused my heart to turn over upon itself. I dropped my gaze from his and tried to fasten my attentions on Polly's concert. But the chords of my heart seemed to vibrate with a new awareness. What had once been forbidden was forbidden no longer. What I once despaired of having, could, quite possibly, become mine. I dared to look up at him again. "How did . . . what did thee do? When that happened?"

"I kept going on. I kept living. And eventually I found something else to love."

Something else to love. I walked up the stair with a smile on my face and a song in my heart. Jenny had arranged my things in the spare room so I slept that night on a true bed once more. My dreams were sweet and I woke with the echo of Polly's songs in my head. I was actually bold enough to start humming one!

Everything was different. Everything that was old had fallen away. There were no calls to make and no Friends to visit. There were no letters to search out. There was nothing that had to be done. I would have to ask Aunt how it was for her. What she did as she waited for her new life to begin.

There were so many good things to look forward to.

When I went down to breakfast, only Aunt was there. She was finishing up her tea as I entered. "Hannah! Come. Sit. We can talk as you eat."

Doll placed a plate before me.

"Now, then. We need to introduce you around the city as my niece. I would like to obtain invitations for you to all of the events that Polly is attending."

"Thee should not feel obliged."

"Society needs to understand your new position."

"And what is that?"

"Let's think of you as our ward. Mr. Pennington's and mine. How would that be?"

I ate in silence for a while as I thought on it.

"You're past the age for that, of course, but it will make it easier for everyone else to understand that you're no longer a Friend. They'll treat you as one of us now."

"It's not that I don't generally agree with the Friends."

"Of course not."

"Or even that I don't want to be one of them. I still would be if . . . well."

Aunt Rebekah sighed. "That is exactly why it's so complicated. And why it's best to keep things plain." She smiled as she said that, knowing, I suppose, that I would appreciate the irony.

"I can't live my life as a lie."

"I'm not asking you to lie. I'm just asking you to help people understand how to think of you now."

Dare I speak of my dreams? Of my fondness for Jeremiah? Would it be presumptuous to think I might not have need of my aunt's patronage for very long?

She took both Polly and me to the mantua-maker and the milliner that afternoon. And the next day she escorted me, alone, to the glover as well. By the end of the week I had six new gowns on order with slippers to match, four new hats, and six pairs of gloves. Though I hadn't chosen trimmings

511

as fancy as Polly might have liked, I was well pleased with the choices I had made.

I had feared seventh day's visit to the jail, but I wasn't even allowed into the building. I showed my pass, but then was told the new general's orders were inviolable: There were to be no more visits to the prisoners. I left that place light in heart and buoyant in spirit. My time as a spy was finished.

I had wondered how my new life would be. It became apparent once the first of my gowns was delivered the following week that it would consist of accompanying my aunt and my cousin on their rounds of calls and on the Penningtons' circuit of evening entertainments. There were suppers to attend and concerts to hear, and very soon I came close to regretting the life I had left behind. I may have despaired of ever fitting in had it not been for the presence of Jeremiah at nearly all of the events.

By the first seventh day in June, Aunt's remaining purchases on my behalf had been delivered. She now considered me possessed of a presentable wardrobe, and I had come to learn those customs that society required of me. I felt, finally, able to manage what my life had become. But then Aunt announced over breakfast that it was time to begin thinking about a wardrobe for autumn.

A knock sounded at the door.

We could hear Davy's quick steps as he crossed the front hall.

Aunt resumed speaking. "At the very least I'd like you to look over some of the new styles from London with me. And perhaps —"

"Mrs. Pennington, ma'am?" Davy stood at the entrance to the dining room.

"What is it?"

"They's some soldiers here. Asking 'bout Miss Hannah."

Aunt Rebekah's brow furrowed, but she placed her teacup back atop its saucer and rose. She hadn't taken two steps when the soldiers pushed Davy aside. "We've come to arrest Hannah Sunderland in the name of the King."

Aunt's mouth dropped into an *O*. She placed a hand on the soldier's arm to halt him as she stretched out an arm toward me. "Just — you must — there's a mistake." Her gaze shot back and forth between the soldier and me. "There has to be a mistake! My niece is a Quaker. She can't have done — anything!"

"Aunt Rebekah."

Her eyes fixed upon me. "You haven't

done anything. Tell them." She was beseeching me with a stricken face.

Much as I loved her, I could not lie. "I must go with them."

"But . . . why?" The words came out in a wail.

"They've reason for their accusations."

"But — I can't — what have you done?"

"I'm sorry." I only said the words because I meant them. I was sorry that I couldn't be the niece she wanted. The one who would benefit from and blossom under her tutelage.

The soldier seized me by the shoulder and marched me out of the house.

In all of the upheaval of the past weeks, I had somehow managed to forget that what I had done in helping the prisoners escape was anathema to people like her. An abomination to all those who considered themselves Loyalists. Had I truly thought I could leave my old life behind?

Then I had become the worst of liars. And I had only deceived myself.

46

JEREMIAH

"Wait." I put a hand to Doll's shoulder to steady her. To try to make sense of what she was saying. "Slow down. I don't understand."

She batted my hand away. Punched the air. "I'm saying they came for Miss Hannah."

"Who came?"

"The soldiers."

"Soldiers came for Hannah?" My heart began to gallop within my chest. "Why? Did they say why?"

"No. They just marched into the house and they took her off. Like she was some criminal."

"What did they say? Exactly. I have to know what they said."

"They say they was arresting her. Like I just told you!"

They knew then. Somehow they had

discovered what she'd done. What we'd done.

"You going to do something about it or just stand there?"

"I'll do something about it." I didn't know what. I didn't know how. But if General Clinton was demanding a head in exchange for the escape, I would make sure it was mine they took. Not hers.

I shoved a hat on my head and took off for headquarters at a run. Beat a tattoo up the stair to John's office. "Hannah's been arrested."

"Your *Friendly* maid? Yes. I know."

"Why?"

"You really oughtn't be consorting with that kind of company."

"Why!"

"It seems you got yourself involved with a spy. That's why."

It wasn't difficult to affix the appropriate look of horror on my face. How had they discovered her? Who had given her up?

"We hang spies, you know."

I knew it. All too well. "A spy?" I tried to laugh, but it came out in a mangled cough. "You can't believe she's a spy."

"I've known stranger things to be true."

"But she's a Quaker!"

"Yes. I've never had much use for those

516

people. And now I know why."

"I can't believe you'd think —"

He came around from behind his desk and placed a gentle hand to my arm. "Can't say I wanted to believe it either. Knowing how fond you were of her. But some things can't be ignored. It's seems she was just using you for your connection to me."

"I don't understand what you're saying."

"I'm saying she's a spy. There's irrefutable evidence. She deceived both of us. All of us."

"Can I at least see her? Talk to her?"

"Don't know why you'd want to." He settled himself back behind his desk. Then, sighing, he pulled a piece of paper toward himself. Scrawled a few sentences across it. Folded it, dripped a meager drop of wax upon it, and pressed a seal into it. He shoved it across the table. "Take this down to the jail. Maybe they'll let you in."

I handed John's letter to the guard in the front hall at the jail.

He disappeared with it into one of the front rooms. My letter reappeared a moment later in the hands of a different guard "You're here for the lady spy, then?"

"I'm here to see Miss Sunderland."

"Been a while since we've caught a spy.

People's getting excited for the hanging."

"She's not a spy."

"Tricked you as well, eh?"

"May I see her?"

He spat toward a spittoon at the back of the hall. Missed. "No."

"That letter is from headquarters. It says I can see her."

He shrugged. "And I say you can't."

"Why not?"

"I have my own orders. You can't see her."

No argument would sway him.

I returned the next day and the next day and the one after that. Each time we had the same conversation. Each conversation yielded the same result. I brought food every day and I begged the guard to see that she got it, though I didn't have much hope that she would. Although I repeatedly entreated John to intervene, he would not do it. "She's a spy, Jonesy. You have to face the truth."

I couldn't.

I wouldn't believe that they had the proof. I returned to the jail on Thursday, letter in hand. I thrust it at the guard the same way I usually did. "I'm here to see Miss Sunderland." I was through yelling at the man. It hadn't done any good the previous times. I was done with planning to break her out. And I had no hope that I could save her. I simply wanted to see her.

"You know I'm not to let you."

"May I see her?"

He narrowed his eyes as he looked at me. Then he shrugged. "Don't see why not." He didn't seem to be in any hurry, however, to go get her.

"May I see her *today?*"

"Don't have to be so rude about it. I've got nothing to do with it. Have to be careful where you bury your dead bodies, you know!" He laughed uproariously, as if he'd told some magnificent joke. I could hear his heavy footsteps as he descended the stair into the basement. Just as I feared that he had disappeared altogether, I heard that same weighted tread come back up.

The door pushed open and Hannah came through it. No cuts. No bruises. No tears. Her gown was soiled and she brought the stench of the cells with her, but the barest hint of a smile crossed her face when she saw me.

I stepped toward her. "Are you — ?"

"No touching the prisoner!"

She was squinting as if the hall's dim light was too bright for her eyes.

"Did they hurt you?"

She eyed the guard who was hovering at her side.

I addressed myself to him. "Is it possible that you could leave us?"

He tossed a look at me. "No."

"Then can she at least have a chair to sit in?"

He looked as if he was mightily tempted to say no again. But then he frowned. "Fine." He stumped down the hall and evicted one of the other guards from a chair. Taking hold of it by the back, he dragged it toward us.

I took the moment when his back was turned to give Hannah the food I had brought. I reached out and touched her cheek. "Are you well?"

Her eyes softened as she looked into mine. "Ironic that I should end up here. Now."

"Have they questioned you?"

She leaned into my hand. Closed her eyes. "No."

"Hannah. Listen to me."

The guard shoved the chair into the wall with a thump. Took her by the shoulder and pushed her into it. She winced as her bottom made contact with the seat.

"There's no call to be so rough!"

"Don't see why you'd care any? She's a spy, isn't she?"

"She's not!"

Her hand slipped into mine. It was cool. And so very small. "Thee mustn't growl so. He is only doing his job."

I turned on her, willing to fight, to shout, to . . . tear someone apart. Anyone! I would do whatever it took to gain her freedom. But as she looked at me, I saw such hope shining from her eyes that I came undone. Kneeling beside her, I pressed her hand to my cheek. "You must promise me you will not tell the truth when they question you. Not this time." I was having trouble speaking through the fear that had gripped my throat. I tried to swallow it down.

She was already shaking her head. Sadly. As if, in the end, I had managed to disappoint her after all. "I can't start lying. Not now."

"Then promise me you won't tell them anything at all!"

"Hush, thee." She reached out a hand to my hair, letting it linger there for a moment. And then she gathered my head to her chest. "I can't." She kissed me on the head as she released me. "What would my word be worth then? When I say that I love thee, I want thee to know always that I meant it. If anything is to remain, it must be truth. I did what I did because it was right. Why

521

ought I to conceal it?"

"Because they're going to hang you."

Her face went white. She grasped at my hand with both of hers as if she feared I might slip away. She closed her eyes for a moment. When she opened them, a look of resignation had replaced that look of hope. "I have done what I have done. There is nothing more to say."

The guard was clomping back down the hall toward us. "Time's up. I haven't got all day."

"Just — !" I spun to my feet, rounding on the man.

A tug from Hannah's hand held me back. "No, Jeremiah. Thee must not fight this. I know it quite plainly. I hear it in my heart."

Thee must not fight this. I know it quite plainly. I hear it in my heart.

Her voice had taken on the cadence of my steps. Faster and faster and faster she spoke until her words were running through my head the same way my feet were running through the streets. I reached the wharves and all of their commotion, and I could run no more. I panted, trying to recover my breath, as I dodged carts and porters. Finally, my energy spent and my breath returned, I stood there watching ships sail out of the port.

What had she been trying to say? Did she mean she'd had a message for me — from God? What did He know about anything? And yet . . . she'd been right before. About the things she'd said at the Meeting, though she'd kept herself from saying them for a very long time. But how could it be right not to try and secure her release? Someone had to fight for her. She clearly wasn't going to do it herself. Because she couldn't lie. No. She *wouldn't* lie. She was the most stubborn, most vexing woman in the colony.

And she wouldn't lie to save her life.

I started to laugh, but then a great cry tore from my throat and rose up through my lips. It gave voice to all my rage and loss and grief. I'd been knocked right round to where I had started: Contemplating how to free a prisoner from the jail. And I came to no conclusion but what I'd known from the beginning: I could do nothing.

Do not fight this.

I had already grown tired of those words. Though . . . the voice was new. It wasn't Hannah I was hearing. It was something else. Something different. Something new.

Do not fight.

They were odd, those words. It was as if I was . . . *hearing them with my heart.* But if I

523

wasn't to fight, did that mean I was to . . .
give myself up? I waited. For something.
But . . . there was nothing.

I didn't have time for this Quaker nonsense!

I wouldn't fight. But that didn't mean I
would do nothing at all. I turned around
and headed back for High Street. I was going back to John. If there was anyone who
held any power to free Hannah, it was him.

After returning to his office and making
every argument I could think of, he still
claimed he could do nothing. The new
general, General Clinton, was my only
recourse, and he was too busy to consult
with citizens. So I spent the next two days
pacing the halls at headquarters, making a
nuisance of myself, trying to see him.

At least I'd been able to see her. One time
more. When I'd tried again, the guard had
laughed at me and marched me to the door.
I could only hope the food I left had actually been given to her.

On Sunday I was surprised to see John
walking down Walnut Street, arms filled
with books. Many other officers were doing
the same. His young sergeant was trailing
him, carrying several portfolios. They
dumped their armloads into one of many
carts that lined the street. It was already

nearly filled to overflowing.

He looked up as I approached. Straightened as he slipped a hand beneath his coat. "I was just coming to see you. Looks as if you've saved me the trouble." His hand reappeared, grasping a pistol.

"What's this?"

"You were part of it."

"Part of what?"

"You and she together. You were both spies."

Do not fight this.

"I don't know why you'd say that."

"There was one thing that kept bothering me. I couldn't figure out why you were always so interested in her. I couldn't understand what you saw in her. At first I thought you'd given up. Because of . . ." He gestured toward my armless sleeve. "She wasn't like any of the girls you used to flirt with. And now I know why. So." He cocked the pistol. "Do you deny it?"

Do not fight.

He may have drawn the wrong conclusion but there was no point in denying anything any longer. "No."

His face puckered with disappointment and disbelief. "You *are* a spy, then?"

"Yes."

"Blast it all! Why? You were one of the best

soldiers the army had. You could have . . . you could have . . ." His gaze had been drawn to my empty sleeve again.

"I became a spy because I could no longer hold a musket. And I was tired of never quite being good enough. I was ten times the officer you ever were and yet you were the one who was given the commission. I would never have been offered it. Not even if Devil's Hole hadn't happened."

"This is about your *arm?*"

"It was. I'll admit that I once hated you. I spent years wishing it had been you who'd lost your arm instead of me. But I've realized these past months that hate never got me anything at all."

"How very noble of you." He'd taken a step closer with every word. And no one in the street even seemed to notice. They all just continued filling their carts.

"Not noble. I finally realized that you weren't worth it."

"Well, this puts us in a bit of a bind, doesn't it? Can't exactly accuse you of trying to attack me, considering you've only got the one arm."

"You're going to shoot me? Now?" A tingling began behind my ears and a deathly chill swept over me. But then there came a great and comforting peace. A stillness in my soul.

Do not fight.

"I want to shoot you. I long to shoot you! But I'm a better man than that." He yelled for his sergeant.

"Sir!"

"Take this spy down to the jail."

47

HANNAH

When I'd been arrested, I was taken straight to the jail and placed in my brother's old cell. It was empty, Robert's body was gone, and the tunnel had been filled back in with dirt. I wished I'd been put in a cell with some of the others, for there in Robert's cell I was alone.

I had never known terror before. I thought I had, but true terror lived in the darkness where there was no possibility of light, where the rats scuffled at all hours through the filthy straw. I had the presence of mind to think only one thought: I was going to be hanged. How much would it hurt at the end, when I dangled from the noose? How much pain would I feel? How long would it take to die?

Be still and know that I am God.

Be still. When everything within me longed to cry out, to strike out, to do what I could to free myself!

It seemed to me sometimes that I could still hear William Addison and the others, their whispered conversations, their shuffling and rustling through the straw.

I heard coughs come from the men in the other cells. And I heard muffled moans.

At least I could no longer smell the filth. I had tired of standing after that first day and so I had allowed myself to settle down into it. There was nothing else to do, for there was nothing unspoiled down there. There was no clean thing. And there was no hope.

There was only a meager light that seeped through a broken, grime-covered window in the day and an inky blackness that blotted out everything in the night. All the hours passed the same. Without notice, without observation, they merged and bled into each other. Once in a while the guard that used to let me in to see Robert would open the door and throw in a roll. And sometimes the first guard, the one in the outer room, would stand by the door and taunt me.

I saw Jeremiah, twice. The memory of him, of his touch, was almost too much to bear.

I had begun to think that I had been forgotten. But then I heard the scuff of boots coming down the hall. And there was light. It was so feeble I could not see it at first, but as the sound of footsteps came nearer, the reach of the light increased until there was a fumbling at my door. My eyes ached from the sudden brightness. The light was so terrible that I threw an arm up over my face as I withdrew into the corner.

"Who — who's there?" I did not know whether it was better to have been forgotten or remembered. The door protested movement. And then . . . there were voices. "You don't have to keep us down here. You know you don't."

Was that . . . "Jeremiah?" I lowered my arm, but still I could not see for the light.

"Major's orders."

"Aye. But who's to know if you did or didn't follow them? No one here will tell."

Jeremiah's protests went unanswered, and I could hear him enter the room as the door was drawn shut and the key turned in the lock. "Hannah?"

"Jeremiah?" I could see, but dimly. He was standing over by the door.

As I went to him, he suddenly keeled over and retched. Straightened. "Sorry, I —" He bent and retched again. "How did they — how did anyone survive this?" He wiped his mouth on his coat sleeve.

"It's why I had to keep coming."

He looked around in that squalid room,

gaze probing the dark recesses. "I didn't know. If I'd known what it was like down here, I would never have asked you to come."

As he put his arm around me, I felt tears spill from my eyes. There were so many tears to be shed for the injustice of all that had happened. But there was one thing still to be thankful for. "Had I never come, I would have never known thee."

As we stood together in the middle of the room, Jeremiah's gaze traveled once more the length and breadth of it. "If I'd been able to join the honest fight, then I might have been one of them. One of those sad, pitiful wretches. I might have perished here alongside them."

I put an arm about his waist.

He looked down at me.

"They weren't to be pitied. They wouldn't have wanted it." Of that, I was certain. "There were many opportunities to leave. They freed any who would swear allegiance to the king. Those who stayed did so because they wanted to."

"No." Jeremiah was shaking his head. "They didn't stay because they wanted to. No one would have wanted to stay here. They stayed because their hearts were honest. It was the only thing they could do."

"Thee must know that they needed us. Brave as they were, they needed people like us, Jeremiah. There's no shame in what we did."

We weren't alone for long. Once again, there came the sound of footsteps, a flare of light, and the squeal of the door. And with them a flurry of profanity.

Jeremiah gripped my hand in his.

"How could anyone survive in this wretched place?" It was Major Lindley. He was accompanied by another soldier, and they were both holding handkerchiefs to their noses. I knew from experience that it wasn't helping the slightest bit.

"I came down here because there's not enough time left. There won't be a trial."

My heart stopped beating for the space of a moment.

"You told me everything I need to know, Jones, but I still don't understand why." He was no longer talking to Jeremiah. He had addressed himself to me. "Why would you pretend an interest in someone like him?"

"Someone like . . . ?"

"You're a Quaker."

"I was." But I'd found what happened when a person valued politics over God and a cause above a person. I'd always known that to Robert everything was personal. I just hadn't realized that's the way it was meant to be.

"You want to know how you were discovered?"

I'd assumed that they'd tortured one of the sick men who'd been left behind.

"None of the prisoners would tell us anything. Not one. Did you know that? Not until we started finding the bodies. Until we told them we wanted to notify families." He stopped for a moment and took in a deep breath through his nose. His face folded as he leaned over and retched into the straw, which caused his sergeant to do the same. He coughed and then dabbed at his lips with the handkerchief. "In any case, it was your own family that gave you away, Miss Sunderland."

My family? But who . . . ?

"We found your brother."

Robert.

"He'd been buried in the straw. And he'd been dead for quite some time."

Jeremiah's face had gone white and then flushed red. "But —"

I shook my head at him, though I said nothing to the major.

"He'd been dead long enough that you ought to have stopped visiting. And yet they tell me you came every week, even after you should have known." He smiled. "And they say dead men don't talk!" He turned his gaze to Jeremiah. "I never figured you for a traitor. Had our roles been reversed, I would have joined your army in an instant. I would have fought beside you, not against you. But . . . I forget." He gestured toward Jeremiah's missing arm. "You're useless."

"Not useless. I was once. Once, I was just like you. But not anymore."

"You didn't used to be so provincial. But I suppose, breeding will show. And there's none of it — none that I've noticed — anywhere to be had in this godforsaken colony."

"God does not forsake, John. 'Tis man who does the discarding. And the discounting. There is that of God in all of us." Jeremiah's use of the familiar phrase resounded in my ears.

"I've had enough of you and your army and — and God!" He turned from us to his soldier. "I ought to have them shot." He faced us once more. "I *would* have you shot, only there's no time. And I'll not have my reputation tainted by an unauthorized execution."

As they left and locked the door behind them, my heart regained its proper beat. I looked up at Jeremiah. "He didn't mean those things. Thee must know that. He only said them because he was hurt."

"I didn't care, not nearly as much as I once might have. Now . . . why didn't you tell me about Robert?"

Tears threatened again. "What would it have changed?"

"I would have wanted to know."

"Thee mightn't have let me come here if thee had known."

He tipped my chin up, forcing me to look at him. "I wouldn't have. But still . . . I would have wanted to know."

"Why? What good would it have done?"

"I could have told you how sorry I was."

I opened my mouth to reply, but no words came out. My chin began to tremble, and I felt the corners of my lips being wrenched downward as if by an unseen hand. "I didn't — I couldn't — he died digging the tunnel. It collapsed on him. They didn't tell me, not at first. But I *knew*." He opened his arm to me and I came to him. He drew my head to his chest and placed a kiss atop my head.

I clung to him as great, ugly, wrenching sobs tore from my soul. "I couldn't just leave the rest of them to die."

"You didn't. Seven officers escaped. And forty-nine other men."

535

"That many?"

"Aye. Thanks to you. And to Robert."

"He wasn't the only one who died in the digging."

"But fifty-six men went free."

"Why does it always have to be that way? Why do good men always have to sacrifice themselves for others?"

"Because they believe that the rest of us are worth it."

We moved toward a wall, the one where William Addison had always been, and sat down in the straw side by side. We stayed there for a long while. The window's dim light faded and finally there was nothing left to see. And nothing left to hear, save the snores of the men in the cells next to ours and the scurrying of rats.

In that place of hopelessness and despair a surprising thought came to me. "Major Lindley did thee a favor: He left us here. There should be no doubt as to thy loyalties now, when the patriots come."

Jeremiah shifted beside me. "I had not thought of it in quite that way."

We were silent again for a great long while.

It was Jeremiah who finally spoke. "Does your family know you're here?"

"I don't know. They arrested me at Pennington House." I wondered if anyone had sent a message to my family. "I'm sure they won't want me now."

"If I had known at the first how much my proposal would cost you . . ."

"Do not apologize, Jeremiah, or I shall rebuke thee as thee have often accused me of doing in the past." I heard both a promise and a threat in my tone, but there was a quaver there as well.

"I was not going to. I was only going to ask . . . ?" He lifted his arm, what was left of it, in invitation.

It was the only place I had ever felt safe and I fled to it.

"I have only one arm to offer you."

"And I have only one heart to give thee."

The bolt in the door at the end of the hall shrieked. Footsteps sounded against the packed earth and a ring of keys jangled. A door somewhere along the hall was unlocked. "Come out! Come out of there. Let's go. Come out."

There were protests and moans, but soon we heard the sounds of many footsteps in the hall. And then another door was opened. "Come out! Let's go. Rouse yourselves. You're leaving."

Jeremiah and I looked at each other. Perhaps there was some hope still.

"Come out. Let's go." The call was repeated and the footsteps came closer.

Finally someone in one of the other cells thought to ask what was happening.

"It's the prison ships for you. General's orders."

Suddenly those shouts and the clanking of the keys sounded more like a summons to death than an invitation to freedom.

"They're not going to take us." Jeremiah had pushed to his feet and was holding his hand out to me.

Another door was opened. More prisoners were called out into the hall.

"You're going to stand in the corner over there" — he gestured to the one farthest from the window — "and I'm going to stand in front of you. If they try to make us leave, just be still. No matter what happens, don't move. They won't notice you in the shadow."

"Thee can't — what are thee saying?"

"They're not taking you."

"But —" Fear grabbed at my stomach. I clutched his hand. "They can't take thee."

"They can. They probably will. But they won't have you."

"I don't want to stay if thee are not here." Panic began to claw at my throat.

"Listen to me!"

I stilled.

He cupped his hand to my face. "You're

the only one of us worth saving."

"That isn't true! I want to come with thee. I would rather perish by thy side than live without thee." He would not free me from the corner, so I threw my arms about him and wept into his unyielding back. We waited there in the darkness as the footsteps drew near.

But they never came for us.

We had been forgotten.

A jail abandoned by men was worse than one filled with them. Without the sounds of those souls in misery, we could hear people passing on the street outside. We heard the rumble of carts and the clop of horses' hooves. We heard rats, many more than we had been hearing. And there was a constant dripping somewhere in the dark.

My head was beginning to feel as if it were trying to float away from my shoulders, and my throat was so dry that I could no longer swallow. I began to shiver and I wandered in and out of sleep.

Eventually, Jeremiah roused me. "Listen."

There were footsteps again. And then — thank God! — the shriek of the door at the end of the hall. "Is anyone there?" A voice called out into our darkness.

I opened my mouth to answer, but Jeremiah stopped me. "If we tell them we're here, they might throw us onto the ships with the others."

"Anyone there?"

The footsteps were joined by another pair. They scuffed slowly toward us, pausing along the way. We heard doors being pushed open.

"We never treated their men so poorly!" The voice was heavy with judgment.

"General Washington agreed to an exchange!" And that voice sounded of outrage. "How are we going to tell him there's no one left to trade?"

General Washington. They sounded as if they were going to talk to him . . . as if they actually knew him.

"The blackguards. I hope they rot in hell!"

Beside me, Jeremiah shouted out. "We're here! Two of us were left behind."

"Who — ? Where are you?"

"Here!" He got up, strode to the door, and began to beat against it. "In the last cell."

"How could anyone survive down here? Just a minute. We need to find a taper. We'll have you out in no time."

I joined Jeremiah at the door, holding on to his hand, and together we waited for the light we knew would soon come.

A NOTE FROM THE AUTHOR

I've always been fascinated by the Revolutionary War. I can date that interest to a particular time and place: the gift shop at Valley Forge in 1976. That's when my parents bought me a copy of *Patriots in Petticoats.* It's a book filled with stories of female revolutionary spies. I will always be thankful to Patricia Edwards Cline for writing a book that taught an eight-year-old that girls can participate in history too.

Historians believe that when the Revolutionary War started, one-third of the colonists supported the patriots, one-third remained loyal to the crown, and one-third had made no decision either way. The British army was the mightiest army on earth. In funds, soldiers, and equipment, they vastly outnumbered the colonists. The war was Britain's to lose and they did an admirable job of it. Many of those who had cheered when the British army marched into Philadelphia cheered even louder as it left.

The condition of the patriot army at Valley Forge the winter of 1777/78 was truly pitiful. It was a miracle the colonists ever won the war at all. The patriot army starved at Valley Forge because the quartermasters charged with supplying the troops were not given the resources with which to do it. The Continental Congress refused to believe that things were as dire as General Washington claimed. And even when they were persuaded things needed to change, they were only willing to offer worthless continental paper money in payment. Pennsylvania's colonial government might have helped, but they didn't feel the need to canvas the countryside for supplies. Their philosophy decreed their fellow countrymen would offer supplies freely from the goodness of their hearts, even as the British army was paying for its supplies in gold. It wasn't the weather that killed so many soldiers that winter. They starved to death from greed, ineptitude, political inertia, and lofty philosophies.

In 1778, Philadelphia was the fourth largest city in the British Empire. They were only a ship's journey behind in news, fashions, and letters from London. Like many in the colonies, Philadelphians considered themselves upstanding British citizens. Which makes what happened at the Walnut Street Jail even more incomprehensible.

Although there was a flurry of visits to the jail's prisoners when the occupation first began in October, those visits quickly tapered off as food became increasingly difficult and expensive to come by. In fact, the historical record only indicates that one person visited regularly, outside of General Washington's appointed advocate. She was a black woman. Historians are divided on whether she was enslaved or free.

From what is known of General Howe, he never would have condoned the cruel treatment by the jailers. He and General Washington corresponded all winter long about how best to care for prisoners on both sides of the lines. One of the difficulties lay in the era's convention that the welfare of the prisoners was the fiscal and physical responsibility of their own army. If supplies weren't allowed to pass the lines, then the prisoners didn't get anything to eat. In fact, there was a three-week period early in the occupation during which prisoners received nothing at all.

Captain Cunningham was all too real. Reports of atrocities followed the man wherever he went. Unfortunately, in times of war, such atrocities were easily overlooked. But we can see his descendants at work today whenever we allow ourselves to treat others as second-class citizens. Intolerance, xenophobia, and prejudice provide the training that make things like the Walnut Street Jail, the enslavement of millions of Africans, the Holocaust, and the Rwanda and Darfur massacres possible.

If the prisoners did not die of their wounds or through slow starvation, diseases like putrid fever (typhus), dysentery, and smallpox killed them by the hundreds. By April 1777 (nine months before this story starts), nearly two thousand soldiers had already been buried in potter's field in Southeast Square, most of them prisoners from the city's jails and hospitals.

There were at least two escapes from the Walnut Street Jail. The first took place in December. After that, General Howe allowed no communication with the prisoners. The second escape was the one undertaken by the prisoners in this novel. Fifty-six men escaped that night in May. And when their absence was discovered, the bodies of five men who had died digging the tunnel were found buried beneath the straw of their cell.

Undoubtedly there had to have been coordination between the patriot camp and the prisoners inside the jail. Could it have been the work of a Quaker spy? Perhaps. At least one other Quaker spy operated during the occupation of Philadelphia. Lydia Darragh's story makes for fascinating reading, though her concern was for an enlisted son rather than a brother. And she seems to only have operated during a period of weeks rather than months.

Hannah Sunderland and Jeremiah Jones are figments of my imagination, but someone very much like them must have helped in the escape. It was timed, just as I wrote, to coincide with the festivities of the Meschianza. As officers feted General Howe, Captain McLane created a diversion at the lines, which allowed the prisoners to escape.

Earlier that spring, a prisoner exchange had been discussed with the British, but the Continental Congress was more interested in one-upmanship than in saving soldiers' lives. They appointed men to the congressional committee with explicit instructions to avoid an exchange by any means possible. After haggling over details, rules for the exchange were finally agreed upon by both sides. Unfortunately, General Howe's replacement suffered from impatience and sent the patriot prisoners off in prison ships before the exchange could be transacted.

People of common sense in every era since the Revolutionary War have always wondered what possessed a handful of British majors to plan such a spectacularly lavish party for a general who had failed to quench the rebellion. I like to think they were encouraged in their folly, though I have no proof of it. There is a legend that Peggy Shippen (Benedict Arnold's wife-to-be) was kept from attending the Meschianza by her father. He'd been persuaded by a group of Quakers that the Turkish costumes supplied for the event were immodest. Always known for her histrionics, her sulk that day must have been magnificent.

Major John André was one of the masterminds behind the event. His sketches of the Meschianza's costumes are still available, and the report he made in a letter to *Gentleman's Magazine* about the festivities was widely read, and roundly mocked. He was well liked by both sides during the war. He was a gentleman's gentleman and a ladies' man. He was also General Benedict Arnold's handler. He would leave with the British when they evacuated Philadelphia, only to be captured in New York two years later. On October 2, 1780, he was hanged as a spy.

The British army did indeed leave in a hurry. After a month of whispered rumors and expectations of a withdrawal, the actual leaving was accomplished almost overnight. Elizabeth Drinker, a Quaker diarist of the period, noted on June 19:

> last night it was said there was 9,000 of the British Troops left in Town 11,000 in the Jersyes (sic): this Morning when we arose, there was not one Red-Coat to be seen in Town; and the encampment, in the Jersys (sic) vanish'd.

When the patriots entered Philadelphia on the heels of the British evacuation, devastation greeted them. The northern part of the city was completely destroyed. Those who had abandoned or had been forced to give up their homes to quarter troops very often found them looted. Quakers' possessions had been especially targeted.

It took weeks to clean out the filth in the city's public buildings like the hospital and the State House. In such places, as in the private homes they had commandeered, the British had taken up the practice of punching holes in the floors at the ground level and then sweeping excrement and other waste into the basements. The once beautiful and elegant city was overcome by depredation, filth, and the constant swarming of flies. The reason for the third amendment to the United States Constitution used to be unclear to me, but after researching this book, I have a much better understanding of its significance.

Once the city and its government were stabilized, the corruption and social whirl began anew with the very same set of leading families. Many of the ladies of the Meschianza went on to marry patriot officers, though most of them would consider that evening in May 1778 the high point of their lives. Through old age, they looked back on those British officers and the British occupation with nostalgia.

Reprisals came swiftly once the patriots retook the city under the command of General Benedict Arnold. The first order of business was evening the score. Under the new regime, suspected British collaborators were jailed. Some were even hanged. It was not unknown for Washington's spies to have to produce proof of their true loyalties to avoid being lynched.

Scientists have long remarked on the ability of twins to share emotions, dreams, and even pain. Hannah's special link with her brother is based on true incidents.

Phantom pain, as scientists now understand it, occurs when a limb has been amputated and the brain mixes or rewires its signaling as it remaps the body. Many times phantom pain is associated with nerve damage from an amputation that has been poorly executed. The pain can be described as a shooting, boring, stabbing, or burning sensation. Some amputees experience it rarely, others on a daily basis.

The names for those enslaved at Pennington House were chosen from among the rosters of George Washington's slaves at Mt. Vernon.

THE QUAKERS

The Society of Friends is a Christian movement that originated in seventeenth-century Britain. Originally called dissenters, they reacted to societal and political upheaval by trying to reform the church. They were nicknamed Quakers when their founder, George Fox, was brought before a judge, who noted that they bid everyone tremble at the Word of God. In spite of heavy persecution, Friends in England sent scores of missionaries to the New World in the seventeenth and eighteenth centuries — men and women both. They traveled up and down the eastern seaboard and pushed inland to the frontier in order to spread the Gospel. Their creed was simple: God was willing to communicate with any person directly. The emphasis was not on hearing *about* God, but on hearing *from* God.

Though Friends ordained no preachers, they quickly fastened upon an effective organization. They met together weekly, on first day. Monthly they met with other Meetings in the local area. Quarterly and yearly they sent delegates to Meetings of groups from increasingly larger geographical areas.

In 1681, Friend William Penn convinced the King of England to take care of the dual problems of the kingdom's Quakers and a royal debt owed the Penn family by granting him the charter for Pennsylvania. For nearly a hundred years, the Quaker-led colony was able to coexist with the Native American population by treating them with respect and integrity. But the French and Indian Wars of the 1750s challenged the Friends sitting in the colony's legislature to either compromise their pacifist principles or to withdraw from public life. They chose the latter and their influence over the colony's laws and politics soon disappeared.

Friends were the first faith to advocate against slavery in America. They became active members of the Underground Railroad in the nineteenth century. Whenever possible, they taught former slaves to read and write and care for themselves in preparation for freedom. For Friends to have taken the stand they did on not visiting the prisoners in Walnut Street Jail seems uncharacteristically callous. But after having watched the radical element seize control of the government and experiencing firsthand the devastating consequences of war, it's not surprising that they decided to wash their hands of everything associated with it.

The Society of Friends is still active throughout the world, though it is not generally aggressive in seeking converts. The faith developed without a creed. Traditionally, Friends believed that Christ — not the Bible — was the Word of God. Though Friends initially never expected a message from Christ to contradict the Bible, emphasis on the Inner Voice has led to an increased reliance on revealed truth and personal testimony. In some branches of the faith, it is possible to encounter Quaker Buddhists, Quaker Agnostics, or Quaker Pagans at Meeting.

Friends believe that there is that of God in everyone, in women as well as in men. It is one of the few faiths that allowed women to preach and teach from its very beginnings. They call themselves Children of Light, proclaiming that Christ's light within will reveal the state of the heart.

In America there have been many examples of religions that preach the person of God as a wrathful avenger. There have also been many groups that emphasize the person of Jesus and seem to preach a cheap grace. In the history of America, the Society of Friends was one of the only faiths to emphasize the person of the Holy Spirit. They believed, quite literally, that if one could just be still and learn to listen, the Holy Spirit would make His voice heard.

The concept of the Trinity seems very esoteric and irrelevant in today's world, but it seems to me that only a faith embracing each person of the Trinity can save us from imbalance. While love without faith offers no hope, faith without love offers no mercy. We must have both faith and love or run the danger of discovering that, in the end, we have nothing at all.

ACKNOWLEDGMENTS

It is a commonly held belief in the publishing industry that Revolutionary War–era novels don't sell, so I am extremely grateful to my editors, Dave and Sarah Long, who took a chance on this book. My critique partner, Maureen Lang, encouraged me during my first drafts when it seemed as if this story would never get written. And my agent, Natasha Kern, spurred me on at the end with some insightful suggestions. But most of all, I'd like to thank my husband, who kept insisting on calling this my "spy book" even as I kept referring to it as my "Quaker book." *Tu as raison.*

DISCUSSION QUESTIONS

1. James Bond, Benedict Arnold, Nathan Hale, Mata Hari. In what cases is spying admirable? In what cases is it dishonorable?

2. Do you have a disability or know anyone who does? How does this affect self-image? What sort of limitations does it place upon interactions with other people?

3. What causes is your church passionate about? What causes are you passionate about? How do these causes affect your faith?

4. What did you know about the Quaker faith before reading this book? Did any of the things you learned about it surprise you? What parts of the Quaker faith do you find admirable?

5. Quakers believe strife is caused by lust. Do you agree?

6. What are your thoughts about pacifism? How do they fit with your views about faith? Did your thoughts change any while you were reading this book?

7. In Chapter 23, Jeremiah Jones says, "You can't base your faith on a position. You can't live your life as a protest. Because sooner or later positions resolve themselves. And then what's left?" Do you agree with him?

8. Have you ever had to choose between a cause and your faith? A person and your faith? What parameters or criteria did you use to guide you?

9. Why is it that prisoners of war seem so often to be abused? Why is it that our modern world hasn't been able to stop this from happening?

10. Have you ever felt burdened by a message from God? Did you share it or did you keep it to yourself? Why?